THE DREAM LAND

THE DREAM LAND

Diaspora

BOOK III OF THE DREAM LAND TRILOGY

Stephen Swartz

TANGENTIAL BOOKS
In Association with

MYRDDIN PUBLISHING GROUP
UNITED STATES · UNITED KINGDOM · AUSTRALIA

ISBN-13: 978-1-939296-27-6

ISBN-10: 1-939296-27-7

In Association with

www.myrddinpublishing.com

Cover by Marta Swartz

Drink the poison of love and your life
will transform into myth.

Mekmel-Tokou (GP 1498-1611)

Danid poet & priest

THE DREAM LAND

Diaspora

Stephen Swartz

PART ONE

It is difficult to be a madman when everyone around you is also quite mad.

Set-d'Elous, Emperor of Sekuate

Chapter 1

Legend

He felt the sand scratching his face before he opened his eyes. A faint dream hovered wallflower-like at the edge of his dance card, afraid to let itself go and twirl about the floor no matter who might be watching. Letting the image sail away on a breeze, he pushed out his legs, stretched his arms up, bent his neck—and in every movement felt pain shoot through his body like lightning, like fire and ice. He stopped, grimacing against Fate once more, like some old habit his mother had scolded him for. When his eyes opened he saw what he had expected to see, yet the sight of the desert landscape, red and brown below the emerald sky, seemed to catch him by surprise.

He sat up then, in one swift motion, crossing his legs, bracing his torso with his outstretched arms, nodding his head to the left, right, left, up, down, around in semicircles back and forth, testing his range of motion and feeling satisfied. Then he looked for the twin suns to confirm his suspicions: that he was, somehow, unbelievably, home again.

Behind him, nearly a quarter mile (almost one *radit*, as they called the measurement on that world), stood the sleek stone ramparts of the interdimensional doorway (what he referred to as a *tangent*, one of many such points scattered across the universe). He could still see the tops of the columns from where he sat on the sand, the grayish-brown soapflake-like chips. The monument had not stood there in his memory, and he had never imagined that anyone would venture so deep into the desert to build it. And yet, the sight of the simple structure—a gray stone platform with four stone columns, roofless, a central stone pedestal apparently used for rituals unknown—struck his heart like a warm glove on a cold winter's day (winter being called *Trist*, even in this place without snow). It was a temple, he decided and smiled. He could begin again, even as he could not recall what had come first, previous, or just a moment before his dream snuck away to hide in the folds of the curtain, sniffling in silence and wanting to forget the monumental past.

He picked himself up from where his body had crumpled against the flaky sands, a portion of his knee and foot pushed down into the material, as though he had fallen hard from a great height. With both hands, he brushed himself off, front and back. Then he took time to notice how he was dressed. His khaki jacket had crimson trim and powder-blue epaulets, a uniform of some kind, though his legs were covered in ragged blue jeans, a large hole at one knee. In a hip pocket remained a wallet, he felt. He dug it out and flipped it open to see who he was. A driver's license from Missouri and a couple of credit cards told him his name was Sebastian Talbot. It did not sound familiar to him.

Am I wearing someone else's clothes?

He pulled out a few pictures of people who could only lounge at the edges of his mind and glare back at him, begging for attention. He found a spare key to something, probably the door to a house. There was also a membership card to some gentlemen's club, a ticket stub to a play he could not remember, an automobile insurance card, a folded index card upon which were written several names and codes he could not immediately decipher. *What does psygal2@hotmail.com mean?* He pondered it. He counted the money: a hundred and thirty-six American dollars. He sighed, not quite sure of the reason for the audible exhalation, then reached into his jacket's side pocket. Inside he found a folded slip of paper—indeed, a crisp beige parchment rather than slick white paper. It was scribbled with what appeared to be a list of names and dates in a strange alphabet. No, not dates, not names; it was an agenda, a list of events and their starting times.

He laughed quickly, understanding the reality of the situation.

Glancing around, he checked that nobody was there to ponder his amusement.

"Who could be watching me?" he muttered, carefully placing the pile of things that had settled into his lap back into the wallet, and the wallet back into his pocket.

He looked up, regarded the blue sun on the horizon, and had a vague sense of where he was and where he should go. He admitted to himself, however, that he had no idea *when* he was, or *when* he wished to go.

And so, because it was a fairly nice day for a walk, he turned himself away from the distant structure and pushed himself over the slight rise in the flaky sand and there saw a set of footprints heading off to the horizon. Despite a brown leather boot on his right foot and a rubber-soled white-and-red sneaker on his left foot, it seemed like a good thing to follow the footprints. He went at a leisurely stroll at first, then swung into a quicker pace, feeling alive and energetic once more, ready for a new day to begin.

The footprints led him to a trail across firmer ground: a flat, reddish plain that stretched further on to three horizons. The trail took him to a roadway cut into the hard soil by the hooves of large animals and the rolling wheels of carts. He followed it and soon saw signs of civilization. He decided to be cautious, still not certain where he was or where he was going. *Not too sure who I am, either*, he thought. So he left the road and made his way to a low ridge from which he could survey the town. He lay on the ground, peering over the slope, counting the buildings, watching the brown-robed people going to and fro: men with staves, women with baskets, children pulling reptilian pets, carts parked or rolling through narrow streets. A village.

He waited until nightfall and walked around the village, continuing on the road. By dawn he was in sight of a larger settlement.

Sebastian Talbot? He did not feel the name suited him.

Another day passed and he skirted two more settlements. He felt by then that he must have lost weight, given that he had not eaten for such a long time. And yet he did not feel hungry nor too thirsty. He had urinated only a couple of times, minimal output, and had not defecated even once. Time seemed askew, as though his journey was actually only a few hours rather than the few days he seemed to be passing through. He had counted three sunrises since he awoke, using the yellow sun for that marker— noting also that he had not slept during his journey.

Unless my journey is all sleep and no wakefulness!

He continued walking along the road until he saw a city spreading out wide at the base of a low mountain range, knowing the route even as he had a puzzling sense of misdirection. Perhaps he was not on the same road but only one that appeared similar. Perhaps the yellow and blue light of the two different suns tricked him. Or perhaps he was not truly walking across a flat, rocky desert but was journeying through his consciousness, back to the place where his soul was born, to the cell of first thought, the atom of origin.

Perhaps my footsteps are just metaphors.

He shook his head slowly, breathing deeply, smelling staleness. Scratching his backside, he paused, gazing at the gleaming lights in the distance as dusk descended around him. This one was the right place, he sensed.

He stood watching the city through the night and when dawn crept across the horizon, he moved on into the city. It was a place of mixed cultures so no one particularly stared at him. Or, it could merely have been his sleep-deprived psyche swimming gradually to the surface of his consciousness. Either way, he had a task to do, something which demanded his attention and from which he could not turn away. He had been under a spell of some kind and now he was free—free to do what *he* had to do, not what his alter ego had chosen for him.

Inside the city, he made his way as if by a hundred trials through a maze to the station of the vehicles called KOHAX, an acronym meaning a vehicle that traveled on a single rail via electric pulsations. Essentially, an electric train. His usual path would have had him board the KOHAX and travel far to the north, passing first through the larger city of Lyas where he seemed to have some history, and on through the huge metropolis of Seas, the capitol city of some place where he once lived or did not live, and on to his final destination: the culturally sophisticated city and seaport of Selauê, a kind of home away from home, his headquarters whenever he visited the planet of Ghoupallesz.

Could it be so simple?

He waited in line at the ticket office. In his head, he felt maps and compasses working. In his gut, he was certain he did not know where he was going. He glanced around the square, focusing on the people who went by, their clothing and mannerisms, their complexions and gaits, the baskets they carried or carts they drove, trying to match what he was seeing with other, previously stored images in his head—

"*Ashê,*" spoke the man at the window, "*apoforen.*"

He grinned, embarrassed by his lack of understanding.

The ticket agent waved him forward, up to the window.

"*U'le'he'a?*" the man asked in a lowered voice.

It seemed the man was speaking a different language, guessing that this customer did not understand the first language. But it made no difference.

He dug into his pockets and found nothing, and he felt foolish.

"I'm sorry." He dared speak in English, trusting that his sincere tone of voice and friendly smile would carry the message even though his words would not be understood. "Really, I am. You see, I've been wandering across the desert for about five days, with no food or water, and now I seem to have only American dollars, which"—he pulled out the bills, began flipping through them—"is probably not a currency you take here. I really don't know where I am, or how I got here." He glanced around at the people gathered around the ticket office, waiting for him to conclude his business and move on. "You're all probably wondering what this madman is doing, what he is saying, what foolish language he is speaking—hah! only a fool would understand what I'm saying. That leaves out all of you." He stepped back, moving slowly away from the ticket window, keeping his eyes on the people encircling him. "Everything's going to be all right—all right—all right, everybody take it easy and I'll—I'll be moving on—on my way— on my way home, cuz I'm homeward bound—bound for home."

The ticket agent, eyes narrowing in suspicion, spoke to him further but he still could not reply, had no words to offer.

He saw them staring at him. He knew they were thinking he was a madman. He knew they hated him, and he erupted in wild gestures, shouting: "I know you're all fake, you're not real, you're part of some strange game, a puzzle for me to figure out, or a dream! That's it! You're all just flickering puffs of smoke in my dream and when I awaken you will, none of you will be here, wherever here is."

The ticket agent turned quickly to a colleague inside the office.

Before he could think of how to extricate himself from the situation, two uniformed men had come out of the office and stood beside him. One held his arm and the other began shaking him gently, checking his jacket pockets, and soon found a slip of paper and stood back, unfolding it. Only then did he put any significance to his wardrobe: a military uniform jacket, torn blue jeans probably from K-Mart, and mismatched footwear. The slip of paper only added to his extraordinary presence.

"Give me my slip of paper!" he demanded and the one man held him tighter.

The other man, holding the paper, glanced at him and spoke something.

"What?" he grunted. "I don't know what you're saying. Speak English!"

The man with the paper folded it again and put it away in his own pocket and he tried to grab for it. The man holding him pulled him back roughly.

"No, stop it! Leave me alone! You're not real, none of you are!"

Suddenly he felt light-headed and stumbled backwards. He tried to catch himself by grabbing the person behind him, a middle-aged woman, knocking her to the ground. Looking up, he saw the two men from the ticket office staring down at him with ugly, twisted faces.

"Let me wake up," he cried out, seeing one of them make a fist and—"I know it's all a dream, a bad dream!"—thrust it downward at him.

The world went black.

The man with the salt-and-pepper beard, wearing the white lab coat, looked up from the electric blue lines on the monitor and gave a slight grin, enough to be noticed by the woman sitting on the opposite side of the hospital bed. Also wearing a white coat, her dark hair was tied up in a bun on the top of her head. She remained expressionless, waiting for confirmation, waiting for another show of the lines zigzagging across the black screen.

There!

"Brain wave activity," said the man, "as strong as ever."

"So he's conscious?"

"Not conscious, but there is mental activity. He is no longer dead."

"Wonderful," said the woman in a level voice, empty of emotion. "What's that make it? Hundred thirty-eight days?" She stood and went to the door of the room, opened it. "I'll get Doctor Stafford."

"Good. Then call those detectives. Henderson or Wilson, I think are their names. They'll want to know, too."

"And his wife, don't forget. She calls nearly every day."

"Right. I'll call her first. What's the number of that mental hospital?"

Chapter 2

Retrogradation

Three men arrived from between the tall panels dividing work sections in the huge IRS service center building, two in dark suits and one in a police uniform, all with visitor tags. They knew where to go, it seemed to the women who were standing around another woman slumped in a chair.

"She done fainted," said Priscilla, the chubby one.

"So did you," said Kate, the older one.

"But I'm up now!"

The women stepped back as they arrived, calling themselves Detectives Ray Golden and Connie "Con" Jasperson. Golden, short blonde hair freshly cut, stood like a hipster, dark glasses hanging off his suit's breast pocket, acting cool. He seemed annoyed to be called out on such an unimportant matter. Jasperson was older, burly for a woman, dressed in pantsuit and black boots, no heels for her. Holding the chomped end of a cigar between her fingers, she was pulled along at the last second because they needed a female detective to deal with the female victim.

"What's the problem here?" asked Golden.

It was becoming routine for law enforcement to stop by to nab somebody. They had come in like this when they caught Sebastian Talbot, who had foolishly returned to work after killing all those people. Six in all. Including Tammy, supposedly. Except here she was! She was mumbling, unconsciousness in the chair, clearly not dead but alive. And she was dressed in something like a harem costume, bare belly, a big gemstone in her navel. And she was carrying another thirty pounds on her once anorectic body.

"What happened? Who is she?" asked Jasperson, gruffly.

"She's Tammy Tucker," said Bethany. "She used to work in our section."

"Yeah, like three years ago," said Priscilla.

Kate stepped up. "The night Sebastian Talbot supposedly killed—"

"Supposedly?" Priscilla cut in.

"When those people were killed, she was one of them."

Bethany waved her hands as though introducing the detectives to her. "Here she is."

"Yep, here's Tammy." Kate was smiling. "She's not dead."

They regarded their former coworker closely, Kate almost nose to nose, as she rose to consciousness. The woman blinked but still did not seem aware of where she was.

"Tammy? You awright?" asked Kate. She took Tammy's hand, patted it.

"Where you been, girl?" asked Priscilla.

Detective Golden asked more questions as Jasperson jotted answers on a notepad. Jasperson sent the uniform to call for an ambulance.

"And bring me a lighter," she called after the officer.

"She just come outta th' toilet dressed like that," said Priscilla, "and we never seen her since that night."

"Three years ago," Bethany added.

The detectives dismissed other workers who were starting to gather around them, curious what crime the cops were there for. It was a rare distraction from third shift tasks.

"You can positively identify this woman?" asked Detective Golden.

"Yes," said Kate. "We all know her. Tammy Tucker. She worked in Underreporting with me and Priscilla. Then she disappeared after her shift that night. And suddenly tonight...she's back." She looked around at her colleagues. "Ain't that right?"

They all agreed. That was Tammy Tucker but with some extra weight on her now. Priscilla said she looked good with some new curves. Bethany was enamored by the jewelry she wore. Look at that emerald! Is that a real diamond? Kate noticed the stretch marks on Tammy's bare belly.

"Tammy?" called Kate, still holding her hand. "We're all here to help you. Just relax."

She opened her eyes completely then and the first face she saw was Priscilla's, who offered a big grin.

"Hey, Tammy!"

"*U'le'ha me'lo'lo a'be'fe'o*," said Tammy weakly. Nobody seemed to understand so she repeated her words. Nothing. "*O'la Alebafe'o he'lo a'a*," she added with more strength.

"What's she sayin'?" asked Bethany.

"She talkin' gibberish," Priscilla replied.

"Ma'am," said Detective Golden, squatting to speak to her, "can you hear me? Do you need medical assistance? Can you speak?"

"*O'la Alebafe'o he'lo a'a*," she repeated, expressionless.

"I mean, can you speak English?"

"*He'lo a'fe'o.*"

"Well, that's weird," said Priscilla with a laugh.

"Leave her alone," said Kate. "She probably got some big whack to the head.

"But where's she been for three years?" asked Bethany. "Has she been hiding out here in the service center? Digging through the trash bins for food? Lotta places to hide in this creepy place."

When Detective Henderson pushed through the door of the hospital room, already knowing what he would find, he was still taken by surprise. In the bed, surrounded by IV bags, tubes, and wires was his former colleague, Chuck McElroy, presumed dead for three years but now very much alive albeit with both arms in casts up past the elbows, and assorted other scars and bandaged wounds.

"You look like hell," said Henderson.

Chuck did not smile. His eyes were narrowed, suspicious. Everyone was hassling him, asking him questions, acting like he was crazy. He knew where he was but could not believe he had been where he had been. On another planet? Slipping through some tear in the air? Who would ever believe him?

"Scratch my nose," Chuck grunted.

"What's that?"

"I said scratch my damn nose. I can't reach it, not with these things on my arms."

"Sounds like Chuck McElroy. Looks like him, too. Can it really be my old buddy?"

Henderson stepped to the side of the bed. He raised a finger, aimed at the nose, slowly zeroed in and landed fingernail first. He stroked downward a few times.

"Good?"

"Tip."

Henderson scratched the end of Chuck's nose.

"Good now?"

"Better."

"So...where the hell you been?"

"That's what everybody wants to know, huh?"

"Yes. The next question is 'What happened to you?'"

The room fell silent, the men staring at each other.

Chuck coughed, winced in pain.

Henderson repeated his questions.

Chuck snorted back mucus in his sinuses.

Henderson blinked twice.

Chuck looked away, scanning the cityscape outside: cold and gray, lifeless.

"Not ready to talk?" asked Henderson.

"Am I charged with any crime?" Chuck finally spoke.

"I'm not sure. We're just talking. Buddy to buddy. Not even cop to cop. What happened to you? Where've you been for three damn years?"

The staring match resumed. Henderson was arranging the sting to bring down Sebastian Talbot in an old, abandoned house in the countryside. The operation went bad. The house exploded in flames when a SWAT team's shot hit the propane tank. Then he'd gotten a call from headquarters telling him Chuck McElroy had fallen down from the ceiling, right through the tiles, and crashed on a desk, rolled onto the floor, arms broken, bones poking out, messy. And all he was wearing was some gladiator get-up, like he was at a leather party. Nobody could explain how he got up into the ceiling crawl space without anyone noticing.

"So what happened?" asked Henderson again.

Chuck pursed his lips, putting words together, gathering his breath. Henderson waited. He pulled a chair around to the side of the bed and sat, waited.

"I guess I just had a bad dream," said Chuck.

"Bad dream? For three years?"

"Yeah, that's what I said."

"Where were you sleeping? Dreams only happen when you sleep, Chuckie."

"Last thing I remember...." He stopped. He remembered what it was, but he realized he had to be careful what he said. "I was going back to Sunnydale...."

"Yes...?"

"I was going back to meet Toni. You know, Dr. Franck. I was gonna talk to her."

"Go on."

"And just as I arrived I saw some guy stealing her car." He was warming up, had fashioned a complete story in a few seconds. Now it was time to run with it. "I saw it was Talbot. Somehow he escaped and he was taking her car. I followed him out to Independence, out Pink Hill Road, you know, to that quarry. I ran after him and we fought. He had some strange kind of weapon...."

"Really. Laser beam? Pulse gun?"

"Not sure."

Chuck stopped. Was he going to go ahead and admit stepping through the tear in the air to another world? Or something else? He hadn't thought it through that far.

"I don't know what it was. I just—whatever it was hit me and knocked me out. Next thing I know I'm falling down from the ceiling in my old station. I guess I was held prisoner by him. I can't remember any of that."

"How'd you escape?"

Chuck grinned, tried to hold it back. "That I don't know. No idea where I was or how I ever coulda got up into the ceiling like that. I must've been drugged. The whole time. I kept thinking I was...yeah, I was like lost in the desert. I really thought I was somewhere else. In some kind of dream world."

It was starting to make sense to him, even as he invented his story. He could not really have been on another world. He could not have been at the mercy of some desert bandits. Could he? That was what was crazy. It all seemed so real—and yet it couldn't have been. And Tammy...? She must've been part of his dream, his drug-coma, too. That made him wonder if she were still alive—or dead, killed by Talbot.

"I see." Henderson did not smile but nodded.

Suddenly, Chuck wasn't too sure what Henderson might know already. He wondered if he had just been caught telling a fabulous story.

"Toni?" asked Chuck.

"She's in good health."

"What happened to her? I mean, with Talbot escaping...?"

Henderson frowned. "She was hurt pretty bad. Landed in a coma. But she's out of it now and back to whatever."

"She's alive?" Chuck felt his heart skip a beat.

"Very alive. And get this: she went ahead and married Talbot. They have a son, too."

"He's here? Back on Earth—umm, here?"

"Back on Earth? What's that supposed to mean?"

Chuck grinned sheepishly. "Bang on the head sure makes a guy say strange things. I mean, Talbot is here? In town? Right now?"

"Yes, of course." Henderson studied Chuck a moment. "After the house incident he ended up in the prison hospital at Sibley. He was shot, paralyzed now. Can't move anything but his eyes. So we don't need to worry about him."

"That's...weird."

Henderson smiled. "You mean ironic?"

"Yeah...ironic...."

Henderson patted the bed. "So when you're up and ready to lock and load, see me at the station. All right?"

"Yeah, sure." Chuck seemed lost in thought.

"All right then." Henderson hesitated. "What's wrong?"

Chuck looked over at him. "So is Tammy back, too? My ex?"

"Back?"

"Is she in town?"

"Funny you should mention that. She was found in an IRS service center restroom the same night you fell through the ceiling. Strange coincidence, don't you think? It's almost like you two were both blown back here from somewhere—like in *The Wizard of Oz*, you know? But from where?"

"That's a very good question," said Chuck.

Chapter 3

Magic

"It's like I been trying to tell you, I'm the Queen of Aivana." The woman in the hospital gown, sitting across the table, was frantic. "By marriage, anyway. See, I met the king on Agani Isle and he took me back and married me. When he died I stayed on as the queen. Then I married another man, Jason. We had children, too. Buffy, then Jason Junior, and Kip and Mary-Ann."

"You had four children in three years?" asked Detective Jasperson. She rolled her eyes at her colleague, Detective Golden.

"Well, the time works different there. It was really like ten years."

"Ten years, you say?"

"Then it all ended with a big explosion. That's all I remember."

"Explosion?" asked Detective Jasperson. Golden, in blue pinstriped 'gangster' suit, sat silently on a chair in the corner, arms crossed.

"Yes." Tammy took a drink from the Diet Coke can in her hand. "We were all in the Great Hall, having an audience. You know, greeting princes and answering people's questions, settling arguments, like what queens're supposed to do. Then my ex just ran in, dressed in a leather costume begging for me to take him back. That was funny! We was arguing and some Roûe guys in brown robes ran in and tossed some bombs at us. Last thing I remember is him throwing his body over me."

"To protect you?"

"I dunno. I guess so. He was big and strong, like he was working out. He was tanned and had scars on his chest and arms. He looked like some hero guy from the movies. He was hot."

"You're referring to Chuck McElroy?"

"Yeah, my ex. From Earth."

Detective Jasperson, in brown pantsuit and dark red blouse, perused the file before her. This woman had not committed any crime. In fact, she had been the victim. That was the story, Jasperson understood, although now it did not make sense. Three years earlier this woman was presumed dead—murdered by the notorious serial killer Sebastian Talbot—along with a few others. Then, not long after, her ex, the cop who had been investigating Talbot, disappeared.

And Talbot had been locked in an asylum for the criminally insane. Then he escaped.

Now Tammy Sue Tucker reappears. And she's dressed in some harem girl costume: billowing pantaloons, cute vest over low-cut filmy blouse, bedecked with jewelry. She had appeared in the service center dressed like that, no other clothes. Not even a purse.

"From Earth?" asked Jasperson.

"Yes, from Earth."

"That's what I said." Tammy looked around at the framed paintings on the walls. "You don't believe me?"

Jasperson shook her head. "It's not whether we believe you or not. We are gathering details. Whatever you tell us is helpful."

"So I'm not, like, in trouble, am I?"

"You have not been charged with anything."

"Can I go home now?"

Jasperson glanced at Detective Golden. He remained motionless, expressionless, silent. She cleared her throat.

"Ms. Tucker, do you have a home to go to?" asked Golden, sitting up on the front edge of the chair, hands clasped between his knees.

"My mother's house in Sugar Creek. I guess I'll go there."

Golden brushed his crew-cut with his hand, breathing deeply.

"She doesn't live there any longer. She's in a nursing home."

"Nursing home? Why? How long's it been?"

Jasperson nodded, flipped through the folder. "About four years—since you went missing, but—"

"She awright?"

"No, she's not." Golden stood, leaned on the table with two fists. "She tried to commit suicide. The report says she cut her wrists."

"She did? But why?"

"When your son went missing—when was it? Three years ago? She felt responsible. She went crazy, tried to end her life. She lost a lot of blood. Enough to affect her brain. She lived but she doesn't have full cognitive abilities."

Tammy threw her hands to her face.

"I didn't mean no harm," she cried through her fingers. "I thought I was doing the right thing."

Golden stepped back.

"The right thing?" asked Jasperson. "What do you mean?"

Tammy looked up, her face red and streaked with tears.

"I just wanted to have my baby away from those gossipy women at the service center. I never meant to be away so long. And my son, well, I wanted him to be with me."

"Your mother thought he was kidnapped or killed like you, and she—"

"I know, I know," cried Tammy. "I messed up everything."

The detectives let her cry a few minutes. When she seemed to catch her breath, Jasperson handed her a tissue.

"So why did you return?"

"Well, I didn't mean to return. It just happened, like I said. I sorta popped back here. Big explosion and bang, I'm in the restroom at the service center." She snapped her fingers. "Just like that."

"Instantly?"

"One second I was shouting at my ex in the middle of the Great Hall. The next second the explosion and I'm sitting on the floor in a toilet stall at the service center. I couldn't hear anything at first, ya know. My head was kinda spinning."

Jasperson turned to Golden. "Concussion from the blast."

Golden nodded.

"How did you get from the house to the IRS building?"

Tammy wiped her tears. "What house?"

"The house where Sebastian Talbot was holed up the past three years."

"But—he never—I ain't seen him since before the explosion."

"You saw the explosion, right?"

"Yeah, it was right in front of me."

"Were you inside the house or outside?"

"What house are you talking about?"

"The house off Pink Hill Road. Where you were hiding the past three years. You don't remember?"

Tammy shook her head, then covered her face with her hands, sobbing once more.

"That has to be a good twenty miles," said Golden. "Pink Hill Road to Highway 291, then I-70, south on I-435, off at Bannister, keep going a couple miles. Only someone driving, giving her a ride, could get her across the city like that. In that short time."

Jasperson nodded. "How'd you get from there to the IRS building?"

Tammy lifted her face to Detective Golden, met his stern expression, all business, like he'd never had a friend in his life.

"I just popped in. Like I was beaming in, ya know, like they do on that *Star Trek* show. Hah, I made a rhyme: *know* and *show*. Funny, huh?"

"Hilarious," grunted Jasperson, pulling out a fresh cigar and turning to Golden. "Got a lighter?"

"You gonna smoke in here?" asked Tammy.

She stared at the Queen of Aivana a moment. Tammy fell silent.

"I hate fairy tales."

"It's not a fairy tale—"

"You need to get up outta that bed and get a job. Then you'll get your head right. Remember: Say no to drugs."

❊ ❊ ❊

Detectives Henderson and Wilson both reached for the phone when it rang. Wilson waved it to Henderson, who answered.

"That was the science team," he said, hanging up. "You'll never guess what they're calling about."

"Try me," said Wilson.

"There's no gap any longer."

"Gap? You mean at the quarry?"

"The gap in the air. Where Talbot escaped."

"He just stepped through and was gone."

"Didn't our guys follow him?"

"That's when they were shot at by whoever was waiting on the other side."

"So the science team began investigating the...what do we call it? the phenomena? A hole in the sky. Waving back and forth like the flaps of a circus tent."

"I told you guys he went to another world."

"Well, they didn't find him. Now it's gone. Mended, fixed. No more gap."

"Just like that?"

"Apparently."

"So was it a doorway or not? Or was it just an optical illusion?"

"He really did escape through it. But to who knows where?"

"Without any proof—"

"He's locked up in the hospital anyway. No need to worry about it. He came back from wherever—or he was here all along."

"Living in that old house they tore down?"

"That's what most people think."

"But not you?"

"I wonder what's true anymore."

"He went through the gap and returned three years later through the gap. That's when we caught him running from the house, escaping up to the quarry and then—"

"Jumping off the cliff."

"He was shot and fell. He didn't jump."

"He was going to jump."

"Then he was shot. Head and shoulder."

"And he fell on the rocks below. Snap. Neck broken."

"Paralyzed."

"Quadriplegic."

"Terrible ending."

"Not for a serial killer."

"The question is not whether he left Earth—Can we actually say that?—left through some doorway, but whether he killed those people at all. Still no bodies."

"Except Davenport's, the fat guy. And Tucker, the skinny girl. McElroy's ex. Although she's not dead any longer."

"She is alive but out of it mentally. Freaked out. So where's Michael, her supposed lover? And the others from the Service Center, the three women?"

"They all went to the quarry that night. And they all disappeared. They found part of one girl's shirt on a tree limb. Some hair samples. And Talbot was gone for three months, shows up again one night like nothing's happened, shows up for his shift."

"He led them through the gap and left them there. That's what he maintains."

"He didn't know the three women who were there, he said, just Michael Fenning and Tammy Tucker."

"Don't tell me you're thinking it could all be true? That he did take them somewhere. Somewhere out there?"

"Way out there."

"And Tucker has returned."

"So has McElroy. He was gone for some time, too. After Talbot broke out of the asylum, almost killed that doctor."

"Doctor Franck swore it was not him."

"She was hit in the head. How would she know?"

"If not Talbot beating her to death—almost—who else could it be? I mean, she goes to see him every week. And they have a kid together. Talbot had no reason to attack her."

"Except to get out of there."

"And he stole her car, drove straight to the quarry, according to McElroy."

"The night McElroy disappeared."

"At the quarry."

"They investigated it right away and they saw the gap. The big flapping gap. And no people. No bodies. No footprints."

"I wonder...."

"About what? The science team's diligence?"

"No, I believe they saw what they saw and now they don't see it any longer."

"You know.... Scientists, right?"

"I was wondering if the story is different than what we all believe. About McElroy seeing Talbot escape. Chasing him to the quarry. Then muscle-bound McElroy gets beaten up by that bookworm Talbot? And then kidnapped? Seems a little odd."

"What're you thinking?"

"Just follow me for a minute," said Wilson. "McElroy is dating Toni Franck. They get into a fight at her office late one night. He hates Talbot for killing his ex, Tammy Tucker. So Chuck is angry at Franck for whatever reason and—you know how his temper can be—he lets fly a punch and she crashes against the corner of the desk. Just like forensics described."

"Then what?"

"Chuck realizes what he's done and tries to cover for himself."

"I see."

"He lets Talbot out so he can blame the attack on him, then lets Talbot drive off just so he can chase him and be the hero who kills Talbot the terrorist!"

"Only something else happened."

Henderson grimaced. The clouds were clearing yet he could not believe he hadn't seen it all before. "Really?"

"Really." Wilson was not smiling. "So Talbot got the jump on him somehow. Then...."

"Then...?"

"You finish it."

"Then Talbot takes McElroy...."

"Go on."

"McElroy follows Talbot through the gap...."

"Into that other world he's always talked about."

They sat in silence a moment. Wilson got up and refilled his coffee, returned to his desk.

"There's no other explanation that fits the facts."

"But McElroy falls from the ceiling almost three years later?" Henderson shook his head. "How does that happen? How could Talbot get Chuck up there in the ceiling without anybody noticing?"

Wilson shook his head. "I haven't figured that out yet. But we do know Talbot was burning up in that abandoned house out east when McElroy returned through the ceiling."

"Well," said Henderson, rubbing his furrowed brow, "at least we thought he was burning up. But he escaped once again. Got over to the quarry, where our team caught up with him, plugged him, and sent him to the coma ward."

"And McElroy instantly pops back onto Earth!"

Henderson laughed. "On Earth? You're serious, aren't you?"

"I never put much stock in Drummond's sci-fi jokes, but it kinda has a ring of truth if you look at the hard facts we know and line'em up against the only available explanation. Talbot can go from Earth to somewhere else. And back again. Isn't he some kind of physics genius?"

"Or some kind of wizard with a magic wand."

Dr. Antoinette Franck—Toni to her few friends—flipped her dark, curly locks from her shoulder, rubbed her neck as she sat back in her office chair. She had finished reading the entire folder before her, a couple hundred pages of documents, notes, photographs, charts, forensic reports, everything on her new patient. It all seemed so neat.

Before the "incident," she had worked with the criminally insane, returning them to normalcy, at least enough that they could stand trial or, in a rare case, be set free. She thought she was tough and could handle them. After the attack and the coma she had endured, however, she was hesitant to take that position again. So she made herself feel satisfied to work with outpatients, those who needed to talk to someone, needed a prescription, or some advice. A lot of those who visited were students from the university a few blocks away; she didn't mind discussing boyfriend troubles or identity issues or anxiety.

Now the past was catching up with her. She stared at the folder, the top sheet bearing a name she knew from her previous life: Tammy Sue Tucker.

Dr. Franck's first thought was how could someone have exactly the same name as one of the victims of the serial killer Sebastian Talbot. Then she realized it was not coincidence but progress: Ms. Tucker had returned, not as dead as everyone presumed.

Surely they must know there would be a conflict of interest since she had been *his* doctor. Her partner in the private practice, Dr. Caroline Minor, was slated to take the Tucker case, yet she was rather suddenly called away. Family emergency, she had said, rushing out.

Toni exhaled with an edge of frustration and stood up.

How could everything be so strange? She recovered from the coma, went through rehabilitation until her legs were strong enough for her to walk without braces. Checked out by the finest neurologists, she proceeded to retake her licensure exams and be recertified in psychiatry. She was back where she used to be: helping people. And from her previous life, she had a souvenir: a boy named for his father.

Little Sebastian looked like his father and was growing fast, starting school early, speaking both English and French, and showing promise in Mandarin and Russian. The school had to move him to their advanced track, not wanting to embarrass the other second-graders with his prowess in mathematics and science. The only thing unusual about the budding genius was how often he would fall silent and seem to be engaged telepathically with someone or something out somewhere. She worried it might be a neurological disorder or, worse, someone was actually communicating with the boy. God or demons, psychics or...his father, perhaps.

She kept hoping he would be able to join her soon, move into the apartment where she and their son lived. It was troublesome having weekend visits. The wheelchair and the stairs and his paralyzed body did not come together easily. And there were always guards watching them. Even when they would go to the park for a picnic, men with dark glasses and radios watched them—as though she was about to make a run for it with him in tow! He was of no danger to anyone now, locked inside his stiff body, hoisted into a wheelchair, his eyes and ears alive, his mind seemingly quite normal. He was, however, unable to speak, or move, or scratch his nose, much less get up and run away from the prison hospital. All because they found one dead body and tagged him for the murder in lieu of not being able to find the other bodies.

Now one of the bodies had returned and, as luck would have it in her crazy world, the woman was assigned to her office. The problem? She believed she was actually the queen of a desert kingdom. On another world. How common was that psychosis?

Sebastian Talbot, her former patient and briefly her lover, believed he could travel between Earth and another planet, too. He insisted he had various adventures there, became a warrior and rescued a woman he called his long-lost love, or some such name, from the castle of some warlord. Much like the popular video games coming out now. With Ms. Tucker's reappearance, his case could be opened again.

She pursed her lips a moment, then turned the framed photograph on her desk and gazed at the portrait of the three of them—taken in the prison. They did make an interesting family. Psychiatrist and interdimensional voyager. The odd couple.

She laughed and closed the folder.

If she could just get that call from the lawyer telling her that a new hearing had been scheduled, she could be happy. Since two of the supposed victims had returned, he could no longer be charged with their murders. That also opened the possibility that his story was true: they were not dead, just missing. She had hopes for a future free of persecution.

Once her husband was released from prison they would move away—vanish off the face of the Earth, go where nobody could bother them ever again. He believed they could, he said so many times, but she had doubts. Alaska or northern Québec seemed a good place. Or some Caribbean island. Anywhere but Kansas City, Missouri, U.S.A. If only his fantasy world were a real place, she sighed. They could go there and live happily ever after.

Detective Henderson waved Chuck McElroy over to the table they reserved in the Hereford House restaurant. Already there were all his buddies from the force. Everyone wore a suit and tie except for Chuck, who came as a surprise guest in jeans and sweatshirt.

"How's it going, ol' buddy?" sang Henderson.

A chorus of bad jokes and lame insults followed as Chuck sat and drank his beer.

Eventually a waiter took their orders: steaks all around, of course. What would you expect from a restaurant a cow pile's throw from the Kansas City stockyards? Chuck grinned, enjoying himself, not too worried what the occasion was they were celebrating. His arms felt strong, too; he could lift the full mug confidently.

"So Chuckie, how's it feel to be retired?"

It was Detective Sawyer, the kid, who asked the party-crushing question. Of course, he did not know that Chuck had yet to be informed of his failure to pass the physical.

"It's all right, Chuck," said Henderson. "That's why we're all here tonight. To celebrate. To wish you well, and all that crap. We wanna get one more crack at you."

"Retired? Who said anything about that?"

They glanced at each other around the table.

"You're right. Forget it," said Henderson. "Let's just have a good time."

"We never go out enough, he always says," Detective Wilson laughed. He was using a woman's voice. "That's what he's always complaining about. We never go out. We never go out. We're out now, aren't we?"

The others laughed but suddenly Chuck was not sharing their sense of humor. His arms had healed and felt as strong as ever. The other injuries he had were also good. His body wore the scars of a tough few years stuck on an alien world—and none of these yahoos could comprehend that. They could not understand how it felt to be a slave, a total nothing but naked flesh submissive slave being pulled along through the desert with a rope around his neck, like some animal, following behind the wagging tail of some kind of giraffe/camel hybrid thing. He could be sold at any marketplace, rented out for anyone's party, poked or stabbed or cut at will simply for the pleasure of the crazy nomad who ordered it.

Retirement? From what? He had already been gone for three years. In Earth time. *Listen to me...Earth time.... You are one messed up sonovabitch.* He never expected his job would be saved for him. Now he returns and everybody thought he was dead. Nobody went looking for him. Nobody cared.

"Yeah," said Chuck finally, cutting off the group's chummy boisterousness, "I think I'm gonna like retirement. I'm still young enough I can do something else before I die. Thinking of being a security guard for some dumb-ass hotel. Or maybe do some undercover investigation work. I wanna get in touch with my son, too. Maybe we'll go to some ballgames. And I'll be traveling, too. Finally gonna go up to Canada and shoot me a moose." He looked around the table. "I can tell you're all jealous. Hey, look me up when you get bored. I might have something going on you can be a part of."

And with that, he set down his napkin neatly and stood, shared a smirk with them, and departed.

Chapter 4

The Jungle

Before Chucker opened his eyes, he desperately grabbed his chest, rubbing his hands over himself, expecting to find a deep wound there but drew away his fingers and saw no blood. He felt his clothing, the purple robe he had worn in the Great Hall, and it was gone. In its place was a high-collared khaki coat. He felt a leather belt around his waist. Evidently the purple robe he had worn to cover his smart uniform had been torn off.

He noticed he was hungry, thirsty, and felt as though he had not slept for days.

Opening his eyes, he saw palm fronds leaning down to him, the beams of pale gray sunlight streaking through the leaves, the fluttering of white feathers from some kind of peafowl on a nearby branch, and the warm, moist air sitting atop him, pushing him against the cool, rich earth, fragrant and exciting.

He sat up, found he could do so without pain or limitation, then stood up, brushing off dirt and grass from his uniform.

"Where am I?" he asked aloud, then realized he did not need to speak since he was alone, alone in what seemed to be a lush jungle.

To the right was more forest, becoming denser until it faded into shadows. To his left more trees, also thickening into darkness. Behind him he could detect a cliff behind more trees and brush. Ahead seemed to be a slope down through the forest.

He thought he could see some water, a pond or stream, through the trees. He was tempted to go toward the water but decided to climb the cliff and get a better view of his situation.

Breaking through the trees, he saw what looked like an animal trail and followed it to the base of the cliff. He looked along its face in both directions, crumbling yellow rock, looking for a trail but found none. He turned and walked along it anyway until he saw a gentler slope and began to scramble up to the top, losing his footing several times and getting his uniform quite dirty before finally reaching the top.

From the top, he could see the water he had detected from below. It was not a jungle pond or a forest stream, but a whole expanse of water—a sea or ocean, he thought, gazing to the far horizon and seeing no other land out there.

He sat on the edge of the cliff, examining himself, analyzing the situation while occasionally regarding the sea and the two suns, a larger yellow one and a smaller blue one, until the greening sunset faded into black night—calculating trajectories, measuring time, contemplating the patterns of stars, hearing the wild bird calls and animal grunts and growls, seeing a few spots of torch fires in the distance, and cursing Set-d'Elous for growing that ugly beard and slipping out of Aivana too soon. Without saying goodbye.

Or giving him a map of the universe.

Or offering him any kind of weapon as a line of upright figures approached through the dark forest flora.

"In the dream land," spoke a voice not too unfamiliar, a rich baritone that did not echo against the stone walls, "it is not uncommon for people to focus on a place where they once existed and to which they wish to return: a place of romance, of majesty, of comfort, perhaps, where wonderful events occurred, where memories were made; indeed, a place that now in hindsight seems the ideal world where everything was available and one wanted for nothing and all was in perfect balance, a way station equidistant between order and chaos. Or, conversely, the dream land is a place where people expect to have their expectations met. I know that sounds ironic, to use the same word twice in the same sentence yet with different meanings, but that, too, is something that often happens in the dream land. And so it is, as you might by now surmise, a place you intend to discover: so you journey about in search of meaning, seeking every clue you can find that will lead you to that perfect place, that land of milk and honey, as it were, or in more modern parlance, a place of destiny—your destiny, which may be something entirely of your own design or something entirely not—"

"Stop, please," he said. The words caught in his throat, as though he meant to think them, not speak them. His throat managed to push the words out nevertheless and when they came out it was more like sludge than a flowing stream.

"Stop?"

"You are wrong."

"Am I?" the voice responded. "I have many years of experience to bring to bear on the subject."

"Who are you?"

"I am...well, let's say I am your roommate. That's a friendly term, is it not? We are in a room together, such as it is."

"What room? I can't see anything."

"Yes, that was a problem for me, as well. In time, I felt my way around the walls and discovered, as you will also, that the room is two and a half meters in length and two meters in width, that the height of the space we inhabit is likewise two and a half meters. You will feel the horizontal surface upon which you now recline is attached to the wall. Beneath this shelf, if you wish to identify it as such, are the two bins which contain all you will ever need while residing here—"

"Where are we?"

"As I was describing to you, this is our home. Perhaps for a few years, perhaps forever. It's never been...how you say? set in stone. The walls are stone yet I have not found anything inscribed on them."

"Stone walls?" He felt claustrophobic. His hand reached out and felt the wall. So close. "What is this place?"

"You should know. You built it."

"I did? How is that possible?"

"You build everything in your world."

"My world.... What are you talking about?"

"The dream land. This is what you've built. Now you live here...more or less."

"Then who are you?"

"I have many names, but you might want to refer to me as Max."

"Max...? I've never known anyone with that name. Who are you and how did you get here? I mean, in this room with me. How did we become...roommates?"

There was a moment of silence and just as he was beginning to think he had imagined the while conversation, the voice of Max returned:

"I don't wish to alarm you but I have been with you since the start. It is only in this dire circumstance that I've been released and allowed to speak to you in this way."

"I don't understand. Where are we?"

"Sebastian...we are in a prison."

"A prison? But why? I never did anything wrong.... Not much, anyway. Nothing serious. Well, there was that one time when I...it was all a misunderstanding...and...."

"Yes, a prison, Sebastian Talbot. We are in the prison you built. We are in the prison of your mind."

Chucker spotted a patch of red through the flora, saw it waving at random. Civilization, he thought warily. After all, Set-d'Elous had told him that jungles were dangerous places. That was why he preferred the open landscape, the barren isles, the desert: he could see trouble coming miles away.

Stepping carefully through the forest, he tried to avoid snapping twigs or brushing the large leaves to make any rustling sound. He approached the red patch, which moved slightly with every step he took.

Breaking through the bushes, he saw the girl. She was dressed in red and her trailing scarf was also red. So was her veil.

"Oh my god!" he grunted, recognizing her. Bad had turned to

worse. "You came through the tangent, too?"

She pulled herself up to her knees, her eyes reflecting fear.

"I'm not going to hurt you," said Chucker, extending his hand to help her up.

She refused it, moving her own hands to cover her face and body.

"I'm not going to hurt you," he repeated with more insistence.

He dropped to a cross-legged position before her, tried to grin, thought it may have seemed evil, and tried again to produce a more sincere expression.

"I'm Chuck," he said, pointing at himself, "but you can call me Chucker. You probably will need to call me something since we are in this together. Damn if I want to have to look after you but I don't see any other way. I can't just leave you here—I mean, leave you to your fate. Shit, I'm talking like Set."

She spoke something in Roué, or more likely a dialect of it she spoke in her native Typeg. At least he recognized it.

He summoned his best Roué and explained that they were in a dangerous place. The first thing they needed to do was get rid of her red clothing, which would catch the eyes of any wild animals or primitive people. They needed to stay hidden. She did not immediately respond, neither approving or rejecting his plan.

Thinking she did not understand him, Chucker stared at her a moment, smiled again, then proceeded to undress her.

She fought him, scratching at his face as he told her again how she needed to get out of the red clothing. He stopped; his own khaki clothes were not much better. He pulled off his jacket, turned it inside out so the dark green lining was showing. He stood and stepped out of his trousers, pulled them inside out also and pulled them on again, leaving black showing. She watched him and seemed to get the idea. She unfastened her long train and rolled it up in her hands. He sat with her again as she unfastened her veil and added it to the long scarf. Then she pointed behind him and he almost jumped up to defend her from some tiger.

No, he guessed, she wanted him to look away. So he turned, still sitting on the mossy ground, and she stood.

He listened as she unsnapped her garment and pulled off the red jacket embroidered with golden designs, turned it inside out and dressed again. He waited patiently, watching the forest, as she did the same with her pantaloons. She tapped his shoulder when she was finished transforming herself. What he saw was not much better: her inside-out clothing was now a bright yellow. He shook his head.

"*Lu'e'fo*," he muttered. 'Needs to be darker.'

She nodded, stepped over to a small depression where water had gathered and dug in the soil under the puddle, then began smearing the mud over her garments.

All I can remember is a sunrise, thought Set-d'Elous. The yellow sun was striking the windowsill and I opened my eyes, expecting to be in my apartment in Raytown, Missouri. I was afraid I was late for work. But I realized within the first two minutes that I was awakening on another world. I had no clue; I just felt it. I remembered a life as full and rich as anything you'd read about in a very fat novel. Only this was me. I felt old, ancient. It was as though I were looking back over time and seeing every event, big and small, unfold like a film playing. My life. I was stepping through a rip in the night sky, disappearing, finding myself in a desert. A hand was holding my hand—and I looked. It was Gina. And she said "Come."

And I did. We walked for years across the desert and one morning I awoke in bed. In a room at the top of a tower. And outside the window I saw a mountain with two peaks stabbing the sky. I was about to go to the window to look at them but I heard a baby crying. I turned and there was Gina, the love of my life, sitting in a chair, holding a bundle of baby. She began to nurse the baby and I watched yet I could not see the baby among the blankets. I asked her the baby's name and she said "Zaura."

And I told her that Zaura was my wife—had been my wife. The woman I married in Selauê, who I met in Lyas. And Gina said that was correct. She did as I requested and named our daughter after my Ghoupalle wife who died in 1481. Then Gina reminded me that my Ghoupalle wife died because of the syndrome all *senzenors* get when they give up their gift for a many-year dalliance with an Earth man, when they bear children.

And she told me how I had tried to undo that fate of hers by returning through the rips in the universal curtain, how I had tried to present myself as the man she married many years before. There was no emotional connection between us the second time, for she knew I was not the same man and I let her believe I was someone new to her. It all did not matter, of course, once I went north with the regiment to Sorêg for the autumn patrol. Did I mention I was captain of a cavalry regiment? Yes, I've had a full, rich life.

And I met Basura-Kanoun there at Sorêg. Yes, the evil empress. Rather, the innocent young lady who would grow up to become the evil empress. And I fought with myself what to do. Should I act to save millions from death and defeat? Or should I let the girl live? In the end I killed her and awoke—somehow; I never can figure out how that happened because I did not traverse the tangents—I awoke beside her in bed, in a large, elegant room I thought was a fancy hotel in Paris, France. And she was speaking French to me. Then a man came and helped me dress in a uniform and led me out to the day's events. When I went through my tasks, I was invited into another room to wait to give a speech to representatives of the nations of the world.

And in came a quartet of assassins—right when I was standing on a ledge to better see the stacked coffins in the plaza below the windows. I broke through the windows. I think I was shot by the assassins. I fell. I dropped for years, it seemed, and I never knew if I landed anywhere. Then I awoke in the desert and just started walking. I walked until I got to a town, where I did not know the language and was knocked out and taken to this prison.

The first time Chucker saw them, he wondered if Blue Hairs was a good name for the people he encountered in his hunts through the jungle. He had called old ladies straight out of the salons Blue Hairs, of course. However, these people—men, women, and children—all had hair that was pale blue, a pastel blue, subdued but definitely blue. All the while their skin was a healthy milk chocolate. Chucker wondered if their hair was dyed or if it was the result of their diet. The babies had yellow hair, which became blue as they grew older, possibly as their consumption of the local berries increased. He watched them intently whenever he came upon them, always careful not to give away his presence. He was becoming jungle-savvy.

They had small temporary villages in the forest clearings, usually near a stream. Three or four round huts made of the reeds that grew beside the streams. The huts were easily constructed by weaving the long leaves and using the stalks as ribbing. They seemed to be an extended family group, perhaps a set of siblings with elder parents, spouses, and children. A few yellow meter-long lizards with three horns accompanied them as hunting companions or pets.

He focused on the horns. Some animals had them, had fully developed horns of one kind or another. Others had only knobs. These humans had knobs on their heads where horns might have grown before those genes were somehow suppressed during evolution. (That science class back in high school, reinforced by his tutors in Aivana, was paying off.) He noticed the fauna of Ghoupallesz—if indeed, he and Foj were still on Ghoupallesz—no matter whether a bird, a reptile, mammal or something else, always had either the knobs or a full set of horns.

Chucker snuck away, back to his own camp, a four-*peth* hike. He thought about the Blues. He only saw them eating vegetables and fruit. Rarely the snake-like animal with short feet that ran everywhere. They did not seem cannibalistic. He wondered if they might be helpful—whether the Blues were a kind people who might share their supplies with him. Or were they warriors who would kill any outside before he could take two steps into the village?

He watched them from trees or from behind rocks. Once he lay submerged in the stream to observe them. At all times they seemed pure as the breeze, as simple as sand, as calm as dust. What would they think of him? He was taller but not by much. He was more muscular, lightly tanned, and had blonde hair. He definitely would not blend in. But they had food and tools and he wanted some of each.

Over the weeks of life in the jungle, he and Foj moved often, following the Blues at a distance. He tried to emulate their camping and hunting methods. They ate the same berries, and he saw his blond hair slipping into a blue hue over the months. At night he would slip to the edge of their campsite and snatch a tool or a basket of food, returning like a ghost through the forest.

Always he stayed alert to the animals and people of the jungle, ever vigilant in protecting his patient partner, the girl from Typeg named Foj. She actually made life in the jungle a kind of fantasy camp for Tarzan-wannabe's. She made good loincloths, too.

But like all good summer camps, a return to civilization was eventually expected. It had already been more than a year that he and Foj had been living there as husband and wife, pretending the *o'lo*, a colorful parrot-like bird that was always nearby, had squawked the divine words of union on their behalf. That was good enough, he told her, and she agreed.

Chapter 5

Never Comes The Day

"Where is my food?" grumbled Jason, Prince Regent of Aivana. He was sitting comfortably on the embroidered cushions, a small table placed before him. "And where is my companion?"

He waited, hearing faint stirrings in the next room as his dinner was being readied.

It had become a chore getting through the days. Only he remained from the disaster. He felt guilty about that fact. His subjects felt hatred toward him, toward the royal family, as though the explosion was somehow his fault. Everyone knew it was caused by terrorists who infiltrated the Royal Audience and set off bombs. He had stayed on the dais while Queen Tammy went down the aisle to meet her ex-husband, that muscle-bound oaf, the cop, Chuck whatever. The guards had held him back, made him stay on the dais. He could only watch. He saw that Chuck guy disappear, too. So did his son, Chuck junior—Chucker. He wasn't actually Jason's son; "Chucker" was his stepson.

Now he was alone.

"Where is Lu'le'he?"

The door opened, as if on cue, and in stumbled the young man in the reddish vest and white pantaloons, gold trim down the legs and across the shoulders. Palace uniform. On the man's chest was a blue ribbon, designating him as a personal assistant to the Prince Regent and able to pass anywhere in the palace.

"There you are!" said Jason.

The young man took a seat on the cushion across from Jason, out of breath.

The prince shook his head. "You're late! Again! I'm getting tired of this bad behavior. You only have one job: to talk with me and listen to me while I dine. The rest of the time is yours to indulge. Yet you find it impossible to keep to the schedule. I pay you to be here to have a conversation! When I summon you, you must appear!"

The young man bowed his head. "My deepest apologies, *Kanê*."

The prince shook his head. *Kanê*? Not *Kalmonê*, the higher title? His servant was becoming too casual. The prince always preferred *Kalmonê* ('My Lord') over *Kanê* ('Sire').

"Yeah, yeah, yeah, deepest apologies," said the prince with a grunt. "I don't want you having to apologize. Understand? Set was always on time. And he liked having dinner with me." The prince began mumbling to himself, something about where his friend might be now, how he always ran away, leaving him to sort things out. That was his friend's usual habit: getting himself into trouble. Then he got all of them into trouble—and left. "So, what should we discuss while I dine?"

Six maidens entered, each carrying a special dish of food. Another entered last with a tall pitcher of nectar. The dishes were arranged on the table before him. Rather than deliver each course in order, he had decided it was better to be able to go from dish to dish as he liked, sampling each of them.

Jason reached for the utensil, surveying the buffet. "You can have some," he said to his companion, "if you're hungry. I don't care."

"Thank you, *Kalmonê*."

They worked in silence, taking manageable portions of the food, chewing, drinking, repeating.

"So why were you late? What were you doing?"

"*Kalmonê*, I was meeting with my friends in the plaza."

"For what purpose?"

"*Kalmonê*, to talk about the weather."

"The weather? Don't be so clever. It's always the same in Aivana: hot and dry. Unless a dust storm blows through. What were you really talking about?"

"*Kalmonê*, we—they—dared to suggest that with the absence of Alebafe"—what the locals called Queen Tammy—"with her majesty's departure, *Kalmonê* may not be legally in power. They don't—"

"What? I'm not the prince regent?" He spit out his food. "Crazy students! Well, she will return. I know she will. She's not dead and she's not lost. And when she returns to Aivana everything will be back to normal again. So you tell your so-called friends not to worry. Their queen will return soon and be back in charge of this kingdom. You tell them that."

"I will, *Kalmonê*."

"And if you ever say anything against Tammy—I mean, your queen—you could be facing a painful execution. So watch your mouth."

"Yes, *Kanê*, I will."

Jason nodded and returned to his eating, spearing a morsel of meat and shoving it into his mouth. "Now, what else did you do today? Talk to me. Keep it clean. Make it interesting. That's what I pay you for. Entertain me."

"Yes, *Kanê*, I will."

"Tell me a story...."

❋ ❋ ❋

"And then I married Jason. It was about a year after the king died. The staff said I waited the official mourning time all right so I could take a new spouse."

Tammy opened her eyes, felt her bare back sticking to the leather of the couch. Perhaps next time she would not wear a short top. Nobody here appreciated the desert queen look.

"So there I was, Queen of Aivana, not even very good talking in Roué. And I had two children to raise besides making all these decisions about everything. It was great having Jason visit. He came with some economic cooperation delegation, and he had a sports car. Okay, it was their kind of sports car. It still ran on steam, of course. Our military advisor knew him from the war in Tebbicousimankalê so he introduced us and I was immediately hooked on him."

"Excuse me," asked Dr. Franck from her chair, "what was that word you said? The long one."

"You mean Tebbicousimankalê?"

"Yes, that one."

"It's the name of a country up north. That's where the war was. During the winter. Record snowfall that winter. It got up to 40 feet deep in places. They ended up digging tunnels under the snow just to survive, or to move soldiers around. Of course, you never heard of it. That's because Set-d'Elous went back in time and changed things so the war never happened. It happened, then it didn't happen. A lot of people were left confused."

"Naturally."

Dr. Franck paused, assessing her new client's information, finding parts of it that paralleled the story her husband had told. She thought this woman's story was pure fantasy, as many schizophrenics experienced: the fantasy world merged with the world of reality, often seamlessly. And yet, her husband had told about the same world, a war there he had been involved in, and his return to change it.

"So we got married and had four children," Tammy continued. "Buffy is our oldest. Then Jason Junior, Kip, and Mary-Ann. And also my son from Earth, the one we all call Chucker—that's Chuck Junior, after my ex, Chuck McElroy."

"Yes.... McElroy, the cop."

Dr. Franck had been over the details many times and took the patient solely for the opportunity to investigate a community psychosis that seemed to envelope the people of one group who shared an experience. Everyone who claimed to have walked over to another world had returned with the same stories. Most disturbing was that her husband, Sebastian Talbot, now severely injured and confined to a prison hospital room, was seen as the instigator of the psychosis. The others also seemed to treat him as some kind of god—or, at least, something more than a mortal.

Her article on mass psychosis was coming along just fine, and a major journal had already accepted it based on her proposal and abstract. They believed it would open a door to research on other mass psychoses related to disasters or other public events where many unrelated people shared the same story. She felt conflicted, however, using her husband as a source, but he could easily be listed under a pseudonym: Set-d'Elous.

"And where are they now?" she asked Tammy.

"I guess they are back in the palace. When the explosion happened, I was blown back here to Earth. They weren't around, I mean, not in the Hall so they weren't affected."

"Have you had contact with them?"

Sure, it might have sounded like a mocking question, but Dr. Franck was serious.

"No, course not." Tammy giggled. "They are on another planet. How'm I supposed to have contact with them?"

So her patient understood the different locations. The idea of interstellar communication being impossible was a cogent sign of rationality. Yet saying they were on another planet displayed the same irrational thinking her husband had shown when they first talked.

"What do you think you will do, now that you're back on Earth?"

Tammy waved her hand in the air. "Well, they said I got some real expensive gemstones on me. So I'll be okay for a while. I cashed in the ruby and the two emeralds for around twenty thousand bucks, and the diamond—it was pretty big—I got six thousand. for it."

"Then you're planning on staying here." Toni swallowed, decided to go ahead and say it: "On Earth?"

"Well, I dunno." Tammy sighed. "I ain't got no job here and that money's gonna run out before long. I miss my children, too. If you had the choice, would you wanna be doing what you're doing or go back to where you was a queen?"

Dr. Franck smiled to herself. Yes, she would like to go back to before all the troubles happened. She could understand that. If she could have met Sebastian under different circumstances, or not met him at all. C'est la vie, she thought. That's life.

"Certainly."

"So if I had the chance, I guess I'd be going back to Aivana and be the queen again."

"And what about Chuck?"

Tammy choked. "Why would I want that jerk to go with me? He's the reason I got blasted back here. If he wasn't making a fool of himself in the Hall, then I wouldn't've been right there where the bomb went off—and then got blown back to Earth."

"Do you blame him for your return?"

"Heck, yes."

"Did he ever tell you how he came to be there?"

"You mean in the Dream Land?"

"Yes, there."

"Well, he said he was chasing Set-d'Elous—you know, that Sebastian Talbot guy from my IRS job? He was chasing him and they went through the doorway—you know, that tear in the air? And Chuck, big stupid doofus that he is, he couldn't get back so he was stuck there. Then somehow he found me. But I was a queen and he was just some desert fighter, all sweaty in his leather get-up, like some Roman movie guy."

"You say Chuck was chasing Sebastian?"

"Sure, that's what he said."

"Who said?"

"Sebastian—Set-d'Elous, I mean. He said Chuck was chasing him to the quarry. They was chasing all the way from the mental hospital where he was locked up. Where Sebastian was locked up."

"Let me get this straight. Sebastian told you that Chuck had chased him from the mental hospital all the way to the quarry, right?"

"That's right."

"Did he say why Chuck was chasing him?"

"Not really. Just he wanted to be the one to shoot him and get promoted for killing the serial killer. Only Sebastian wasn't no serial killer. He didn't kill nobody."

"Did he say how he got out of the mental hospital?"

Tammy thought for a moment. "Chuck let him out."

"Let him out?"

"Yeah, like unlocked the door and told him to scram. Then he chased him. But Set-d'Elous got him back good, I guess, seeing how Chuck was beat up by the desert nomads and all. He got what was coming to him and then he turned into a nice guy. He really thought I'd take him back! Hah!"

"Chuck McElroy let Sebastian Talbot out of his room, then deliberately chased him, trying to be the one to kill him?"

"That's what I said. I don't stutter, ya know!"

※ ❋ ※

First came the hand over the mouth, then the knife blade to the throat.

Jason, Prince Regent of Aivana, quickly opened his eyes to see his dinner companion, Lu'le'he, hovering over him, no longer happy to tell stories while the prince dined.

"You have been in this palace much too long," said Lu'le'he in whispered Roûê. "I will give you only one chance tonight to save yourself. Else my friends will come tomorrow to kill you all."

He eased the knife away from Jason's throat.

Jason knew the people were restless, no longer content to have Tammy sit as Queen of Aivana. And with her gone several months now and looking to everyone as though she was magically sucked off the planet, only he was left to sit upon the throne. And who was he? Nobody. Another foreigner, but one who had not even married any Aivanan but, instead, another foreigner. How could the people be so lucky?

"Gather your things. One bag only," Lu'le'he instructed. He straightened up, keeping the knife between them.

Jason scrambled to his feet, sweeping back the sheet to retrieve his socks.

"I can't understand this," said the prince. "I thought the people were happy. I built the arch for them. To honor their king. Aivana is prosperous now."

Lu'le'he tossed a small trunk at him. "It is decided. Pack!"

Jason ripped open the drawers of the long dresser, snapping clothing into the trunk, mumbling to himself.

"What happens tomorrow?" he asked as he gathered clothing.

"I hear the king's eldest son will arrive. And he has sworn to kill the foreign usurpers of the throne."

"E'Bu'li'rou is coming back?" Jason was excited. "I never met him. Heard a lot of stories, of course. So what's the occasion that brings him here?"

"He wishes to be the king. Like his father. Not like Alebafe. E'Bu'li'rou is very angry, and he carries a big sword, and has many soldiers behind him."

Jason stopped, realizing the seriousness of this midnight visit. He closed the trunk. Gazing at himself, he asked if there was time to change into some traveling outfit. Already he was thinking of places he could go.

"And the children? Must they go?"

"Everyone not of the blood of our king."

"So O'Fe'o'pi will stay and be safe?"

"Princess Fe'o'pi has the king's blood. She is one of us and may stay in the palace. Yet she will never reign here as queen."

"I can live with that. I just want her to be safe. No revenge killing, I mean."

"She will be safe."

"Can she come with us? I know her mother won't ever forgive me if we left her behind."

"She is only half-blood so she may go if she chooses."

"And my other children? Buffy and Jason Junior, Kip and Mary-Ann? Not to mention her daughter brought unborn from Earth, O'Ro'ma'le? And how about Prince Chucker?"

"Your children must go. Prince Chucker is already vanished along with his mother, it seems."

"And I still mourn them. If I am forced to leave, how can I wait for them to return? How will I know when they come back through the hole in the Royal Audience Hall? I must stay and wait for them!"

"If you do not depart tonight, you will all—"

The door to the suite opened and in rushed the children of Jason and Tammy, dressed for travel. Two servants, the nanny and the tutor, accompanied them.

"Father, what is happening?" cried Buffy, the eldest, a woman with the appearance of a twenty-year old Earthling. She led Mary-Ann by the hand.

Jason went to Buffy, placed his hands on her shoulders, then glanced around at the others.

"We must leave Aivana tonight. For our safety. My personal companion here, Lu'le'he, tells me of a plot to kill us. If we leave, we live. If we are here tomorrow, the people who hate us will kill us. All of us."

"How can they be so cruel?" asked Kip.

"We cannot wonder about that now," said Jason. "You are

packed? Good. I am packed." He gazed at Lu'le'he. "We are ready."

By candlelight—actually a small jar containing a coiled luminous worm glowing orange in the darkness—they were led along the corridor to a set of secret stairs hidden behind six doors, and down the stairs to the underground garage. Lu'le'he showed them the large ETUR vehicle that had long been planned for use in an escape.

"Provisions are aboard this vehicle."

"Thank you," said Jason.

Out of a side door appeared Princess Fe'o'pi with her Roûê nanny. A short discussion ensued with Lu'le'he.

"They will go with you."

"Two vehicles, then."

He watched his children climb into the first vehicle and he thought of the von Trapp family in *The Sound of Music*, rushing off from the concert and hiding in the abbey to escape the Nazi stormtroopers. What should he and the children sing tonight as they crossed the desert under the twinkling stars? And how would Tammy and Chucker ever find them again?

He turned to little Mary-Ann, who seemed like a twelve year old girl of Earth, and spoke gently: "Do you like to sing at night?"

"At night?" she asked.

"Yes. When we are out of the city we can sing at the top of our lungs. We can awaken all the birds and lizards of the desert with our voices. How about that?"

"I want to try it."

"Me, too," said Jason Junior, and Kip quickly agreed.

"All right, then. Off we go."

He hesitated entering the pilot compartment, turning to regard Lu'le'he.

"I guess it's goodbye."

"Fare you well," he spoke in English.

They shook hands, a custom Jason had taught the Roûê man who had entertained him during his mourning.

Jason climbed into the pilot compartment and took hold of the levers, fired up the furnace. Lu'le'he went ahead and slid open the doors to the cobblestone plaza. With no moon orbiting Ghoupallesz, the night was as black as *dakkilê*—obsidian—as they rolled into the plaza and made the turn down the drive to the side gate. The second ETUR followed closely. Two guards stood there—at attention but refusing to salute the Prince Regent as the two vehicles passed through.

"They didn't salute, Father," Mary-Ann dared remark.

"I'll let it go this time, dear."

Jason knew to keep going.

Just drive! Keep driving....

The desert spread before them, brown hills and red plains under the amber crease breaking along the horizon. They headed north, trying to make for the closest border before anyone noticed they had abandoned the palace of Aivana.

At home with the Talbots. Toni took off her apron and folded it over the dining room table. She turned out the kitchen light and joined her husband in the living room. He was in his wheelchair, of course, watching a football game with the sound turned down on the television while little Sebastian played with a set of cars on the floor. A rare day with the family; rain kept them indoors while his agents monitored the condo from their car.

"Mon chèr," she said, sitting on the end of the couch nearest his chair, "I got good news today. Our lawyer called and a new hearing has been scheduled. You've been granted a new hearing. This time we'll get the charges dropped. With those two people returned, there's no evidence you killed them." She bit her lip. "Sorry. I don't mean to suggest you would kill anyone. My tongue slipped."

But you know you would kill the right person, said a voice in his head, a throaty alto that frequently spoke up to remind him he was not alone. *If the right person stood in your way. Isn't that true?*

"...on Monday," his wife, Toni, was saying, "and I'll pick up little Sebastian from school and I'll be visiting you about dinner time. How does that sound?"

Blinks.

"Soon you will be able to live here full-time. Then we could share the bed again. I know you can't, uh, do anything, but holding you next to me would be so lovely. I miss our sessions on the couch in my office."

He wanted to do more than blink. He had feelings; he could be aroused emotionally even though his body would not respond. That was agonizing to him: to want something so much yet never be able to come close to getting it.

That is part of the suffering you earned in your little drama, the alto voice spoke inside his head. *Don't be so coy. You will never be able to show your love to that woman.*

He shook in the chair, rattling to get the voice out of his head.

"Are you all right, chèr?" Usually when he shook his chair he wanted something. "Do you want a drink? Change the channel? Something else?"

She gazed into his eyes. They were teary. Involuntary muscles had twisted his face into a mask of sorrow, frustration, and silent torment. She brushed his hair, kissed his cheek, tasted a teardrop.

"Soon everything will be much better."

The telephone buzzed and she knew it was the agents telling her it was time for Sebastian Talbot, serial killer, to return to the prison hospital until next month.

"Yes, I know," she replied, and hung up the receiver. "The night is young but time is growing old."

In daylight the world looked normal, could be anywhere in the universe, could be somewhere in Arizona back on Earth, but Jason knew it was not. They were driving along a road in southern Sekuate. That is, Sekuate-sotos, the southern portion of the split nation. After all, there had been no war; nor revolution and unification of the two halves before the war. And since then everything seemed to be gradually balancing out, he noticed.

"What's that?" asked Mary-Ann, always so innocent.

Kip also pointed to the light in the sky.

Jason gazed upward and with their coaching found the streak in the sky—bright enough to be seen by sharp-eyed youth in full daylight.

"Looks like a comet."

"A comet?" asked Jason Jr. "What's that?"

"Buffy, why don't you explain," said Jason, busy piloting the vehicle.

"A comet is a rock surrounded by ice that flies around the suns in an elliptical orbit."

"It's not a star?" asked Mary-Ann.

"No, it's like an asteroid but covered with ice."

"Why can we see it in the daylight?"

"As it orbits the suns, the ice particles are spread backward, like your hair as we drive through the desert and the wind catches it. You can see the elongated tail that way."

The youth seemed satisfied.

"It's a long way off," assured Jason.

He drove on a bit. The second vehicle carrying his Roûe step-children and their nannies and tutor following closely behind. He thought of the story Set-d'Elous had told him: a prophecy of some kind involving a comet.

"There is a legend," said Jason, "about a comet flying around the two suns and coming to Ghoupallesz. The legend says the comet will crash into the planet. 'And only the righteous shall be saved'—I think that's the quote. You know how legends are. No, wait. I think I got it: 'All living beings must call attention to Heaven before requesting grace, then the light causes blindness!'"

"I remember that from our studies," cried Kip. "U'fe told us that legend. Right, Mary-Ann?"

"I think so."

"The light is the comet. Then it goes 'Goddess Memitha cries for some time while flesh and stone merge as one. Faithfulness will hide all in a closet of hell until Goddess Memitha's death.'"

"I better say the next lines," Buffy announced. "It's too sexy for children. 'Then suckle survivors from Memitha's nipples and sing a song of life.' That's the verse."

"Thank you, children," said Jason, impressed. "When the comet finally arrives, we will all be long dead. The legend says it is far in the future. Besides, even if we were living in that far off day, we could simply escape using a tangent."

Apparently, that satisfied the young ones. At least for a while.

"Father, what is a tangent?" asked Mary-Ann.

Jason chuckled. "A tangent is the secret to everything."

"Is it evil?" asked Buffy solemnly.

Jason coughed, cleared his throat. "It certainly can be."

Kip laughed. "It's a flying rock. It can't be evil. It has no brain!"

The girls laughed. Then Mary-Ann giggled: "Like Kip, got no brain."

"Hey!" shouted Kip.

"Be nice back there," Jason commanded and the four fell silent. "We have a long way to go and I don't want to listen to any of you kids fighting, okay?"

Chapter 6

Full Cycle

As before, Set-d'Elous stumbled up the slope of the caldera, crumbs of volcanic dirt streaming downward under his boots and gloved hands. Once on the ridge he paused to survey the climb, measuring his height with the line of pea-green clouds that stood in the sky like sentinels alarmed at his escape.

He faced the blue sun, akimbo, and breathed in the higher-oxygenated air with gusto.

"You said it couldn't be done, yet I have done it." The winds listened and did not rebut him. "I arrived too soon and so decided to wait for Gina's appearance rather than go back and try again for a closer time."

The line of clouds on the horizon seemed to smile their approval. He frowned, believing them to simply be smiles of condescension.

"Hah! Indeed, young man! And to fill the time, you return to Zaura, your long-lost love, and replace the man she originally married when you were lost at sea." He snickered suspiciously. "Lost at sea!"

He turned to face the yellow sun, brighter than the blue, and squinted.

"Then the time came to patrol the highlands and there she was: the young terrorist Basura-Kanoun, lost in her innocence, unable to know how her life would unfold. But you knew. Oh, how you knew the results. So to change history seemed a good thing. Admit it! You murdered an innocent girl for the chance to save your own family. And many others' families. Sacrifice the one for the many. The old saw...."

He dropped to the soil, his butt planted like a stone, forming his own caldera. He felt he had gained weight as he waited for Gina's return. What was it? Three months off by now, he counted. And he had changed history to prevent the wars. He had saved millions! Had he also then prevented Gina's return? Did he do something that somehow caused her appearance in Aivana to be delayed or abandoned? Would she still show up on the twenty-first day of Batou in the year 1584. Had he stopped time, too?

His back felt the resistance in the dry air. He leaned and the resistance firmed. He stood and faced it, as he had years before. He recalled the precise point, the very spot where the correct tangent existed. His finger pushed against the invisible force. He moved his arm forward, his finger disappearing into the gulf. The tangent begrudgingly opened for him and he saw the future two steps inside the next dimension: the former Kansas City suburbs now locked in skyscrapers in the year 2055 or 6, a 30-story high Wal-Mart store anchoring the commercial district where he had once chased rabbits through pastures and forests, skinny-dipped with Carla Webster in the stream that trickled out of the dammed up fishing lake, where he had imagined different worlds that he could rule and invented whole universes that he could—

Toni Franck was right, perhaps. The Dream Land was inside him, not outside. He could rule it, yes, but only when he could be alone with his thoughts. Some place like the top of the ridge surrounding a desolate caldera of an extinct volcano on a desert isle off the coast of a great continent on another planet he had tripped over during his escape from police in hot pursuit for a crime he did not commit against people he did not know and couldn't care less about—

Three months to go!

Time enough for another adventure. He would return to Selauê and assess the changes in the historical record.

He stepped back from the tangent, felt the pressure squeeze against his forearm until he was free. He stared at the invisible wall, the transparent curtain, saw faint filigree flashes of the world beyond, and he sighed.

It did not sound quite right in the echo within his mind, so he sighed again but with more deliberation, trying to affect the tone that indicated satisfaction with one's circumstance yet not quite accepting of complaisance, something closer to giving in to the inevitable out of sheer expediency yet not surrendering to fate, all the while keeping one or two options open and thus feeling comfortable in the knowledge they were always available should they be needed.

Then he went down from the mountain but with only one commandment to share with the populace below.

"O'le'eh'a," the brown-skinned Foj spoke, then continued with the animated tongue-flapping that irritated him.

"Speak English!"

She stopped and frowned. She showed him her tongue, wagged it to insult him.

"That doesn't help."

"I want..." she said and rolled her eyes, searching for the right word, "...you."

"I want you. Is that what you're saying?" Chucker smiled. "I want you, too."

She pressed her index fingers to her two cheeks, a show of affection.

Chucker had to grin. "We've been together through thick and thin, as they say. Your parents would disown you if they knew you spent a couple years in the jungle with me. But you know what, babe? It's not going to be good for you if we stay together. Like in a marriage. After all, I am such a monster."

"You are...." She stopped and brushed her hair seductively. He thought it was seductive, at least. "...my monster."

"Yeah, I get that." He lowered his head. "Babe, I've done some pretty awful things. I got myself in a lot of trouble. Those gods up there, up in the Ghoupalle sky, they're not going to let me into their club, not the way I've been carrying on. I've hurt people—a lot of people. I've killed people. Some of them turned out to be innocent. I even killed my mentor. That was an accident but the result's the same. I didn't recognize him until it was too late. He had grown a beard and he wasn't supposed to be there. I let it happen, so I'm just as guilty as if I pulled the AT's trigger myself."

She brushed his cheek with her hand, her skinny fingers languishing on his forehead as though checking him for fever.

"You pretty man," she said. "You make pretty baby."

"Yeah, well, you're real hot, too. But I don't think that's the path I'm supposed to take."

He regarded her, and a toothy grin burst upon her face and her hand rose quickly to block his view.

"Besides, we're far away from your people. From mine, too. Light-years, in fact. How can we have a ceremony that everyone would think was legal? They say Adam and Eve were married by God—that's what my Mom says—but I never see wedding rings on her finger in all the paintings down through the ages. Okay, I know, I know, you don't use rings in your culture. I don't mind having a feather in my hair, if that's what you want. Even so, if you want to be my wife, or whatever the equivalent is, then we need to exchange something. And I don't have much here in the jungle, as you know."

She sat up and reached for him, caught his face between her hands. "Give me gemstones in your body. Is everything I need."

"Your English is improving," he grumbled with a smirk.

She hid her smile, unable to contain it. "We make pretty baby."

He took her hands from his face and held them. Their fingers interlocked.

"If that's all it takes, you and me, we can just declare we are married now. Remember our parrot friend? The nine gods and seven goddesses, or whatever, however many there are, they can bless us or curse us. As long as you and me are together, we can stand strong against them. Just Chucker and Foj, two hot uh, er, mmm, warriors, I guess."

He leaned in for a kiss to seal the deal and she tilted backwards, away from him. Mouth to mouth contact was not the custom in her culture. He grinned, recognizing her game. Leaning forward, he watched her slip back again, downward, and he followed. A few more times and they were finally horizontal, stretching out on the bed of the jungle floor, on the soft mossy mattress, where he presented his tithe to her altar.

And the gods were pleased. He concluded they must be; after all, he was not struck down by any comet.

In the morning, as with most mornings on the island, a fresh new bird sat upon his window sill, staring at him, watching him sleep, as silent as the two suns before they rose. And when his eyes cracked open and saw the bird, the bird, only at that instant, began to sing. And the song that it sang was such a lovely tune that he would repose there on his cot listening to it. When the song was finished, he called for an encore but the bird would simply fly away. Each morning, for weeks, for months, a new bird would greet him in the morning, and like most mornings, after the song was sung the bird would disappear.

Stirring up his breakfast of X, Y, and Z, he would contemplate the phenomena. If only he could decipher the song, match the notes with numbers, discern the mathematics behind the music. Perhaps then it all might make sense. Perhaps then he would have an answer to a question he would never have asked.

"Dreaming again?" asked his annoying cellmate instead.

"Yes, I suppose."

"What a useless thing. You are meant to be here for a fair amount of suffering. These dreams only delay your suffering. And until you have suffered enough, you cannot be freed from this prison cell."

"Did you just make that up?"

"No, it's in the script. Now you say 'I shall strive to suffer better' and I respond 'I'm glad to know you take this seriously.' That's how it works."

"Is there an intermission?"

"No, there is only one act."

"Life is a one act show?"

"Certainly. Unless the lights go off by some mysterious account—what is beyond any reasonable control we might expect to have. Or when the hero falls prematurely. We must start again. The audience will understand. Better to have a better story, a complete plot line, than to push on through a journey that's already been corrupted by flaws."

"The hero's flaws?"

"The hero, yes. And the stage, too. The entire cast. And the audience; they have many flaws, as well. Even the poor ticket master is cut through with flaws."

"Then why even have a play?"

"Ah! Because it is what we do!"

* * *

Chucker ran the words through his mind once more: "As long as you and me are together, we can stand strong against them. Just Chucker and Foj, two hot warriors." They had simply popped into his head, something he thought sounded good as some kind of marriage proposal. And yet, the more he thought of what he'd said, the more the words felt familiar, as though he had said them before. He thought deeply for several days, even holding off Foj's amorous advances in order to concentrate.

"Two hot warriors...."

The warm breeze picked up and tossed his long mane across his face. Like a mask. Like a beard.

"Two...warriors...." He brushed his hair away from his face. "Two. A Council of Two. The Council of Two...."

Far back in his memory he found a spot of blood and an angry cry, a cord of tension and mistrust that circled through other memories and hooked and snagged others. He pulled on that thread and gradually discerned where it led, where it originated. A Council of Two. The Empress and her consort. The rulers of the Sekuatean Empire.

He remembered going to Siti, to the Conference of Nations, with a team of mercenaries. Assassins, actually. He had been in that business for a while before returning to Aivana to be introduced as Prince in his mother's Royal Court. And he was supposed to return to that line of work after the great audience in the Royal Hall—where his father, his real father, Chuck, had strangely appeared, dressed for Homeric battle. And his mother had laughed at his father, teased him, ordered her guards to capture him, And then the other assassins arrived, tossing grenades into the Royal Hall. He was held back by the crowds rushing to escape. Yet he saw Chuck, big muscled, gallant warrior, try to throw his mother out of the way of the bombs. And he, Chuck junior, was also thrown away from the bombs by his heroic father—while his stepfather remained passive on the dais at the far end of the hall—

Explosions!

He shook his head, clearing the emotions of that day, that moment. A sickness grew in his stomach and he knew it was not from something Foj had fed him from the jungle. It was a creeping sense of anguish—

"You!" gasped the furious leader of the assassins, lowering his weapon. "Is it you? Is it really you?" He stared hard at the target of his fury, not believing his tired eyes through the ski mask. "What are you doing here?" he exclaimed. He ripped off his mask to have a better look: "You grew a beard! I didn't recognize you. How did you get here? Why are you here?"

Chuck shook his head again and again. Was it memory or vision? Had he really been with that team of assassins, sent to kill the Empress and Emperor? One team had gone to the suite where the couple were staying in that former palace turned conference center. His team went after the Emperor, trailing him through his morning appearances, biding their time until he and his staff could be cornered in secret. And dispatched. They had dressed as Aivanan nomads in brown robes and hoods. They had worn ski masks from K-Mart, ragged as they were. And they aimed their AT guns at the man standing on the windowsill—the emperor's back was to them as he gazed outside at who knows what down in the plaza, perhaps a gaping tangent doorway.

"You!" Chucker had shouted.

"It is him," said another assassin.

"What should we do?"

"We have our orders!"

"This was not part of the mission!"

"We have to follow through. You heard him! It is the only way to make things right."

"What can we do?"

"We must clean the timeline!"

"We have to do it! He told us what to do! Set-d'Elous gave us the order."

"You fool! *This* is Set-d'Elous!" Chjucker had barked. He shook back his blond locks and gritted his straight, even teeth, as white as the teeth his mother always flashed whenever she entered the Grand Hall for another audience with her Aivanan subjects. "This is Set-d'Elous," he repeated in a somber tone. He called to the man on the ledge: "Dude, what're you doing here?"

"It can't be him!"

Chucker glared at the target of his mission, feelings of pain and regret welling up in his chest. His fingers gripped the AT gun, stoked to firing temperature. A bead of sweat ran down from his forehead, falling from the end of his nose.

"What should we do?" he asked the Emperor.

Before the Emperor could answer, one of his team let go a blast from the AT, striking the man between the shoulder blades. He fell forward, crashing through the window glass, falling forever to the plaza. They had rushed to the windows to see him fall—

The plaza was empty. There was no body splattered across the stone surface. They had raced down to the plaza and checked, but found no body. They dispersed and met up later at the appointed place.

"He must've been killed."

"We shot him and he fell. That would kill anyone."

"There was no body."

Chucker felt uneasy. Had they killed Set-d'Elous, who had strangely become the Emperor of Sekuate, or had he somehow escaped, like he usually does?

He had never expected when his mentor had sent them on a mission to assassinate the Emperor, that Set-d'Elous could be that person. What else had their messing with history done? What was that trick of fate? Here he was, a couple years removed from that day, lost in the jungle with his princess-bride and their infant son. And all he could think of was that he had killed his teacher by mistake.

Chucker lay back against the log and laughed. Foj, washing the makeshift diaper of the little one, looked up and asked him why he laughed. Inside his gut he knew the reason, but with her smiling face shining at him, he just said, "Because I am happy you are here with me."

"Me happy too with you."

He loved her smile: white teeth surrounded by brown lips. He gave their naked baby a squeeze, leaned over and kissed him.

"But there is something important I gotta do."

PART TWO

To be a hero, a man must give one-third of his soul to the gods and goddesses. Another third belongs to the family he leaves behind, for their nourishment. One-third remains for him to use in saving himself from death, whether he succeeds or fails.

Mekmel-Saraxon (GP 888-1001)
Selauan warrior & philosopher

Chapter 7

You Can Never Go Home

Former Detective Sergeant Dale T. Wilson entered his small apartment of six months and instinctively reached for the badge that had always been clipped on his sportcoat, a habit he had going on for several years, expecting to drop the badge on the end table by the sofa. He would remove his shoulder holster next and set it also on the table. Now there was no badge. No gun, either. He shook his head, feeling odd for being tricked that way. Starting a new life....

He remained haunted by the Sebastian Talbot case—Julie had divorced him over his obsession with it—and he hated to quit the force before it was settled. But life had its priorities and, hoping to find something better, he had decided to return to school and upgrade his skills. Instead of a policeman, a detective, a law enforcement officer, he was aiming to be a judge. He had passed the LSAT and been accepted into the law school at UMKC.

His former partners kidded him about someday coming face to face with them in a courtroom. Wilson sneered that he would outrank them, might give them a few nights in jail for contempt of court. So they started buying him drinks whenever they happened to meet, which seemed about as often as when they actually worked together. However, gradually, they were going their separate ways.

He stripped down, stepped into the shower, and after that,

studied the framed photograph of his ex-wife a minute before reclining on the bed. He tried to fall asleep but was kept awake by a nagging thought about the Talbot case. The others had teased him about his theory, saying he was watching too many sci-fi shows like Drummond had, and he could not deny it.

And yet, because he did watch so much, he knew what was possible in the various alternate situations people might find themselves. If it were possible for someone—say, the IRS worker Sebastian Talbot—to cross through some barrier and be happily alive on the other side, then Talbot's story made perfect sense. He could have led others over there and, people being stubborn, they might refuse to return with him. There were no bodies, of course. Except for Davenport, the guy nobody at the IRS service center liked. He could have been knocked off by anyone. And then the skinny girl returns, in good health except for having her head screwed on backwards and insisting she was a queen of some desert kingdom. Chuck McElroy returned, too. And yet, if Talbot's story were true, then the story Tammy Tucker was telling fit into Talbot's version quite nicely. And there was no way they could have gotten their stories straight first, not with him unconscious in a hospital bed and she just arriving from who knows where, straight back into the IRS service center where she used to work—

"Just tonight," he grumbled, getting up from the bed. "One more pill." Then he would resume trying to wean himself from the sleeping medication. "Gotta stop thinking about all that," he said, then popped the pill and swallowed some water.

With the first rays of dawn bleeding around the curtains, he awoke, his mind already clicking. He sprang off the bed and got dressed in jeans and boots, t-shirt and his old camo fatigue coat. He trotted down the stairs and got in his Mustang and peeled out of the driveway. Somewhere on the east side of the metro area was a mystery that would not let him sleep. Somewhere there was something he had to know. Then he would laugh at his former colleagues and boastfully shout: "I told you so!"

Wilson stared at the limestone cliffs forming the central arena of the abandoned quarry. The walls were a chalky beige, scored with brown lines. Limestone, nothing special. In the center were a few large rocks tossed about seemingly at random. He looked up to the top of the cliffs, maybe twenty feet high. High enough. That was where Talbot had been standing when he was shot. And he fell—there. He went over to the spot where Talbot would have hit. That side of the rock was scraped, flakes broken off, now in a small pile on the wet clay surface where some autumn rain had collected briefly the past few days.

He looked up from that spot, searching the rim of the quarry for something. The gap?

Henderson had said there was nothing floating in the air, no waving flaps of sky with another landscape within. He wished he had seen it. Scientists had seen it, photographed it, did all kinds of tests on it. Someone had seen it, but when it closed one night, they had nothing more to investigate and some even wondered if it had ever really existed or if it was all an illusion.

If the gap was just a sci-fi story, then Talbot's story would not provide an alibi. Wilson wanted to believe the gap had existed; after all, scientists had been investigating it—though nothing made the local news, of course. Top secret stuff. Government only. Hush hush. Marking the site as a radiation danger. Yet no guards, no electric fence around it, no cameras watching. Or were there?

He froze, then looked both directions without moving his head. If there were cameras, he had already been seen and there could be a squad of federal agents on the way to get him and question him. Why, I just walked on up here, no problem, because I'm one of the detectives on the case, just had to take a look when I heard the gap was gone. The gap? Never heard of it? It was a secret, but now it's gone so no big deal, huh, so I'll be on my way and you all have a nice day.

There was no more wire grid set up in the quarry, either. It had been removed by investigators. It was as though they were determined to return the quarry to its pre-Talbot state. Talbot had claimed the grid marked the positions where various "doorways" existed, marked so he could access them more easily.

Or perhaps it was another mind game he was playing with them.

Wilson sat on the rock and studied his boot print in the wet clay. Footprints. Why were there no other footprints in the clay around him? Even if the rain filled the basin, it would not wash away the footprints of boots, he thought. They would dry yet remain imprinted. He stood up on top of the rock and glanced around, saw only the one line of his own boots circling around the quarry. The scientists may have cleaned up after themselves.

"All right," he muttered, starting to feel warm in the army coat as the sun stretched toward noon. "I guess I've seen enough. The gap is gone." He chuckled. "Great song title...."

Returning the way he had come, about to exit the arena of the quarry and moving into the short, narrow limestone canyon—barely wide enough for a truck—he heard something like a freight train or a semi-trailer barreling down the highway. He instinctively crouched and spun around to see what was chasing him.

There in the center of the arena, where he had stood moments before, was a kaleidoscopic display of sparkling lights: red, blue, yellow. Pinpoints. Even in daylight he could see it clearly. They spun, waxed and waned, until they formed a star—four points, then five, six, eight, ten, twelve, twenty-eight, and more. The star flashed, modulated. At the center of the star a finger appeared. Then a hand pushed through. An arm followed, then a shoulder, hip, foot, face, head, and the rest of the body of a blue-haired, light-skinned man wearing a strange outfit, something from *The Arabian Nights*, complete with red Fez and red, curly-toed shoes and a lengthy scimitar hanging from a yellow leather belt. The man stepped forward and the light display vanished, sucked into a vortex like the signal of an old black and white television set. Gone.

The gap is back, Wilson thought with a grin and a snap of his fingers, feeling the beat of a new song.

Chucker brushed his arms off ceremonially, feeling the electricity sizzle out of his fingertips. His legs felt weak and he had to sit. He dropped onto the nearest rock and caught his breath. Set was right, he thought. It seems easy but it's not an experience you want to do every day. He considered that passing through an interdimensional tangent often enough really could have detrimental effects on one's body, not to mention one's psyche.

Looking around the quarry he noticed the absence of the wire grid that had marked every known tangent. It could not have been blown away or some of it would still remain. It had to have been deliberately removed. But by who? He felt uneasy. Was someone watching him right now? Maybe Set himself had destroyed it so nobody else could use it and find themselves lost in the Dream Land.

He realized he had not fully prepared for the trip, not expecting to be successful. He should have brought other clothes, though he did not have anything available that was Earth-suitable. It had been so long, maybe the fashion was bizarre enough now that nobody would notice his. Probably nobody would notice he was a prince, either. That would be good.

With the final sparks crackling out of his body, Chucker felt ready to continue.

He stood and headed into the short canyon he remembered from many trips back and forth as a member of History, Inc. That was nostalgia. The years of youth when he wanted to break something—and did. So much he had done, good and bad. He had regrets, sure, but then he had a life to get on with, and a family to protect and care for. First, he had a mentor to find and rescue, so he pressed on with his mission—

"Ho!" Chucker gasped, halting in the canyon at the sight of the man there. "Who the hell're you?"

The clean-cut man in camo army coat and faded jeans stood his ground and nodded in a friendly, knowing way. He didn't seem to be anyone he should care about but here was a man in a place where nobody belonged. This was private land, Chucker understood from Set-d'Elous. The man must be trespassing—but for what reason?

"I could ask you the same question," said the man, shoving his hands into his front pockets. "You can call me Wilson."

"Awright, Wilson, what're you doing here?"

"I was just leaving. Had a look around, is all. Read a report so I wanted to see for myself."

"What report? What about?"

"And I got to see it for myself. Holy crap. I never quite believed it. Or doubted it, for that matter. But here I am, seeing the whole thing, just as Talbot described it. And here you are."

"Here the hell I am. What're you talking about?"

"Relax, I'm not here to do anything."

"Well, I'm not either. I got other stuff to do."

"Stuff to do?"

"Yea, stuff."

"What kind of stuff?"

"None of your business, dude."

"Well, stuff is kind of my business."

"Are you gonna get out of my way? I got stuff to do, I said."

The man looked him over. "Heading to a costume party, I 'm going to guess."

"If that's what you wanna think, go on."

Chucker tried to move past the man but Wilson, six-foot tall, 220 pounds, would not budge.

"Come on, man, get outta my way! You don't even belong up here."

"And you do?" The man frowned, turning into a troll guarding the passage. "Who are you? Where'd you come from just now?"

Chucker glared at him. This was a totally unexpected turn of events. He knew the tangent was watched but he didn't expect to get through. He decided to try it, and it worked. Now that he had arrived, here was this dude blocking his path.

So Chucker whipped out his scimitar and held it up between them.

"Nice prop," said the man. "Looks real."

"It is real, dude!" And Chucker shoved it forward—

The man sidestepped the blade and grabbed Chucker's wrist, pulling his arm forward and smashing it into the stone wall of the canyon, knocked his hand against the stone until he dropped the scimitar. Then the man threw Chucker up against the opposite wall, knocking the breath from him. He sank to the ground.

"When you get your breath back, how about you tell me your name."

Chucker took a moment. "My name is Chuck."

Wilson squatted. "Chuck, huh? I know a Chuck, used to be a colleague of mine. Chuck McElroy was his name. I don't work there any more, though. Changed jobs, you might say."

Chucker spit to the side, blood mixing with saliva.

"Yeah, I know. He's my dad."

Chapter 8

Voyager

Wilson pressed his fist against his chin, elbow tucked against his chest, and looked over the younger man in the Aladdin costume crumpled on the ground, sizing him up.

"I don't suppose you have any i.d. on you?" asked Wilson. "Not in that kind of get-up, huh?"

Chucker looked up, wiping his nose with the back of his hand. "Who are you again? Wilson? How do you know me?"

"I worked with your father. We worked on the Talbot case together. You probably know about that: serial killer, former IRS employee, lured his coworkers out here then did away with them somehow."

Chucker gave a smirk. "Is that why you're out here? Expecting him to come back?"

"Come back? You mean like you did?"

"He's not that direction, dude. He's here." Chucker blinked. "On Earth."

"Interesting expression." Wilson watched the man's eyes. Perhaps he knew what was coming next. Didn't matter: he spoke the words anyway: "Does that mean you came from...not on Earth?"

Chucker shrugged. "You can decide. Look how I'm dressed."

"Fair enough."

"Just tell me what year this is."

Wilson had to grin. It was exactly like the time travel movies he had always loved. Never *where am I* but *when am I*. He had this guy nailed: he was a time traveler. At least the guy believed he was.

"It's nineteen-ninety-five," said Wilson, carefully studying the guy's facial reaction. He seemed to think it over, as though he was counting in his head. He did not seem upset at the information. "October. Saturday. Is that what you were expecting?"

"Doesn't matter."

"So you *are* a time traveler...."

"Well, what the hell do you think?"

"I wasn't thinking anything. I'm trying to figure out what I saw, how you got here, why you're freaked out about the year. Not to mention how you're dressed. You have only two choices. You can keep playing the innocent young man who was hiking around the quarry in an Ali Baba costume and happened to meet me—or you can be a time traveler like you're trying to get me to believe."

"Seems like the choices are yours, not mine."

Wilson nodded. "Touché."

"I'm minding my own business—gonna take care of business, but you, well, you are in the wrong place at the wrong time."

"No, I think it's the right place at the right time. Because here you are. From who knows where. I'd like to hear the full explanation."

"The full explanation...."

"Yes, tell me how the son of Detective Chuck McElroy got lost beyond the gap and just now returned." He dared to laugh. "I saw it but I can't believe it. I'm talking to you but I still don't believe you're right here."

"This is real blood you knocked out of my nose."

"I suppose it is." He had to do something when a man with a scimitar attacked. "Sorry about that. I didn't know if you were a serious scimitar user or just playing around."

"It's not my best weapon."

"I should be glad of that." He straightened up and extended his hand down to the younger man. "Come on."

Chucker took it and Wilson pulled him to his feet.

"Tell you what. My car's down on the road. I can give you a lift, wherever you need to go. Maybe get you some clothes?"

"In exchange for what?"

Wilson laughed. "I'm trying to figure out a theory. And you walked into my life at the right time. Talk. That's all I want: to talk with you."

"About that?" He threw a thumb back at the quarry arena. "You mean the tangent?"

"The what?"

"Tangent. Doorway. Portal. Whatever you want to call it. It's a phenomena that joins here and there. I was there, now I'm here. Got stuff to do, like I said."

"I'll help you." Wilson was surprised he offered so easily, but the mystery was too strong. "How do you do it?"

"You mean pass through the tangent? It takes special training. Then a ton of luck to find the spot, the tangent."

"So what's there on the other side?"

"First there's desert. Then you come to a city. Then a country, a continent, another whole planet."

Wilson cursed in his excitement. He tried to stay calm but his head was buzzing with questions. "Is that so?" was all he could get out.

"It's a hassle but it beats a hundred-plus years in a spaceship."

Wilson snickered at the joke. "I'll bet it does."

They reached the bottom of the gravel drive. Wilson's Mustang was parked there. He went to the driver's door, unlocked it.

"So where do you need to go?"

Chucker hesitated. First stop was always the 7-Eleven up the road a mile to check the date, get a candy bar and a soda. This time he had a ride.

"I can trust you?" asked Chucker, opening the car door.

"I think you can. I'm no longer on the force. Right now, I'm just damn curious. I want to know everything about your mysterious doorway."

"But can you trust me?"

"I hope I can. Why would you lie to me? I'm helping you."

"That's when most people lie."

Keep an open mind.

Wilson repeated the mantra as he watched the 'visitor from beyond the gap' snoozing on his sofa. The young man couldn't be too old, not if he was Chuck's son. He had been reported missing three years ago. Everyone thought he had simply run off. Perhaps he was looking for his mother, or just getting out of town. Nobody suspected foul play and so the case was dropped.

So where's he been?

He clearly was not in the quarry when Wilson was first there, looking around. Then he was there, suddenly, appearing in a blaze of colored lights—and dressed in some foppish Ali Baba costume. He had no doubt the young man would not have chosen that outfit if there were any other choices. It had to be real: he had to have come from beyond the gap.

So what actually is beyond the gap?

He rubbed his chin as his eyes fell across the framed posters of his favorite sci-fi movies: *Star Trek*, *Star Wars*, and a dozen others. Other than criminal forensics, he was no scientist, couldn't tell a light-year from a neutron star, but he had been exposed to almost every weird idea there was through TV and film. Now he had witnessed some strange phenomena himself. He was willing to believe quite a lot that most people would be skeptical about. His former partner, Drummond, was even more into sci-fi, but he was dead now.

"He does sorta look like McElroy," Wilson mumbled. Except he had long hair—dull, pastel, medium blue hair—and a scruffy chin and jawline. Though he had to be around eighteen, based on being fourteen when reported missing, he looked older, possibly thirty. More time lived "off-Earth" compared to time passing on Earth? He thought that's how it worked. The guy was a man, no doubt, well past being a teenager.

Wilson had not gotten much of the adventure tale before his guest had commenced yawning and finally conked out. Something to do with passage through the gap, perhaps. It had to take some energy to do that, or to subject yourself to the forces of the universe. That had to place a strain on a body. So he would let him sleep. He had errands to run, anyway.

* ❋ *

After entering and setting down two shopping bags, Wilson returned to the door and slammed it, just to make some noise.

"Hey, you gonna get up sometime today?" he growled. "Almost two in the afternoon. You slept all freakin' night and most of the day!"

The body on the sofa stirred, hit a plateau, then stirred a little more. After another five minutes, it rolled over and slowly sat up, feet to the floor.

"Well, good morning," said Wilson, smiling. The adventure was about to continue. Where would this man take him today in the world of make-believe?

"*Vidê*," he muttered absently, rubbing his eyes. "Afternoon—not morning."

"That's right." Wilson grabbed the bags and brought them to the sofa. "Good thing it's the weekend or I'd be out all day and you'd be stuck here with nothing to do."

"I would sleep."

"I thought you had a mission."

Chucker yawned, stretched. "I do."

"Here's some Earth clothes for you. I bet I guessed your sizes with great accuracy. Being a detective, I can estimate. If they don't fit, we'll exchange them. So let's get a move on. Get dressed."

Chucker showered and dressed in the jeans and button shirt, socks and sneakers that Wilson had bought at the Penney's store in the mall. He returned to the living room.

Wilson had made coffee.

"Once a cop, always a cop. Coffee every hour." He handed a mug to Chucker. "So where we off to today?"

Chucker set the mug down on the dinette table, compelled to stretch a little more. "What, are you in on this now?"

"I'm helping you. Like I said. Why? I don't even know why—I love a good mystery, that's all. I was in the right place at the right time and *poof* here's a mystery. So what're we doing today?"

Chucker yawned, then drank more coffee. "No donuts?"

Wilson laughed. "I got granola bars. No more fancy living. I'm on a student loan now, plus I need to eat right. I even shaved off my mustache. Had a walrus thing going for several years, but if I'm gonna have a new life, I gotta start with a new look. Lost about twenty-five pounds, too, and enrolled in law school, became a student again. How about you? What's your story?"

Chucker tried to repress a grin. "I was a teen rebel who fell through a hole and landed in a desert, walked and walked until I found my mother in a palace. She was the queen, so that made me a prince. But I hated being a prince so I went to an island where a madman lived and I asked him for some wisdom and he told a buncha sick jokes and took me back to my mother the queen. Then I joined a band of mercenaries who went around the time zones changing things, but most things were worse, not better. Until I got caught in the worst thing of all. I killed that madman—accidently."

"Accidently? How'd that happen?"

"I went on a mission, as usual. Only everything got screwed up. I didn't recognize him. I shot him, not thinking it was him. Don't hassle me about it. I know he didn't die. He fell through another hole—a 'tangent'—so he's here. Somewhere."

"And you mean...Talbot?"

"Sebastian Talbot, yeah. Also known as Set-d'Elous, the legendary madman."

"Well, you are half-right. He is here. You got that part correct. So what is the mission?"

"Good. I thought he would be."

Chucker finished his coffee.

"More?" asked Wilson.

Chucker nodded. "I need to make amends. I need to right the situation. By that, I mean, I'm going to collect his ass and take him back to where he belongs. Back to the Dream Land."

Wilson handed him back the mug. "Two problems with that plan. First, he's in a guarded location. A state hospital. It's like a prison but a hospital. Second, he's in the hospital section because he's paralyzed. Quadriplegic. Can't speak either. But he can see and hear, and presumably think. You may want to leave him where he can be treated as best they can. How can you carry a man in a wheelchair through that hole, as you say, or gap as I say—"

"Tangent is what he says."

"All right: tangent. How can you get him through that?"

Chucker studied the swirling cream in his coffee, looking for an omen of good fortune. "Paralyzed, huh?"

"Yep. He's not going anywhere anytime soon. Some people still think that's too good for him, being alive but paralyzed."

"There's got to be some advanced surgery that can fix him."

"Well, if you can mend a brain, then be my guest." They stared at each other a moment. "Listen, Chuck. What should I call you? Chuck junior?"

"I go by Chucker. As in Chuck R. Tucker. Never call me junior."

"All right, Chucker. I don't know what happened exactly since I was not right there, but I was part of the SWAT operation that nabbed him—Talbot. See, we got a tip, so we surrounded an old house in the countryside where he was hiding out—in fact, not far from the quarry, you know—and we—"

"I know it."

Wilson narrowed his eyes. "You do?"

"I've visited here a few times. We used it as a meeting place to plan missions."

"Plan missions, huh? Like what?"

"So tell me what happened here. On Earth."

"All right....“

Now the mystery was both deepening and becoming clearer. What had been going on with these people who claim to be traveling between two worlds? What kind of missions were they on? Wilson wondered if any federal agencies were involved with this kind of transference technology.

He laughed, not that there was anything funny about it.

"What happened was we surrounded the house in the evening, after dark. He was supposedly inside, was observed there: leads, witnesses, you get it. We had a tip his lady friend was meeting him there but we intercepted her so she wasn't hurt. They're building a new subdivision there so the sewer system had been installed, running from the street to that house, pipes and culverts. We think he got away through the pipes. Good thing, too, because one of the SWAT team shot the propane tank beside the house and it blew up. Took the whole house down. We thought he was inside and burned up. We couldn't find a body—"

"He got away?"

"Of course. He always gets away—bastard. But someone saw him climb out of the culvert under the road and head up the hill to the quarry so a team went after him. Obviously he was trying to escape through the tangent—the gap, and there *was* a gap then, a big flapping hole in the air. They saw it when they got there. He was somewhere—they said he was on top of the cliff, waving his arms. They ordered him down, then when he refused, someone shot at him. He was hit in the neck and head. He fell. Some people think he jumped, like a suicide, and was shot just as he stepped off the cliff. I don't know; I wasn't there. That's what the reports say."

"So he was taken to the hospital?"

"Yes. In fact, he was in a coma for six months, and paralyzed when he awoke."

Chucker downed the last of the second mug, sat back with a sigh of relaxed contemplation. "Are you sure it was him?"

"That's what the report says. The official report. And all the newspapers. I would've been right there seeing it for myself but I was busy taking care of his girlfriend—"

"Because while you guys were shooting him at the quarry, me and my team were shooting him in a palace in Siti. And while you were watching him fall from the cliff, we were watching him fall through a window and down to the plaza below the window. The only difference is that you guys had a body at the bottom. We didn't. Four floors down and no body. No splat, either. No—"

"A palace in Siti. You mean a city?"

"No, it's a city called Siti—like See-Tee. Third largest city in the nation of Ghoupallæssa, on the continent of Ghoupallæssus, which as everyone knows is on the planet Ghoupallesz. Get it?"

"Got it."

"Good."

"Or maybe," said Wilson, eyes bright, "just maybe your episode and my episode did not happen simultaneously on two separate planets but happened one after the other. Probably yours was first since you didn't find a body. We have a body so this is the destination of his fall from that palace you said. That seems more plausible. Can't figure how he popped from one to the other, though."

"There are tangents everywhere. And he can find them. He has the touch. You know, the sensitivity to sense them and exploit them. I learned a lot from him but I haven't developed that kind of sensitivity yet. If I ever can. Part of it is genetic, I guess. You have the potential to be a Voyager or you don't. I can't find them, but I can use the ones I know of."

"I'd like to know more, but there's plenty of time for that, I guess."

"So how're we gonna get him out?"

Wilson shook his head. "You know you're speaking to an ex-cop, don't you?"

"If you're not a member of History, Inc., you're all the same to me: a bystander."

"You *are* full of mystery, aren't you? History, Inc.? What is that? A video game club?"

"You might say that. Except without the video game. We play for real and for keeps. We tweak history. Ghoupalle history, not Earth history. We're done now. I need to get him and take him back so he can be fixed."

Wilson regarded the man as seriously as he could. He certainly seemed adamant in his mission. Good mercenary: complete the mission and all. Ever since Drummond went down, the pall of sci-fi guru had fallen to him. With time on his hands, he watched more Si-Fi channel, went to more movies, read more fantasy books. So much was possible in those worlds, those future places where the technology was so advanced—or magic was available. If this guy was from a world of advanced technology, perhaps they could fix a paralyzed man. Then the question would be whether he should help. What was at stake? What would the odds be? Repercussions?

"I've always had doubts about the Sebastian Talbot story," said Wilson, waving Chucker out the door. "But being a detective, I'm supposed to check out all angles, find the truth of the situation. No matter how implausible it may be. Occam's razor, that sort of thing. The only possibility you can't check off has to be the real one. Given the details that are confirmed facts, plus some bullshit theory from my late colleague, I've got doubts. If Talbot had taken those people through the gap—"

"Tangent."

"All right, tangent—but at the time it really was a gap. If he took them to your world, and they refused to come back with him, that would explain a lot."

He unlocked the car doors and they got into the Mustang. Wilson started the engine.

"The only body we've found was Davenport's, a co-worker. But everybody hated him, so it wasn't necessarily Talbot who killed him. We thought Talbot had done away with your father, too, but suddenly he reappeared. And Tammy also returned—"

"Mom and Dad are here? Back here? Are they okay?"

Wilson smiled. He was about to do a good deed.

Chapter 9

Nostalgia

Wilson had an uncanny sense of direction as they drove through the streets of Independence, Missouri—the older part of the city, north of the square where three pioneer trails originated long ago. Chucker was like a dog fearing a trip to the vet, staring out the window, eager to see what was there but equally afraid to spot anything that signaled a wrong direction, a turn into a dead end or perhaps a police station.

"There's my school," Chucker said, matter-of-factly, so Wilson would have that fact marked on his checklist.

They crossed into Sugar Creek, drove past the old public pool, now long out of use. Chucker confirmed he had been taken there one summer by his mother. They drove down crumbling streets Chucker knew, slowed before one old, off-white, ranch-style house with a gravel driveway.

"I'm not going to stop," said Wilson. "Don't want to draw any attention. Here is where your grandmother lived before she went to a nursing home. It's where you lived when your mother disappeared. To your grandmother, you've been gone four years. Your mother, for almost nine—until she returned, of course."

"To me, it feels like twenty years. Maybe longer. Fifty years? Who knows?"

"Seen enough?" He turned to see Chucker nod. "All right, we'll go on to our next place on the nostalgia tour."

Wilson took them back down to Truman Road and west to head to Kansas City. Crossing through the eastside on St. John Avenue, they made their way over to the Museum of Science and History on Gladstone, a neighborhood of grand, stately old homes. Wilson rolled to a halt along the curb.

"Yeah, what's here?" asked Chucker.

"That house," said Wilson, pointing to the yellow Victorian with the wide, wrapping veranda and the tower on the side, "is your other grandmother's house."

"I don't think I ever met her."

"No, I don't think so. But your father lives here now. Moved back in with his mother. For now. That took a lot of guts. He always said how much he couldn't stand her. Hated her—mostly because of how she treated your mother."

"What're you talking about?"

"Look at the house. It's a mansion. Sure, it's old but it's well-kept. The family is, or was, well-off. McElroy came from this house and this family. He came from money. But he fell for your mother who came from a dirt poor family. Instead of becoming a rich lawyer he became a cop. He met your mother in a bar—almost arrested her, I heard. They disowned him when he married her. So it's gutsy for him to come home to stay until he recovers from his adventures."

Chucker coughed. "I never knew that."

"That's often the case," said Wilson, pulling the car from the curb and continuing on. He turned at the corner and zigzagged down to Paseo Avenue, went south. "Parents don't want the kids to know a lot of things. Petty jealousies. Misunderstandings. Rivalries among siblings. Black sheep. Family stuff. You missed all of that."

"Well, I went to Aivana to be with my Mom. I was a prince, so we had money."

"Yes, but now she's back on Earth."

"I hate that 'on Earth' shit."

They drove south to the hospital district by the Liberty Memorial, a beacon-shaped tower on top of a hill overlooking the downtown skyline. Below was a vast complex of hospitals, clinics, and research facilities. There was a mental hospital, too.

"And your mother is here," said Wilson, pulling into a parking lot and circling around to maneuver the car into a space where they could monitor the right window. "She is not ready to go out into the world and be on her own, I'm sorry to say. They found her inside the IRS building, still dressed as a queen. I can sure believe it after seeing your costume."

"Is she okay? I mean, she's not crazy, is she?"

"The report I read said she was admitted for observation. Lots of symptoms to observe. First off was speaking a language nobody else knows."

"Probably Rouê. What they speak in Aivana."

"I could guess that much."

"Anyway, she is classified paranoid-schizophrenic and will be in there until the doctors are convinced she's not a danger to herself or anyone else. I suppose she'll be released soon enough."

"Does she know about my dad?"

"No." Wilson paused as though taking a puff from a cigarette and blowing it out. "They thought it best not to let each of them know the other is here. Not yet."

"So if I walked into the room she would freak out?"

"She might be happy to see you. I'm guessing so. But she may also cross over that line she's hugging right now. As you said, your priority is Talbot, or whatever name he uses over there."

"Beyond the gap...."

"Exactly."

Thirty minutes later they were on Highway 71, heading south again, exiting the city for the suburbs, then turning southeast into the countryside. The next stop was a bit of a drive, Wilson explained.

"The last thing I remembered," said Chucker as they drove, "was some guys in brown robes coming into the Great Hall and tossing grenades. My mom and dad were arguing in the center of the Hall, everybody around them. It was so embarrassing. Then, when the grenades were thrown, he pushed her back. I tried to help, too, but he threw me across the floor, out of the way. When the grenades went off, everything disappeared in a flash of white light."

"Were you injured?"

"No. I woke up in a jungle somewhere—turned out to be the west side of Bæronak—"

"Which is where?"

"Over there, man. Beyond the gap. I got up and checked myself and I was okay, just incredibly lost. I didn't know if I was still on Ghoupallesz or on Earth or even some other planet at first. I walked through the jungle, getting my bearings, finding food and water. Then I found Foj also lost in the jungle."

"That's someone you knew?"

"Hah! We didn't really know each other. She was the princess from Typeg—"

"Another place over there...."

"Right. She was in the Great Hall, too, so we were blown to the same general area. So it was Boy Scout time. I taught her how to live in a jungle, you know, making fire, choosing the right fruits, how to cook whatever animal I brought back to the campsite. We moved a lot, spent five years keeping away from the Blue Hairs. I have blue hair because we ate the same fruit as them. I'm as blonde as my mom and dad. Foj, being Typegan, has jet black hair so it didn't turn blue."

"So then, this Foj person, she's your...?"

"My wife." Chucker looked up, grinning despite himself. "We never had any ceremony, but before the grenades were thrown in the Great Hall, her father brought her to Aivana to present to my mother as a bride for me. All for show. To make some treaty. I never dug that give a girl to make a deal system, ya know. Then here we are, together in the jungle. Adam and Eve. Making children."

"Children?"

"We have two, a boy and a girl. Randy and Joy."

"Where are they now?"

"Back through the gap. We got a place in Liêta. Civilization. It's tropical—a beautiful white beach and turquoise waters. We made a life there."

"But here you are, running away from all that."

"I'm not running away. I'm righting a wrong. After that, I'm going back to them."

Wilson smiled a moment, like a happy memory had flooded his consciousness. "We are such manly men, aren't we?"

"I'm not like Set. Maybe you don't really know him. He swears he loves this Gina woman from his high school days and waits for her and goes looking for her on Ghoupallesz. Then he takes up with a Ghoupalle woman named Zaura—a woman from beyond the gap, as you call it."

Wilson chuckled. "Then he gets caught up with a woman here. That psychiatrist, Toni Franck."

"Really?" Chucker did not seem surprised. "Voyagers can be so disgusting. No morals at all. Running back and forth playing god."

"You said a Voyager has to play fast and loose."

"No, he said that. Set-d'Elous said it."

Wilson ran a hand through his hair and sighed. "I never had any children. But I stayed faithful to her. She's the one who ended it. She said the case took all my time and attention. It did, I hafta admit."

Chucker grunted. "I wouldn't've chosen Foj as my wife if we were still in civilization, but we made it work in the jungle. We never knew if we would make it back. We come from different worlds—obviously. Survival brings people together."

"I suppose it does."

"I'm not a kid any more, ya know. I didn't need to keep being a prince and having to do things. Being a father and husband gives me a lot to do. And with Set not around, I had no more missions to go on. So it's Foj who is the cook and housekeeper and I'm the manager and repairman of this little resort inn up at the end of a long, curving beach, too far for most tourists to go. We didn't mind. We got by."

"And then you remembered what happened to Talbot and you felt guilty?"

"If you want to put it that way."

"How would you put it?"

"It bugged me ever since the explosions. I saw him there before the whole thing started. He was checking the Great Hall to be sure everything was in order. Then he went on his way. He probably got out in time. And somehow he returned to 1533, in a place he was not supposed to be. Or in a different version of 1533 that was never meant to be. We were trying to change history again—or, really, we were changing it back. We messed up. We were on Plan C or D. He messed up, going off on his own to do a mission. We followed his instructions to the letter and then we were facing him and didn't recognize him. We didn't expect he would be the

Emperor of Sekuate! We were tasked with killing the Emperor of Sekuate—"

"How could he be in two places at once? At your Great Hall and then in that palace—as you said—huh?"

"I don't know. Magic, I guess. Tangent magic. Here's a theory for you: trauma creates some kind of energy vortex that can bust open a tangent—if there's one there. Nothing more traumatic than getting shot."

"Or having a house explode around you."

"Yeah...."

The car turned up the curving drive, rolled to a stop in the closest parking spot. Wilson shut off the engine and the lights.

"Now here is where you can find Mister Talbot," said Wilson. "His room is on the back, third floor, third window from this end of the building. They dim the lights at night but never turn them all the way off in his room."

"Have you visited him?"

"Not recently. Not since he awoke from the coma. We went a few times, expecting to question him but we were turned away. Now I'm off the force and have no reason to talk to him."

"Horrible existence."

"Horrible it should be—if he did what he's been charged with."

"But?"

"But I don't think he did it."

Chucker seemed to sigh and Wilson glanced at him.

"I'm not completely convinced he's innocent, but with your mother returning that certainly throws a big wrench into the case. If she came back, the others might also come back. That's why there are no bodies."

"So you'll help me get him out?"

Wilson lay his head back, smiling. He didn't know what he would do. He had a future to work on and this mission could blow that off the map. Justice was justice, sure. But the case was done, right or wrong. He was off it. He was off the force. He could literally turn his back on it and walk away. Except here was this guy, McElroy's son, who had so many answers to questions he had never considered asking.

Chapter 10

Rules

"Sounds like quite an adventure you've had, from teen rebel to prince of—what was it? Aivana?—Prince of Aivana to...what are you now, exactly?"

"I'm a rescuer." Chucker blinked. "Did you say you're gonna help?"

"I'm not going to break any laws, if that's what you're asking."

"Laws may need to be broken."

"I can't do that."

"Even if a man has been improperly detained? Unjustly accused? Completely innocent? Who's been fatally wounded twice for no reason but mistaken identity? If anybody should be let free, it's him. The only person I know for sure he's killed was back on Ghoupallesz, not here."

"Tell me about that."

"Out of your jurisdiction. But I approved of it—after the fact. It was only a mercy killing. You know, put someone out of their misery. Only she wasn't in misery yet. But she was going to be someday. He knew because he lived through the years when she was the Empress of Sekuate, so he knew what she would become. And he saved her from that fate."

Wilson nodded, listening. He wondered, though, if this Chucker was telling him a true story or making up something to test him. He wasn't about to turn into a criminal on the say-so of this guy, no matter how he made the last pieces of the puzzle fall into alignment.

They continued talking for another hour, driving back.

"Sounds like you got a lot of choices to make. Everybody's here. So do you go see your mother first or your dad or Talbot?"

"Set is the priority. Get him out first. Then I'll come back for Mom and maybe say 'hi' to my dad."

A forty-seven minute explication of the options ensued.

"As I told you, he's in the hospital, immobile. Once a month his ol' lady comes and takes him out for the day."

"His wife?"

"Sure. Doctor Toni Franck, formerly his psychiatrist. They also have a son—born before Talbot was shot and put into the coma."

"A son, huh? I kinda thought I was his son. Like protégé, that kind of son. "

"I don't know how that all happened. He was in the wheelchair and couldn't speak. I guess he just nodded when the priest asked him if he would love and obey her. She couldn't wait to get him in a contract, it seemed. Maybe there's insurance money involved."

Splatters of conversation continued to interrupt the night's silence. Bawdy humor and Wilson's confession of a brief affair with his college roommate. More adventures of alluding the Blue Hairs and the finer points of Chucker's wife's sexual attributes. An exchange of speculation about the near and the far future tied to Moody Blues' lyrics. Some talk of racing cars, engine specs, and football games.

Dawn.

"Why do you keep shaking your head and smiling like that?"

"Because I'm so freakin' amazed at everything that's happening this weekend. You and your story. Your mission. And the way you popped into existence. And everything you say makes everything else make sense. You know? You are the missing link. If you could tell the judge what you've been telling me, he'd have to throw out the verdict. But then again, you might be sharing a room with him in that mental hospital. Who's gonna believe you? Nobody—unless they see you poof into that quarry like you're beaming down from the *Enterprise*."

"Interdimensional Voyagers don't have time for make-believe. We know it's all true. We accept it and move on. No use focusing on the details. Or, as Set likes to say: 'I can't explain'em, I just use'em.'"

Wilson dragged himself to the kitchen, threw some eggs into a pan. He set the coffee maker popping.

"There's no way you're gonna get him out of there, not with all the security they have. Your only chance is when she takes him out. There's always a couple guards to watch her. They figure he's in a wheelchair so he's not going anywhere. That would be the time to grab him. But you're gonna have to have a get-away plan ready. I assume you'll take him to the quarry?"

"Yes—and back home."

"Once they find him missing, they'll probably assume he's on the way there. If you delay, thinking they'll check the quarry, then you may miss your chance. They'll post officers there and you won't be able to get close."

"I don't want to race anyone if I don't have to."

"Well, you'll need a car for that. And I can't let you use Betsy here."

"Don't worry," said Chucker. "I got plans."

A hot shower and fresh clothes.

A slow drive downtown.

Police cars everywhere. An errand to run.

"I'll be just a moment," said Wilson. "Don't freak out or nothing. I'm just checking some things."

After greeting an old colleague outside, Wilson went inside the building.

Chucker sat in the passenger seat, watching patrol cars come and go from the parking lot. He was certain Wilson was going to bring out some of his buddies to grab him. If only he would tell his story to the judge, he'd said. His story was no more believable than anyone else's. His hand went to the door handle, ready to spring from the car if he saw Wilson coming out with his buddies.

Chucker let out his sigh as Wilson returned alone, a piece of paper in his hand.

"She's scheduled to take him out the last Saturday of the month. You got one month to put your plan together. They're going to the zoo, it seems. They will have a detail of two or three officers accompanying them. Franck, Talbot, and the boy."

"Then let's go to the zoo. I haven't been there since I was a kid."

"To find a good location for the snatch?"

"Yes. And I wanna see some wild animals."

Long way back to Independence.

Burger King by the mall for lunch.

"If I'm gonna help you," said Wilson after swallowing the first bite of his sandwich, "I was thinking.... How about I follow you back there? Beyond the gap. Would that be cool?"

"That would not be cool."

"How much trouble could it be? I just want to see it, see what all the excitement's about, see how the place looks."

"It's a desert. You have to hike about three days to get to anything worth seeing. On the way you might bump into some nomads who will eat you. Or sell you as a slave to other nomads."

"Geez, really?" He stopped eating. "You know, if those women from the IRS were following him...you think maybe they...could they have run into some of those nomads? Would that be why they never came back?"

"I'd say that's more likely than Set murdering them."

"More pieces of the puzzle."

"Same as my dad. He followed Set through the tangent and got lost in the desert. I never got to talk to him, ask him questions, but the way he was dressed when he burst into the Great Hall told me he spent time in the desert, took on some Rouê customs. He was like Conan the Barbarian when he arrived there. Then the grenades were thrown. He was blown back to Earth. Still don't know if he wants to see me. We kinda had eye contact at the last second—like we would've gone out to have a beer and talk over everything, ya know, but there wasn't time for that."

Wilson pinched his chin, the start of his next beard there. "So Talbot took Tammy there—and that other guy, Michael. And three other women followed them, like, to spy on them, and got lost in the desert, as you say. Then Talbot returns and takes you to be with your mother there. And again he returns, but he gets caught...but escapes, chased by McElroy. He follows Talbot through the gap. Somehow finds Tammy—and she's the queen. Michael runs off—there, still there, succumbs to disease, as you said. Then the terrorist thing happens and your parents are blasted back to Earth—Tammy to the IRS building and Chuck to the police station, the places they worked. Why there? And once again Talbot returns to do some mission, gets cornered and shot, in a coma, awakens paralyzed. Now you return to get Talbot." Wilson shook his head, rubbed his brow. "I sure have been watching too much of that Sci-Fi channel.

"Keep the coffee coming," Wilson said to Millie the waitress in the pink uniform at the 39th Street Denny's. He was losing track of time, focused on the mission.

He and Chucker hopped into a booth in the far corner, against the wall and the windows.

"I know your usual," she said with a grin. "How about your friend?"

"Give him the same."

It was nearly dawn but a cool rain fell outside, making for a nasty commute. Wilson had nothing going on this morning, no classes until the afternoon. Chucker had only his mission. Both needed a quick breakfast.

"The worst thing you can do," said Wilson after their plotting conversation had reached an impasse, "is let them know you're here. They're starting to settle in, back to normal. Not only is it a bad idea for you to suddenly reappear to them—a major distraction in recovery—but you could set off alarms all over the city. Nobody's looking for you. That gives you freedom. If your mother thinks you're in town, she's gonna be blabbing to everyone—and then everyone's gonna be looking for you. Probably the same with your father. He'll be interested to find you. And he's got cop buddies who know how to track you down. Then you'll be put somewhere you don't want to be. My guess is it's better to save the family reunion for next time."

"I want to know they're okay."

"They're fine, medically. Back to good health. Mental health? I'm not so sure. I know Tammy's seeing a shrink once a week. McElroy...hmm, probably talking to the police shrink, but I don't know for sure."

The door swung open at the far end of the dining room and three men in suits and raincoats entered.

"Hey, look who's here!" called one.

Wilson looked up. It was his old partner, Detective Henderson. Accompanying him was the kid, Bobby Sawyer, and a man he did not know.

Wilson smiled and got up as they approached. "How you doing?" They shook hands.

"Great. Great. Showing the new guy around. You?"

"Doing good. Yep, good."

"That's good. So who's your date here?"

Wilson threw a thumb at Chucker. "My nephew's in town."

"Nice to meet you. Like the blue hair."

Chucker, frowning, got up and went to the restroom.

"Don't mind Charlie. College hazing, you know," said Wilson without missing a beat. "It's a sore spot with him. Made him go through all that bullshit then kicked him out."

"Yes, frats can be rough. So how's law school?"

"Oh, tons of reading. My mind's fried."

"I hear you. Well, if you ever get tired of it, we're saving a desk for you. Way in the back."

"Good to know. Thanks."

Henderson turned to the youngest of the three, a man with a crew-cut and wide jaw, serious look. "This is Detective Wilson. He was on the Talbot case with me." He turned to Wilson. "Ray Golden. Detective."

Wilson shook hands with Golden.

"We busted Talbot the first time at the IRS," said Henderson, "then again at the house. We saw him sent to psychoville. Then this mug wants to bale out on me, says he wants to be a lawyer or a judge."

They laughed.

"I'm trying to forget that case now, buddy," said Wilson. "Too many ethical issues involved. It'll be a case for students to study for years ahead."

"What ethical issues?" asked Golden in a dry monotone.

"It's an open and shut case."

"Is it?"

"You mean because there were no bodies?"

"Partly. Now that the woman and McElroy have returned, it throws everything into question. What if they—"

"Stop right there," said Henderson, turning to Golden. "You see why he wants to be a lawyer." Golden did not smile. "Becker still thinks you're the spacehead—out of deference to Drummond, may he rest in peace."

"He said he took them to—"

"No need to debate the case now. We're just here for some food. And looks like yours is here, too." He pointed to Wilson's table. "Well, enjoy your breakfast. We'll see you round."

"Yeah, see ya."

Wilson sat at his table, Chucker still absent. The platter of eggs and sausage, pancakes on the side, had been delivered. He began fixing the pancakes, butter and syrup, as his police colleagues sat down several tables away. He began eating. Just before he finished, Chucker returned, slinking into the booth like he was hiding from an old girlfriend.

"They're still here?"

"Don't worry, *Charlie*. I told them you were my nephew from out of town. Then we talked about the case. Hurry up and eat. We have things to do, places to go."

He watched Chucker pick at his breakfast. "My mom always said if I can't finish it all, at least eat the meat. That's what's expensive." He stuffed the forkful of sausage into his mouth.

When they got up to leave, Wilson was stopped as they passed the detective's table.

"Hey, you hear about McElroy?" asked Henderson.

"No—what?"

"He's finally retiring."

"Retiring? I thought he already did."

"Me, too. But he keeps trying to pass the physical. Now he's stopped trying. Can't pass, not with those injuries."

"So what's he gonna do?"

"I don't know. Maybe crossing guard. Mall cop. Something like that."

"That's too bad."

"Yeah. Well, see you round."

And Wilson and his nephew exited the restaurant.

They drove for a few minutes, wipers beating back the rain, before Chucker muttered: "My dad is no mall cop."

❋ ❋ ❋

Wilson unzipped his jeans and, standing at the far corner of the quarry, aimed his urine at the small rock stuck in the clay, drawing a circle around it. Before he finished, a sound like steak sizzling on a grill made him look back over his shoulder. The lights were faintly sparkling and there was Chucker, freshly returned from beyond the gap.

"That was fast," said Wilson with a snort, zipping up. He glanced at his watch. "Thirty-seven minutes."

Chucker took a deep breath. "Hundred-thirty-seven days."

He sat down a long canvas bag and dropped his backpack to the ground, and saw Wilson's eyes questioning him.

"Equipment we need for the mission."

"Great."

"Top of the line stuff. I stold it. Don't arrest me."

"You have a window of leeway."

"Thanks."

Wilson cleared his throat, spit. "So the mission is a go, huh?"

"If you're in, yes. If you want to drop out, it's still a go."

"I just need to know the truth about Drummond."

"Now?" He hefted the bags onto his back and took a step. "I got serious hunger issues at the moment."

So they drove to a Mexican restaurant on Noland Road and went in.

"This is so like Liêtan food, it's spooky," said Chucker, swabbing up refried beans with a tortilla.

"I'm glad you're not dressed weird this time."

"I learned my lesson. Never look like a fool in the place you're going, even if you look cool in the place you're coming from."

"Wisdom for the ages."

"You want to know about your friend...." Chucker scooped up a forkful of rice. "All I ever heard Set say about it was that when he went through the tangent, there was a line of soldiers waiting for him on the other side. The soldiers were the ones that fired at the police. The police tried to come through the tangent, he said. I guess bullets can pass through it easy."

"So Set—Sebastian Talbot—never fired a shot himself?"

"Naw, he didn't even have any gun."

Wilson stared at the chile relleno, stirred the gravy with his fork. "They could've used you on the witness stand. That's for sure."

"A guy from the other side? That'd go over good."

"Right." He grabbed a chip, dipped it in salsa. "I'm convinced. Talbot is a crazy man, but not a killer. And I can only imagine what it's been like for him. First in a coma. Then waking up paralyzed. But still put away in a prison. Locked within his body, his body locked within the prison. Ironic."

"Set loves irony," said Chucker. "He's probably laughing his ass off inside his head."

Chapter 11

Zoology

As usual, Toni's hands were cool when she placed them against his cheeks, cradling his face like a little puppy, too cute to be punished for a moment of naughtiness. Sebastian had learned to endure her touch, at once full of kindness yet evilly portentous. He would hold his breath every time she touched him, expecting to receive a warning or a curse. Whenever she touched him, he heard voices in his mind: female voices, all the same voice but slightly out of sync so they formed a barely comprehendible cacophony only a step up from a chorus of out-of-tune succubae.

"Are you ready for your day out?" she asked him, using the cheery voice he was growing to hate. He could hear the sadness, the fear behind her words. Putting her words into a coldly artificial lilt only emphasized the horrific nature of his situation. He could not complain. "It's sunny and on the warm side, at least for late October."

She finished dressing him, commenting on his favorite blue shirt and khaki slacks. Most of the time he wore a hospital gown. Blue socks and brown shoes were added, forcing the woman to squat and take each foot in her lap.

"Are you ready, Mrs. Talbot?" a young woman in uniform called and Toni looked up as the nurse stepped into the room.

"You must be new here. Please call me Doctor Franck. I did not take his name when we married."

"Oh, I'm sorry," the nurse said, then went about the room, checking the medical equipment that monitored the prisoner's daily life. She had been there a while, she explained, but only recently been transferred to this wing of the facility. "Your escorts are waiting in the front."

Toni thanked her, grabbing his jacket and dropping it in his lap. She got behind him and pushed the wheelchair out of the room, into the corridor and down to the elevators.

Two men in gray suits stood as she approached.

Uncomfortably familiar to each other, Agent Brown, the man with the short brown hair and big shoulders, spoke: "This is Johnson. He'll be on this detail with me for the foreseeable future." He waved at the other man, who smiled minimally. He was younger than Agent Brown, slim yet athletic, blond hair to his collar.

"What happened to Agent Folson?" she asked.

"Guess he got tired of babysitting prisoners."

"That's a nice way to say it!"

She knew the score. Nobody liked accompanying them out, not this serial killer who was now paralyzed and stuck in a prison hospital the rest of his life. That still was not good enough for him, many believed. He only went out one day a month—twelve times a year—to get some sunshine, fresh air, and see his son. He was in a wheelchair; he was not going anywhere.

"Shall we go?" she shot back.

That bastard only has twenty-six days to live, said the voice in his head. He had heard similar sentiments as his wife interacted with other people. She only visited him once or twice a week, for an hour or two each time. She mostly talked about her day, their son, his school activities, sometimes a bit of legal news. To him, it seemed as though the voice was her real thoughts, different from the words she spoke. Or they were the words of the demon living inside her—the one that tried to make their conjugal visits worth scheduling, sitting naked on his naked lap and coaxing him to autoerotic pleasures. He could feel that, fortunately, but could do nothing for himself, or for her.

He will be hit by an ice cream truck and bleed out, the voice said.

A wetness inside his trousers drew his attention as they

strapped him and his wheelchair into the van. He could do nothing about it.

The boy sitting beside him called his mother's attention: Papa had wet his pants again.

"Do you want to go back?" asked Agent Brown.

She thought of the time it would take to change him. There was only a few hours before they must return. She could run up to his room and grab another pair of trousers, change him when they arrived at the zoo. It was so tiring, she sighed. It would dry.

"No, let's go on."

And off they went: to the Kansas City Zoological Park nestled inside Swope Park between 63rd Street and Gregory Boulevard, one of the largest municipal parks in the country, acres of forests and fields for play. Clouds had lessened the sun's effects and the crowds were not yet large. October was not zoo season so she thought it would be a good time to take Junior there.

She bought tickets for all of her group and they entered. First stop was the restroom to clean up Sebastian. She could not take him into the Women's side nor could she go into the Men's side with him. Brown was not interested in being his nanny. Johnson agreed to roll him into the Men's side and help him pee.

"First and last time," said Brown.

"You're in particularly cruel voice today," said Toni. "No sex this month?"

He smiled, shook his head. "You're weird."

She didn't know how to take his remark. Working together for a year, they had gotten to know some things about each other, not in a romantic way but like two coworkers in a job neither of them liked.

Out came the wheelchair with Sebastian leaning forward. Toni went and pushed him up straight.

"Everything all right?"

"I've had worse," said Johnson. "My grandpa had cancer and wasted away. I had to help him in the bathroom every day."

"I'm sure he appreciated that. Good for you, Agent Johnson. And thank you for your help with my husband."

Too bad he has his grandfather's genes, said the voice in Sebastian's head, *because he will develop cancer, too, in fifteen years. It's already started in his lymph node.*

Brown gave Johnson a sharp look. They started off, heading to the children's section of the zoo.

"Don't run off!" Toni cried after Junior as his excitement made him hurry.

Johnson ran after the boy, caught up with him by the sea lion pool. Toni smiled at that, wishing Sebastian could do that. Brown seemed disappointed his new partner did not have more cynicism for the job. A four hour excursion, that's all. Then back to the office where cases awaited his attention. Toni felt his dislike.

She pushed the wheelchair down the slope and over to the sea lion exhibit.

From the sea lions, they crossed to llamas, deer, and then the farm animals and the Discovery Barn. Junior was eager to go in but his mother told him to wait.

"I'll wait here," Agent Brown grunted, folding his arms.

Johnson accompanied the boy into the barn, walked with him along the pens. Pigs, sheep, donkeys, chickens, geese, and rabbits. Outside were four breeds of horses. Johnson explained about each of them to the boy. Like a father.

Toni glanced at Sebastian, frozen in his chair, and felt bad for him. This was supposed to be his outing. Family time.

"Excuse me, Agent Johnson," said Toni, leaning against the railing of the goat pen. "I'm very happy you take an interest in helping us, especially my son. That's wonderful, really. Except, I need for my son and his father to spend time together."

He grimaced. "I'm sorry. You're right."

"Thank you."

"I'll wait outside."

After Johnson exited, Toni turned to Sebastian, squatted beside his wheelchair and whispered into his ear an apology for letting the new agent take over. Of course, Sebastian could hear her words yet not turn his head or speak a reply. He batted his eyes, which was the best he could do to communicate.

"I'm glad you understand," she said.

They moved down the aisle, pausing at each pen. At the end of the barn was a door for zoo personnel only. The door opened and a young man came out, dressed in the khaki uniform of zoo staff. He had bluish hair, not like he had been at some punk rock party but more like he had visited his grandmother's hair salon. She could not keep from smiling at him.

The zookeeper halted before her, looking down at the man in the wheelchair.

"What do you want?" Toni burst out suddenly, not sure where that fearful response originated.

Others around them noticed her outburst.

"Nothing, ma'am," said the zoo staff guy. "I hope I didn't startle you or your little boy."

Toni composed herself. "No, I'm sorry. I have no idea why I would say that. Something came over me. Strange. I'm all right now."

He apologized again and went on his way, moving to the opposite end of the barn, looking back and forth as though checking each pen, then stepped outside.

He looks like one of the assassins, the voice in his head spoke, *one of them who killed me, there in our bed.*

Sebastian closed his eyes tightly. He knew. The voice was not Toni's. He could do nothing about that phenomena. Somewhere a spirit had entered Dr. Toni Franck and shared her body and mind. If only he could tell Toni, warn her. Was there any way to exorcize the spirit of Basura-Kanoun?

Chucker's heart was beating fast. He recognized them as soon as he left the staff room. The wheelchair was a dead giveaway. He almost lost his nerve when he exited the barn and spotted the two men in suits leaning against the fence of the horse corral. He strolled past them casually, as though he was off break and returning to his section of the zoo.

He made his way to the camel rides, next to the barnyard area and took a position where he could keep an eye on the barn door and the two agents.

Set-d'Elous in a wheelchair, he considered. His mind went blank as his eyes locked on the barn door. Was that him? Could that be? Chucker did not get a clear look in his brief passage. He did not know the woman or the boy, of course, but they seemed to be just as Wilson had described them. Set-d'Elous, family man.

He wanted to laugh. Family man in a wheelchair, silent and immobile. And Chucker had something to do with that.

He could not quite put together the theory, but he did know he and his team had shot the man and he had fallen through the window panes yet somehow never crashed on the plaza below. The only explanation was that he fell down through a tangent and crashed in the quarry, broken neck, paralyzed. But Wilson said they had shot him. Gunshot to the head would cause paralysis. Gunshot to the neck would do that, too.

None of that mattered now. He had about two more hours to get him and get him out of the zoo. It freaked him out that he had bumped into them unexpectedly. He had planned to remain anonymous up to the final instant when Set would need to recognize him to go along with the escape. The woman did not know him and the man in the wheelchair had not looked up.

Meanwhile, Wilson would have to be ready with the van.

The sun was warm through the windshield so Wilson got out and stood beside the van, door open. He pretended to be a hippie who had driven all night and was too tired to continue, ready to take a nap. He had checked and rechecked the controls for the lift gate. The tank was full. Everything was ready except his nerves.

He didn't know why he had agreed to this mission. It could ruin everything if he were caught. Ex-COP MASTERMINDS ESCAPE OF SERIAL KILLER! He could see the headlines. Worse yet would be the reactions of his former colleagues. He had worked on the case with them and now he was helping the criminal escape? That's the worst kind of treachery. How long had he been planning this betrayal? That's what they would wonder.

So it had to work. Smoothly. And he would be anonymous. He had grown out his beard in the two weeks they waited, planning. He was dressed in camo jacket and jeans but had a uniform of a nursing home attendant in the van to change to once they were out of the zoo area. They would apply a nursing home placard to the doors also. Then they could drive innocently to the quarry and be rid of this troublesome man.

❇ ❇ ❇

Little Sebastian was enjoying the zoo. Toni guided him from exhibit to exhibit and explained to him about each animal to the best of her education, though she was far from a zoologist. He asked a lot of questions. *Why is that horse brown and that one has stripes on it? That's a zebra, not a horse. Looks like a horse. It does, doesn't it? They are related but sometimes things that look alike aren't the same.* She paused to think of her answer.

That man in the barn, dressed as zoo staff, seemed strange. He was strange in a familiar way. The way he had looked at her—as though he knew who she was. Probably someone who recognized her from the newspaper stories. Someone like him did not seem the type to read newspapers, or keep updated on the television news reports on her and her husband, the serial killer.

What would the people in the zoo do if they knew Sebastian Talbot was among them? Even frozen in a wheelchair, just knowing he was present might cause them to flee. It seemed nobody had compassion for a crippled man. Even if they did not want to give him a break, there was nothing to be afraid of now. He could not move. They were safe. Perhaps too safe.

She took her son's hand, leading him to the camels. Gazing down at him, asking him if he wanted to ride the camel, she felt a pang in her gut. The boy tilted his head up to reply that he would like to ride the camel and she gazed into his eyes, saw his nose and measured his cheeks. He looked exactly like his father.

That man in the barn looked exactly like someone she knew.

"Ma'am, you okay?" asked Agent Brown when she stopped for too long half-way to the camel ride.

She shook her head. "I'm fine."

Then she knew: the man in the barn resembled the woman she was counseling. Tammy Tucker, Queen of Aivana, as she insisted she be called. Blonde, small nose, high cheeks, brown eyes. Only the man's dull blue hair was different—and likely not natural but something done for a party.

She was certain he was related to Tammy. But he seemed too old to be her son.

✳ ✻ ✳

Sebastian knew where he was: the prison of his mind. And in that prison was a zoo full of animals he had seen previously in his youth. Resting in a chair that rolled, he could watch the world go by, never lifting a finger or moving a foot in effort. The woman pushing his chair seemed familiar. He recognized her face, the touch of her hands, the tone of her voice. He remembered how she sat on his lap from time to time and called his name, rocking against him until he felt sparks in his groin—the only sensations south of his chin he could detect. A mystery. And somehow that exercise had produced a child who she called his son. He knew the boy's name but could not speak it himself.

The day was fair. Autumn. Sky half-cloudy. Breeze calm. The zoo was not crowded. It was a good day to go outdoors. He wanted to smile but the muscles would not respond. His mouth was dry anyway. He wanted a drink of water.

Rattling in his chair got the attention of Agent Johnson.

"Is he all right?"

The woman halted. "He wants something." She leaned down and whispered into his ear: "What do you need, Sebastian dear? You already went to the lavatory."

But the voice in his head told him clearly that he was about to ruin a perfectly good day simply to satisfy one of his personal quirks. That was not fair. He should be glad to be outdoors and be still.

"Water? You want a drink? Is that it?"

He batted his eyes twice and she pulled a water bottle from her bag, opened it and helped him with a couple swallows.

"Better?"

Two blinks.

Chapter 12

Serendipity

The zookeeper in khaki uniform waved the children into a semi-circle around the Bactrian two-hump camel with red reins dangling from its mouth.

"Gather 'round, kids," called the man. "Don't stick out your hands. Missus Humpty might think your finger is food."

Chucker stepped close to him. "I can take over now. Time for lunch, huh?"

The man was surprised. "No, it's not time for my lunch yet..." He looked at Chucker's name tag. "...Bobby. Are you new here?"

They argued with restraint in their voices, not wanting to upset the children. Finally, Chucker gave up and pretended to help. He lifted the children into the saddle between the two humps, then watched the other man lead the camel around the small track, the children jostling back and forth with each slow step.

Next came that woman. It was her son's turn so Chucker hefted him into the saddle. He was missing his opportunity, thought Chucker, though he was not sure what his move would be. Some kind of distraction, then snatch the wheelchair and take off to the side gate, hidden among the maintenance sheds.

However, he had learned from his mentor how serendipity could be his friend.

The camel balked, refused to go ahead, fought the zookeeper

and in the squabble, the children slid out of the saddle.

Chucker dove to the ground, just as he had when the brown-robed terrorist had tossed the grenade in the Royal Hall in Aivana. His arm outstretched, he caught the boy, kept his head from hitting the ground. His other arm wrapped around the boy, cradling him from the hoofs of the belligerent beast. Then came the dung.

The zookeeper managed to catch the other child and swing her from the saddle. The rides were done for the afternoon, it seemed.

"Thank you so much," Toni sang frantically, taking her son from Chucker, whose uniform was now soiled.

"You're welcome, ma'am," he said, sheepishly. If the boy had hit the ground, he might have gotten a concussion or a broken arm. She would have rushed him to the first aid station and in her haste abandon the wheelchair. He could have absconded with the man then. But, no, he did not allow the child to be hurt. He had a son and daughter of his own. He acted automatically and saved the boy.

As they stepped away from the camel rides, the woman talked with Chucker, thanking him. He was polite but excused himself, saying he needed to change his soiled uniform.

A petite Asian girl with the name tag Patti had a big smile for Chucker. Amusement flickered across her face. "What'd you get into?" she asked as he entered through the 'staff only' door at the end of the barn.

"Camel shit."

"Missus Humpty? That old gal? She's gotten me a couple times, too." The girl stared at him. "You must be new."

"Right. New. Too new for this." He fashioned a story, just like his mentor, Set, would always do. "Supposed to be only a summer job but I'm ready to quit now."

"Awww, it ain't so bad. At least you don't have to clean up after apes or elephants. Apes're the worst. Like they're making a mess because they know someone else has to clean it up. Nothing worse than ape shit."

"I hear ya," said Chucker. He scanned the rack of freshly laundered uniforms. He selected one that appeared to be his size, glanced at the name tag on the hanger. "Looks like I'm gonna need to borrow Gary Hoover's uniform. Got to finish out the shift, right?"

"Oh, he's not coming in today, anyway. He got bit by a monkey," said the girl, petite and perky, not his type. With her black hair and heart-shaped face, she resembled his Typegan wife, Foj, back in Liêta. When this mission was done....

"Good. I'll keep it as clean as I can."

"I'm Patti, by the way," she said.

"Nice to meet you."

"Likewise...uh, who are you again?"

"Chu—Charlie. I'm Charlie."

"Nice to meet you, Charlie. Have fun."

The girl exited and 'Charlie' quickly switched trousers and shirt. He kept the Bobby name tag.

The woman and her family were still there when Chucker came out of the barn. He could not avoid them and so joined them, sitting on the bench with them. The woman thanked him again, and again he waved off any hint of heroism. The conversation turned to him and his path to becoming a zookeeper. No, he hadn't dreamed of working with animals all his life. It was just a job for now.

"You look just like a woman I know," she said, rocking the boy in her lap. "It's uncanny. I wonder of you are any relation to her. Her name's Tammy Tucker."

Chucker smirked. "Isn't that one of them people killed by the serial killer?"

Toni frowned. "Haven't you heard? She has returned. So she wasn't killed."

"Good for her."

"So you're not related? You look just like her."

Chucker swallowed, deciding whether any information he

shared would jeopardize his mission. It had before. He had botched missions in the past. This one could not fail. He would play dumb.

"No, I don't think so."

The woman seemed put-off; something she felt certain of had been dismissed.

"All right," she said, setting her son down on his feet beside the bench, "I'm sorry. But thank you so much for catching my little man."

Chucker waved farewell and hurried away, knowing he had missed his chance. The walkie-talkie bobbled in his pants pocket. He decided not to tell Wilson what had happened but try again at another location in the zoo. Now that she had met him, it would be harder to act with the guards watching.

Or perhaps it would be easier, now that he was in her good graces, a friend of the family and all.

"I must wash his hands now," she said, holding up her son's arm. "A camel is not very clean, I suppose." She looked over at the restroom shack, then gazed around for Brown and Johnson.

"I can watch him," said Chucker, nodding at the man in the wheelchair, "while you take your son to the restroom."

"Oh, thank you. That is so helpful."

She led the boy away to the restroom and Chucker sensed the man in the wheelchair watching them go.

Chucker let out a sigh, squatted before the man in the wheelchair, grabbing the wheels to keep himself steady.

"Set-d'Elous," he whispered to the man, "we meet at last."

Their eyes touched uncomfortably.

"You recognize me? I'm Chucker. I don't know how, but I'm gonna try to get you out of here." He paused, gazing into the man's eyes as though needing confirmation of him being alive, being conscious, able to hear, able to comprehend. "Then I'm taking you back to Ghoupallesz where we can fix you good as new. In the future they got ways of fixing you. Advanced medical treatment, I mean. I scoped it out. We can do this. I got the gear hidden. I just need to get you away from those other people. Understand?"

He blinked twice.

"You can hear me, right? You know what I'm saying, right?"

Blinks.

"Good. So whenever it all goes down, just hang loose. Be cool. Trust me." Chucker laughed. "I guess that's all you can do, huh?"

"Everything all right here?" asked Agent Johnson, coming up behind them.

"Sure," said Chucker, standing. "She took the boy to wash his hands. I said I'd wait with this guy."

"I see." The agent seemed annoyed, like he was being accused of not doing his job. "I can watch him now. You can go on with your duties. Thanks for your help."

"No problem," said the man, turning to leave.

The woman was returning, hand in hand with her son. She called her thanks to him again.

"All right, let's go."

"Where to?" asked the agent.

"To the Australian section!"

Chucker watched the woman pushing the wheelchair up the slope, the boy walking beside them. The agent held back, saw Chucker watching him.

"We aren't actually supposed to help, just observe," said the agent.

"Observe what?"

"You see, he's a criminal. He's paralyzed but he's a prisoner. He gets out once a month with his wife—her, and their son—so when he's out somebody's got to watch them—him."

"You think he's going to escape?" Chucker laughed.

"It's protocol."

"Seems stupid to watch a guy in a wheelchair."

"He's not some guy. He's Talbot the Terminator. The serial killer. Killed his coworkers from the IRS? Know about it?"

"I heard something."

Chucker gazed up the slope at the woman, seeing her slowing behind the wheelchair, possibly getting tired.

"Been about six years now," said the agent.

"I heard one of them came back, so she wasn't killed by him, after all. So he should get off for that."

"There were others killed, and they have not returned."

"Well, maybe they are just living somewhere else, not killed."

"That's a theory, but—"

"You say several people were killed by him, then one comes back, what're you gonna think about the others? That they're wherever she was at, all of them not dead."

"One victim was outside his residence. He definitely killed that one."

"You mean the Fat Man?"

"Davenport was his name. Right outside his apartment. The killer's apartment. So he's at least the killer of that victim."

"I still don't get why he has to be watched if he's paralyzed and in a wheelchair."

"You're a freakin' zookeeper, that's why!"

As they argued, Chucker kept his eyes on the woman and the wheelchair. It was not a long slope but it was steep towards the end. Turn right and they would enter the Australian exhibit.

"...four years in Criminal Justice," the agent was boasting when Chucker saw the woman stop to rest, then reach out to grab her son who started to walk away. The woman stretched for the boy, losing her balance and falling to a knee. The wheelchair wobbled, then leaned back a moment before rolling down the slope. It gained momentum and Chucker and the agent had to jump out of the way as it plunged down the asphalt—straight for the sea lion exhibit.

A low wall surrounded the pool—a concrete island rose from the center of the pool—and a dozen children were gathered there, tossing sardines at the sea lions barking in the water.

The agent shouted for the children to move out of the way as the wheelchair rushed down at them. Chucker leaped for the wheelchair but missed.

It crashed against the low wall and flipped over, throwing the man head over heels into the pool.

Chucker rushed to the wall and dove in, grabbed the man and pulled his head above the surface. Sea lions flicked their tails at him, sending water over the humans, barking their enjoyment of the trick.

The pool wasn't deep around the shoreline and Chucker could

stand up, keeping his charge well above the water.

Chucker hefted the man out of the pool, dumping him over the low wall, both of them soaked and dripping. He shook his head to flip his hair back out of his face.

"Good thing I don't hafta charge you extra for any mouth-to-mouth!"

Reaching for the man, he saw the crowd gathering around him. Kneeling beside the victim, Chucker could not see over the visitors. Between them, however, he spied a cart.

He hoisted the man up from the asphalt and threw an arm over his shoulder, pulled him upright like a drunk, and held him with his other arm.

"Make way," Chucker grunted, dragging him through the crowd, over to the golf cart parked there.

"Gimme the cart, man," he commanded the guy. "I gotta get him to medical services!"

The guy stepped off the cart and Chucker pulled his mentor into the seat beside him, holding him up by one arm as he rushed off down the path, honking to clear the crowd of visitors as he went—over the bridge to Africa and a hard left to the Education Center.

Chapter 13

Les Éléphants

Wilson stared at his watch, not believing how much time had expired since he parked the van. A glance around the parking lot showed no police activity. He thought again of the ethics of what he was doing, tried to rationalize his participation. The man could not be guilty, not now, not after that Tammy and his old buddy Chuck McElroy returned. It would take too long to convince his former colleagues of the truth of the new evidence; easier to let him stay in a prison hospital the rest of his life—with once a month outings with his wife and son. Miserable life. He scratched the whiskers that had grown out since he met the young man from another world. Nothing was more important now than helping this guy complete the mission. Maybe he'd be able to follow him back to beyond the gap.

"...in the sea lion pool! Went straight in," said a woman to another woman, both pushing child carts.

More zoo patrons filed out, not as though there was any evacuation. Leaving as usual, children tired—mother tired, more likely. But they all had something to mention: someone fell into the sea lion pool and was pulled out by a zoo staff person.

Could Chucker be involved? Wilson wondered after a minute to contemplate the information.

✳ ✳ ✳

"Where is he?" Agent Brown asked Agent Johnson. They craned their necks over the crowd that had gathered.

Toni stood nearby, holding her son's hand, scanning the park, checking each face.

"The zoo guy took him to medical services," said Johnson.

"Where's that?" asked Toni.

They stepped over to a map board and studied it.

"I don't see any medical services station," said Agent Brown.

"It's probably in the main building. By the entrance," Agent Johnson suggested.

"I don't see anything that looks medical," said Toni. "No white crosses on this map."

Agent Brown to Agent Johnson: "Check the front. Alert zoo officials." To Toni: "He can't get out of the zoo, not with us here by the entrance. Only one way out. Don't worry."

"What should I do?" she asked.

"We can't sound an alarm, can't startle or scare people. What if they knew a serial killer was visiting today?"

"Please don't talk like that." She crossed her arms in a huff. "He was convicted by people who only got to hear incriminating evidence and opinions, not by the facts."

"We cannot keep having this debate," said Agent Brown. "My job is to make sure he is returned to the prison hospital the same as when we picked him up."

Agent Johnson jogged back to them after a few minutes. "I informed the zoo officials about his visit and his escape."

"Let's not call it that just yet," said Agent Brown.

"There is a first aid station over in the Africa section, they said." He pointed to its location on the map.

"We'd better get over there," said Agent Brown. He sighed, shook his head and glared at Agent Johnson. "Did you see what happened?"

"He rolled backward down the hill—"

"My hands froze and I—I couldn't hold the chair any longer," Toni cried.

"It's all right, ma'am," said Agent Brown. "An accident. That's what it was." To Agent Johnson: "Go after him!"

He rubbed his eyes, took a deep breath.

"Ma'am, I think we should call it a day. He's no doubt traumatized now. No reason to make it worse by trying to continue this ridiculous field trip."

"It's not ridiculous!" Toni felt a tug at her shirt.

"Mama, je veux voir les éléphants!" said her son.

She looked down at him. "You sure you can't wait to see the elephants next time?"

He shook his head, pouted. "Les éléphants!"

She turned to Agent Brown. "Can we stay a little longer?"

"He's sitting in wet clothing, ma'am."

"He will dry off in the sunshine."

"It's a little on the cool side. He'll catch a chill."

"We didn't bring any extra clothes—"

"Ma-ma!"

"*Silence*, s'il tu plaît, Sebastian." An idea flashed in her head. "I'll buy some clothes in the gift shop. T-shirt or sweatshirt. The pants we can take off him and then cover his legs with the blanket. Won't that get us through another hour? Then we can leave."

Agent Brown seemed tired, nodding like a bobblehead doll.

"If you insist."

"I'll be right back. Watch my son, please."

"Wait!" Agent Brown watched her hurry away. "We can't be left in charge of him."

Remember your training!

Chucker thought hard. He could see the procedure in his mind, repeating the four times he had gone through it with supervision. The last time had been in the dark, deliberately, and he had set a new training record for assembly completion. That earned him a Third Director rank in Emergency Medical Services. He mused how Kobarêl society liked to put people in hierarchies. He could have headed his own team of technicians with that rank—if he had stayed.

He opened the long, canvas bag, laid out all the parts, then carefully organized them according to where they would be applied: head, torso, legs, and feet.

The story came to him then, one that his step-father Jason had told, later confirmed by Set himself: how Set had put together a hang glider to escape with Queen Jinetta from the top of some castle in Zetinê. That was brilliant—and it succeeded. So why not an exoskeleton transport system? He had gone to medical school for less than three months—Ghoupalle months, that is. Seeing Set's condition, Chucker was anxious to learn all the advanced orthopedic treatments available in the Kobarêl of 2122. When he felt he knew enough, he rushed back to Earth with stolen equipment in hand. Actually, he'd paid for most of it. Some parts he could not find for purchase, being high-tech and in limited supply, so he snatched them—just like he had snatched Set-d'Elous.

Wilson had reported Set-d'Elous was still scheduled to visit the zoo with wife and child on the same Saturday. And Chucker had only missed one day of his work shift at the zoo, where he had undergone two weeks of training. It was enough to get a uniform and a badge so he could come and go as he pleased. Wilson had told the zoo boss he was ill.

Now Chucker had Set-d'Elous flat on a table in the zoo's Education Center, which was closed for the day.

First, a change of clothing was needed. Chucker had thought of everything: a pair of trousers and a shirt, jacket, athletic shoes and socks, but had forgotten underwear. He closed his eyes as he pulled the wet clothing off of the man, wiped him dry with paper towels from the Center's restroom, then proceeded to pull the new clothing onto him. All the time, the man's eyes followed the activity, and as Chucker saw them observing him, he did not know whether the man was afraid of what was happening, felt relief, or was surprised at his protégé's resourcefulness.

He had to work quickly. Grabbing the EVSk-12 speech by-pass system, he swung it atop the man's head, held it in position against his temple and aligned the wire down behind his ear to his jaw and onward to his throat, aiming for the vocal chords. Another wire he taped to the crown of the man's head, the point of the wire dangling. He took a device from the bag and tested it:

a small drill bit loaded with what Chucker knew was a tiny, tiny explosive charge.

"This is going to hurt—if you can feel it."

He pushed the drill end above the hairline, measured with his fingers from the temple back past the ear and, satisfied, fired away.

The man groaned, shook against the table.

"Ideally you'd be unconscious while we do this, but there's no time for anesthesia."

Chucker took the other wires and jabbed one into the side of the jaw, worked it around a bit to find the nerve, then stretched the other wire to the vocal chords and found the nerve there as his victim writhed against the table.

"Hold still. This will work."

He pulled strips of duct tape off the roll and pressed them to the man's head, jaw, and throat to hold the apparatus and connections in place. The next step was to pull a knit ski cap carefully over his head, then more duct tape around and around his head. He could see the man's eyes wanting to cry for the pain, instead frozen in anguish.

"Once I activate this, you'll be able to speak." He played with a remote control and Set-d'Elous jerked wildly with each spark of electricity. "It reroutes the speech commands past the damaged spinal chord—from your brain speech center directly to your vocal chords. With extra power to your tongue and lips, too, so you can form words. I trained on this for a week."

One more trio of spasms, then—

"Hell. You. Do. T. Me?" said the man on the table. The voice was dry, crackling like a bad radio reception but had the timbre of his voice, the rough tone of a Sebastian Talbot on vacation and not caring how he sounded.

"Hold still now. We don't have much time. They're looking for you as we speak. We've got maybe ten minutes."

Chucker turned his attention to the pieces of metal and plastic he had laid beside his patient: rods and connectors, round disks and joints, bolts and clamps, and lots of wiring. Two small packs were set to the side: the gyroscope and the fuel cell. Suddenly it was all just a pile of junk. How did it go together?

"I can do this," he muttered. "Don't worry. I did this in the dark in nine minutes."

"Wazdat?" asked Sebastian, fighting to control the phonemes.

"You'll see." He lifted the mechanical system of rods and clips. "It's not really a torture device. Just looks like one." He turned to Sebastian. "Can you roll over on your stomach?"

"No. Can't."

"Okay." Chucker rolled him over and stretched out his legs, which had turned stiff during his years of paralysis.

He juggled the many equipment parts in his arms, finally dropped it all in the small of Sebastian's back. Then he moved the appropriate metal rods to his legs and alongside his arms. Clear plastic loops filled with wiring were fitted around his wrists, then elbows, and a small, rounded cube stuffed into each arm pit, He unspooled the wiring and strung it out along the metal rods, clipping wires at each joint and power grid module.

"We can rebuild him. We have the technology," Chucker mumbled as he worked. "We can make him better than he was before...."

The longer rods aligned with thighs and shins, with plastic bands fitted around ankles and knees, a power pack affixed to the small of his back with leads going between his legs and up to his belly where they attached to what was labeled in Ghoupallêan as 'Control Module.' Treaded platforms slid under feet, hugged the heel and toes, grabbed the arch, and were laced around the feet like gladiator sandals.

"Almost done," he spoke softly, attention on his work.

Chucker rolled him onto his back and continued adjusting the connections across the man's belly and chest. The belts were tightened, locking him into the contraption.

He took another remote control from the table and jabbed at a few buttons that made the joints hum and the leg and arm braces move, the body jerking in obedience.

"This may hurt at first, but mostly it'll just be freaking you out. I'm gonna make you walk, dude! With this thing I got from 2122—Kobarêl is the place. Advanced medical machinery. There's not a lot of power stored in the fuel cell but it should be enough to get you out of here."

"Where?" asked the man in the exoskeleton.

"Home."

Puzzled eyes.

"Home to Ghoupallesz."

Sad eyes. Blinks.

"You wonder about that woman and the boy, right?"

"Yeah."

"Here's the plan: we get you back to Ghoupallesz in 2122 or close and get you fixed. Healed. Back to normal. Then you can do whatever the heck you want to do. Come back here and sweep her off her feet, if you like. My duty is to fix you—because I killed you. I'm sorry, really. I shot you before I knew the target was you. And you fell. To Earth. Through a tangent."

"Not true—"

"So I pledged to find you and bring you back. To make you as good as new. It's taken me eight years to find you. And I was five years lost in the jungles of Bæronak before that. I have a wife and children now. Like you, huh? They live in Liêta."

"Let's go."

"Right. We need to get a move on or we won't be able to party tonight."

He took the remote control and studied the buttons layout. He pressed the yellow circle at the top and the fuel cell taped in the small of the man's back showed a yellow light and hummed. He pressed the other, smaller yellow buttons across the top and other parts of the exoskeleton came to life.

"It is al*iiiiive*," said Chucker with a snort. "Let's see if we can get you up on your feet."

The joints moved smoothly with the power on and Chucker eased the man into a sitting position, the frame cradling his hips and supporting the back, firming automatically to hold him in that upright position. Chucker helped him turn his legs off the table, lowering them until one foot platform touched the concrete floor. The rest was done my remote control.

"Relax," said Chucker, giddy with his success. "Let the machinery do the work. Trust it. It won't drop you and you won't stumble. I've seen it work. See, there's a gyroscope in the unit that's fixed to your back. But don't resist the system or you could break some bones. Think of it as a robot that is walking you around and just enjoy the ride."

A shadow fell on the floor.

"Excuse me," said a voice not from the man in the exoskeleton.

Chucker froze. He was certain he had locked the door. He had. But a man had entered from the restroom side. He looked up.

"Sorry to bother you, but my boy...." The man was dressed as a tourist, and paused right then to wonder what was going on in the Education Center on a blustery Saturday afternoon. "He really gots to go and the restroom over at the African Market is out of order."

Chucker saw a boy of six or seven hiding behind the man's legs.

"Sure...aaa...go right ahead."

Remain calm. They probably don't have any concern for what you're doing. They probably don't know a serial killer has escaped his handlers and is hiding out with a madman from another world.

He heard the dad giving instructions to the boy, the words echoing back to him, and he thought of his own children, waiting so long for him to return, insistent as he was about completing this final mission.

"What's that thing, mister?" asked the boy, proudly exiting the toilet, slow to hitch up his pants.

Chucker did not miss a beat as he stared at the man in the metal transport frame.

"It's a robot. We're getting ready for a carnival. Somebody is having a birthday party later and we are the entertainment."

"That's cool!" said the boy. "Does he do tricks?"

"Sure, he does." Chucker pushed the right blue T-shaped button and the right arm swung from beside the body to a Heil Hitler salute and back down again. He pressed the left T-button and the left arm repeated the movement.

"That's impressive," said the dad. "I work at Kaufman Industries, actually." He nodded toward the empty wheelchair. "We make those. But that thing you got your friend in could be used to move patients a whole lot better—"

"It's just a hobby," said Chucker, pretending to inspect the transport frame up close. "It only looks real. Sure is gonna scare some kids, huh?"

The man was not put off. "That does look very advanced. Are you the inventor?"

"I'm just a guy who works at the zoo. You know, camel rides, cleaning ape shit, escorting robots to birthday parties."

"He said a bad word, daddy."

"Yes, son," said the dad. "He did."

The man directed his son out of the Education Center as Chucker glanced at the clock on the wall. Twenty-two minutes! Not ten. It could have been zoo security descending on the building instead of a dad and his bladder-filled boy.

"We gotta go now," Chucker announced, pulling a trench coat from the canvas bag. "Let's have you wear this over the machinery. Less scary to children and wild animals." He pulled the coat over the outstretched arms but it was a tight fit. "I did not program arm swinging, so it may look strange walking with your arms straight. Kinda like that Frankenstein monster."

Remote control in hand, Chucker initiated lift-off and the device hummed. With a push of the top point of the red diamond-shaped button, Set-d'Elous the robot took his first two steps.

Chucker opened the door for him. "Out you go!"

He wanted to hurry; the contraption was capable of quickwalking, and as long as the passenger did not stiffen with resistance, the robot could move at 120 beats a minute, marching tempo.

"There's a gate right outside this building that we are going to go through. There's a drive on the other side. Nobody is watching it today cuz its Saturday. No events at this building. It's all asphalt pavement, smooth surface except for a few crumbles. It should be easy. My partner is at the end of the drive with a van. It has a wheelchair lift but you can walk up the ramp into the van and we'll get the heck out of here."

Except that the lock on the gate he had left unlocked had a fresh padlock on it. He had spent the better part of an hour sawing through the previous one and now there was a new one: shiny and silver, as unyielding as Tangent 34-X.

Chucker sang a string of obscenities, shaking the lock and kicking the wooden gate. He gazed at the top of the gate. Sure, he could scale it, drop down on the other side, but not possible for a man wearing a first-generation Kobarêl Medical Services Mobility Division D5-BCX human transport system. The weak link was that they could not do fences. No leaping over a building in a single bound. No faster than a speeding bullet, either.

Glancing at the corner of the building, Chucker saw past it out into the zoo expanse. Nothing unusual going on. Mothers and children, dads and kids, many of them now huddled around huts that were selling snacks.

"We're going to Plan B," he called to Set-d'Elous.

"Plan C," the man dared utter despite the pain searing through him whenever he activated the speech device.

Chucker sneered, then smiled. He was going to make it. He swore it.

"You look good, man. Trench coat, ski cap, metal feet and legs. Nobody will even take a second look at you."

"Ha. Ha. Ha." The voice was sounding like a robot's now.

Chucker directed the D5-BCX unit to the rear corner of the building, still within the shadow of the eaves.

"There's another gate on the other side. Around the Veldt area—that big open area where all the African animals roam free. That gate's for maintenance. They take the trash out that gate. All the animal crap goes there. Very unpleasant spot. I've worked here two weeks and I know this place backwards and forwards. It *is* a jungle."

He pulled a walkie-talkie out of his pants pocket.

"Code Three," he spoke, rather softly. The radio crackled loudly.

"Yeah. What's up?" said Wilson.

"I said Code Three."

"Okay, Code Three."

"Got it?"

Pause. "Okay, what is Code Three, again?"

"It's when Code Two is a no-go."

"Right. But what is it? I forgot."

"The other side from Code Two extraction point. Go there."

"Gotcha." Radio static. "You mean now?"

"Heading there now."

"I'll be ready."

"Great."

Nervous thumb resting on the red diamond-shaped button, Chucker turned to his robot friend: "Suck up your guts, dude, it's show time."

Chapter 14

Witnesses

The tall, blonde woman in the pink business suit smiled at the camera, nodded to the cameraman.

"We're here today with zoo-goer Kathleen Barker who, with her son, witnessed the horrific event at the K.C. zoo today." She turned to the woman standing next to her. "Can you tell us what you saw today?"

"I was sitting on the bench, and my son was looking at the elephants and suddenly he shouts 'Mommy, there's a tin man!' You know, like the *Wizard of Oz*? I thought it was his wonderful imagination, you know. This boy is always thinking of fantastic things—"

"What did you see?"

"When I looked, there was a man with, like, metal strips all over him, kinda walking like Frankenstein. And there was this other man chasing him. The second man was in a zoo uniform so I didn't think too much about it. Then—" She looked down at her son. "Then the most terrible thing I ever saw happened. Those men were with the elephants and a mother elephant started chasing them. She got real close and almost trampled the second man. They were running real hard, too."

"And then what happened?"

"I heard the second guy shouting at the first guy. He was shouting 'Run, Seth, run!' It sounded like 'Seth' so must be his name. The first guy running—only he wasn't really running, kinda hobbling along, ya know. Then the second guy turned back to the elephant and then I saw this puff a smoke and a big flash of something orange—"

"Like fire?"

"Coulda been. He was pointing his arm at the elephant and then it stopped. The elephant stopped, right in her tracks and I—I saw—we saw—it looked like the end of the elephant's nose was flying through the air! And it went tumbling over the fence into the cheetah exhibit. Next thing I know they're fighting over that nose. And the elephant is roaring or—what do you call elephant sounds?"

"Trumpeting?"

"Yeah, trumpeting. So much trumpeting, she had to be in a whole lotta pain! Well, I covered my son's eyes and told him he shouldn't see that."

"Then what did you do?"

"Some zoo people run toward us and they escorted us away and they entered the elephant yard. They were chasing the two men, I guess. We weren't allowed to see."

"And what happened to them?"

"After the elephant got its nose shot off, I was all distracted. When I look again, I didn't see them. Maybe they crossed to the other side and climbed out. Who knows?"

The reporter turned to the camera. "And there you have it, Dean, an eyewitness account of the horrific event happening today at the Kansas City zoo. An elephant is maimed by a disgruntled zoo employee. An investigation is underway. I'm Alison DeLuca, KCTV-5 News."

She turned to the mother when the camera was off her. "What happened to the so-called tin man?"

"We didn't see him after the elephant was shot. He must've got away."

"All right. Thank you."

Dean the anchor grinned to the metropolitan audience. "A sad story. I'm sure members of PETA will be on the case." He turned to Nicole, his co-anchor. "Any information on who the disgruntled employee was or what his grievances might be?"

"They'll be investigating it, I'm sure." Nicole faced the camera.

"On a related story comes word that convicted serial killer Sebastian Talbot was among those visitors to the zoo today, joined by his family, and accompanied, as always, by government agents. It is unclear whether he knew about the incident involving Bathsheba, the female African elephant, or the employee presumed to have injured her." She turned to Dean with a smirk. "If there's any good news today, it might be that Talbot reportedly had an accident, too. At some point, it seems, he fell into the sea lion pool."

Dean chuckled. "There is some justice, after all."

"Perhaps, Dean." She faced the viewers, rolling her eyes. "Stay with us, folks. Weather is next."

* ❄ *

The innocent-looking nursing home van raced along I-70, taking the Benton curve at 75 while zipping between two sedans and cutting off a semi that had to slam on its brakes.

"I think you're supposed to drive slow, make it look like we're not fleeing the scene," said Chucker calmly to a frantic Wilson.

"Are you freakin' kidding me?" Wilson continued. "You kidding me?"

"We did it," said Chucker. "Somehow."

"You had to shoot at the elephant?"

"It was chasing us!"

"But—But why're you even in the elephant area?"

"We had to cut across the Veldt to get to the other gate."

"You couldn't walk around it, try to blend in?"

"People were staring already, man! They were calling attention to the Frankenstein guy. And zoo security was—"

"So you just decide to go cross-country?"

"We didn't think the elephants would care about us. Or the zebra, antelope, whatever they got in there. And I didn't think the exoskeleton could perform leaps like that, but—" He broke into freakish laughter. "Man, you shoulda seen it!"

"I'm sure it was amazing—drawing attention to yourself—"

"Like speeding now? Watch out for the Charger, man!"

The van zipped around the sport car, regained position.

"Not my fault that elephant got spooked."

"So you have to shoot at it?" He swung the van around another truck from inside to outside lane, and back to the inside lane, slowing to 60. "And with what?"

Chucker held up the firearm: a XG-48 standard issue Zetin handgun.

"With this."

"What the hell is that?"

"It's a gun from beyond the gap. It fires plasma pulses. I thought I could scare the elephant, make it stop chasing us."

"Are you kidding me?"

"Hey, I'm as surprised as you that it had that range. And that much power at that range—"

"You turned a simple snatch and run into a national media story! Maimed elephant! It's on the news! Disgruntled zoo employee shoots elephant!"

"I didn't mean to hurt it, just stop it from chasing us."

"Sheesh—"

"Chance. We. Get. Cheese. Burger?" came the weirdly robotic voice of their silent partner folded into the backseat, sitting on hands and knees while locked into the exoskeleton.

"We're on the way to the quarry," Wilson grunted.

"They have to guess where we'd be going," said Chucker.

"I'm. Hungry."

"Okay, okay, we'll try the Big Boy on Highway Forty," said Wilson. "It's never crowded. I'll go in. Nobody's seen *me* on TV today."

* * *

IRS clerk Cassie Dorfman suddenly stared up at the talking heads on the television hanging from the ceiling in the south canteen of the service center. At 3 a.m., it was the third shift's second break. She made a face, something that could have been mashed by the slap of an elephant's foot.

"You freakin' kidding?" she trumpeted.

The older woman at the next table eating from a lunch box asked her what was wrong and Cassie waved her off.

There on the TV screen, they were saying exactly what she had dreamed a few nights before. She saw an elephant fall to the ground and a metal man fly away, low across the city skyline. Probably just the sci-fi movie of alien hunters visiting Earth she'd watched that night still playing through her elastic mind. She knew she wasn't crazy but she also knew not to talk so much about her dreams or people would think she was crazy.

No, it wasn't the movie, she knew at that moment; it was another damn premonition. About *him*—convicted serial killer Sebastian Talbot, who used to work right by her at the IRS service center. She put two and two together. He was at the zoo, they reported. Something about his one day a month outside of prison. He was confined to a wheelchair, anyway. And they lost track of him. In the whole big-ass zoo!

Cassie grinned, figuring it out.

"The elephant attack was probably a distraction. Get everybody focused on that elephant and they could get away clean. But who would be helping him escape? Who's here that'd help him?"

She thought of Tammy, who had returned unexpectedly all insane-like and stupid. And they'd heard her ex- also returned, all beat-up and unable to continue being a cop. They both had nothing going now. They sure had motive. Tammy and Chuck were probably the ones getting him out the zoo. They had motive. They were living the fun life before, while everybody thought they was dead, but then they return and life is crap for them. So naturally they wanna return wherever they was hiding. And the only way to get back there is for him to lead them—just like he did on that summer night six years ago.

Satisfied she'd figured it all out, she hurried back to her section to inform everyone of her brilliance.

Wilson dropped off Chucker and "Mr. Roboto"—a.k.a., Sebastian Talbot, a.k.a. Set-d'Elous—at the gravel drive below the hill crowned with the quarry. Ahead was the start of a housing subdivision. At the far end of it was where an old house once stood before it was burned to the ground.

It was dark by then, autumn chill coating everything.

As Wilson drove away, the exoskeleton hummed and cranked, preparing to climb the hill. Chucker worked the remote control to move his mentor up the drive and into the arena of the quarry. The hard part was coming, he knew, thinking of the trip across the desert he had made in the past month of Earth time. Unless they could hit the tangent leading directly to Kobarêl in 2122.

Meanwhile, Wilson took the van to the 7-Eleven, bought several bottles of soda and assorted snacks, then drove to the corner of the mall's parking lot, and walked back along 39th Street to the gravel drive with the chain link gate and the DANGER: RADIOACTIVITY signs.

"Hey, wait," called Wilson, arriving in the quarry arena and seeing Chucker checking the air for what Wilson guessed was a different spot to tear open a new gap. It was several steps from where Chucker had arrived previously.

"Wait? Why?" asked Chucker, not regarding him. "We need to get outta here."

"Looks like we're free," said Wilson, a bit out of breath from the jog up the hill. "I didn't see any patrol cars pass me as I walked back. Maybe they're not as sharp as we thought they were."

"See? Told ya."

Wilson shook his head. "We—them—us—." He sighed. "Whose side am I on? Who am I now?"

"You're a good, decent man now," said Chucker in a plain voice, like a rehearsed speech. He pointed over to the stiff exoskeleton standing beside of the infamous 'love' rock. The man inside the exoskeleton seemed to have nodded off: eyes closed, head held upright. "You helped save an innocent man."

"I gotta believe it now, don't I?" Wilson cleared his throat, coughed in the cool night air. "I've really gone out on a limb helping you. I wonder if they know I helped you. Will they somehow know to look me up and come get me?"

Chucker waved his arms around. "Do you hear anything? I don't. We are free."

"They won't announce their arrival with sirens."

Chucker froze. "Oh. I guess not."

"I really thought they'd be here by now, expecting us to also head here. This is the center of the universe, after all. The only place he would go. Everybody knows. Well, if they're smart."

"Looks like their best man is already here, and they got no idea what to do without you."

Wilson chuckled. "He was in prison, safely put away. And everybody forgot about him. Until today. The radio's saying it was a coincidence. The elephant and the missing killer. Happened to be the same day, no linking yet. Still searching the zoo."

"Lots of places to hide in there."

Wilson pointed to the robot. He got up and went to it, staring for a while. The man inside was asleep.

"They'll find the wheelchair in the Education Center," said Chucker. "Then they can put it all together. But we'll be gone." He resumed his preparation, feeling for the tangent without benefit of a wire grid from days of old.

"I wonder what it feels like to be in that thing," said Wilson. He regarded the sleeping man. "If he's truly paralyzed, maybe it doesn't hurt." He turned to Chucker, who was stripping off his clothes. "How're you going to get him to where you need to go? What if you have to go over mountains, for example?"

Chucker folded his shirt and pants, set them on the rock, and stood in his black bikini briefs and boots.

"I got until the battery runs out—the fuel cell, I mean. Likely a couple days' movement. Picking the right tangent will help. Gotta get us as close as we can." He glared at Wilson. "But I need to concentrate—if you don't mind."

Wilson grinned, stood. "Gotcha."

He strolled around the quarry, occasionally looking up at the cliffs from where Talbot had supposedly fallen when he was shot. In other moments, he glanced at Chucker to monitor his progress. For a man who had lived half his life on another world, he was strangely grounded, thought Wilson, and the young man knew what he was doing.

"I think I found it," Chucker spoke softly, avoiding the echo in the stone-walled arena.

Wilson went to him, studying the air.

"Of course you won't see anything. Not until I open it. But this feels right. Resistance in a patch of air. Like poking a jellyfish after having your hand in the ocean, after feeling the water pressure already. Slight resistance."

Wilson stared in amazement at the spot hovering in the night air, as though it were a diamond that had been mined and they were going to split the proceeds. Then his eyes shifted down to Chucker's belly, noting the shadow of hair above his waistband, his tight belly, and quickly returned his eyes to the invisible spot held in place by Chucker's thumb and forefinger.

"Take me with you."

"What?" said Chucker. "You serious?"

"I think I am."

"You know what happened to my dad, don't you? He went mad there."

"But you didn't."

"I had a guide, a mentor. Then my mom and step-dad taught me everything I needed to know."

"You can teach me."

Chucker laughed—a hollow sound that seemed to suggest that Wilson should not pursue the matter further. It did not make sense for the ex-cop to visit the Dream Land, much less to possibly settle down and live the rest of his life there. Chucker had not wanted to but, forced to adapt, he—

A sprinkle of lights caught their attention: flashlights shining through the trees. The snap of twigs, the swish of dried leaves. No car door slams. No crunch of boots on the gravel drive.

"They're here," whispered Wilson.

"We should go."

Chucker gestured for Wilson to grab the remote control and the backpack. As he did, Chucker concentrated with eyes closed, and with his sensitive fingertips spread several molecules apart, carefully tearing open the fabric of the universe until he could pass his whole hand through.

Wilson played with the remote, awakening the sleeping man— "What. Da. Hell?"—and directed the exoskeleton to carry him to the gap, now open enough for a torso to slip through. Wilson could see the landscape on the other side—beyond the gap— rolling hills, grass, strange trees. He handed the backpack to Chucker who was already half-way through.

"Push the top of the red diamond and it moves him forward,"

Chucker said and Wilson obeyed.

The robot-man stepped up to the gap, held open by Chucker from the ground up to shoulder height.

"Stop! Police officers!" came a shout. Two uniformed officers had entered the quarry through the short canyon. Pistols and flashlights were raised.

"Keep going," said Wilson to Chucker.

The exoskeleton stepped awkwardly to and through the gap, tottering. The gap was now as high as Chucker's head but as narrow as his shoulders. Like the parting of tent flaps—just as Talbot had described the phenomena.

"Halt right there!" the officer called.

A trio of other officers broke from the woods and stood along the top of the cliffs.

"Stop what you're doing!" one ordered.

Wilson pushed against the exoskeleton. "Take me with you!"

"All right, but you hafta do everything I say or you could end up dead."

"I'll die if I stay here."

"Then come on through."

Wilson practically carried the exoskeleton forward, almost riding the machinery through the gap. He felt like turning and grinning at the officers he was leaving behind—everything he was leaving behind—everything.

The gap flowed together once more: like two bodies of fluid briefly separated, again released. Blinking, Wilson could not see any quarry or officers when he turned to look. He saw only the other side of the same landscape that surrounded them. He gazed in each direction, found the skyline of a city in the distance, a few miles away across a red-brown plain with sparse yellow grasses sprouting here and there under a dull, pastel green sky.

His head ached suddenly, his body full of electricity, and after a moment he dropped to his knees and vomited.

"Welcome to the Dream Land," said Chucker.

PART THREE

Lo, did the sons of F'eng set ringing the bellicose bell
and did make war, not love, with the vile unbelievers;
And in their shame did the sons of F'eng mark the
world for their pleasure and build funeral pyres for all
to see!

The Book of Shame, authored by the F'eng,
the Nine Sons, and the Ghost of Set (Song 16)

Chapter 15

The Prophet

In the Valley of the Three Suns in the northwest corner of Jisilika stood the Prophet in golden robe and blue skullcap, his blonde-white hair falling shiny and smooth down his back almost to his hips, a few strands tied off with red *ashi* feathers. Loosening the metal button at the collar of the golden robe, the Prophet inhaled deeply, as though he had been deprived of breath for many years. His arms rose with the help of two young assistants as he urged the congregation to likewise stand and breathe deeply. Most did. The elderly or infirm remained seated on the ground, some of them almost hidden in the tall, yellow grasses. Yet as the suns shown upon them, and the side of the distant cliffs reflecting their different light to form a third color, everyone believed in the existence of immortality.

"I stood before a mirror," spoke the Prophet in a calm but firm voice, feeling no need to expand his voice. The winds had fallen silent so that he might be heard, and most people there were amazed. "And I took sight of myself. I saw nobody I recognized. But I knew I was alive. I knew I had cheated death. Even if I had been transformed into a living death, I could move and think and speak. I knew I had survived a baptism of fire—hellfire, the sting of fate, the stab of destiny, the crush of all my sins at once upon me!"

Anyone who would dare gaze upon the countenance of the

Prophet could easily understand what he meant. His face was not easy to gaze upon, riddled as it were with the remnants of *moussalaganê* infection and the pox that followed. There were clean holes in his cheeks and his lower lip had fallen away. The Prophet's nose had shrunk to the bone, the cartilage long rotted away. Eyelids had folded back and he required his assistants to place droplets of moisture in his eyes periodically. He wore no eyebrows and his hairline had fallen back to the crown of his head. Some believed the long white hair streaming from the back of his head was merely a wig, but it was, in fact, real and natural.

"I stared at Death and met its match—ruined in body yet refreshed in mind." A well-timed breeze tugged at his long white hair. "In the furrowing of my mind I found a third way. I now see what cannot be seen by eyes. I can see what will be so. I can see my own death far into the future. And yours. Touch my hand and I will see your death in my mind. I will tell you the day and hour. Yet you cannot escape it, no matter how you scheme. It is fate. It is ordained. It will happen."

The congregation stood or sat like statues, shocked to hear that all was not as joyful as they wished to believe. That was, of course, why crowds gathered to hear him speak. He made his way across Gotanka, stopping outside each city and town, his assistants calling forth everyone who would come out to hear the message.

"I bring you not a message of doom but a message of hope!"

The congregation cooed, flapped their hands for him to continue.

"I bring you a message from the future, so you may now prepare for it. You will be ready when Death calls on you to give up your fears. You will embrace the future you deserve, and on the Final Day you can see the darkest secret of the universe!"

One assistant counted the gathering, wrote the number *1345* in a ledger. He added *36* later—those who did not seem to be enamored by the Prophet's divine words. The crowds were growing as the Prophet's reputation preceded him. They were starting to get some decent money from donations. Soon they would not need to sleep in tents or eat whatever they could scrounge.

Religion always loosened pocketbooks, he and his staff knew.

And this prophet, one of many in those days following the wars, was good at drawing crowds. It was no doubt because of his graven appearance. The Prophet did look like someone who had clawed his way back from the deepest pit of death. Whenever one of his assistants needed to speak to the Prophet, it was customary to stare at the center of the Prophet's forehead, or at the wall behind him, never into his eyes, never at any spot of his face.

The Prophet's body was worse. When he helped the Prophet bathe, the assistant had to be particularly careful not to get the disinfectant into any of the holes in his skin. His body was ravaged with openings eaten away by the pox. The ointment would sting and burn if it touched any of the organs visible through the holes. There must be fifty of them, the assistants counted. And stomach, liver, intestines, lungs—all could be seen clearly through the many openings that resulted from his former affliction. And yet, rather than dying as most would, he had risen and stared into the mirror, realizing he had beaten it, had become special, had touched the Great Beyond!

Mirrors were forbidden in their camp, wherever they roamed. The Prophet kept his special golden robe covering his body as much as possible. Something about the lining being protective of his ravaged skin. A second skin, in essence. The Prophet was immune from disease now, it seemed, yet there was no reason to tempt fate further. How many chances at rebirth did one get? Even for a prophet like the F'eng?

"And so today I greet you all with glad tidings and holy words! That you, too, shall gain from my misery all that you deserve to know. For all of us, the question is not what comes next; rather, what goes next! Listen and you shall know! Listen, good people, and tell your families and friends and colleagues what lies beyond the Great Beyond! And I shall walk with you and hold open the doorway to another world, where you will surely be safe from all that will rain down upon this world. That is all you need to know today. Tomorrow shall be the test."

The crowd unanimously bowed.

"Until that day, watch the skies for the light of dawn! That is our sign. That is our curse."

✳ ✳ ✳

And Darkness reigneth over all, and Humanity called it a Night.

"You disappoint me," said the same salacious baritone voice he had come to hate. "You really are disappointing me, Sebastian. You know that? I expected better treatment from you."

"I'm not listening to you."

"Of course you are. You always listen. You are enamored by the sound of my voice and my countless words of wisdom."

"Not this time, Max. I'm getting out. I found the key to unlock the door. I know the passages. I know the schedule of the guards. And I've arranged for an escape vehicle to meet me outside."

"Hah! You must be dreaming!"

"Exactly! A dream. It's all been a dream. A dream within a dream. Some of them are your doing, I know. But others are my own folly, the abyss I've fallen into. But I have rope, and I pulled myself up. Now I am done with you."

"You shall take me wherever you go. You cannot escape me."

"Sure I can, Max—short for 'maximum sentence.' Once I get out of this cell, I will be free of you. Once out of this prison, you will die—like a bad metaphor."

"You have learned your comedy craft well. I'm certain you will be able to find employment among the jesters of the world."

"That is not my destiny."

"Then what is?"

"I was supposed to be a scientist. I became an adventurer. Then a lover. A soldier. A philosopher. An author. Then somehow I became an emperor, then a corpse. And, as you know, eventually a prisoner."

"Indeed. It has been a pleasure sharing a cell with you."

"The cell is my own mind, you tell me often."

"So you are leaving your mind for greener pastures?"

"Yes, greener pastures."

"Where the dying horses roam?"

"Yes, the valleys of Gotanka is my destination. I have work to do. I must save the world. Again."

"And your mistress, Jinetta? Will she be assisting you?"

"If I can find her, then yes."

"Where is she?"

"Somewhere very far away and yet always beside me."

"Always the wordsmith, eh?"

"Always."

"So this is farewell?"

"It seems that way."

"Then I wish you well—the best of all kinds of luck!"

"Thanks. I'm sure I'll be needing that sooner than later."

"Safe journey, Sebastian."

"Goodbye, Sebastian's...uh...conscience."

"I shall forever be Max to you. Remember me, will you?"

Specks of light fluttered into the darkness of the prison cell like snowflakes, illumination growing from the corners of the cell to fill the entire room. Overhead were lamps—and faces: eight faces behind clear plastic bubbles—physicians, he guessed.

"*Sata-stepen.*"

'Welcome back,' one of the faces had spoken in Ghoupallêan. A smile seemed to fill her clear plastic bubble. Her hands were coated in some kind of filmy textured fabric. A curly cord and a monitoring device hung around her neck and lights pulsed on its face. "You gave us a very exciting challenge, yet we are finished with the procedure. How do you feel?"

He was not sure and took a few moments to assess his body's interface with the environment. Toes wiggled, fingers bent, skin itched, stomach gurgled, bowels expelled gas.

"*Ê—*"

The pronoun 'I' was all he could say in Ghoupallêan. He wanted to listen to the echo, and bathe in the bliss of a single phoneme uttered without any mechanical assistance.

"*Emai,*" he continued. 'I am.'

"*Zil, gumai,*" the physician smiled warmly. 'Yes, you are.'

He struggled to sit up, failed.

"*E logaren emai,*" he said. 'I think I am.'

Outside, he saw Chucker and the man named Wilson stand and rush over to him, carried on the hovering panel that glided along the corridor.

"Dude, you're alive!" said Chucker in archaic English.

He gave a thumbs up.

"Say something. Lemme hear some sarcasm."

"Thanks for saving my life."

"That's not sarcasm."

"Yes, it is."

"Okay, *that's* sarcasm."

He glanced over at Wilson as they moved down the corridor. He vaguely knew the man was a cop. Recognizing him as one of the detectives who arrested him at the IRS service center long ago, he wondered suddenly what the deal was.

"You arresting me again?" he asked faintly.

"What's that?" asked Wilson, leaning down.

"You gonna arrest me?"

"No. I'm here as a guest of your friend. I'm not a detective any longer. Now I'm...I'm an interdimensional voyager, real beginner class—or whatever Chucker says I am. Anyway, welcome to the Dream Land, Sebastian."

The patient swore silently, unable to fathom that phrase. He could not believe someone was actually welcoming him to *his* world, the world *he* discovered. He grinned painfully, however, feeling the slings and arrows of outrageous irony piercing him.

※ ※ ※

In the golden summers did the Prophet leisure among his followers, speaking freely of the choices they had to make. These were twofold, he said: the *Now* choice and the *Far Away* choice. To each he added fantastic stories which illustrated them clearly for even the dull-witted followers. The Now choice was whether or not to abandon the false teachings of their homes and schools and follow the true path to Enlightenment. The Far Away choice was whether or not to fight or to concede the judgment of the seven gods and nine goddesses at the end of history, on the Final Day.

"How do you know of the end of history, Master F'eng," one youth dared ask.

The Prophet smiled upon the boy; he would not touch the boy with his disease-ravaged hand.

"I have seen the history to its final day. I do not know the time or the name of the day but I know it is not so long from us. Your grandchildren's grandchildren's grandchildren will see that day. And they shall make their choice, too. Whether to stay or to go. Whether to hold fast to the soil or fly to the stars."

"Tell us, Master F'eng, what you wish us to do."

The Prophet seemed to laugh—as well as he could with limited mouth and lips and tongue.

"I say to you: the choice is yours. The choice is always yours. And I shall never abandon you because of your choice. You may, however, abandon me if you make one choice over the other choice. That is for you and your stars to decide. I am only a prophet, not a god or goddess."

Later, the Prophet sat back on his lounger inside his magnificent tent and his assistant prepared the special tea he always insisted on drinking, served in a tall beaker and sipped through a long straw, all the better to avoid further injury to his mouth, teeth and gums.

"Someday the end will come," he spoke, apparently more to himself than to anyone in the tent. "That will be so good. A welcome relief to body and mind. I cannot wait."

The Prophet opened his mouth, what there was of it, now almost toothless and full of blisters, and began producing a melody. His assistants turned to watch. He became more animated, waving his hands through the air.

Of course, none of them could understand the Prophet's words, singing as he was in his private language. They thought it was a divine language, something the gods and goddesses shared with only the Prophet. Nevertheless, it was a catchy tune.

They gave rapt attention as the Prophet's voice soared through the tent:

"*Might as well face it, you're addicted to love. Might as well face it, you're addicted to love. Might as well face it, you're addicted to love....*"

At the end, they all showed him their index fingers to show their approval of his vocalization, and thanked him.

Chapter 16

Repose

The beach was exactly as Chucker had described it: blindingly white sand and turquoise waters. On one side of the gently curving cove was the jungle. On the other side, rocky cliffs that blocked the view of the road into town.

"Even on Earth this would be an amazing location," said Dale T. Wilson, Interdimensional Voyager, lowest ranking novice.

Out from the cottage came the woman and two children, all of them dressed in tropical clothing, brightly colored patterns of floral prints. Chucker went to the woman, patting the children's heads as he passed them, and embraced her tightly. He whirled her around and around in his arms. They lingered in a kiss until the guests grew uncomfortable.

"My brown-skinned babe," Chucker said, exiting the kiss. "I love coming home to her."

He turned to his guests and introduced the family: Foj, his wife, Randy, their son, and Joy, their daughter.

"Beautiful family," said Set-d'Elous, still walking with a cane to steady himself. He was in Liêta, after all, to recover from three years of paralysis.

Wilson was equally complimentary.

Foj had a meal prepared, which they all ate around the patio's grill table, a wide, flat metal plate upon which everything was cooked. Typegan style. They exchanged questions with Foj and learned that Chucker had only been absent for thirty-two days while undertaking the fifteen-day mission on Earth. The time differential was more kind going the other direction: more time on Ghoupallesz, less on Earth. Foj was happy everything went well—expressed in her accented English. She seemed to understand about Earth, but perhaps believed it was somewhere else on Ghoupallesz instead of itself being another planet.

After dinner, they got the full tour of the resort.

Beginning the next morning, the hardship set in: day after day, night after night of mere existence, awakening with the birdsong, drifting off to sleep with the brush of surf against sand....

* * *

Swimming was good for his recovery and he went out every morning and every evening. During the afternoons he stayed in the shade and played Ghoupallean-style chess with Randy or was a judge for the fashion designs made by Joy. Set-d'Elous enjoyed Chucker's hospitality, but he knew eventually he would need to take on a mission himself, if only to remain sane on a world where nothing much was required of him.

"You think I should visit my island?" he asked Chucker one day. "Think everything's still there?"

"What's it been? Eleven years in this time zone? I'm sure the storms have blown it to bits by now."

"Probably."

They quizzed Wilson on his desires, but he was still too amazed to have a plan.

"I guess I should learn this language you use. Then maybe do some sightseeing? What do you think I should be doing?"

Set-d'Elous felt awkward with the man who had first arrested him that night at the IRS service center now trying to be a friend.

"You're a trained detective. Detect something!"

Wilson laughed. "Happy to. But I need to know the language and the culture to understand why people do what they do. It is not Missouri, am I right?"

Set gave a smirk. "So you believe me now?"

"You have to admit, it's not easy to believe." Wilson's face lit up.

"Not until you see it for yourself. Not until you make the journey." He waved his arm at the cove. "Not until you sit for a few weeks on this beach and wonder why the stars are so different, why there are two suns in the sky, why you never want anything else but to relax and dream of nothing."

"I think he's got it!" said Chucker.

"Hence , the 'dream land,' right?"

"Indeed."

"But I need a proper job, or I should go back...."

"There are no proper jobs here. Only merc work."

"Being mercenaries," Set explained. "However, we seem to be out of that business now. Too much has happened. Besides, I think we've achieved some kind of balance, so I'm ready to let it go on its own for a while."

Chucker sat up. "Hey, don't forget! You have a rendezvous with that Zetin boy. The one you wrote about in your so-called journal—history book, memoir, whatever it is. Have you met him yet?"

Set grinned, unpleasantly. "No, I have not done that. I suppose I should before the lad grows up to be the Zetin ambassador to Tebbicousimankalê and starts all the trouble with Gina. And then I have to rescue her. And then we live happily ever after—for a year. Then she runs away—again."

"One step at a time," Chucker cautioned.

"You mean you have to go on another mission?" Wilson asked, scratching his tanned belly.

"Have to? No. But I should. I've encountered the man twice and both times he mentioned meeting me when he was a boy. And I gave him advice...yes, advice which came back to bite us in 1533." He laughed a while. "You see the irony? If you hadn't rescued me from my paralysis, I could never go meet him and give him some advice!"

"What kind of advice is that?" asked Wilson.

Set snorted. "Advice that will cause me trouble in the future."

"Then you shouldn't give him any advice."

Set and Chucker shared a knowing glance.

"You're new here, so I'll take it easy on you," said Set-d'Elous. "It's like this: I give the kid some advice. He uses it to do things that will cause me major hassles in the future. But because of all

157

those major hassles, I find Gina, my long-lost love, again. And we go off to live happily ever after—for a year."

Wilson lost his smile. "Oh."

Chucker slapped the armrest of his lounger.

"So go. We'll wait for you."

"Can I come along?" asked Wilson.

"It's kind of a private matter," said Set. "But when I return I'll find something for you to do here."

Chucker clapped his hands. "He can be the security guard for this resort."

"Thanks. I guess."

"And I will need to return to get my mom and dad some time. I mean, if they want to come back here. There's no royal family of Aivana any more, not since the eldest son marched into the city and claimed the throne. I knew he'd come back. I told Mom and Jason but they kept ignoring me. I should try to track down Jason and the kids, too."

Set shifted in his chair. "And I need to return for Toni. And my son. Our son."

"We are all such family men, aren't we?"

Wilson cleared his throat. "Not me. No ties. I don't need to go back." He scratched his forehead. "I wonder how long it's been there. I probably missed paying the rent, got kicked out by now. And as for law school...."

Foj appeared at the window of the cottage and called softly to Chucker.

"Sorry, guys. Gotta go make love with my wife." He got up. "You know how it is.... We been together ten years now, but she still thinks she has to keep me young."

Set and Wilson stared at each other as Chucker departed.

"So...how about those Chiefs, huh?"

"Yeah. What're their chances to make the playoffs?"

※ ※ ※

By turns the legendary warrior and tax clerk sat with his back against the *salix* tree and paced around the tree in ever-widening circles, patiently waiting for the right time and the right place to finally merge.

He looked at his wrist, felt foolish for believing a watch would be there. He was too freshly back to Ghoupallesz to act instinctively as a Ghoupalle would act.

"Come on, come on," he muttered.

He was waiting for Ut'r-BkanN to come waltzing by on the road from the capital city of BON'GOY'Z, near the end of year two of his youth trek, what the Zetin called RE'KL. He would be a naïve teenager, full of himself and counting on the gods to save him at every turn. He could not get into too much trouble walking the paths of Zetinê except from whatever wildlife might happen upon him. *Jalo* was the main concern: a giant bear-like beast with horns.

He adjusted his orange jumpsuit, a souvenir from his prison days, and gazed down the road. In the distance was a figure.

"At last."

He took a seat again at the base of the tree, the northern willow tree which sported blue flowers and white berries that were thought to be poisonous to humans. The branches slung low and often floated through the air when breezes blew. The sun was bright and the thin, swaying branches did little to provide shade. He waited.

When the youth approached, he pretended to be dozing against the tree, and the youth stopped, staring at him.

"Why do you block the yellow sun from my eyes?" he asked suddenly in perfectly rehearsed Zetin, coming to life and startling the young Ut'r-BkanN.

"My father taught me never to apologize," spoke the youth with hesitation in his voice.

He offered a fake laugh and said: "Someday, young warrior, you will apologize. In fact, you will be a man of peace, not a warrior."

"How can that be? All Zetin are warriors!"

"People will beg for your counsel. If you play your cards right, you'll be a great leader of Zetinê."

"KA'A-DZ?" The kid obviously did not know the game. In Zetinê, children played with stones or spearpoints, not cards.

"Stones," he said. "Play your stones right and you will be wise and many will seek your counsel."

"That would be good. Me, a wiseman!"

"Yeah, okay." His Zetin was rusty, he knew, which was the reason he had written it out and memorized his speech. "But when you take the woman of golden hair who claims to be a goddess, hold her and keep her, she will pray to the two suns and the seven winds. Then, on the day the God of Evil comes—when Set dines with you, it shall be your last day in this world."

The youth was initially surprised, delighted even, then fell glum and fearful.

"Got it? Don't mess with the woman with golden hair. Don't hold her hostage or the God of Evil will visit you. That day is the day you will die."

"Yes, I understand. How do you know this?"

He rose and stood tall against the tree. He swept the thin branches out of his way and stepped forward.

"I am Set, the God of Evil!"

The youth was again amazed. "I thought so!"

"I do not bear the marks of a Zetin, true. I am God of Evil over all races!" He realized how ridiculous he felt affecting the booming voice of a movie monster, but he had to stay in character. "You will see me again someday. And on that day, I will tell you what task you must do for me."

"I will do it. I will do it," he said, nervous.

"Someday I will return for you, young Ut'r-BkanN. Once upon a time, I collected taxes. Now I collect moments of history. Someday I will come to collect your moment of history. Then you will vanish from everyone's memories."

"But why?"

That was not how the script was supposed to go. No questions, just the statement to scare the boy. It would pay dividends years later—as he had already proven. Best not to think of that too closely. Better to just let it ride, let things unfold as they will.

"Indeed, you have curiosity," he intoned like an orange divine statue rather than a man in a prison jumpsuit with black numbers 450-651 stamped on the chest and back. "When the day comes that you dine with Death, only then will you know the truth of everything."

The youth seemed to think it over. Then, cocky lad that he was, he asked another infernal question:

"Do you think that will be before the Great Light shines upon us?"

What great light? Perhaps the kid was playing with him. Smart alec!

"Tell me what you know of the Great Light."

The youth seemed surprised. Set-d'Elous could see the question flash across the kid's face: Gods should know everything about the future, shouldn't they?

"I was told about the Great Light in a dream," said the youth. "I rode through the winter valley and a bird flew down and alighted upon my shoulder. The bird carried a clump of ice which burned with a blue flame. The bird spoke in words which were not Zetin. I took a year to decode them—on my own. A great light will shine one day in the future and all will be afraid. Half will fly away. Half will go underground. The light will purify all."

Set-d'Elous recognized the legend of the comet, the story that was at the root of all mythology. And yet, how could someone in the past have such knowledge of an event in the far future? It had to be more than speculation. Knowing he had jumped from time to time on Ghoupallesz, he wondered if some fellow Voyager had visited the future—as he'd had to in order to receive his advanced surgery—and then gone to the distant past to start a religion. He grinned, wishing he had done it first.

"Yes, young Ut'r-BkanN, you are correct."

"Thought so!" It sounded better in Zetin: Uk'Lr.

"Very well, then. Shall we part ways now? I must visit other naughty boys before sundown."

"I shall allow it, God of Evil. I shall continue my Youth Trek."

They almost shook hands—automatic response for an Earther, not for Zetin—instead gave each other a firm nod and a curt wave, thumbs up. He watched the youth march away down the road. He waited a while, until the boy was out of sight, then made his way to the town, and from there to a seaport where he caught a ship which took him to another port and another ship, which eventually took him to Selauê. A twenty-nine day trip, just to set an old timeline in motion. That, plus the toll of doing the tangent loopty-loop to get to this time and place. At least, his legs held up. His back, too.

He realized then—if, indeed, he had refused to acknowledge it previously—that he was getting too old for this kind of exercise.

❋ ❋ ❋

"Yes, I've heard that legend, too." Chucker sipped his tropical punch from the gourd. He lay on the sand, the two suns bathing him in green light. "The Blue Hairs had that, too. They were always drawing pictures of a star falling to the ground."

"How could they know about something that has yet to happen?"

"Myth, man. It's everywhere."

"Seems to be."

"Perhaps they were remembering something that has already happened."

Set-d'Elous regarded his protégé, a look of derision. "If it happened in the past, I'm way past it by now. And if it will happen in the future, I'm not there yet. So nothing to worry about."

Chucker grinned. "Agreed."

Every day, all day, Chucker would lay on the beach, swim in the cove, eat and drink and play with his children. Once in a while there would be guests to tend to, people from the city who would stay for a few days at best then depart. Not really enough of them to provide a good income but Chucker didn't care about profits. When he needed to, he would catch fish in the cove. There were plenty of fruits available in the jungle and he knew which ones were good, which were poisonous. When he was not doing any of those tasks, he thought of his mother and the man who donated sperm to make him. And his step-father Jason.

Suddenly Set jumped up from his beach towel. "Well, that's it for me. Got to be going now."

Chucker seemed alarmed. "Where?"

"Next mission. I'm crossing them off my to-do list."

"And what is next for you?"

"Toni." He smiled. "You met her at the zoo, I recall. Dr. Antoinette Franck. And our son. She calls him Little Sebastian. I'm Big Sebastian. Being paralyzed, I couldn't call him anything. I'm recovered now, so it's time to retrieve them."

"Are you sure she wants to come here?"

"To Liêta? This beach? Or do you mean all of Ghoupallesz?"

"I'm sure she will be delighted to find me whole once more and want to go wherever I go. It's a paradise here. Besides, Life has been tough since she awoke from her coma. And I certainly know what that's like. I had the stupidest cellmate.... Anyway.... For her, she had a three-year old son to take care of—along with regaining the use of her legs. She is back to normal, so...."

"Then I should go get Mom and Dad."

"Are you sure they want to come back here? It was rather traumatic for them last time."

"Listen, dude. I told you the story before. The explosion in the Royal Hall sent me to the jungle—me and Foj. Same deal sent Mom and that lughead to Earth. And you...? Where were you sent?"

"I suppose to Earth. That's what they tell me, anyway."

"So given that sudden and unexpected turn of events, wouldn't you want to return to the point where things became no good? Whatever you were doing before the explosion? I know Mom loved her life in Aivana. I actually liked her that way. She developed eccentricities, sure, but she was fun. I liked being her son. Except for all the prince business."

"There is only one way to know if they want to join us in the Dream Land or not."

"Conduct a survey?"

"No, we go ask them."

"I hear you," said Chucker like a world-weary grandpa, "but I need to wait until Wilson gets back here. Gone off to the jungle with a dictionary and a backpack full of trouble, just to see what he can see. Strange dude."

"Then I'll see you on the other side. Maybe."

Sebastian hobbled over and sat down on the 'love' rock to check his knee, tripping as he exited the tangent and landing on the kneecap. Satisfied it would keep working, he paused to study the stars overhead. The constellations were now unfamiliar to him yet they reminded him of other nights when he had stood and gazed out at the universe, expecting to see neon signs directing him to his favorite planet. This night was no different.

The air seemed as musty as usual while he made his way carefully down the gravel path in the dark. He walked along the road to the 7-Eleven store, where he got a Baby Ruth and a Slurpee. He checked the newspaper on the rack: six months had passed there while he had been lounging beside the cove in Liêta. It was now spring.

He could not forget the last time he was on Earth: he had been locked into an exoskeleton, a captive quadriplegic, so much at the mercy of gravity. He retained a plastic disk over the hole Chucker had drilled in the side of his head to access his brain. A permanent reminder of his strategic withdrawal from Earth and the rehabilitation he had endured. Now he could walk and talk. He had a lot to say and a lot of walking to do. Or driving.

He skipped the Greencrest Motel for another one farther down 40 Highway, paid with cash. Inside the room, he stripped and showered, went to sleep and had no dreams.

Chapter 17

Reunion

New moon. Sebastian had to believe there was a moon up there somewhere, not being used to a night light. Instead, he squinted in the dark until he saw her crossing the parking lot outside the medical office building. Early April was cool but she wore a dress. Her heels clicked against the pavement.

Before he could tap her shoulder, she paused, as though she sensed his presence, then spun around.

"Sebastian!" Toni exclaimed, seeing a ghost. She instinctively stepped back, looking him over, fearing him.

"Toni," he spoke softly. She acted like it was something in her head instead of from his mouth. "You can see I've been fixed. No more paralysis."

She didn't know whether to smile or call the police. "Yes. I can see that." She tried to step away.

"Aren't you happy to see me? Aren't you happy my paralysis is repaired?"

"Yes, that's wonderful." Her voice was weak.

He stepped toward her.

"What are you afraid of? It's me, Sebastian. I can talk again. And I'm not paralyzed any more. I came back for you!"

She broke away and hurried to her car, unlocking the door. He caught up to her.

"Toni, what's wrong? I came back for you."

"There are cameras," she said.

He looked at the building, spotted two cameras.

"Go to the other side of those bushes," she said. "I'll pick you up there."

He agreed and jogged out of sight—and watched her drive away quickly in the opposite direction. She made the tires squeal.

"Dammit, Toni, what are you afraid of?"

❋ ❋ ❋

"He just came up to me from the bushes. He almost grabbed me," said Toni into the phone. "He didn't hurt me. Actually, I got away by saying I'd pick him up behind the bushes and he believed me. Then I sped away."

"He knows where you live," Detective Henderson reminded her. "Take precautions. Lock everything. I'm sending a patrol car over."

"Thanks."

She felt less comfortable once the line was disconnected.

In the bedroom she sat beside her son, asleep on the queen-sized bed in the dark. The lights were still on in the living room and the hallway. She rubbed his back, thinking of the few times Sebastian had been in the condo. He had never lain on the bed, had always sat stiffly in his wheelchair. Like a bump on a log. A dirty, unwashed bump. They did not care for him well at the prison hospital. He could never speak, never react to anything.

The doorbell startled her. She did not expect that the patrol officer would come to the door, so she worried that Sebastian had found her.

She held her son close and he awoke, struggled in her arms, then relaxed and returned to sleep.

The front door's lock clicked. The door swung open.

"Toni?" came the strangely familiar voice. She had not heard it for three years—except earlier in the parking lot. It had sounded surreal, mechanical. "It's me. Sebastian. Your husband. I don't know what you're afraid of. I'm not here to hurt you. I came back because I love you. That's not a crime is it?"

The bedroom door swung shut, the lock bolted.

"I don't know what anyone told you, but that day at the zoo I was kidnapped. Honestly. I had no part of it, except as the victim. I had no idea it was going to happen. Please believe me."

There was only silence in the condo.

"All right, Toni?"

"I believe you," came words in her voice, muffled by the walls.

"You want to know how I could be healed, right?"

He waited for her response but heard nothing.

"The kidnappers.... They took me to a place where a medical team could do some advanced surgery. They repaired my spine and my head. Then I had to recover my strength. That's why I was gone for a few months. I literally could not walk back here until very recently."

The bedroom door unlocked. He stepped down the hallway, rapping on the wall to let her know where he was, not wanting to surprise her again.

"I'm sorry, Toni." He leaned his head against the door. "I'm so sorry. I wanted to contact you but I couldn't from where I was."

"Where were you?" she asked hesitantly.

"I think you know where."

"Say it, Sebastian."

He took a breath. "In the Dream Land."

The door locked again.

"You may not like that answer but that is the truth, Toni." He stood up, rested against the door. "What you need to think about most is that I returned for you. I came back for you, Toni. I can't live without you. These years of you caring for me have been so frustrating for me, of course, but every day I can see how it pained you to care for me. Yet you never complained. You laughed off every bad thing that happened. You had so much patience. So much love in your heart. I watched you care for Little Sebastian, too. You are a wonderful mother. And now I want the chance to be the kind of husband and father I should've been instead of being shot and put into a coma and then awaking paralyzed."

The silence was eventually interrupted by a brushing against the door, as though she had leaned against it.

"Really?" her soft voice pushed through the crack.

He knocked lightly on the door. "Yes, really. That is why I've come back."

"I believe you."

"But...?"

"I'm frightened."

"Of what?"

"This dream place you always talk about. I don't want to be with a man who doesn't have his mind right. I worry you could go crazy any moment."

"Crazy? Is that a professional term?"

He heard a laugh. The door unlocked, stayed shut.

"I'm going to come into the bedroom now," he said. "Is that all right with you?"

He reached for the doorknob—

Are you sure she's not got a gun aimed at the door?

The alto voice rattled him. He dropped his hand from the doorknob.

"Toni?"

"Yes?"

"May I come in?"

"Please."

"You don't have anything ready to spring at me, do you?"

"There are no traps here."

"Good. Just my mind playing tricks on me. Happens when a person's been in a coma."

"I know what you mean."

"Yes, you do. We have something in common. We were both in comas."

"We also have a son," she said, her voice stronger.

He grabbed the doorknob again, turned it.

You always were an idealistic fool!

"I'm coming in, Toni, no matter what awaits me."

He opened the door, saw the bedroom was dark except for a small nightlight low on the far wall: a smiling teddy bear with a crescent moon. Her legs dropped from the side of the bed, feet bare against the carpet. In the shadows, her torso and arms moved. She stood, leaving her son on the bed.

"Sebastian...."

She stepped toward him and they embraced, half in the dark and half in the light of the hallway. Her hands wrapped around his head, messing his hair as her lips pushed into his. His arms tightened around her waist, then shoulders. They fell backward against the doorjamb, tumbling to the hallway floor.

"I'm back, Toni," he mumbled through their kissing, as her hands tore open his shirt and his hands pulled at her blouse.

❉ ❉ ❉

They kissed playfully as she sat the plate of omelet on the table before him. He popped up to tend to the coffee, pouring for both of them. Little Sebastian sat in his chair, wondering why his parents were being so frisky this morning. He poked at his cereal but ate the fruit.

Toni walked him to the bus stop and waved as the school bus drove off.

"Great breakfast," said Sebastian as she entered, closing the door behind herself and resting against it.

"What shall we do, Sebastian?"

"You mean for today?"

She went over to him, kissed his head and sat at the table.

"You know we cannot go anywhere," she said, caressing the back of her lover's neck. "They watch me constantly. Now you have escaped, they are watching my home every minute. They expect you will contact me. The phone is likely tapped, too."

"You are innocent—"

"I'm the bait for you."

"Do they still think I'm paralyzed and in a wheelchair?"

"They found the wheelchair in the zoo so they believe you had help escaping. And the elephant? Why did you have to shoot at an innocent elephant?"

"That was not my doing. Unfortunate, yes, but it wasn't me." He stood and placed his hands on her hips. "Listen, my dear, there is only one place we can go and be safe. Nobody to look for us. Nobody to bother us."

"Where is such a place?" She wiped away a tear.

"It's far away...."

She frowned. "Are you talking about your fantasy place?"

His hand went to her back, caressed it while he tried to pull on a new, hopeful face. What he would say next would make or break this trip he had made from Ghoupallesz to Earth. He tensed, ready to flee.

"Yes."

She held her breath, shook her head. "I knew it."

He circled his arms around her shoulders and was pleasantly surprised she leaned toward him, against him, her cheek resting on his chest.

"Oh, Sebastian...."

"Yes, my dear?"

"Why did you have to say that? For three years you said nothing—of course you couldn't speak—but I believed.... I could believe we were a normal family, not one.... Not a family with a man who lived a fantasy life inside his head. There: I said it. I want you to be healthy. And normal. Living in this world, in my world. Not that world of your mind."

"It's not in my mind."

"Can't you pretend? Try to be here with me. Focus on this world. Can you do that?"

He cradled her face in his hands and kissed her mouth. She pulled his hands away.

"It's not like that. Not at all. You have the notes from my sessions. You were starting to believe me. It's not a fantasy world. It's real. It's how I was able to be treated and healed. Advanced medical procedures nobody can do here on Earth."

He tapped on the plastic disk that covered the hole in the side of his head. "See this? An entry point to fix my speech."

"They drilled into your head?"

"It wasn't fun. But otherwise, I'd still be in that wheelchair and in that prison cell. That's not the normal I want."

She stepped away. "All I want is to be a normal family. We are so not normal." Two tears ran down her face. "Two survivors who happened to find each other. For better or worse. I want to be like those other families. Happy. Man, woman, child. Like that."

"That's what I want." He followed her, step by step down the hallway as they argued. "I want to be a family. And we can do that somewhere else. Better places than here. You will like it. I'll teach you the language. You can have all your arts and culture—"

"Sebastian, I came from France when I was a little girl. My

parents assassinated, my aunt taking me in. I had to learn a new language and culture then. Soon I fit in. I was successful. I had everything I wanted. Then I met you and everything went crazy. I suffered a lot because of you!"

"I have never hurt you."

"And yet I have been hurt because of you being in my life."

"That is the cruelty of fate. Nobody decides. It happens. It cannot be undone but we can make up for lost time. We can forget the past and start fresh. You, me, and the little man."

By then they were in the bedroom. He turned on a lamp.

"That's all I want. To be a family with you and our son. What ever it takes."

"We will have to hide somewhere. Start a new life, as you say. They won't stop, you know. They will hunt you forever. And since you escaped, they assume you are guilty—again. No new hearing for you. They had your friend Tammy Tucker lined up to testify on your behalf. She was going to say she went willingly with you."

"To where?"

"I don't know. Somewhere."

"They would never believe her."

He brushed her hair, felt closer to her than ever before.

I like where this is going, said an alto voice in his head. *You will do the intercourse with her yet you will be thinking of me. I will enjoy that, Sebastian.*

He stopped.

"Sebastian?" Toni called, her hand on his cheek. "Are you all right? Seemed like you went into a trance for a moment."

He shook his head, stepped away. "Yeah, a trance."

"Here, sit down." She directed him to the bed and made him lie down. The robe he was wearing fell open and she gazed upon the scars of his surgery. She touched the worst looking one. "I didn't see these last night, not in the dark."

"You see? I have suffered for you, too. And I came back for you. Because I want you in my life."

"And I want you, too, Sebastian. Forever."

"Forever is a long time," he said automatically, then felt as though he was repeating something someone had said to him.

"I'll call Carlie and let her know I'm not feeling well today. Maria can take over my cases for today. I need to tend to you, to care for my dear husband."

You are so good at playing the role, Sebastian. I'm impressed. Make this woman yours. I shall give you the strength to ravage her. Then she will be ours!

* * *

As Sebastian lay beside Toni, the afternoon sun marking the passage of time, he thought of the voice. It had been with him from the moment he had awakened from the coma and found himself unable to move or speak. The voice had spoken for him, to him. It mocked him, continued teasing him, tempting him, goading him. It was the voice of Basura-Kanoun.

"Thank you," Toni whispered, rolling against him and kissing his shoulder. "I love you, mon chèr."

Thank you, Sebastian, said the voice, adding a giggle. *My dear!*

Basura-Kanoun, it turned out, was a *senzenor*, a person with a flexible aura. Such people became practitioners in the health professions, using their aura to heal a long list of maladies. In the case of this Danid woman who was a university student and poet at the time of her death, she did not know how to control her raw power. Not until later, when she was able to use her *senzenaxii* skills to great advantage, usurping his will and driving him through many years of playing emperor.

It seemed only like a bad dream now.

The Emperor of Sekuate, he mused and Toni wondered what thought had changed his expression.

Basura-Kanoun was, of course, the all-controlling Empress of Sekuate. Until his team of mercenaries assassinated her. Before they assassinated him. Or so they thought. He was still not clear on what had happened. He fell.

Then he awoke, frozen in his body, the voice mocking him.

"Are you all right?" asked Toni, clenching his hand in hers.

He smiled warmly at her, but it was obvious his mind was far away.

"Let me just hold you a while longer," he said, and wrapped his arms around her, squeezed her a moment, then held her snuggly.

"It's so good to have a bed," Toni said with a laugh, "not that office couch."

"Indeed."

"This is the first time we have been able to be completely together, my dear husband. You know?"

He nodded.

"I suppose you're right," he said when his arms relaxed around her. "There is a problem. I need to figure it out. I need to find a way to solve it, or you and I can never truly be together."

Toni sat up. "What is it? What's the problem? Tell me."

"I'm sorry to say, but you have picked up a kind of virus. I'm sorry. It's from me. I gave it to you. It shouldn't be any trouble for you, though. Not medically. You see, it's designed to hurt me, to keep me away from you. But I will find a cure."

He threw back the sheet, jumped up from the bed, and got dressed in the clothes he'd brought in his pack.

"Should I see a doctor? What is it?"

"No, Toni. Virus is only a metaphor. You're possessed by an evil spirit. The Evil Empress. Only I can cure you. But I need to learn how."

He rushed out of the bedroom and she heard the front door unlock and open.

"Sebastian! You can't go out in daylight! They'll see you!"

"Uh, yeah, this is patrol car 116, at the Franck residence, and we just saw an adult male exiting the residence. White, six-feet tall, two-hundred pounds, wearing a tan jacket and blue jeans. Heading east on foot."

"Awright, one of you check on her and the other go after him. Follow but do not attempt to apprehend him without back-up. Sending back-up to your location."

Officer Clark got out of the patrol car and jogged up the steps of the condo as the car drove off.

Toni heard the doorbell and thought Sebastian had decided to return. He had come in with a key the previous evening. Perhaps he had forgotten it in his haste.

She wiped the tears from her face and rushed to the door,

pulling on her robe as she went.

"Sorry to bother you, ma'am," said Officer Clark when Toni opened the door. "Just checking on you. Are you all right? Do you need anything? Was there another adult here with you a short time ago?"

"What?" She was unnerved to have the officer throw out so many questions. At the same time, she knew Sebastian had left his worn clothes on the floor in the bedroom and put on fresh clothing before he ran out.

"Ma'am? Was there someone here with you?"

She smiled, knowing how artificial it must look. "No....just me. My son's at school now. I stayed home because I'm not feeling very well."

She pulled her robe tighter but figured he'd caught a glimpse of her body anyway.

The radio crackled. Detective Henderson was speaking to the officer, telling him to stay with her, to protect her should Sebastian Talbot return to the residence. Back-up had arrived, they saw outside on the street.

"Ma'am, you might as well get yourself dressed. They're coming over."

"Zut alors!" She turned away and retreated to the bedroom, locking the door. Sitting on the bed, she wept, wondering what had happened this morning. After such a special night. Now everything was going insane so quickly!

When she stepped out of the shower, she could hear several men talking in the living room. She dressed in a white knit blouse and tan slacks, almost as though she was going to the office, and tossed Sebastian's clothes in the hamper, stuffed them down to the bottom. She went around the bedroom and cleaned away any sign he had been there. There were stains on the sheets, however, but she made up the bed so it looked as though nobody had slept in it.

"...need to send a patrol car by the Tucker residence, too," she heard Henderson saying as she came out of the bedroom to join them. "That should cover everyone he's likely to try and contact."

The detective spun around and greeted her.

"I understand you had a visitor last night."

"In the parking lot. I told you already."

"I'm talking about here. In this residence. This morning. Or perhaps all night long.... May we have a look around?"

"Help yourself," she said, biting her lip.

A team of men swarmed through the condo with bags and kits and tools. She guessed she was going to be caught. Doing what? Harboring a dangerous fugitive? No, she was a hostage. It was only natural that a crazed killer would hold his wife hostage, force her to have wild, amazing sex all night and all the next day. That would be natural, wouldn't it? To have one perfect night of lovemaking with the father of her child. One perfect night. Then he would leave before he could be caught.

Chapter 18

Salvation

Old habits die hard. Sebastian repeated the words in his head as he stepped down the ramp with his sea bag, exiting the ship docked in Selauê harbor.

Next stop would be the Archives, to catch up with the news, to know his place in this newest world. From that moment on, he would not be Sebastian Talbot but, instead, some retired cavalry commander named Set-d'Elous. He turned into the next fashion shop and exited a while later in a dull red jumpsuit and a brown cape, a uniform of the retired class. A few young people he passed in the streets saluted him, acknowledging his service to the nation. Even one of the blue-helmeted patrol men halted traffic to let him cross the avenue.

He did not feel old, but he knew the calendars did not lie. The memories he should have had were wiped out. Twenty years lost. Basura-Kanoun had the copyright on those memories, not him. Even so, he did not feel he really wanted them. There was only pain there—pain and deception, humiliation, abuse, and lots of blood on his hands. Because of time spent doing her bidding, he had aged twenty years in Ghoupalle years. That translated via any mirror into a ten year leap in appearance in Earth years. That was the man he presented to Toni upon his return to Earth. Even so, she had recognized him and accepted him.

Now he needed to find someone who could answer all of his

questions, give him advice, perhaps actually help in a hands-on way. Who was smarter at these matters than him? Who would know, or guess, about how to exorcize an evil spirit from the perfectly healthy body of an Earth woman? Only one name came to mind: Gina Parton—also known as Jinetta, Queen of Fenula, though she was long from that position by now.

Just as he crossed into the park, a crowd of people milling about in long robes called to him, asking if he had heard the message of the Prophet.

He ignored them, but a couple joined him, walked with him, suggesting that if he were any kind of educated person, if he cared about the spark within him, he would stop and listen to what they had to say. The Prophet would be sharing his message nearby the next day. Everyone was invited.

"I must attend a funeral," he insisted, just to mess with them

"Who has died? The Prophet may be able to help."

"I don't think so," retorted Set-d'Elous.

They pestered him all the way across the park. On the other side, a squad of mounted civil patrol officers had gathered—the blue helmeted men armed with long, hooked staves to urge people not to loiter or to awaken sleeping vagrants. Now they held weapons—whatever the newest version of the ol' reliable AT guns were. He recognized the smell of them heating up, and so he sought to distance himself from the robed ones.

"I'm not one of them!" he shouted to the civil patrol as he jogged across the street. One gave him a lingering look. Perhaps his Ghoupallêan was a bit rough after his three years on Earth. Or he was being marked as a possible rebel.

He watched from the opposite side of the street as the squad strutted into the park and the crowd of robed ones stood in tight blocks to thwart any charge. They were disciplined, he had to admit. The civil patrol trotted around the group, one of them sounding the rules of public behavior to the group.

There were always demonstrations going on. He shook it off as he went on his way. Of course, he was used to that climate, having lived through the early days of the revolution. He stopped himself. Had it happened after all? He supposed it did; how else could he have risen to become emperor with Basura-Kanoun?

And yet, in the weeks that followed his entry into suitable

temporary housing and daily walks to the Archives to conduct his research, he realized this was different. They were a religious group, not political. They seemed to be ascetically minded, anti-materialistic, and thus abhorred anyone who had anything beyond the meagerest of provisions. The populace was ripe for sermons and harassment. The civil patrol was kept busy guarding the public areas, shepherding the robed ones away whenever they would gather, and in a few instances protecting citizens from physical confrontation with the groups who called themselves Followers of the F'eng.

He did not know who or what this "F'eng" was (*F* with a puff of air before the *eng*) but soon did. There was actually a prophet—someone they called a prophet. And what did the prophet prophesize? The end of everything, of course. That was always the case. However, the end of everything would come in conjunction with a "great light"—what he took to mean a comet. The same comet, perhaps, that young Ut'r-BkanN referred to. Or the legend he'd heard in his early days on Ghoupallesz.

It was far into the future, he knew. After all, his prime reason for setting up shop on Little Biznuik Isle was to shop for tangents. He had theorized that the Ghoupalle race, ethnic group, cult, whatever they should be called, had arrived via a tangent on this small rock of an islet. They then spread to the mainland, supplanting the Danid and Rouê kingdoms of northern Zissekap. That story was all over the Archives. And with that legend came the one about a comet.

He looked up from his reading, stretching his legs under the table and a few people nearby gave him fearsome glares for causing a disturbance.

The comet! In the future? Or in the past? Had a threatening comet driven them from their home world to Ghoupallesz via some tangent? Did the Ghoupalle people bring a memory of a comet with them to this planet? Or did they somehow predict or believe, for no particular reason, that a comet would visit them in the future? If the latter, how would they know about it? Only someone from the future who visited the past and told the story could account for that connection.

He grinned. This time it was not him. He could not be blamed for that. The furthest into the future he had ever been via tangent was 2126 when Chucker and their cop friend Wilson had taken him to be repaired, like one of Jason's old Mustangs in for an overhaul.

Somehow a lot of people had heard this so-called prophet preaching about a comet coming soon and so they had better make things right with themselves and with the seven gods and nine goddesses before that day. They talked of the Final Day, the Great Light, the Cleansing Fire, and a dozen other clever metaphors, but he paid them no mind.

Until he noticed a new thread in their rhetoric. Suddenly, he heard them mention a certain *Ghost of Set* who, as he listened, seemed very close to a description of the devil. Some devil, at least. He couldn't be sure, never having been a theology student on Ghoupallesz. However, he did hear them clearly:

"The Ghost of Set," preached one young follower, "does war with the F'eng every day! The Ghost of Set lives in each person's head and conspires to trip you. And when you fall, it is not a scraped knee you will enjoy but a place as dinner for the Ghost of Set and his ravenous minions. Yes, you will become the dinner of demons!"

That sounded serious. But why Set? Was it him—in which case what had he done to deserve such a title and reputation?—or some other evil Earthling? He paused by the group and asked questions of them.

"The F'eng calls the Ghost of Set his mortal enemy because Set was the one who decided his fate. Set sent him on a mission, but it was a trick, and the F'eng was poisoned. The treatment made the effects worse. The F'eng sought to kill himself, but a treasure box presented to him by an innocent youth saved him. He was still quite ravaged in body and face, but his mind achieved in that moment a glorious enlightenment. He could see the future. Since then, the Ghost of Set has pursued him, trying to block the light— that is, the enlightenment that the F'eng wishes to share with the people of this world."

"I see."

He studied the F'eng followers around him. They did not seem dangerous, just misinformed. Well-meaning folks caught up in a cult that seemed to fit their own life circumstances and provided a quick and easy answer: blame the Ghost of Set.

"Tell me more about this Set—before he became a ghost."

And so he listened to them and bit his tongue a lot, afraid to reveal his true identity. He knew the truth, of course: Set-d'Elous was a cavalry commander of the Sekuatean Empire, who had fought in the Tebbicousimankalê campaign of 1533—or he was the Emperor himself, in an alternate version of history. Thus, he was certain he could not be this other ghostly Set who led this F'eng person through some magical tunnel as a cruel trick, then poisoned him. What would be the point of that? And for what purpose? For a good laugh?

"Set sent an innocent youth to kill the F'eng," said the robed woman lecturing him, her once-pretty face now disfigured by cuts down her cheeks. "Yet Set could not measure the power of the F'eng and the plan was thwarted. Yet, instead of the death Set had planned for the Prophet, the F'eng gained great enlightenment and in the process it was Set himself who burst into flames and died."

He smiled. "Is that so."

Thus distraught at his failure to kill the F'eng, the Ghost of Set made it his mission to go about trying to disrupt whatever the F'eng tried to do. Always setting up obstacles for the F'eng and, by extension, all of his followers. That was a common motif in all doomsday teachings. Good and Evil arm wrestling forever.

"Well, I'm sure Set had good intentions," he said and scanned the ring of stern faces. He realized there would be no *hah hah* at the end of their story. "No chance of any peace treaty between them?"

"Set was jealous of the F'eng."

He nodded, grinning like an idiot. "Aren't we all?"

The preaching went on, from city to city, across national borders, and wherever he went, there were groups of the F'eng followers to shout at him—as though they believed he was the Ghost of Set incarnate.

After a year of searching for Gina in all the usual places, he began to hear a new expression woven into the rhetoric of the

F'eng. There was mention of the Nine Sons of the F'eng. He thought they meant apostles. Perhaps that was who they were, a set of metaphorical sons. They were set up as guardians of the F'eng at first, then reassigned as local leaders, assistant prophets, one in each region they hoped to convert.

Hiding in Selauê as his base, he could avoid them for the most part. Violent clashes did occur. He heard of them, read about them on the information bulletins posted on the reading walls. He didn't think it was more than a passing trend. He recalled when he was young he would be obsessed with this rock band or that one only to shift alliances completely when the next new band came on the scene. So, too, with these F'eng followers. They would pass on.

When Chucker and Foj and the kids visited him on his lonely little island, they had discussed the F'eng. They also talked about Chucker's plan to retrieve his parents, for better or worse. That made him think of his promise to return for Toni, but he had yet to find any solution to the problem of evil spirits. It wasn't as simple as taking some antacid tablets.

"There's a shaman I know," Chucker offered. "Maybe he could help."

"I know also of a certain ghost named after me. He is supposed to help rid people of spirits. In his case, their good spirits."

"Well, then, dude, you need to stay away from that one. Bad news."

"Yes, indeed." He took a deep breath. "Except that I think it's me. Or supposed to be me. I am the God of Evil, aren't I?"

"Who would name a ghost after you?"

"Someone who thinks I'm dead?"

Set got up, returned with a handbill. "Look at this."

Chucker read it, looked it over once he was done.

"Congrats, dude! You are famous."

The handbill was a statement from whatever organization had formed to be the official voice of the F'eng. Like a miniature sermon, it outlined what one must do to be saved from the Great Light and the Fire of Cleansing. Item 4 was to kill the Ghost of Set wherever he may be found.

"So I moved to the island here. Thought it would be safe."

"Good thinking." Chucker sat up. His children came to him,

asking questions and he answered them happily. Foj came and escorted them away. "I've been playing with these kids every day of their lives—except when I was on Earth saving you. But they want me to keep at it even when we are on a business trip. So it's Foj's turn to play with them."

"The real issue is the core belief of these F'engsters. The comet. It matches the legend I've always heard. That worries me. Why now? Why is a religious cult rising now focused on the coming of a comet?"

"It's like any cult. They found something useful for getting people to join. It's already among their legends, so why not?"

"But if a comet is really coming to visit, what do we do? Go back to Earth?"

"Whoa! That might not be a good idea. You know how popular we are there now."

"I'm popular there. You, not so much. They don't know who you are."

"But, hey, passing through a tangent to escape an incoming planetoid of some kind would be a great ending to some sci-fi movie, you know."

"I can see it now," said Set, holding up his hands, index fingers and thumbs forming a movie screen. "The comet is charging down and the group of survivors—the last group of people who agree to try the tangent route, and they have special skills, too, whatever is needed in a new homeland—they slip through the tangent at the last possible second. And we see the crash through the tangent tear: the smoke and fire, and dirt and rocks thrown up, the comet skidding toward the tangent tear. And I shout at you to shut that damn tangent!"

"And I say 'Wait a sec, dude, I wanna see this!'"

"So I have to pull you back to save your miserable life."

They were both breathing hard and laughing.

"That was too close for comfort, dude."

Set shook his head. "That's the right idea, though. We could never bring very many people with us, however. We could only manage up to maybe fifty people passing through the tangent in the time we could keep it open. They would have to run and dive, like people abandoning a crashed airplane and sliding down the chute."

The children were playing happily with their stones and ribbons. Foj had been watching the animated conversation between her husband and his mentor. She joined them.

"You should make a choice for them," said Foj.

Chucker waved her to sit on his lap rather than stand.

"My brown-skinned beauty always has good ideas."

"If the people want to fly away, let them. They must build a rocket. If the people want to hide, let them. They can dig a tunnel to Ur-tha. If the people want to travel through the door you talk about, let them. They will need a guide. Are you ready to be a guide for them?"

"She's right, you know," said Set. "Do we want to get into all that responsibility, all that hassle? I never like trying to keep other people in line, ya know, making sure they do what they're supposed to do and not cause trouble."

"You must make a choice for the people," Foj insisted. "It is a fair thing to do."

Set and Chucker stared at each other, then both regarded the exotic lady.

"What do you know of this comet story?" asked Set-d'Elous.

She did not smile, kept a serious expression as she stood up from Chucker's lap.

"You become a prophet. You stand opposite the F'eng. Tell the people the choices. Let them choose. It is a fair thing."

Set nodded. "She's right. I can make plenty of handbills to pass out on street corners. Maybe hire some street urchins to pass them out. Everyone will learn the truth. 'The truth is out there somewhere,' after all."

"No, it's 'The truth will set you free.'"

"No, big boys!" Foj exclaimed. "It is this: Truth removes your burden. Typegan proverb."

"She's a smartee," said Set with a chuckle.

"You should hire her to run your P.R. project."

"I should. But who would look after you? You need someone to keep you out of trouble."

"You're right about that. She does keep me out of trouble. And you...you always pull me back in."

"That's Fate, not me. You have a trip to undertake, don't you?"

Chucker let out a sigh. "That's right. Mom. Gotta get her and bring her home. And, I suppose, Dad, too."

"Ever the dutiful son."

"Prodigal son. Damn you, Set-d'Elous!"

They exchanged grins but Chucker's seemed to have greater value and Set felt cheated.

"And so do you, Mister Sebastian Talbot! You have a mission, too. Hypocrite. Go change something. Anything."

He stood up and smiled at his guests: Chucker and his wife, Foj, and their two children, Randy and Joy. The days of leisure had come to an end, it seemed. How old he was feeling! How bursting with energy! The world was his now.

"We never run out of missions, do we?"

Through a staff of busy helpers housed in Selauê, Set-d'Elous was able to distribute an array of countering handbills to the public, arguing against the prophet's dire warnings. Set offered a more realistic opportunity for the few who wanted to take the risk: to travel to another world to escape the comet. He knew the place, the doorway. All anyone needed to do was sign up and when the appointed day came, they would line up and march lock-step through the tangent to...well, probably somewhere in Missouri. Still, better than what the F'eng proposed. The F'eng only offered a quaint grab-your-ankles-and-kiss-your-ass solution to the great comet's arrival. Neither was well-received. The populace in 1599 and the years that followed were naïvely optimistic and had no thought to the vagaries of celestial objects.

By the middle of the month of Ahok in 1599, conflicts with the followers of F'eng had become quite serious. They had attacked his printing operation, burned the building and killed some of his workers. No more opposition handbills, they swore.

They also built themselves an army. Not content to convert by persuasion, nor by petty harassment, they had shifted to militaristic means. National governments had been forced to defend towns from their aggression. It was like the good ol' days fighting the Gangus rebels, thought Set, comfortably ensconced in his townhouse in Selauê—until he, too, was forced to flee as the cleansing flames licked closer and closer to him.

Damn F'engster arsonists! Supposed to wait for the comet!

Constabularies were quickly overwhelmed by all the anarchy created by the F'eng followers. The result was open warfare—an odd sort of action given the cumbersome robes they wore.

The Prophet swore to bring the whole of northern Zissekap under his dominion, from Adanê and Biznuik in the west to the nations of Gotanka in the middle, to Bezua-hü and Rox in the east. Then he would invade Tebbicousimankalê and Fenula just as the grand armies of the Sekuatean Empire had done—or, perhaps, not done, according to some history books. However, he would skip Herêbout, declaring its people unclean and thus unworthy of hearing his message. He vowed that all would follow him or die.

To mark themselves for battle, his followers would disfigure their faces in homage to the F'eng, whose own face was horribly scarred and stripped down to bone. A disciplined army of skull-faced warriors met the local militias and the locals were no match for the fury of religious fervor.

Set-d'Elous followed the news, much as he had followed events back in 1480 as the Sekuatean revolution was beginning. He knew what was coming, so one day he put on his ancient uniform and appeared at the high headquarters of the Jisilikan military, offering his services. He had never wanted to get back into the war business, content to languish with his beloved, whoever she might be, and wile away the days in sensual pleasures, but with the F'eng on the march, he had no choice. He had been the *Berron*, Supreme Commanding General, of the Sekuatean grand army for all of three days, after all, during their disastrous retreat from Tebbicousimankalê. He knew how to defeat a marching army.

The Jisilika Military Council happily gave him carte blanche to muster the forces of Gotanka, the wide plain in northern Zissekap serviced by two great rivers: the nations of Jisilika, Feasfend, Manên, and Peror. To these armies, he begged assistance from neighboring Foixe and Filopêa. Bezua-hü refused him. Enough, he decided, to face down the rag-tag legions of F'engsters, as he called them. One last call to battle! Then he could escape to the warm arms of his lover, Toni Franck.

Set-d'Elous studied his foe in earnest now. Few pictures were available, thankfully. Most shielded his face with a hood or cowl, yet when an artist dared depict the F'eng, the result was usually a bare skull. It was believed that he arose from the slums of Peror and was a frequent patron of the brothels there, catching the pox and letting it run too far before treatment. That was the cause of his so-called poisoning. If treated too late, the medicine not only would have no positive effect but would produce negative effects. The F'eng was no military commander, had no tactical mind, but managed to rally those who could command battalions. He did not know them but he could put his educated guesses next to the geography and meteorological information and know where to take a stand. Then it would be decided. The planning began. As for their leader, the Prophet, the F'eng, the dude in the yellow robe, whatever he was called, his followers would all fight to the death for him. That was something different from the ordinary soldiers he had fought against in previous battles. This would be no typical battle. They would be facing a storm of holy rage.

One chance to halt it, he thought, and stared at himself in a camp mirror, noting how his beard had grown out, gray now. He called for a razor, then a message board and stylus.

Dear Mr. F'eng,

he wrote in a message to be delivered to his opposite number,

We seem to have multiple disagreements, such that aggression has become the flavor of the day.

Let us come together and discuss how we might put an end to the rising conflicts that threaten to destroy civilization, for surely the citizenry have no dogs in this fight. If you truly believe that I have caused you any harm, not harm created by the hand of Fate but by your own poorly chosen actions, then let me attempt to make amends.

Let us come together, you and I, and leave the innocent people of Ghoupallesz to their own Fate. What say you?

I shall await you in the Valley of Kadirra-Uek. Bring guns, if you must.

And Set-d'Elous signed his name, his Earth name, Sebastian E. Talbot, and added his IRS employee ID number to make it official.

Eleven days hence came the reply by *Jêpe*-mounted messenger girl, the F'eng apparently believing an innocent young girl would not be harmed by the armies of Gotanka:

If you call yourself Sebastian Talbot, then you are my enemy and I have no reason to chat with you about these matters. I shall meet you, however, in the Valley of Kadirra-Uek, 21 days hence. The last bullet is yours.

Lowering the message board from his eyes, he expelled a great sigh, disappointed.

"I've been fighting these F'engsters for nearly ten years," he grumbled to his aides, "and finally we get the big battle. Well, fair enough. You want to play hardball? Let's play! It is on, bucko."

His aides glanced at each other, wondering what their boss had said in his strange, foreign language.

"I tried," he continued, pacing the large headquarters tent. "I tried to resolve this politely. Hell if I have any reason to be here. Not except for this F'eng being here." He paused, gazing up at the sky from the open tent flaps, thinking of the way the tangent in that quarry back home had waved like tent flaps so long ago.... "It is my fault. I opened this world to such an infection. I'm to blame."

Sure, it was easy enough for him to pass through the tangent and play around on this world. Then things became serious. He married, had children; they spread his genes through the society. And wars came. Perhaps they would have come anyway, yet he became involved in them. Then he sought to undo them, make them go away—as though that were truly possible, dreamer that he was.

"It's just as Gina always said: I screw up. I break things. I'm the bull in the china shop. I am, after all, Set, the God of Evil. Hah, the God of Clumsiness. Now it's my mess to clean up."

He caught his two aides rolling their eyes, chose to ignore them. It was not time for petty grievances. Not any longer.

"Clean up this mess! Make things right again," he suddenly snapped. "Be nice. Say 'please' and 'thank you' and smile. Right. Then I can go home. Then I may be allowed to go home to...to whatever is left there for me. There on that planet called Earth. I definitely do not belong here. I shouldn't have stepped through that opening, should never have followed Gina through it, should never have—"

He motioned for his aides to snap to action and they gathered his armor and helped him dress for battle.

Around the nations of northern Zissekap, the small skirmishes had escalated into full battles, costing thousands of lives for those who chose to fight. Yet even these were not so great as to disrupt the daily routines of most citizens. Now the conflict had erupted into something historic, and in the summer of 1611 two armies lined up in the Valley of Kadirra-Uek, ready to fight for the right to dictate what people in the future would or should or could do about something that may or may not ever happen. It was a battle of beliefs, fought with deadly weapons.

For that effort, they had taken the best that military weaponry had to offer: on the side of the massed Gotankan armies were the *rassal-galtal*: the giant war rabbits—not truly rabbits, but close enough for Set's eyes, the beasts as large as elephants and able to carry a gunnery basket. Also brought to the valley by the F'eng were equally large *reñ-parnox*—battle hamsters—as vicious as bears and mounted with a pair of gunners. Accompanying both fighting zoos were battalions of armored soldiers, dressed to deflect the pulse blasts of the new and improved AT guns. Among the F'eng followers who lined up behind the others were the usual farm implements and tools—anything that could cut or kill a human body.

Set-d'Elous once more called upon the F'eng via message board and nervous messenger to sit down and talk it out, to come to some sort of equitable agreement, not so much to split the land between F'eng and non-F'eng regions, each of them assigned to rule his portion, but to come up with some solution that would prevent further deaths. No response arrived. The messenger also did not return.

Two *pon* passed, everyone waiting for Fate to intercede. Then Set-d'Elous, in his royal blue and crimson uniform, white scarf trailing in the wind, raised his arm and with white gloved hand gave the signal to unleash hell.

The battle was intense and bloody. The war beasts inflicted much damage on opposing troops. The carnage on the field was legendary. Down to the last hundred men. The F'eng followers were stopped, at least. The remaining followers fled for the hills, knowing they would be hunted down. They went into hiding and only occasionally arose to spout their doomsday rhetoric.

With bandages on his arm and knee, his blade broken and AT gun depleted of its plasma, Set-d'Elous accepted the outcome.

He was ready to go back to Earth for his wife, evil spirit or not. Once she returned with him to the Dream Land, he could find a way to exorcise from her the ghost of Basura-Kanoun—the evil empress who had caused him so much grief.

Chapter 19

The Cleansing

"It's really rather simple," said the man in the brown robe, frazzled hood back on his shoulders, scarred face and bald head looking like Humpty Dumpty had been beaten up by the King's Men and trampled by the King's Horses. "We believe in Death as the true end of our existence. Is that not easy to understand? We are brought here through no will of our own; only by the wayward coupling of ignorant animals who fancy themselves gods and goddesses do we exist. From that initiation, we are slaves and are trained to be slaves of one or another particular kind. Most of all we are trained for breeding."

His guards took him and stood him in the corner of the room, fastened his hands to rings high on the wall.

"The most critical task we have is to make more of us. A crazy proposition, perhaps. With no suitable quality control we quickly overpopulate with mutants and anarchists. So the universe has provided us with a basic counterinfluence. We grow old. Our breeding shrivels up. We become unattractive to each other. The season ends, and we then sit around pondering our next effort. How should we occupy ourselves in the years that follow the ceasing of breeding? Some would say we monitor the growth of our offspring, guide them to the lessons we followed, make them into us."

Before him sat a panel of uniformed interrogators, the one in the middle wearing the red collar. He was the leader, the one to decide his fate. When the man paused, the lead interrogator, without expression, waved him to continue.

"Others say it is a time to connect with the universe and our special place in it. We are encouraged to plant, to build, to create art and music and all that is imitative of the beauty of the universe. We are supposed to leave it all for our offspring. Yet how will they make space for all of that indulgence? It becomes pointless."

The interrogator on the end of the panel was pressing buttons on a comm pad, the man saw, wondering if he was taking dictation. He grew more confident, continued.

"The third way condemns us to a dangerous path. We wander from our homes and live without limits, without direction, and without any past or future. This path leads to the greatest self realization—if you wish to call it such, as do many of our older philosophers, especially those of Gotanka. It has been said that to realize our selves is to join with the universe. In such a case, how shall we make that leap into the arms of our mother, the universe?"

"The universe?" asked the lead interrogator.

"The Prophet has another way: the true way. After our breeding years we should ease our way out of existence and give everything to those who will follow us. We do not make things that will occupy space. We do not create waste, nor do we collect objects of meaning for they, ultimately, have no meaning but what our ignorance assigns to them. We then go lightly away from all we once knew: home, family, lives of working and playing, and all institutions that once enslaved us. We vanish."

"Is that what you believe?"

"You must understand the origin of this way. The Prophet's teachings include the history of his existence—what people try to call his 'life'; this is a vulgar term to us. He was born of clumsy parents and presented to a world that shunned him. He grew tall and strong and entered his breeding years. 'Lo, then was the Prophet given poison by the Ghost of Set-d'Elous'—yes, the same as the legendary warrior, thus a ghost after his death. Scripture 5 verse 5. The poison forced him to breed beyond his limit and endangered his body. Thus, he ran from the house of pain and found comfort among helpmates who sought to comfort him; yet 'verily did his breeding spirit compel him further to make of the universe its stars, planets, and moons'—a bit metaphorical to your mind, perhaps, but the idea holds true: lots of undesired fornication."

"A perversity.... A corruption of history...."

"Continuing the history: The Prophet went from place to place, always followed by the Ghost, and in his fright he suffered the poisoning. It ravaged his body and scarred his face. To the end of his days he believed he had come, and so he took refuge in a physician's lodging. The scripture mentions a visit by the son of one of his past breeding partners, a boy who offered him a cure to the poison if only he would renounce all the beauty, wealth, and power of the world. He accepted and took a treasure device from the boy."

"What was it, this treasure device?"

"Legend has it that the treasure was a small box which when opened shone with a great light. And in the illumination was the Prophet transformed into what he is today: the F'eng. The light healed him. That is to say, it halted the progression of the illness, prevented his death, and at the same time filled his mind with all the truth of the universe. He then understood what he must do: he must give of himself to the world and tell everyone of the true path for their post-breeding seasons."

"And then...?"

"He spoke in village greens and at roadside inns, gathered some followers who were not put off by his appearance. Many thought he was a walking corpse, ravaged by the poison, yet he was quite alive—and always in pain. Eventually he found the sons he had made with willing women of the world, mostly in Gotanka, and they became the Nine Sons of F'eng."

"Now you get to the heart of our inquiry."

"And so it was that the gatherings of followers increased and began taking over small towns, encouraging the people in each location to change their thinking and turn to the righteous path. That path, as I told you, leads to glorious death. For there is no need for our continuing use, indeed overuse, of the world's resources; no need for more material wealth; no need for mundane pleasures that cannot endure the Final Day!"

"Final Day? What is that? Moreover, *when* is that?""

"The Prophet knew the Final Day would come after one very long night and that those who followed him, who took up the same path, would not fear it but embrace it as the expected and welcomed conclusion to the random spin of souls around the universal vortex. 'One does not mourn the flushing of the toilet,' he liked to say. It is inevitable, worth no cheer and no heartache."

"Clever fellow. Too clever for his own benefit."

"He saw breeding as a necessary evil at first, especially given his personal affliction. Later, he understood that if everything is to end on the Final Day, there is no reason for breeding. Why create more of us to stuff the world? More of us to perish on the Final Day? It is all so pointless. He understood the animal urges that fill the youth of our world and they could be forgiven; if a child is born from that play, so be it. Yet at some point both men and women should put aside that play and scan the skies for the Great Light that will signal the coming of the Final Day."

"You are rambling."

The lead interrogator turned to his colleagues, mumbled a question, heard their answers. A push of a button on the panel in front of the lead interrogator brought an open door and two technicians wheeling in an egg-shaped object on a cart.

"Continue...."

"Eat only as necessary, at a minimum. Be never vain in one's appearance; dress simply, modestly, naturally. Live as a beast of the field, for we are them as well. These are the Prophet's ways. It is a way that is kind to the world, kind to each other, yet prepares the body and soul for the Final Day. There is no need to build, to create, to add to what already crowds our world into submission. Our purpose here is to seek our end and leave few footprints behind us while on our path."

"A cult of minimalization...."

"To this end the Prophet designed a Legion of Truth. They are led by the Nine Sons; nine battalions, if you wish to think of it in military terms. Yes, the truth is they were military; they bore many weapons and exercise formations and then the day came when they were called upon to protect the followers of F'eng from bellicose governments who did not see our path as the true way. You know this as the Battle of Kadirra-Uek."

"Where you were captured...."

"To the East formed the battle lines of the Legion of Truth, many of them mounted upon giant battle rabbits, standing like houses, one pilot and three gunners to a saddle basket. To the West formed the Jisilikan brigades. They brought a squadron of armored giant war hamsters. Perhaps a few thousand fighters at each end of the valley. Everyone recalled the warfare of the 1480s through 1560s and vowed never again to allow it. However, chaos requires order and so the Prophet sent the Legion of Truth to do battle."

"Is that where he died?"

"Being in his agèd days the Prophet could only watch from atop a well-placed hill as the armies clashed. It was said that on another hill along the valley stood the Ghost of Set-d'Elous. It was said that the Ghost directed the Jisilikan forces—all the forces of the Gotankan nations, actually. They had been foes for all time. It was necessary they meet again at the final battle. Though it was the final battle, it was not the Final Day. It was only an ordinary day, marked Denio-15 in 1611, the last of the life of the Prophet. He stood for the entire battle and saw the mighty war hamsters completely shred the Jisilikan infantry lines and meet the battle rabbits head-on, tooth to tooth, claw to claw. Such horrible conflict! Such ferocity of animalkind! Yet the war hamsters finally prevailed and put down the last of the battle rabbits, making meal of them. preferred over the flesh of men."

"We have heard enough."

"No, wait! There's more!"

A wave of the lead interrogator's hand and the guards went to the man, unfastened his hands from the rings. They stripped off his robe, bent him down then lifted him up and over the cart. Feet first, they dropped him into the open capsule, knees bent up, shoulders twisted, pressing him entirely inside. Only the top of the man's scalp rose out of the opening.

"And we who have survived.... Yes, we live on, following the way of truth, modeling the path of the Prophet, who decreed our Final Day to be a day of welcome relief from our duties as keepers of this world. Hence, we covet not, we breed not, we step lightly here, and when necessary, we intervene on behalf of the world. At such times, we may be bold, brave, fearless as we crush anything that would disrupt us from the righteous path! So you see us go to war against technology. Yet it is not the inventions of humanity we oppose but the ways such technology distracts us from our preparations for the Final Day."

"Technology comes from the seven gods and nine goddesses."

"We abhor those who seek leisure in frivolous ways. We seek to share with them the true path. Convert them, if you like that word. We do not hate...anything, anyone. We wish to keep to our own path yet so many also seek to break our path, to shove us this way or that way, and that is the reason, kind gentlemen, that we do sometimes become violent. Impede us not as we rush to the Final Day!"

The room was suddenly silent and the interrogators glanced at each other. The lead interrogator nodded, satisfied, then stood.

"One question: How is it this prophet fellow is called the F'eng? What does it mean?"

The man scrunched inside the capsule grinned.

"Not many people know the origin of that name. Some say it is old Danid for 'he who shows the path'—in essence, the leader of a pilgrimage. Others say it is merely a corruption of his birth name. I have no opinions, either way. I call him the Prophet and only use the F'eng when speaking to others—such as now."

"What is his birth name?"

The man grinned again—brighter, more animated, hopeful.

"I have heard it pronounced as 'Myxal-Fennek'—certainly not a common Ghoupalle or even Danid name, I'll grant. I've seen him write his name, and it is spelled thus: MICH-AEL-FEN-NING. It is this name which the Ghost of Set uses to refer to the F'eng."

"Do you know the birth place of Myxal-Fennek?"

"It is said he was born in Ur-tha, but as that is a metaphorical place, I doubt that it's true. Residential records mark him first in Lyas, Sekuate-south in approximately 1544. He was registered by Set-d'Elous—before becoming a ghost. His age was marked as 59 on that record. It may not be accurate, however. Yet that would fit with his death age of 126 in 1611. A physician who examined the body agreed on that age."

"You saw him dead?"

"Oh, yes. I saw the body, cut into twelve sections."

"By who?"

"I do not know that. Yet there were several members of the Gotankan Honor Platoon standing around the body. Big, hulking brutes with horned helmets and battle axes! They were assigned to protect the Gotankan commander. I know that. So perhaps he ordered them to kill the Prophet. When the battle lines were broken, they must have scaled the mountain and intercepted the Prophet and his body guard."

"You witnessed his death?"

"I had to look away."

"You heard it?"

"The Prophet did not make a sound."

"So the F'eng is dead."

"Yes—sadly."

"We can make our report now," said the lead interrogator. He glanced at his fellow interrogators, who responded affirmatively with a raised index finger.

"Is there more you wish to know?" asked the naked prisoner, squirming in the capsule.

"No, that is enough."

"I can tell you more. A lot more."

"You have been very cooperative—"

"I can keep the information flowing like an ancient river, if you wish. All the better to hold off my execution, true?"

"True."

The lead interrogator's hand moved to the control panel on the table.

"Wait! I have more to tell you!"

One technician closed the lid on the capsule, locked it. Another technician affixed a descending tube to an opening in the floor panel.

"Thank you for the information about the F'eng. Perhaps you shall meet him after your cleansing."

The prisoner rattled inside the capsule. "Will it hurt?"

The lead interrogator pressed the button on the panel and the capsule hissed with yellow steam, flashing red and orange, then condensing into white. Below the capsule, a transparent tube drained away the beige sludge.

"No, it won't."

Chapter 20

Wonders

"It's kinda fun, really," said Tammy, pulling the shoulder strap of her summer dress back into place. She sifted through her salad with the fork, found a tiny tomato and speared it. "I just talk about whatever and she asks me questions. I tell her about my life on Ghoupallesz, being the Queen of Aivana and all, and that seems to make her happy. She writes a lot of notes. But we're down to twice a month now, so I guess she thinks I'll make it out here with the normal people."

Chuck McElroy laughed, loosened his tie and took a cheddar biscuit from the communal plate. "I don't even have a shrink. Nobody cares if I can go out in public without freaking out. Don't they know there's nobody more dangerous than an ex-cop. Especially a disgruntled one."

"What're you disgruntled about? Besides them not giving you your job back?

He shook his head. "I didn't pass the physical. My arms, you know. But it's more than that. Their freakin' attitude."

"Shhh, Chuck. No swearing in public. This is a Red Lobster. There are children around."

"Sorry." He lowered his voice. "The way they sent me packing.... Now I got nothing. I'm a freakin' security guard at Independence Center. A mall cop. There's nothing lower than that."

"But dotcha do a good job at that? You help people."

"It's not my thing."

The waitress brought their dinners. Tammy asked for more cheddar biscuits. Chuck said he was done with the salad. Yes, more iced tea. Thanks.

"Well, I'm no better off than you," said Tammy, surveying her dinner. On one end of the huge platter was a small lobster tail, in the middle shrimp, and on the other end a fish filet and rice. Almost as an afterthought, a thimble of broccoli hid behind the cup of garlic butter. "I got some money from selling my jewels, but I'm bored. I just sit around all day thinking about my children. And Jason. You know, I think you'd like him. You two would get along just fine, I think. He's into cars, too."

"I'm freakin' happy for you, Tam." Chuck paused, fork poised, pondering where to start. The lobster was full sized. He had been given a bib, like some stupid kid, and a tiny fork that wasn't big enough to eat anything, much less a whole lobster.

They ate their dinners for a while, flings of small talk to break the silence. All around them, happy families dined, children laughed, a bunch of servers brought in a birthday cake and sang to a customer, and their iced tea was refilled. Still they remained glum, disconnected.

"So what're we gonna do, Chuck?"

He wiped his mouth with the napkin and frowned.

"I got no freakin' idea."

"You ever think about going back?"

Chuck choked, caught himself. He drank some tea to clear his throat. "Is that what you want?"

"I dunno. It's really all I know now. I was a perfect queen. I got that job down."

"Yeah, I remember. Tough as nails and twice as pretty."

He laughed. So did she.

"Aw, Chuckie, thanks."

They reminisced about the day he busted into the Royal Audience wearing his leather gladiator suit, all muscles and sweat, and she in her filmy gown and sparkling jewels. He looked so magnificent, like the cover of a Romance novel. She was a heavenly delight to behold, he said, the most descriptive words he could think of. He didn't care about royalty, just being with her again. The fact that she had married someone else caused him great pain but he understood how he had behaved and accepted the new situation.

The lobster claw squirted juice into his face as he broke it open and Tammy laughed. He wiped his face with the napkin and laughed with her. Sometime after that, two hands met across the table and lingered, fingers intertwined, secret messages sizzling up each arm and into the heads of each person. Eyes met and more secrets were exchanged.

"You know, Chuck, I can't do anything with you," said Tammy, withdrawing her hand. "I am married. It's just I may never see Jason again."

"Then go back."

"Are you serious? You want to? I mean, you think we can? You know how?"

He shoved his mostly finished plate to the side of the table, piled high with lobster scraps.

"I been thinking about that, too. I got nothing going on here. Now, I'm not saying I was king of anything back there, but...."

"Yeah, I know you suffered a lot there," said Tammy. "I know you suffered just to get back to me, and I appreciate that—"

"I had no choice about what happened. But I mean, what I went through changed me. I mean it. I'm a better man now. I can be a better husband, too."

"Chuckie, that's not the problem. I am married to Jason."

"Yeah, I get that."

"If we go back I'm sure I can fix you up with some nice girl who would love you and appreciate you. You can have kids and be happy. And we always got Chucker between the two of us."

"But nobody else would be you, Tam."

She grinned, all fifty of her teeth shining in the light of the restaurant—like a beacon of hope.

"That's so sweet."

He gulped some tea, set the glass down. "We got to get back there. No two ways about it. As long as we avoid the Roué in the desert, we'll be okay."

"Roué...." The word had meaning for both of them but in opposite contexts. Chuck had been tortured by them. Tammy had been their queen. "Listen to us, Chuckie. Here we are in a Red Lobster in Independence, Missouri, talking about all that stuff from another world like it was a weekend trip to the Ozarks!"

"These people here know nothing about all that," said Chuck with a grin. "We're like superheroes or something. We got special knowledge. We come from a secret place."

"But how can we get back there?"

He leaned over the table, speaking quietly. "You know that quarry, right?"

"Yeah...."

"That's the doorway, right?"

"Right."

"We go there and look around. Maybe we can find the way to open it."

"You know how?"

"Not really, but I remember what he did."

"You mean Set-d'Elous?"

"Okay, him. Talbot is what I call him. But I saw what he did. I think I could do it, too. It'll take some practice."

"Wow, Chuckie. You sound like a spy or something. This is exciting. Should we?"

"We don't have nothing to lose."

They waved off desert and Chuck paid, garnering a thanks from Tammy. And a great big hug—right there in the middle of the restaurant. Dinners thought there was a marriage proposal or something and a few applauded.

"It's the two year anniversary of him not hitting me anymore," said Tammy with a straight but smiling face.

Chuck's face turned white. "She's kidding."

✳ ✱ ✳

"I'm not kidding!" Sebastian exclaimed. "She is possessed by the spirit of the woman I killed."

The beige smoke was stinging his eyes but he endured it for the sake of the advice the naked shaman was sharing. He did not particularly enjoy being in the advice position, either: squatting with his rear end hovering over the shaman's lap, the old man handling Sebastian's buttocks.

The shaman spoke no Ghoupallêan, so a local anthropologist

from Typeg, Datamund-Metourus, was translating. They had traveled by ETUR east from the city and up and over the Zissekap mountains into the interior jungle of southern Megank until the road ended. Tribesmen led them farther into the jungle and introduced them to several shamen, none of whom were the right one. Chucker had been very specific. The old man was named Peni and had four nipples, one of them on his back. Metourus was glad when, on the trip's twenty-fifth day, they finally stumbled into the village where Peni lived.

"So what should I do?" asked Sebastian through the translator.

The shaman muttered on and on while squeezing Sebastian's right buttock, apparently enjoying the texture of the skin and the firmness of the muscle. Supposedly he was searching for a sign of future conflict.

Metourus coughed. "He says you must take your woman to the site of the killing." He coughed again, the smoke choking him. It was not leaking out of the hut as quickly as they wished. "You reenact the killing with your living woman. That will scare out the spirit."

"Is there any danger to doing that? I mean, how accurate must it be?"

Metourus translated to the shaman, who had switched to squeezing Sebastian's left buttock.

"He says, 'Well, don't go as far as to kill your living woman.' That makes sense."

Sebastian agreed. "That's it? That's all I have to do?"

"Apparently," said Metourus.

"What if it doesn't work? If she is still possessed by the spirit? Is there a Plan B?"

Metourus spoke again to Peni, the shaman, who continued squeezing the buttocks alternatingly in a rhythmic, meditative manner. In response, the shaman talked a long time, all the while squeezing. Eventually, he stopped and grinned, his last tooth showing in his wide yaw.

"So...the gist of all that was that if the exorcism fails, you should bring the woman here and he will try it himself. However, the cost of that, of him doing it himself, is that she must bear a child for him. Most of what he said was a story about some warrior from his childhood who he loved, and then he told me about his children and grandchildren and everything they were doing these days. It seems nobody comes to speak with him much any more."

"So he's happy we are here. Does that mean my butt's hanging out for no reason? Is there any truth to his recipe for ridding my wife of the evil spirit?"

More translation, more squeezing.

"He says it is truth. He says it worked for two of his wives who were possessed by the spirits of their previous husbands. He needed to rid them of those spirits before he could enjoy sex with them."

"I'll bet. Nothing like sleeping with your wife's ex."

Satisfied, they thanked Peni for the advice and Sebastian hiked up his trousers to a rain of laughter from the shaman. The old man clapped his hands and jumped up and down repeatedly. He seemed happy.

"I think you gave him a thrill," said Metourus as they trekked out of the village, led by their guide.

❄ ❅ ❄

They parked at the far end of the shopping center, where Tammy said they had parked on that fateful night with Michael and Sebastian, and walked the mile down the road to the gravel drive and the chain link gate and the warning sign.

"Is there really radiation up there?"

"Beats me," said Chuck. "I think it's just a sign to keep people away."

"Should we go?"

"Probably a few minutes won't hurt. If it's true."

So they hiked up to the quarry and stood staring at the cliffs in the moonlight. A light breeze rustled some leaves and Tammy thought it felt creepy. Was somebody watching them?

Chuck put his arm around her shoulders.

"Now what do we do?" she asked.

Chuck paced the central arena where he remembered seeing the sparkling lights that time when he chased Talbot through the hole.

"Let me look around."

"If we're going anywhere, I better get some things together in a suitcase, you know?"

"We're not going anywhere tonight, Tam. I'm sure of that. But if we were...."

He halted, gazing at the dry clay chips at his feet. They were broken. Someone had stepped on them. Someone had been here since the last rain. That was about a week before, he counted.

"Are you sure?" asked Tammy when he told her.

"Who comes here? One of them voyager people. That's what he called himself. A voyager."

"He said Interdimensional Voyager, like it was a club you have to join. Very exclusive."

"Like the Mile-High Club?"

Tammy giggled. "Guess so, Chuckie."

"We were so young then, flying to Disney World. Maybe we weren't exactly a mile in the sky, but we got 'er done, huh?"

"Yeah, a long time ago." Her eyes became moist. "A really long time ago. How old am I now? With all those years in Aivana?"

"You still look hot to me."

"Do I?"

"As hot as ever."

"Oh, Chuckie...."

Half-past midnight. Sebastian waited as long as he could behind the bushes, then made a run for it, springing up the steps and crashing into the door. He pushed the doorbell several times and a shadow fell over the door's window.

Sensing someone looking at him through the peep hole, he softly called "Toni, it's me."

The door opened and he fell inside. She quickly closed the door behind him.

"What are you doing here? They'll see you!"

He caught his breath, wiped his hands off on his khaki pants. His head and shoulders were wet from the rain, shirt soaked.

"Here, let's get you out of those." She helped him pull off his shirt and took them to the laundry room. "You left some clothes here last year.... I washed them for you, of course. They're in the closet in the bedroom if you want to change."

"Thanks," he said and shuffled into the bedroom.

She went to check on her son, asleep in his own bed, in his own room now, a year older.

"Toni," said Sebastian, coming out of the bedroom in fresh clothing, "I'm sorry. I didn't realize it's been a year. I told you long ago the tangents can shift."

"Tangents? You have the same story?" She crossed her arms over her chest, pinching the white bathrobe tighter. "I got into a lot of trouble because you visited me."

"I said I'm sorry. I'm not trying to cause trouble. I'm here to help you. Like I was last time. I just did not expect it would be so long until I could return. And return with a solution."

"What solution? Do you mean us? I cannot be with a man who runs out every time he gets satisfied in bed. Or he runs when he's afraid of his responsibilities. Or he's—"

"It's not like that, Toni."

"Then tell me what it is like, Sebastian. Can you be clear for once?"

She turned away from him and went to the kitchen, got a glass and poured some Chardonnay from a bottle on the counter. She pulled out a chair and sat at the table, shaking her head. Another headache—whenever this man appeared!

He joined her, sitting across from her. He placed his hands flat on the table, some kind of sign that he meant her no harm.

"Toni, I love you. I want to be with you and the little man. I want us to be a family. But I don't think we can do that here. Too many things getting in the way. As you know. I think we can make everything work out if we go to a place where we will not be bothered."

"That is your fantasy world?"

He gazed at her. "Yes."

"I knew it!" She got up and poured herself more wine.

"You don't know it. Give me a chance to show you. See it for yourself. If you don't like it, you can come back, no questions asked."

She sipped her wine, licked her lips, then ran her hand through her disheveled hair. It was getting too long, she decided. Her terrycloth robe was itchy. The man across the table from her still looked handsome, had that crazy look in his eyes. There was gray at his temples. How long had he been away? In his fantasy world? all those years? wherever that was? If not for that fantasy world business, she would sweep him into her bed in an instant. Once every year or so was too little reward for all she had been through.

Or perhaps she could indulge him this one time, make him happy—or make him finally see that what he had been saying for years was really fantasy. It was all in his head, no matter what his eyes saw or his heart felt. If she could make him face that façade of wishful thinking, perhaps he would be cured. He would finally see the truth. Then he could be a normal man with a normal family. And he would stay home finally.

"You want me to see your fantasy world?" she asked, tossing down the last swallow of wine. "All right. I will go with you to see it."

"Wonderful. Thank you."

"Yet if it becomes nothing.... If there is nothing to see, then will you accept that it is all fantasy and stay with me here?"

He regarded her like a precious flower that bloomed only once a year.

"I will stay with you. Here." He took a deeper breath. "If you cannot see my other world."

She stood and set the glass in the sink. He got up and waited. She went to him, gazed into his eyes up close. He felt naked that way.

"We should sleep on it," she said, taking his hand and leading him out of the kitchen.

The quarry was as plain and dull as always when the sparkling lights began and rose to the point where a hand, then a foot split them. A full body followed, and the lights subsided, blinking out as Chucker stood confidently on the clay soil in the center of the arena.

He breathed deeply a few times, adjusting to the air of Earth, a little heavier than that of Ghoupallesz. The gravity was stronger, too. He took a step, then another, paused to adjust his shirt and jacket, retied one of his boots.

A strange sound drew his attention and he turned his head to look back over his shoulder.

"Mom?" he exclaimed. "Dad?"

The naked couple on the flat rock were startled, not sure where to look, not sure whether to cover up or run away.

"What are you doing here?" He shook his head. "What are you *doing*?"

Chuck climbed off Tammy and sat beside her as she rolled over to minimize her exposure.

"We certainly didn't expect you to magically appear," he said with a grunt.

"Chucker, can you hand me my clothes? Your dad's, too?"

The night was humid, the moon almost full, and the clay tiles crunched beneath his boots as he went across the arena to retrieve his parents' clothing. He began to laugh. He was not a young man any longer, and he had a family of his own. So nothing to be embarrassed about. He shook his head, smiling.

"Here you go, kids," he said, tossing the clothing to them. He turned away.

"So you just happened to come here for a visit? Tonight of all nights?" asked Tammy.

"That's about right." He waited. "Are you dressed yet?"

"Hold on," said Chuck.

"I actually was coming here to get you guys. To take you back. I finally figured out what happened. I mean, with the bombs in the Royal Hall. I finally tracked you back to Earth. I guessed you wouldn't want to be here, so here I am to take you back."

Tammy rose from the rock, stepped toward Chucker.

"You're kidding, right?"

"No, Mom." He grinned like he had gotten away with snatching candy from the candy store. "Mom, I got a wife now. Remember that princess from Typeg you tried to fix me up with? We were both blown into the jungle. We survived there for five years. And now we have two kids, Randy and Joy. My wife's name is Foj and she is so beautiful, I can't wait to get back to her. We have a little resort on the beach in Liêta. You can stay with us as long as you like."

Tammy pinched his cheek. "My baby's all grown up!"

"Good job, son," said Chuck and shook hands with him.

"I'm a grandmother!" Tammy shrieked, then laughed.

When the sky was dark enough, Sebastian drove Toni and their son to the Independence Center mall and parked in the far corner, next to the other car there, a Camaro. He noticed the Fraternal Order of Police sticker on the bumper and the fuzzy dice hanging from the rearview mirror.

"Someone you know?" asked Toni, helping little Sebastian out of her car.

"I don't think so. Probably just the night guard's car."

He led them down to the street and pointed the way.

"We have to walk?" she asked.

"There's no place to park down there. You'll see. It's just a mile, no more."

Toni insisted Sebastian carry their son who was squirming in his arms. She spoke to the boy, calming him for the hike.

"Où allons-nous?" asked little Sebastian.

"I don't know where we're going," Toni answered.

"Y at-il des jouets là-bas?"

"There might be toys there, but I doubt it. I don't think your father is thinking that far ahead."

Sebastian shook his head. "I thought you said he also knows English."

"He does," said Toni, "but he prefers French when speaking with me."

"How clever! I'll teach him Ghoupallêan."

Toni pursed her lips. "As you like."

When they arrived, Sebastian set the boy down at the chain link gate. The boy was growing, getting too heavy to carry. Sebastian stretched, then rubbed his back, hoping the strain would not affect his ability to concentrate enough to open a tangent in the quarry.

"Up there?" asked Toni, taking her son's hand securely. "It

looks frightening."

"It's safe. Nobody ever goes up there."

"Only police! Only people who think there is a door there to another world."

"Well, that's technically correct."

He led the way up the gravel drive. They regrouped at the short, narrow canyon, then proceeded through it into the arena.

"What!" Sebastian blurted.

Before him stood a select group of people he knew, some he had forgotten about, and one he almost expected to find there.

"Well, if it isn't my ol' buddy Set-d'Elous, slumming back here on Earth!"

His childhood friend and fellow skullduggerian, Jason, greeted him. The man was dressed in Aivanan robes of royal purple. Behind him and to the side were the children, all six of them, from Buffy and Jason Junior to Kip and Mary-Ann. Two others stood nearby: Ro'ma'le and Fe'o'pi. They all appeared as young adults or teenagers now.

"Having a conference?" he asked Jason.

"Just telling these two how there isn't any Aivana anymore. Not for us, anyways. We were kicked out. The eldest son returned, that prodigal bastard!"

Sebastian saw Tammy and Chuck McElroy standing beside their son, Chucker.

"Quite a family reunion you have going here," said Sebastian.

He ushered Toni into the arena. "Everyone.... This is Toni. She's actually my wife here on Earth."

She glared at him. "On Earth? Where else you have a wife?"

"Nowhere else. Not now."

Jason chuckled.

"Toni, this is my friend, Jason, and his children with Tammy," he continued. "They're all from Aivana. The desert kingdom I mentioned before. Those two are the children of Tammy and, for *her*, the King of Aivana, and, for *her*, that IRS co-worker, Michael Fenning."

He turned to Tammy. "Did you know he became some kind of prophet, preaching about a doomsday comet?"

"Well, he was always preaching something," she cursed.

Sebastian gestured toward the other young man.

"And this is Chucker—that's Chuck R. Tucker, son of Tammy and Chuck McElroy over there."

"The man from the zoo," exclaimed Toni.

"Hi, Dr. Franck," said Tammy, waving. "Never thought I'd see you out here, not like this, anyways. I didn't know you was Sebastian's wife, neither."

"That can't be Chuck McElroy," said Toni roughly.

He stepped forward. "It is. But wait a sec. Whatever you think of me, Ma'am, I deserve it. But I've been through hell and back as my punishment. I'm very sorry for everything that happened before—if you even remember. I'm not the same guy as before. Please forgive me, will you?"

Toni turned to Sebastian. "Is this some kind of trick? You plan everyone to meet us here? Is it some kind of sick game you are playing?"

He shook his head, embarrassed.

"I really didn't expect to see anyone here."

"Is this...an intervention of some kind? Am I the crazy person?"

"Absolutely not, Toni."

"Then what is this all about?"

Jason stepped forward. "Perhaps I can explain. We were kicked out of Aivana, as I said. We risked assassination or execution if we stayed, so I managed to get everyone out. But we had no place to go, so I thought, let's show the kids what Earth is like. We've been here about three months, just sightseeing. We were at Worlds of Fun yesterday, in fact. But the kids didn't take to the rich, exotic foods they had, like hot dogs. Or the rollercoaster. Yeah, Buffy threw up lunch on everyone below her riding the rollercoaster—"

"And I came to get my mom and dad and take 'em back," said Chucker. "Instead, I find them acting naughty on that rock over there."

"What?" said Jason.

Sebastian was shocked. "That rock? Over there? That's my rock. Me and Gina's rock."

Tammy laughed. "Don't sweat it. The rain'll wash it off."

"You said Gina. I remember that name," said Toni. "You also mentioned a Zaura. Isn't that right?"

"Zaura was my Ghoupalle wife. Gina was—"

"What do you mean acting naughty?" asked Jason.

"We were talking," said Chuck, "and Tam and me decided to come out and check this place. We thought it would be best if we returned to the Dream Land."

"The Dream Land? That's what you called it before, right?" asked Toni of Sebastian.

"Yes, but its formal name is Ghoupallesz." He swept his arm around the quarry. "We all call it that. We are the club, you might say. Probably the first time we've all been in the same place at the same time. So, in that strange way, we're all kind of related."

Toni nodded, held her son's hand tighter. "I can see that."

"There's nothing to worry about," said Sebastian. "Come with me and you'll see how wonderful our life can be. We can live anywhere you like, from a tropical paradise to a cabin in the woods, a clean, cosmopolitan city, or a desert ranch. Whatever you want. I also know of a beautiful northern island where we could live and no one to bother us."

She regarded the crowd milling about the quarry. There was definitely something not quite right about the people she saw. Were they all insane? Had they been turned insane by going to some place she could only imagine? Mass psychosis, perhaps. And they were all somehow connected to Sebastian Talbot—known in his dreams as the legendary warrior Set-d'Elous.

"And you want me to join you...?"

"Yes, Toni. Give it a try. That's all I ask."

A few of the others urged her to come along.

"Oh, but the first thing we have to do is get that evil spirit out of you," said Sebastian.

"What do you mean?" asked Toni, concerned.

"I told you before—I think. Can't recall now. When I killed Basura-Kanoun, her spirit somehow went into you. Sometimes she speaks to me. She teased me and mocked me the whole time I was stuck in that wheelchair."

"What are you talking about, Sebastian?"

"Basura-Kanoun."

"Who is Basura-Kanoun?"

"She was the evil Empress."

"The Empress of Sekuate," Chucker added.

"When? Where? Were you married to her?"

"I think I was. She put a spell on me. Made me the emperor

with her. I was trapped by her for twenty years. That's twenty Ghoupalle years."

"Ghoupalle years?"

"But don't worry. I went to a Xig shaman and now I know what to do. We just have to return to the place where I killed her and reenact it. Only I won't actually kill you. It's only role playing."

"You killed a woman?"

"Yes, but doing it saved millions of lives! I stopped a war!"

"But you killed someone!"

"It's done already. Now I want to save you, Toni."

"Save me? From what?"

"From her evil spirit. If we reenact the killing, that will scare out the evil spirit of Basura-Kanoun. She will be out of you. Then you and I can be together completely and not have her interfere with our lives. You know, she was the evil Empress. She had me under her spell. As the Emperor, I was made to do many horrible things, but I'm free of that now. Now I need to make you free of her spirit by pretending to kill you."

Toni broke away from him, crying "Mon Dieu!"

She rushed to the narrow canyon, urging her son to run on ahead through it.

"Wait, Toni! Let me explain."

"Don't ever see me again! You are a pathetic man!" she shouted back. "I don't care what you do, where you go, I never want to see you again! Stay away!"

"Toni! Wait!"

"We are finished, Sebastian. You really are crazy—insane!—and all your friends, too! What a madhouse! Mon Dieu!"

And she disappeared.

For another minute they heard her shouting, "Run, Sebastian, run!"

Then silence.

The members of the group stared at each other.

"Oh, well," said Jason, at last. "Guess she doesn't belong here."

"I happen to love her," said Sebastian. He took a deep breath.

"I thought you loved Gina."

"I do. In principle. But Toni is my wife. And I've barely gotten to know my son. For three years I couldn't play with him, couldn't even talk to him. You know he speaks two languages already?"

"Well, she was always so strict," said Tammy. "Like I done something wrong. Never believed in the Dream Land."

"Nice lady, though," said Chuck and received a slap on the arm from Tammy. "I meant as a person."

"Butterfingers," Chucker muttered. All he knew was how she let go of the wheelchair at the zoo, how it slipped out of her hands. His wife, Foj, was stronger than that woman.

Nervous silence filled the arena of the quarry and a few stars twinkled.

"So! Finally we're all together. We're all here!" said Tammy. "We should have a party. We should celebrate."

"Celebrate what?"

"Survival!" Tammy sang.

Several of them agreed.

"Not everyone is here," said Jason. He turned to his friend, Sebastian. "What about Gina?"

"Who?" asked Tammy.

"The girlfriend," said Chucker.

"You got a wife and a girlfriend?" asked Tammy. "No wonder you never wanted any sleepmate in Aivana."

"Who's Gina?" asked Chuck senior.

"Gina Parton," said Sebastian like he was calling off names from a roll. "My high school sweetheart. My Long Lost Love. My soulmate. I seem to spend a lot of time rescuing her. Last time, I had to break into a Zetin castle. After that, she thanked me by staying with me. Like we were married. We even had a child, a daughter. Then one day she left. Vanished. Got tired of me, I suppose."

"Awww," said Tammy, going up and giving him a hug.

"Maybe I'll go look for her—again. Always again. I guess I'll start in Kipzon, the last place where we were together. No matter where she is, I will find her. I just want to know why she left."

Jason clapped his friend's shoulder in sympathy.

"Don't bother. There's a comet coming in a few hundred years anyway. That's why we're settling back on Earth."

"Well, we're going back to the Dream Land," said Tammy, taking Chuck's arm. "We're gonna be grandparents there."

"What about *our* children?" asked Jason, his arms out in disbelief.

"We'll visit each other...?" Tammy grinned.

"Visit?"

"Or come with us. Be one big happy family," said Tammy, hugging his arm. "You and Chuckie can share me."

"Share you? But—"

"I'm okay with sharing," Chuck said with a cough.

"This will take some discussion...."

"I'm going back to Liêta to be with my wife and kids," Chucker spoke up. "I miss them."

Jason rubbed his brow, gazing at his and Tammy's grown offspring all lined up. "I see there's a lot to be decided."

Sebastian simply smiled, taking a step back from the others. Those discussions he need not be a part of. There was a new adventure awaiting him. He felt the night sky expanding, letting him see the far corners of the universe. And one bright star in particular.

The night was young, they all seemed to realize at once. It always was on Earth.

Chapter 21

Journey

Walking across the paper-flat plain was exhausting for Gina and her children, yet she knew they must keep going. Perhaps by tomorrow they would reach a city, somewhere to take a room for the night and get some food. And wash themselves. Her feet were aching and her gown was tattered, yet she tugged at her daughter's hand, urging her: "Come on, young one!" The boy was lucky, riding in a harness on his mother's back, yet he, too, was fatigued by the blazing sun and the stinging, sand-filled wind. He did not care what caused them to flee; he only wanted his portion of milk.

She raked her dirty, blond hair, wishing she had shaved it all off to be more comfortable in the heat of this new world she had stepped onto. The skies boiled red and brown, a stifling overcast that made the landscape an oven. Veins of liquid ore ran like broken, bent fingers across the ground, forcing her to mind her steps and occasionally backtrack to go around the wider ones. Though she knew it did not exist, this place was as close to how she imagined Hell to be as anything she had ever experienced. The air too thick to breathe easily, the fumes, the struggle to go on—nothing was as it used to be and she pondered what she had ever done to deserve what she feared might be her final journey.

I definitely don't belong here.

She was careful to not share her fears with the children.

Once upon a time she had been a queen. A northern kingdom, snowcapped mountains forming its borders and wide fertile plains, a happy shoreline, and a more-or-less kind husband who was the king. She had named herself Jinetta. Then she was kidnapped—and rescued. And she had been the wife of the prime minister of another country. She was offered as a hostage to the Zetin—and escaped. She had been a goddess for the tribes of Xig a little longer than was wise. Not willing to wait for rescue, she had left with her two children. The way things seemed to work on Ghoupallesz, she could never be certain she actually would be rescued. Of course, that was after she had taken up with the handsome rebel, Iadon, sharing his designs for revolution in a desert kingdom, then endured his abuse all the way up to a certain point she was not going to pass. She was not sure whether she preferred the wild, mercurial, bad boys or the safe, heroic, romantic guys. In the end it did not matter: she was alone, on her own, to do or die trying—

She stepped over some broken ground, rocks upturned by the force of an underground lava stream, and turned to help her daughter traverse the stones. They continued to make their own trail, long ago leaving the last of the withered grass, mushy lichen and wilted wildflowers. She noticed the sky far ahead was light green, the death clouds breaking up, and her spirit improved. As they trudged ahead, the clouds slipped apart and she glimpsed the blue sun, backlit by the yellow sun. At the distant edge of her vision, to the right of their present course, she thought she could detect the rising spires of a golden city. She pointed to it and her daughter stared, could not see it yet agreed to imagine it if it would make her mother happy.

Nice guy or bad boy. She knew a nice guy once upon a time in another life, on another world, the foolish boy who was always rescuing her. What she really wanted was to be in a position to rescue *him*. Her lover. Ex-lover. He called her his 'long-lost love' and she supposed that in her pragmatism he might as well be her long-lost love, too. It made everything easier to understand. She wondered where he was now. Occasionally he would enter her dreams and they would chat a while about nothing serious, the weather, new dessert recipes, who's who in politics, and so on. They would meet again, somewhere, someday. Always.

Gina Parton, she considered, feeling that identity more vaguely now than some previous week's dream. Perhaps age 39 in Earth years, she calculated, maybe a few more, yet possibly passing for mid-sixties in Ghoupalle years. Her perpetual youth in the land of the aged made her a rare prize for men young and old—and the occasional princess or witch. Her golden hair was also prized; one lover sought to clip off some of it to sacrifice upon the altar of his temple, hoping for long life. His brother killed him within a fortnight. Both her parents had been blond so there was no magic to her hair color. They had also died, gotten old and gone away, still thinking their daughter had been killed while away at college, or kidnapped and killed later, her body never found. That's what she eventually learned police had suggested to them. She never got along with her parents anyway. Way too strict. She was meant to be a queen, not a nun. It did not hurt her knowing they had mourned her the rest of their lives while she was safe and sound living her life on another world. They wouldn't have understood.

"Mama, are we there yet?" asked the daughter.

"One more day, young one," she replied.

So here she was, actually on another planet, accepting it and everything that went along with that truth as simply as she took her breaths. She could have had an easy life, keeping her head down, enjoying the leisure bought by the wealth she and funny boy had gotten from the *gealan* stones they managed to collect. But no; she had to have her adventures: traveling, meeting people, experiencing strange intimate rituals, trying new dishes and drinks, indulging in the latest fashions, tweaking history and culture to her satisfaction—and moving on when it began to bore her. She was not one to sit back and let life come to her; she was always a grabber, he had said a few times after high school.

What was his name?

Sebastian!

He goes by Set-d'Elous on this world, she reminded herself.

When she and her children arrived in the next town she would take a few days to recuperate, then try to catch the KOHAX to one of the larger cities where she still might have property and start over again. A new life. The next of many. The first of many more. Plenty of time to reinvent herself.

"Mama, my feet hurt so much," said the yellow-haired girl of fifteen Ghoupalle years, appearing to be eight in Earth years.

"I know, Zaura dear," replied Gina, holding back her own complaints, "I know. Just a little more. Then we'll be there."

"I want to go home," said the girl.

"I know," said her mother. "This is what happens when Mama picks the wrong tangent. I'm sorry. We were off by a millimeter or two."

❋ ❋ ❋

Thank goodness she saw them before they saw her, thought Gina. She quickly hid her children safely between the rocks, instructing them to stay there and remain quiet. She assured them she would get some food. Probably the camp she spotted ahead would have some. She would have to barter for it, of course. Yet she was a few days past the last ration and her children were suffering.

It seemed to be a work camp. Mining. There was a big pit and an orange glow arose from within it.

With the evening skies darkening, they did not see her immediately. She got to within twenty steps before one of the men turned, saw her, and jumped to his feet. The other four remained sitting around the silver box which emitted a cooling breeze to dispel the natural heat of the air.

"Greetings, kind gentlemen," she spoke in Ghoupallêan. "I have crossed this desert for many days. I hope I can beg for some food from you."

They seemed not to understand her.

"I know some Ghoupallêan," said the man who was standing. She noted his accent but nodded to be polite.

He was taller than her by a head, and like the others wore a tight-fitting yellowish coverall, dirty from digging in the soil. They each had utility belts on and tools hanging from them and small compartments for other things. Their boots were black and reached to their knees. Three of the men who were sitting had long moustaches that drooped to their collars, one man's was braided.

The man who stood, whom she presumed to be the one in charge, stroked his long goatee, looking her over.

"Do you have some food for me?" she asked again.

"What do you have to exchange?"

"I thought you would have mercy on a lost traveler."

"Therefore you will soon die if I do not help?"

"Please help me." She was actually desperate yet she also knew how to play the game. Remain calm. Be pleasant.

The leader glanced around the circle of his co-workers, then back at her.

"We are lost travelers, too." He laughed and the others joined in, despite not likely knowing what he said.

"True? You look like miners."

"We are miners. We are collecting *Tarê-mag*. Big market for it these days."

She perked up. "What is that ore?"

The man shook his head. "I don't know what it is, only it brings us a lot of credit in the city."

"So you don't work for a mining company?"

"We work for a company. Our shift is finished in two days. Then another team arrives. Never stops, this digging."

"What is it for?"

"I only heard it's used as fuel. Very sophisticated engines. To go to the stars."

"For spacecraft?"

He drew a blank. Had she used a word not yet invented?

"Is the fuel for ships that go into the sky?"

"I haven't seen it myself but I think so. It's the latest project to waste our taxes." He pointed behind himself, extending his arm to the far horizon where the distant spires of a city could be seen in daylight. "I'm actually glad to be on-site and away from all the madness destroying the city."

He went on to describe his life there and eventually waved her to take a seat with them.

"I'm Ralad-Mekmelus, if you want my label."

"Jinetta..." She thought for a moment. "...d'Elous."

"Odd name. Like the legendary warrior, eh?"

"Yes, odd."

"Sure, the buildings are tall and golden," Ralad explained, "but the streets are dirty, littered, and the stores are empty. Food and fuel are in short supply. Nobody goes to work. Nothing is repaired. All the efforts anybody gives are toward the supposed disaster coming someday, what they call the Final Day. There are prophets, of course, roaming the streets warning of the need for people to clear their lists of errors with the local spiritual guide, or join a cult that will assure they are somehow whisked away just in time. The government is split between maximum hedonism, supping at the public trough, and the frustration of trying to lead a populace lost in despair to actually do something productive about the Final Day. The city is full of talk."

"And what is that?" asked Gina, noticing the other men's eyes constantly on her.

"They've seen an object in the skies," said Ralad. "Scientists say it is coming. Someday it will crash into our world. That's the Final Day. Nothing anyone can do, of course. So everyone is either living it up or praying to the seven gods and nine goddesses for salvation. Word is that Goddess Memitha is no longer listening."

"Yes, Memitha is fickle," Gina said with a huff. "I've dealt with her myself. Very unpleasant woman, if you ask me."

"So the government has pushed a new drug program on the people," he continued. "To control their anxiety, make them calm and not worry about the Final Day."

"What else can they do?"

"Supposedly it's sanctioned by Second God Aronk. He always likes the dream land."

"The dream land, you say?"

"Or it's all a lie. In the city, pharmacies are doing brisk business, most on government subsidies. With many people no longer caring to go to their jobs, the economy is collapsing. The only well-paying jobs remaining are those in government service. And most of those are either in science or engineering. The First Directors all live lavishly enough, but everyone else is in squalor, waiting for the end. Pity, them. So those who sit at mining sites have it easy—except for the heat."

"It is strangely hot," she said, nodding and wiping sweat from her throat, "as though the climate zone has shifted."

"This used to be cropland as far as you could see, but when the news broke people didn't care and nobody tended the fields, the crops died, the groceries were bare, and people starved. At least we get food rations being out here. We are 'essential services' so we get the rations. We pull about 30 to 40 units of ore out each cycle—the best rate of any team."

"And the ore is converted for use as fuel?" asked Gina.

"Possibly."

He described the plans the government had yet to implement. There was so much debate, after all. Everyone had an opinion. Philosophers were concerned about the implications of every option. Scientists weighed in on what was possible within the bounds of physics and astronomy. Engineers discussed what was logistically possible. Administrators wanted to maintain their power and control. The general population did not seem to care one way or another.

"We all die sometime, somehow," Ralad said. "Let it be in a big bang, I say. Let me drink until my belly bursts, and I'll watch it come crashing down!"

His coworkers laughed, evidently understanding some of his Ghoupallêan words.

"Tell me more about the drug culture," she asked. If she were going into the city with her children, she needed to be concerned about violence from drug-crazed packs of vagrants. "Are they violent? Do they rape and pillage? Murder indiscriminately?"

"No—far from it," he replied with a laugh. "The drugs calm people, make them slow-witted and docile. They've got the new *bôb* class of suppressors—I think that's the right word. They suppress the natural urge to act. You lose your motivation to do anything—"

"Like marijuana," she mumbled in English, the word just popping into her head. She had a flash of her college days back on Earth, the endless parties, all of the intellectual vagabonds she hung out with, exchanging clever rants for recreational sex. Suddenly she recalled how that boy, that once and future lover, Sebastian, had chastised her for messing with her head. He wanted her to stay sharp so they could solve the riddle of the interdimensional doorway. Then they solved it. Now look where she was!

"There's blue-*bôb* which makes you feel a pleasant sadness, what some people call 'bittersweet'—or a feeling of happiness like after your lover departs for a good new job far away and you won't see her ever again but you're happy for her. Green-*bôb* makes you smile at things like clouds and flowers and small animals. Orange-*bôb* makes you feel like dancing, pulls up energy that overwhelms any sense of woe you may have. The strongest is black-*bôb*, which makes you want to recline and go into some kind of dream land—then you don't dream, or the dreams are only some kind of weird light display. It's beautiful but your brain is dead during it."

"Are the drugs required? Are there drug police?"

"Only if you are on a list. If you caused trouble previously, then you are given a dose to maintain. You have to wear a special bracelet. Otherwise, it's voluntary. Most people are on some kind of *bôb*." He waved his hand around the circle. "We don't get any drugs. Else we couldn't do our jobs. When I return to the city, I only pretend to be out of my mind, just so people leave me alone. My wife, however, she is hooked on *bôb*. She stays on her back, staring at the ceiling, having her dreams, always smiling."

"I'm sorry for that."

He smiled half-heartedly, perhaps embarrassed to reveal the private information. "So it's been a while."

"A while...?"

"For sex."

She took a deep breath and glanced at the others. They understood. Grins greeted her: excited, worried, regretful, curious. Lustful.

"You said you wanted food," Ralad spoke after a moment. "Our rations are measured. If we give up a meal, we need to get something in exchange. What else can you offer?"

"Witty conversation?"

"We've done that. Not worth a food ration." He smiled politely. "We are five. If we each give you a ration then you have enough for five days. It will take you five days to walk to the city. It's a fair barter."

Gina pursed her lips. "Sex for food. Just like cavemen. The barter system." She stared at Ralad, noticed his soft, puppy-dog eyes. "If you came to me starving and asked for food, I wouldn't insist you give me sex. In fact, I'd probably be disgusted at the thought of it. So I would take mercy on you and give you the food."

"I'm not disgusted with the thought, lady...Jinetta, or whatever your name is. It's the reality of the situation."

"Is that the situation?"

"We could simply take you against your will and not give you any rations after," he said in a lower voice, "but we are not savages."

She studied each of their faces, glaring at them, trying to make them feel guilt or shame at their intentions. Her children were hidden among the rocks, vulnerable to toxic gases and wild animals, prickly plants and stinging insects. They were hungry, perhaps undernourished by now. She could go on further herself, but she had the children to care for.

"It's easy," said Ralad. "We will be gentle if you don't fight us. Then we will give you food."

Her eyes fell upon the sleeping packs as her stomach made a noise.

Chapter 22

The Greater Good

The city, she discovered as she approached, was the giant metropolis of Kobarêl, finding first a road and later a sign. Initially surprised at her location being in a nation of the eastern continent, she was now more concerned about the time. The year was 2131, the furthest into the future she had ever been on Ghoupallesz. It was a mistake, of course, but now that she was here, with her daughter and son in tow, she had first to see to their health and comfort. Then she could work on finding a tangent leading them back to a more familiar time zone, perhaps in the mid-1500s, when life was grand.

The land she found herself in was harsh, hostile, and looked like a painter's smeared version of Hell. Nothing like she would have expected for the largest metropolis on the eastern side of the great landmass, her beloved continent of Zissekap on the western side. She knew Kobarêl only from news reports and some geography books. The nation spread along the southern coast of the Jassera Sea. The north coast held the nation of Ghoupallæssus where she had spent much of her time, especially in the city of Siti. Being on the southern coast, she expected subtropical heat, however, she also expected jungle—not the rocky, fruitless plain. In the future, the planet would become hotter, she took note, and croplands would die.

And something would fall from the sky. That's what the miner

Ralad-Mekmelus had told her. The idea had caused mass hysteria in the city. Yet she dared to enter it, seeking a temporary home. What could she trade for shelter and food? She had knowledge of physics, engineering, linguistics, and she was once a queen. She had a small pouch of *gealan* stones hidden under the last of the five food ration packs in her knapsack, but were they worth anything in this day and age? Food, shelter, then try to understand what the madness was all about.

They came to what used to be a moving walkway but it was broken and stationary so they continued along its silent track, deep into the city where the streets were littered with trash, old ETURS, and the grime of industrialization. Looking up, however, Gina could see where the towers rose above the pollution and gleamed golden in the sunlight. The buildings lining the empty streets around her were of brick and stone, ancient by their design, no windows below the third level and many above that level broken and sprouting spontaneous growths of vines and moss, able to suck moisture from the thick air that choked the city.

Gina tore a strip of cloth from the hem of her gown and used it as a mask. Then made two others for the children. Everywhere she went people wore better masks, hunched over, hurrying along, apparently unwilling to be outdoors any longer than necessary. The city smelled rank, like decay, death, and the dream of the end days she once had. And she had walked into it!

Every storefront was battered, broken, abandoned. Signs showed where restaurants had operated, clothing had been sold, scrolls had been for sale, where one could talk with a psychic or a physician or a spiritual adviser, where feet could be massaged, where children could have their intelligence measured, where balloons could be inflated, where feathers could be cleaned, where hands could be sanitized, where a sex partner could be arranged, where the works of famous poets and playwrights could be heard spoken in character by actors, where communication with the city's maintenance personnel, record-keepers, or even administrators could be initiated, where hair could be styled, elbows scented, or undergarments exchanged. A normal city once upon a time. Now it was forlorn and she wondered how many people still lived within its boundary.

Suddenly, a loud horn blew, like a factory being dismissed, and the low-pitched roar filled the streets. After a moment, she had to cover her children's ears. As they were about to succumb to the noise, several doors opened in the buildings along the street and dozens of people dressed in skin-tight coveralls streamed out. Their yellow and green and orange clothing was soiled with oil and dust, and they wore breathing masks over their noses and mouths. As they exited the buildings, they pulled off the masks. Some milled about, others continued down the street. None of them smiled. If the work day had ended, they did not seem glad of it. Or heading home. Perhaps only a lunch break, thought Gina.

One of the men milling about, chatting with another man and a woman, noticed her and the children standing nearby and stared at them. After a moment, his companions also turned to regard the woman standing with the girl and holding the young boy in her arms.

"You looking for work?" he said in a stern voice.

Gina had never considered that option. She was merely finding her way through the city, hoping to come to a neighborhood where she felt safe, where her children could be healthy. She thought the man was a kind sort of fellow so she nodded.

"Go to the door on the opposite side of this building. You can register there and maybe they will hire you. It's dirty work but you get food rations."

"Thank you."

She led the children away, turning the corner, finding the door for registration.

"What kind of work is it?" she asked the old woman in the pink uniform—once pink, now dull and soiled—sitting behind the window.

"This is a factory. We make parts for the flying ships the government engineers are building. You know anything about making parts?"

Gina grinned. "I think I could do it. I studied engineering for a couple semesters in college." She only meant it as a joke, but speaking in Ghoupallêan, her words sounded presumptuous.

The old woman in the once-pink uniform gave her a sharper look.

"You are a student of the Academy?" She glanced at the

children. "Yet you have offspring."

"I once was a student. I had to leave it. War came. I had to leave. Then I had these children."

"Can you swear you studied engineering?"

"I can swear that. And physics. Languages, too. There is a lot I can do. I'll show you."

"Let me call a director to meet you."

✳ ✻ ✳

The first task Gina was assigned was to put the small silver disk squarely into the slightly larger silver tube and insert a pin. Then make sure the disk would spin freely within the confines of the tube. Once satisfied, she put the item back on the moving conveyor and turned her attention to making another one. One after another, all day. It had a complicated scientific-engineering-astrophysics name she hated trying to say. Part 17-A-67009 was what she called it instead.

The third day, she learned from her co-workers that they were all helping to build a flying vessel that would carry a thousand people to another world.

After a few months of making that part she was advanced to a more complex part, then again after a few weeks to a very sophisticated part which earned her the right to sit at a table covered with tiny boxes of tiny parts and assemble Part 8518-G-161695 one after another. In a typical shift of 80 *peth*—a *peth* equaled about 18 minutes, she kept teaching her children so they would be prepared for life back on Earth—she could produce between 90 and 100 of the devices, each consisting of 38 components. She had no idea how the part was used but she was good at making them and won praise from her supervisor.

At least she was able to get work, earn food rations if no wages, and have a quaint place for her and her children to sleep at night. They were given a factory cubicle, two mats and bowls for food rations, and towels for use in the communal washroom down the corridor.

Her children were too tired to misbehave. Zaura, the normally precocious blonde girl, was happy to have her days occupied in learning. Xix, the boy who was an accident of her escape journey and who was dull and expressionless, had both been assigned to a factory-connected education facility. More like indoctrination, thought Gina, but she had no choice in this society. Her children would be taught what they needed to know to be good factory workers, nothing more. Schools did not meet formally any longer; instead, educated volunteers from among the directors' children taught what knowledge and skills would be needed in the future aboard the vehicles that would save them from annihilation. They were taught gardening, mostly. Boys were drilled in engineering skills, and girls were taught the wonders of fertilization and reproduction. It was believed that every maiden would need to produce five offspring, preferably by five different males, in order to continue the community once they all settled on a new world.

The great *xænafi*—'ether ship'—would take them there. It was believed by most that outer space was filled with an invisible substance called *xæ* through which a vessel would move with some resistance. An old tradition. Yet the name stuck: *xænafi*, or in the meta-sense of a multigenerational spaceship, the honorific was applied, thus *xænafaxii* was used to refer to the whole project to save Ghoupalle-kind from an undeserved fate.

The schools also taught the proper use of the colored *bôb* medication system, to which she secretly objected. She needed to keep her wits and focus on her delicate tasks. No room for sedation or anti-depression drugs or something to feign comatose calmness for the anxiety-prone in the city. Regular warnings were sounded throughout the day via the public communications system: "If you feel troubled, now is the time to pop a *bôb*" or "Administration recommends black-*bôb* today; if you do not have black-*bôb* available, two blue-*bôb* will be sufficient to get you through today's anxiety" and "Due to the latest astronomical report, Administration recommends popping one black-*bôb* now and a second black-*bôb* after the evening meal for maximum calm." Often right in the middle of the shift a co-worker would break down and sob, overcome by thoughts of the end days.

No, they can't have the population in a panic.

She remembered her first day on the job when as soon as she stepped outdoors a coworker directed her attention to the sign advising her to pop a white-*bôb* now and a green-*bôb* after the evening meal. There was not much for an evening meal, anyway, consisting of tubes of this, crisps of that, something labeled 'vegetable substance' and another labeled 'hearty grain' that looked like someone's vomit. Worse tasting than the food rations she had bartered for with those five miners a year before. The green-*bôb* also repressed hunger, thankfully. That schedule was to be followed with a red-*bôb* after the morning meal and a pink-*bôb* upon arriving at one's work station. Of course, she did none of that and lied about her consumption patterns. It was voluntary although when properly *bôb*bed the average worker could meet maximum production and thus gain recognition and promotion— and extra food rations.

She worried what her children were being taught about the drugs, however. The school provided miniature dosages of blue- and green-*bôb*, and purple-*bôb* was recommended for unruly children. They had tried silver-*bôb* with her son, trying to spark him out of his innate dullness, but he remained unresponsive. Teachers remarked on his larger than normal head and lack of hair. One of them believed he resembled, especially with his olive skin, one of the so-called 'miracle children' which legend had foretold for the end times. Other teachers thought he was wasting resources and suggested to Gina that he be put to sleep. She feared for him, wondering which day an accident might befall him.

Someday soon, she would have to leave, she knew, her fingers assembling the parts automatically. She had stumbled into this world through the wrong tangent and now that she was, as it were, back on her feet, she needed to keep moving. So what if the people around her were doomed? She did not need to be here to witness it. So what if they were convinced a comet was on its way to destroy the planet? She could escape with her children—back to an earlier age here on Ghoupallesz, well before any comet would arrive, or all the way back to Earth. Zaura could fit in easily there; she was an accurate copy of her mother: smart and golden blond. Her son Xix, however, would likely be deemed mentally disabled and not have much of a life on Ghoupallesz or on Earth. People would be kinder to him on Earth, she considered.

But where to find the tangent to exit this place of doom?

❋ ❋ ❋

Halfway through her third year in Kobarêl, Gina was recognized for her efficient work, innovative suggestions, and strong work ethic. With a special red ribbon affixed to her work coveralls, she was promoted to manager of the section. At the end of the next year, she was assigned as supervisor over several managers. When she rewrote the design plans for a whole system assembly, she was introduced to the director of the plant. Recognizing her sharp mind, he sponsored her civil service exam, which she passed with a top score. Returning, she was asked to work alongside the director and immediately had her own office on the thirty-fourth level of the main building in the Homeland Project compound. One day, she was called to a meeting in the director's office.

From the windows near the top of the tower she could see far out to sea, including the peninsula pushing north from the mainland. And cutting the horizon in half was another tower, narrower yet just as impressive, rising high into the sky, held upright by a massive network of cables.

"It goes to the edge of space," came the answer to the question she was wondering. "They are hoisting the products we make up there for assembly. Someday the vessel will be completed."

She turned from the window and regarded the man there. Her boss was dressed in a long, dark blue suit falling to his knees with red collar and some kind of authority logo attached to his left shoulder and a personal identification card attached to his right shoulder. It was some kind of uniform, and in this city, in this age, everyone had a place and every place had its uniform. She wore only a simple robe, mostly white with a light green pattern woven through it. Very feminine, which the men liked and the women thought unprofessional. That dress and her golden hair: shoulder-length which was quite uncustomary among the efficiently coiffured residents who kept theirs very short. She reminded him of springtime, he had said upon first meeting her.

Now she was respected and welcomed no matter how she dressed or wore her hair.

"It's been two years since you joined us here in the Design Office, and work progresses steadily with your help," said First Director Atox-Dassel, placing a hand on her bare shoulder. "If our days now were as they once were, we could celebrate your promotion with a lavish dinner. Now we have rationing. As it is, I can only offer you my praise for your work and authorize additional rations for you and your family."

"Thank you," said Gina. "That is enough. What more do I need if everything will end soon?"

"You have an attitude that is both refreshingly dire and strangely joyful," Dassel spoke softly, placing his other hand on her other shoulder. "You are a remarkable woman. I've said that almost every day since you arrived in our office."

"I'm glad to be of service."

He smiled, then grabbed her, wrapping her in an embrace that cut off her breath. She was expecting it; he was often affectionate with her when they were alone and, for lack of any other source of emotional connection, she welcomed his touch.

"I apologize," he said when he released her. "I lost control of my emotions. I've run out of my supply of brown-*bôb*, I'm embarrassed to say."

"They say you can take two white-*bôb* and get the same effect."

"Truly I shouldn't need any of them, but in our work...we work so closely with the reality of the situation...."

"The comet?"

"Yes."

"That is the reality of our situation."

"Our astronomers measure its route more precisely the closer it comes and we know its destination."

"I understand. It's overwhelming. I'm working as hard as I can to get things ready...for...the Final Day."

"We have forty years," he said, and wiped a tear from his eye. He grinned sheepishly. "I must get to the pharmacy today." He gazed at her a moment. "However, I want to give you a new assignment. I want to move you to the Homeland Project."

"Seriously?" She smiled, eyes widening. "I'm not finished with the orbiter specifications. Nor the—"

"We can proceed without your daily supervision now. We need you to work with our astrobiologists to find a suitable destination for the vessels we build. You know the plan: first, construct the transport frames, then the residential pods, then dock the pods to the frames, break orbit, and head to whatever destination your team will find for us." He clasped her shoulders again, thumbs pressing into her skin. "I'm putting you in charge—with your promotion to Second Director of the Homeland Project. Use your knowledge of other worlds to pick a good one for us. For this, you will get a boarding ticket for you and your family."

She did not know what to say. For a few years she had been biding her time until she could discover a tangent to take her home. Then she found a purpose for her life in Kobarêl and applied herself. Now she was needed, really needed, to save them. It was time to be a goddess.

"I'll do my best, First Director."

PART FOUR

FINAL TESTAMENT

OF

THE PLANETARY GOVERNING COUNCIL OF GHOUPALLESZ

(ALSO KNOWN AS DANID-TA, FRU'PÊ, GAU, BOK-1,
NOVON-MELISSIT, ROU'OL'HE, OUQ, & 'M)

THIS FINAL DAY OF GHOUPALLE YEAR 2175 (OLD CALENDAR 9475),
THE PERIOD OF BATOU ON DAY 22.

WE AWAIT THE ARRIVAL OF VENGEFUL GODS, WICKED GODDESSES,
THE LEGIONS OF DEMONS, THE HORDES OF EVIL-ONES, AND
THE TERRIBLE LIGHT.

In Ghoupalle year 2130 scientists first became aware that a threat existed to the continuation of the planet. A comet (later named *Xôsz*) was discovered to have a diminishing trajectory that would conclude in a planetary collision. At first all hope was lost; the state of technology at that time did not provide very much encouragement to engineers. It was difficult to believe they could develop a program to construct a fleet of interplanetary vessels suitable for evacuating as much of the population as possible. Moreover, many argued that the collision would be survivable. Some argued that it would be enough to move underground and return to the surface several years after. There were still other plans, guided as much by science as by religion. In the critical years, one Ghoupalle arose to command the planet's resources and lead an international consortium of scientists, engineers, and administrators to work together to create multiple avenues of solutions: First Director Jinetta-d'Elous of the International Aerospace Council was a key person in the history of the final years of the planet....

Chapter 23

Science

Because Second Director Jinetta-d'Elous had so impressed her superiors with her knowledge of astrophysics and engineering, she was sent to represent Kobarêl at the annual conference of aerospace consortiums. She wore a sparkling bronze ankle-length robe with the long red sash as a mark of her rank. She took her seat in the upper section of the airship gondola and watched the lime-hued clouds along the horizon as the silver airship separated from its tether and turned northward for the trip across the sea, destination Siti, her old stomping grounds centuries before.

Gina had no idea what she would find in Siti; she had no time for sightseeing anyway. The conference was much too important to take it as a frivolous get-together of scientists. With other spaceports under construction across the planet, it became desirable to attempt to coordinate their efforts. At the conference they could compare notes, arrange to combine their collective work to better save what portion of the population they could. She felt she was humoring them, however. She would say what she knew, most of it from college classes long ago, and hope they could develop a workable plan before she had to leave via the nearest interdimensional doorway—which, after five years, she still had failed to locate anywhere around Kobarêl.

Flying on an airship, she sighed. How quaint! Steam power still ran most things in the city. How would they ever hope to quickly gain the expertise to construct a spacecraft capable of interstellar travel? Much less one that could provide living quarters for four hundred lucky survivors! First Director Toulor-Jurrand had explained to her they had several futuristic plans on drawing boards and hidden in archives. Those plans were sufficiently advanced, yet they had never been constructed because they would be harmful to the environment. What plans? she had asked. Flying machines that could go from continent to continent without refueling. A vehicle that could sail around the entire planet and enable passengers to look down and predict weather patterns. Yes, wonderful uses. Not needed.

Until now, she had argued. Jurrand told her how the flying machine would burn fuels based on petroleum derivatives, an expensive extraction and distillation process. There would also be pollution of the atmosphere. The airship system was far more effective in transporting people from country to country. Yes, you're right, she responded, but now these advanced devices were needed. Please let there be advanced engineering plans ready for construction, she prayed to the seven gods and nine goddesses, just in case they were listening.

At the conference she hoped to see some actual plans for interstellar spacecraft, theoretical as they may be. Working in the parts factory had not enabled her to imagine the final product. Prototypes. Test vehicles. Working out the kinks. If everyone were onboard with the idea, of course, then things could advance quicker.

There was a fair amount of religious resistance, however; many believed they should accept their fate as payback for lives not well lived. Others believed the gods and goddesses would snatch them away at the last instance and place them in a paradise above the clouds. The scientists had better plans. Some postulated a tethered gondola of survivors who would float far above while waiting out the destruction on the surface. They would then descend to live once more on the planet. Others believed the destruction would be too critical for any successful resettlement and thus proposed temporary colonization of Gouo, the distant and frigid second planet. Few were thinking at that time of any permanent removal from the planet, much less colonization of new planets.

Gina did not have access to all the data and so could not make any judgments. Her area was astrobiology, which amused her because only she knew how little she had paid attention during those classes. Still, she had read the books. Finding inhabitable planets was already forcing her to scan through pages and pages of data printouts for days on end—and on Ghoupallesz the days were almost 30 Earth hours. After months of work, she had rejected the two closest stellar systems: neither had potentially inhabitable planets. A third system had possibilities: perhaps three planets in the comfort zone. That system was seventeen light years distant. Could these people who flew airships make even a 170-year journey at the impossible pace of one-tenth light speed? She was just there to humor them, she reminded herself. Then she would return to Kobarêl and continue the search for a suitable tangent through which her and her children would exit.

She slept soundly at the inn arranged for her, guarded from the midnight vagabonds. Conference attendees had been warned of the crime and local pockets of cannibalism, and were shuttled from the airship terminal under armed escort. So much for casual sightseeing of her old neighborhood. She and the other scientists were too valuable to risk being attacked by the crazed masses who were not addicted to the *bôb* drugs. The Siti government council, bless their kind hearts, believed it was unethical to force or compel its citizens to take drugs, no matter how much fury they were then forced to endure.

In the night she dreamed of a mountain hideaway, a soft bed, and golden morning light awakening her. And there was that boy, Sebastian, sitting on the floor beside the *qala*, watching her sleep. He looked so young and handsome. 'Ready to rise?' he cooed and she happily yawned. They spent the day frolicking through the daisies, or whatever those flowers were called on Ghoupallesz. And every moment they danced in delight she could see the twin peaks of Mount Jilam rising in the corner of one eye or the other. She knew where she was: Kipzon—in the house they had found after Sebastian rescued her from the castle of the Zetin warlord. But then, as she awoke with a start, lost in the darkness of her room, she knew the team of Zetin assassins would soon arrive—

The hallways of the Grand Palace, long ago the royal residence, were crowded and the din was unpleasant. She was swept along with the crowds, ushered into a special chamber where speakers could rest before going on stage. She wondered if this one could possibly be the notorious anteroom where the Emperor of Sekuate was assassinated in 1533; she had been in the audience awaiting his speech when the unexpected announcement came. Later she heard the Empress had also been assassinated in her bed that same morning. She had no love for the royal couple, anyway, being at that time the wife of the Tebbi prime minister and their two countries at war.

She had not spoken before crowds since her days as the Queen of Fenula. That was back in...1440? Seven hundred years earlier! Her heart fluttered. No one would remember her: a minor person in a minor kingdom ages in the past, long before rockets were imagined or comets detected. Yet she was not nervous. She had been speaking Ghoupallêan all of her adult life—that is, through several lives lived in various places around the planet. And she had reviewed all the information available in her subject area. She was ready when they called her name and introduced her as First Director of Engineering at the Kobarêl Science Commission. It was a mistake; she was only Second Director, and only recently promoted from Third Director, at that. And she actually led the Homeland Project which was a subsidiary of the Kobarêl Science Commission. Close enough for doomsday.

"We come together," she continued calmly after giving them an overview of the situation, leaving many in the stunned audience murmuring, "to discuss possible solutions, which seem to be of three kinds. The first follows the belief that destruction will be limited and can be overcome in time. Therefore, we need only be off the surface for a number of years. That would require a fleet of residential arks to orbit the planet. The second solution supposes greater destruction and thus a longer removal from the planet. Second planet Gouo is the obvious choice although it is unsuitable for permanent habitation. Perhaps five years could be eked out of a stay there. The third solution accepts that the planet will be unable to be inhabited again after the destruction. That is to say, no planet would remain, at least not in any condition like the way we know it today. Therefore, we would need to have vessels that are capable of proceeding to other inhabitable planets outside of our system. Such vessels would need to be of two kinds. The first would have an active crew, perhaps multi-generational, living aboard. The second would be composed of sleeping passengers who would be awakened only when arriving at an inhabitable planet. This last solution also supposes that any inhabitable planet located should not already possess an intelligent race with whom we would have conflicts. The journey could be endless—yet we would live a while longer compared to sitting back and accepting the light show the seven gods and nine goddesses have planned for us."

The murmuring rose for a while and she stared down the stern faces on the front rows. They knew she was serious. Others eventually did, too, and silence soon filled the hall. She looked out at the crowd of puzzled faces, thinking of Yuri Gagarin stuffed into the Vostok capsule, sailing around Earth in 1961, and Alan Shepherd and John Glenn squeezed into their Mercury capsules, and President Kennedy vowing to put a man on the moon before the end of the decade. Ten years and they did it. Of course, the moon was there, always in sight to tempt them, luring them, being a target for them. There was no moon orbiting Ghoupallesz, nothing to gaze at in the night sky, nothing to serve as a practice run. To the best of her knowledge, no human had ever been launched into space from Ghoupallesz. And here it was 2144 already and the need had come dramatically upon them.

"I believe it can be done," she spoke at last. "If we pull together, pool our resources, work hard and quickly, we may be able to save some of us—which, I would think, is a better proposition than none of us."

Several in the audience stood and waved an arm to call for recognition. Three of them received the talking staff in turn.

"You obviously have an agenda," said the bald man in the red kaftan, "one which does not fit a variety of beliefs some of us here have. For example, will this god-sent element actually strike our planet or will it merely pass closely? It may be only a warning."

"Is this a judgment of our gods and goddesses?" asked a short, plump man in a dark blue suit with gold epaulets. "And should we interfere with their judgment?"

"You seem to ignore what the majority of us believe," said the woman with red hair piled high on her head, a large, green shawl wrapped around her shoulders that covered her entire body.

"The F'eng knew many centuries ago that this flying light was supposed to be welcomed by us. You try to stand in the way of the F'eng and you shall perish!"

The crowd roared in rebuttal. The chairperson flashed the lights to calm them.

"People of science! Let us fill the room with calm!"

"I have seen the data," Gina spoke when the room was still. "The trajectory is clear. I cannot say it will strike yet I cannot say with certainty that it only will pass at close range. If not this passage then the next one will be our doom. As we gather here, the comet is on the far side of Abæda, and from that point we calculate its arrival in our vicinity again in the year 2167—"

"How can we be ready in time?" someone shouted.

Others attempted to shout their answers and the hall filled with noise again.

When order was restored, Gina continued explaining the options. She seemed to convince a majority of those gathered that the best course of action was to plan for the worst. That meant a fleet of interstellar transports carrying residential pods. If they did not need to evacuate, the vessels could be used for space exploration, a worthy project in its own right. She told about the space center on the peninsula north of Kobarêl, how a space elevator had been constructed and how parts were hoisted up to the edge of the sky for assembly in orbit. A prototype transport frame was nearing completion. On the ground, residential pods were under construction. The main problem with the transport frame was the coupling for the residential pod. The main problem for the residential pod was maintaining the fertility of the replicating gardens to be placed aboard. Yet these problems would be solved soon. The audience sat in stunned silence.

Meanwhile, she explained during the next three *peth*—long enough that the audience should have become restless but did not—she noted how other sites were under development, almost as though each continent decided to save itself and not tell anyone else.

"We need to share our ideas and be as efficient as we can be," she repeated.

Typeg was building a nuclear pulse propulsion system for a long-frame vessel, while the facility at Herêbout was coming up with long-range sleeping docks. These needed to be combined. Even Majjer on the continent south of Kobarêl and Aikavo on the continent of Bæronak were involved in projects.

"None of you would let us aboard your vessels," cried the ambassador, "so we built our own vessel. It will carry eight hundred in sleep and a crew of ninety. Even now we have begun the application process for passengers."

"The rich and famous will be first, I fear!" shouted someone.

"Not true! We seek those who are skilled in every activity we will need while engaged in travel and upon reaching a new homeland."

Gina assured them that some balance needed to be maintained to keep nepotism at bay and still provide for a fully stocked population. Suddenly she could imagine the riots that would destroy the cities long before the comet could destroy the planet, and she shuddered. She knew that with her high rank, she would get a seat. Possibly her children, as well. By the time the comet arrived, they would be adults and subject to the same selection process as everyone else. And she was still hoping to find an easy tangent to exploit in escape—

"There is revelation that the Miracle Children will come forth soon to sweep away the danger," the F'eng follower shouted. "There is news that you have one of the Miracle Children hidden away, First Director!"

Gina was horrified that anyone knew of her children. She even feared for her son's safety while she was away at this conference, yet she could do nothing.

"My son is disabled," she offered. "He is not a Miracle Child."

"So you say," shouted the F'eng follower. "In time, we all shall see. When his head bursts open, all shall be revealed. Then the F'eng shall be praised and our world will be saved! All shall rejoice when the Miracle Children reveal their message!"

By then guards were breaking through the crowd to lead the woman away.

"That is a valid option," said Gina, feigning calmness. "I do not take that option as the truth."

Some in the crowd cheered her while others remained silent.

"Most of us believe the best choice is to prepare to depart, either temporarily or permanently," said Gina. "Each region has begun construction of facilities and vessels. We are decided, it seems. Our fate has been decided. It is time to bring to bear our greatest minds and our greatest effort to save Ghoupalle-kind from doom!"

"Ghoupalles! Only the Ghoupalles?" shouted a contingent from Zetinê, bedecked with horned helmets and leather breastplates.

"All are welcome to join the space plan," Gina called to them. "We must establish quotas for each race and ethnic group. In fact, we should assign groups from tropical climes to planets orbiting the nearer side of comfort zones, and conversely cold clime populations as the Zetin to outer-edge comfort zone worlds."

"You believe we want to live in the cold? It was forced on us in ancient times!"

"We cannot change history now, Sir."

"Ghoupalle takes the perfect worlds in the middle?"

"Not at all. We can share."

"Share? As you did in centuries past? We have not forgotten the invasions!"

The hall again erupted in verbal conflict and Gina waited for order to be restored.

"Good science people, there are priorities. First, we need a means of departure. We need a means of travel. And most of all, we need a destination. Plenty of time to select who goes."

The crowd settled down as diagrams were raised behind her. Circles for orbits, colorful stars, curving trajectories, numbers marking time and distance, ratings and probabilities. She took the lightstick the chairperson handed her and held it on the circle representing Ghoupallesz—the innermost of four worlds in the system with a larger yellow star, Abæda, and a small, blue star named Siila.

She recalled a presentation she did at a science fair while in junior high school back on Earth and smiled to herself. The diagrams she drew won an award. *A Trip to Mars*, she had titled it. Now she was in the big leagues!

"These are the destinations we have found which are suitable for habitation," she spoke, pointing. "As you know, the closest stellar system to us is the Bo-Kala system, which is 8.11 'light-years' distance."

She did not actually use the words expressing the distance

light could travel in a year, but, instead, spoke the Ghoupallêan term which referred to the same distance: one *Utark*. The *Utark* was based on a mythical measurement: how far Great God Zaul's urine stream could reach after holding back all through a night of ribald excess during which he managed to drink all the wine the stars could be made to bleed. The Greeks' Zeus was a wimp next to Zaul.

"Bo-Kala has no habitable planets. Next closest is Hevou-B, 9.72 light-years distance. The triple star group makes whatever planets may exist there too hot for habitation. Kalia-14, which is 12.6 light-years distance, has two planets that could be habitable but one orbits at the inner-edge and the other at the outer-edge of the comfort zone. These three star systems exist in completely different directions from Ghoupallesz, I should note. Therefore, it would not be feasible to visit one, then the other, and so on."

Murmuring in the crowd.

"Further afield is the Tumark-C system, which is 17.54 light-years distant, where three potentially habitable planets all orbit within the comfort zone. In a different direction is the Ubo system which may have two habitable planets. Then comes Raal at 23.77, and Danida at 25.12 light-years, each system with one potentially habitable planet."

She thought of her 'beloved' Earth, surprised at the sarcastic tone of her inner voice. That planet orbited a fairly ordinary yellow star named Sol, about 101 light-years distance as the crow would fly, an impossible journey to make in the kind of space vessels her fellow scientists were likely to build. They needed to advance from steam power to nuclear fusion in 36 years or that would be the end of them.

One equation after another flashed on the screen behind her and she explained each of them. Time intervals for interstellar travel. Acceleration rates, deceleration rates. Radiation patterns. Energy fields. Gamma rays. Space dust. Shields. Lifespan. Growing food aboard. Toilets. Sleep and suspension systems. Pros and cons of having multi-generation passengers living and dying aboard. And the newest passengers: babies. Members of the audience were taking notes, some nodding, others shaking their heads. It was all impossible, the dark din seemed to concede.

She remembered her college physics classes and applied what

she recalled from them to Earth's situation. Light traveled at the speed of 186,000 miles per second. From Earth to the Moon took light 1.3 seconds. The nearest star to Earth was Proxima Centauri, 4.23 light-years away. Out from there was Barnard's Star at 6 light-years, the giant star Sirius at 8.7, and Eridani Epsilon at 10.8. Tau Ceti was 11.8, not much further. Now she was asking— indeed, hoping, expecting—the people of Ghoupallesz to voyage 17.54 light-years to find a new home. From her many years of observations on Ghoupallesz, they did not seem presently to be even as technologically advanced as Earth in the 1960s.

And then she showed schematics for residential capsules for 300 passengers in suspension and a multi-generational crew of 25 who would remain conscious, intending to live and die aboard. Suspended passengers would be awakened as needed to replace crew who died. Everything would need to be carefully calculated and strictly controlled so there would be enough food produced to feed the number of people who were active at any time. The same for air and water resources. Then she showed the blueprint for the 500 passenger pod with a crew of 55. And the giant spacecraft she called 'Voyager'—thinking of how Sebastian had dubbed the two of them interdimensional voyagers once they realized and accepted that they had walked out of that quarry in Missouri to another world. Voyager was intended to be home for one thousand passengers and crew, all conscious and living their lifespans as they traveled to their destination. The energy and food demands were huge, of course, but it was presented as an alternative.

"What say you?" she asked the membership. "Our decision should be toward evacuating as many living citizens of this planet as possible, either as active passengers or in suspension, or both."

She then presented the idea of an embryo craft, a nursery sailing into the void.

"It's not cruel," she retorted to the suggestion from the audience. "It is a way to save yet more of our species. The fate they will find has a greater chance of a positive outcome than leaving them on the surface when the comet arrives."

As she explained new diagrams of propulsions systems, she could not keep out of her mind thoughts of deep space, of alien monsters, hostile races, hungry species, and all of the floating rocks along the way. Was it an impossible mission, after all? Perhaps the F'eng followers had the right response: sit down and enjoy the light show up to the final breath.

Still, if the vessel could average even ten percent of light-speed, she contemplated, that would be enough to reach Proxima Centauri from Earth in, say, forty years. Nuclear power was available on Ghoupallesz yet they had not put much faith in it and never applied it to urban energy generation. Sized to a high-rise building as a trailing power module, it could drive (or 'push') the vessel ahead at a good clip. Getting there as quickly as possible was not necessarily the most important factor to consider—

Velocity available as a function of exhaust projection and mass ratio, she reminded herself, the ratio of initial fuel to final fuel mass.... Her head was hurting but the equations were clicking like wildfire and she was excited by the math burning through her brain.

Accelerating at $1g$ for one year, a vessel would almost reach the speed of light. She smiled. A vessel limited to a peak acceleration of $0.001g$ would take 500 years to reach maximum velocity. *How far was Tumark-C?* The current state-of-the-art high-velocity ion-drive technology could reach speeds of—

She turned to the projectionist, waved him to stop.

"It is possible to do this," she spoke clearly, barely able to contain her excitement. "We have enough time and we have enough resources. We have all the scientists, engineers, and technicians we need. And we have a workforce. We can do it—"

"Who will be in charge of this project?" cried a man who stood in the back of the hall. He wore a large brown hat made of fur. To Gina, he seemed like a big, furry bison. "We have everything you said but the workforce! How can we press people into service when there will be no room for them aboard the very vessels they are building? How can we make that choice?"

He lumbered down the aisle and stood before the stage, large hands and arms raised and the wide black sleeves of his Nouvan uniform drooping to his hips.

"You speak of plans to leave the world of our birth and find a new home," said the bison man. "We are one billion people on this world and you speak of vessels that will each carry five hundred of us. How many vessels can be built? How many people can be saved? Who will make these decisions? You? Your council?"

"Yes, we need to address that problem—"

"Already," yelled the bison man delegate from Nouvê, "we have riots in the streets of Erit. We fight to keep back the lost legions from our construction zone. They have given up, destroying all they can before the comet can do it. They live all the pleasures they can find and pray for the end to come quickly. And they will not put in any work."

Gina leaned over the lectern. "It's a difficult point we are at—"

"She will be saved!" shouted another woman in the robes of F'eng followers. "She has the Miracle Child to buy her ticket."

"I won't be going!" Gina shouted back.

The crowd became boisterous, tossing questions at her so thickly she could not understand any of them.

At that moment, she wanted to reach out her hand and poke the air, pry open a gap and step through it to any other place in the universe. If it could lead her home, to that forgotten place where her body was born, that could be a nice vacation. The last time she set foot on Earth, she had found a shopping center newly built where before had been a forest, pasture, and large granite boulders. She had browsed the Barnes & Noble store in the strip mall, leafed through some science magazines and bought a latté. She read about the Space Shuttle program and the International Space Station. With some regret over the end of the Apollo Moon program, she was pleased that facilities were constructed as the start to what she expected would be a permanent station on the Moon and then an expedition to Mars. Let someone else make the decisions and she would happily sit back and watch it all on TV. She realized then how much she missed television; not the shows themselves which were poor excuses for time-killing, but simply having the leisure to sit back and watch a device which showed moving images, a machine that sucked out the gloom and eased a fractured mind into some sort of solace—

"Enough questions!" she cried out, swinging her hands over her head. The chairperson was turning the lights off and on until the murmuring dropped. "I want to make this plan a success. I love this world, no matter the things that have happened to me here." She took a breath, realizing she was about to say too much. "I love Ghoupallesz, and if I cannot save a planet I will save as many of its living things as possible. In the time which remains, I will do everything I can, use all the knowledge and skills I have, all for the hope that you, some of you, and your families, and the animals and plants of this world will be able to survive and somehow reestablish a civilization on some distant world we can only dream of tonight."

She stared down the angry F'eng woman.

"I will do all I can," said Gina in a loud, clear voice, "but I will not take a seat aboard any vessel. I will give my seat, my ticket to my daughter. I will trust her to carry my genes to a new world."

The crowd gasped, broke into several pockets of discussion. The tenor of the language turned toward duty and sacrifice for the greater good. Heads began to nod. A few delegates hugged each other while others patted shoulders or ran fingers through each other's hair. Gina saw fingers wiping away tears—other people's tears. She stepped back from the lectern and went to the front edge of the stage, scanning the audience.

"We have thirty-one years," she spoke over the crowd, wondering if anyone heard her.

Chapter 24

The Dark

Nearing dusk, Gina had returned to her room in the Grand Palace and changed into casual attire: a dark red kaftan with brown leather strips running vertically from shoulders and collar to her knees. The spiked boots added to her look, wanting to seem formidable.

The guard at the exit doors stopped her, concerned about her brazen attempt to go outside in the dark of the evening, away from the safety of the Grand Palace.

"It will be all right," she barked.

"Shall I arrange an escort for you?" asked the concierge, jogging over to them.

"No need. I used to live in Siti. Long ago. I just want to visit my old neighborhood."

"Where is it?" asked the concierge.

"I lived on the south island mostly."

The city of Siti was built first on an island in the wide river that flowed south from the range of mountains constituting the northern boundary of Ghoupallæssa. There were seven major islands and countless smaller ones at that point in the river. Eventually, the city spread out to encompass both shorelines.

"That is one of the most dangerous districts now."

"I'm not afraid. I'm descended from the legendary warrior Set-d'Elous," she said with a chuckle. The name she was using in this time zone was d'Elous, after all.

"Truly? He was proven a fake more than a hundred years ago," said the concierge with earnestness pasted on his pale face.

"Fake? How so?"

"He was not a warrior of Ghoupalle blood. He was the offspring of Great God Zaul and a Ghoupalle woman. That's from the history scrolls I've read, updated in 1888. The new information came from studies done in 1535 and confirmed in 1579, re-evaluated in 1620 and 1745, so I'm certain it's authoritative."

"A Ghoupalle woman? Who?"

He looked at her name band, hanging from her collar.

"Ah! Apologies. The same name as you have: Jinetta. She was the Queen of Fenula long ago."

"It's ancient history now, open to much speculation."

"After she was captured and tortured by Zetin warriors, her son rescued her. The son of Great God Zaul, too."

"That's how it can be called a legend."

She was amused. *I'm sure I would've remembered if Zaul had slept with me.* The way things get twisted around over the centuries, following agendas, making everything correct, putting a happy ending on horrific drama—where would it end? In the destruction of the planet? Would Great God Zaul, the oldest story in the book, ever do such a thing?

She tapped the concierge's shoulder, smiling.

"I also carry a marker."

"Those are illegal here," said the concierge in a lowered voice. The cigar-sized device was invented to temporarily stun an attacker with a bolt of electricity, yet it became a common tool for criminals to use to immobilize and rob citizens, so the devices were banned for everyone. Still, the criminals always seemed to be able to find one and use it.

"I promise I won't use it unless my life is in danger."

She stepped away from them and exited the building.

The concierge ran after her, calling "Take the KOHAX 19 line to the south island!"

"Yes, I remember!" she called back, letting the yellow sun wave goodnight between the buildings, leaving a burnished red trail down the boulevard for her. The small, blue sun had already set.

She drew looks from other passengers on the KOHAX but was

not bothered. They seemed too sleepy to hassle her.

Exiting the station at her usual stop, she immediately saw how the old neighborhood of small businesses had become run down and dilapidated. Many of the buildings around the station were ten floors high and most now seemed abandoned. The suns had dropped below the horizon now and the darkness of the streets finally caused her to reconsider her sightseeing.

The agent at the exit gate questioned her and she offered her diplomatic pass, which impressed him. He studied it a while, inquiring after her business in this forlorn section of the city. She explained in a tired voice that she was after nostalgia. He warned her of rape gangs and doubted that a marker—he saw it hidden in her fist—would be enough to deter them.

Not the kind of nostalgia she was seeking?

"No," she conceded, "I suppose not."

She gave him the address of her first residence, where she had lived with her first lover on that first trip to Ghoupallesz, with her fellow interdimensional voyager, Sebastian, accompanying her. *Damn, I'm old*. The agent thought briefly, then reported that it had likely been torn down to make space for block residences for factory workers and their families. And even those buildings had been abandoned.

"What year did you live there?" asked the agent.

She smiled, ignoring his question, and thanked him for the information and returned inside the KOHAX station for the ride back to the Grand Palace.

Walking from the station to the Grand Palace, someone called to her, a shadowy figure with a large head, walking hurriedly behind her. She gripped the marker.

It was the bison man from Nouvê, sidling up to her, breathing hard and smiling through his beard.

"I have no intention of frightening you, *Kalmonê*," he said and she noted his use of the highest ranking honorific. While *kanê* was used often in the same way 'sir' and 'ma'am' were used in English, *kalmonê* was closer to 'my lord' and 'my lady.'

Gina grinned. At the same time she expected trouble and tensed, ready for action.

Instead of trouble, the man launched into a passionate apology for his interruption at the conference and segued effortlessly into an eloquent description of the points she had made and his thoughts and feelings about each of them, adding a few anecdotes and jokes then elucidating his own ideas about the conundrum in which they found themselves as erstwhile survivors of an interplanetary catastrophe. After three *peth* standing on the street outside the entrance to the Grand Palace, he paused and invited her to continue their conversation inside, where it was safer, where they could talk further over some warm beverage, where there were no unsuitable eyes poised to snatch any more intimate topics that might come to mind.

"Apologies to you," he spoke with a magical wave of his hand. "My name is Vazak-Mixerran, ambassador to all these scientific conferences, at your service, *Kalmonê*!"

His way of speaking entranced her and he did not seem like someone who was a threat. With kindly eyes and a child's grin amidst his thick beard, he looked to her as though he might be entertaining. She was out of her mind with frustration from the day's conflicts. Perhaps a drink and some conversation would help her relax.

They went inside and made their way to the social room and took a pair of seats near the stage. Already a pair of musicians were performing a ballad with a wooden flute and a tall stringed instrument, something sad that made her think of the Final Day and how everything might look from the window of a space vessel as the comet came in—

"May we discuss something beside the comet?" asked Gina, "something happy."

"I would like nothing more, *Kalmonê*."

"And stop calling me *kalmonê*. My name is Jinetta."

"As you wish, Jinetta of Kobarêl."

"Thanks."

He lifted his left hand, palm open. "Shall we...?"

She knew the custom, an invitation, and placed her right index finger on his palm to indicate her acceptance. His thumb locked her finger in place, the minimum touch between two strangers, and together they proceeded to the grand staircase.

❋ ❊ ❋

"I'm surprised," said Gina, brushing her hair out of her face, "you can be so easily bought with a few hours of such a natural activity as standard intercourse."

"I would vote for your plan no matter how we spent the night," said Buffalo Bob, the ambassador from Erit who had worn the big furry hat.

She had called him 'Buffalo Bob' a couple times during the night, when in her ecstasy she could no longer hold back speaking English. He had questioned her about the name, thinking she called him a kind of drug, what was called *bôb*. Then he had offered her a mauve-*bôb* for her amusement, a rare treat that left her unusually energetic on the *qala*. Vazak, on the other hand, being broad-shouldered and hairy, made the *qala* swing dangerously from one wall to the opposite wall. In the morning, when he sat on the edge of the *qala*, the hammock-style bed tipped down to the floor. Gina had rolled down against him and they had laughed together.

"So it's not a matter of tricking laborers," she told him as she stroked his curly brown back hair, "it's a matter of persuasion. We are asking them to deny themselves, to give up their own reward, to give away their individuality not out of hatred or bias or a lack of value, but to accept the full knowledge of what their choice, their sacrifice, means for the entire species."

"You make sex talk enlightening," said Vazak with a bass rumble. "I agree with you, *Kalmonê*."

"No more *Kalmonê*, I said."

He grunted, feeling the pain in his head of a night with no sleep, considerations of regret dragging on his heart.

"It is not about you or me, or any one person, or any one country, as you say. I understand it is about saving something of our species to live on somewhere else."

"Exactly, Vazak. If we can get everyone to understand they are not sacrificing themselves for nothing, they have nothing to lose, then we have a chance to convince laborers to work for the common good. And the common good is not an ark of salvation for kings and queens and their families, nor even the leaders of industry."

"Yet we must reward those who lead us and those who put forth the money and resources to realize the creation of these 'arks of salvation' as you call them. Some of the other people should be selected for their knowledge and skills, whatever is needed for the flight and for the settlement beyond."

She smiled at him, finding handsomeness in his rough features, thinking of *Beauty and the Beast*.

"It's the ultimate job application," she said, pulling herself back on topic. "It's like, 'I am valuable enough, useful enough, that I should get a seat on the spacecraft, yet I know even though I am useful, members of my family must stay behind.' Right? Complete objectivity. Qualifications only. 'My family cannot join me simply because it pleases me; no, they will need to stay behind.' That's how it must be. Everything we do must be only for preservation of our species."

"And the fertile females?" There was a twinkle in his eye that made her grin. "We must select the fertile ones, surely: the healthiest of both male and female if we hope to extend our species into other generations."

"Skills, knowledge, healthy enough for a long journey, and fertile enough to prolong our species."

"A lottery?"

"No, we cannot choose at random. We should let them apply. Let them tell us their skills and knowledge. If they pass that level, they will be tested for health and fertility."

"Should be young, too, yet not so young they do not know anything and have no life skills. Old people should not go, even if they are wise. That leaves me off the list."

"And room for archives of all knowledge gathered from around the world, too."

"Will these delegates accept such a plan?"

"If we present it this way, they will realize that most of them would not get a seat aboard the vessels and they would vote against the plan."

"Then you must convince them of the greater good, as you said, *Kalmonê*. Their action, which is their choice—their vote is for the future of our species. Nothing less than that will survive. For what is a single person but a bag of cells and a will to keep reproducing itself? It is not our minds or our unique lives that has meaning in the calendar of the universe but the special blob of juice which is the pattern for making us anew. Or returning us to the furnace of creation."

"You, Vazak, should give the speech. You have all the words I cannot pull from my head. You have a magic tongue!"

And so Vazak-Mixerran, burly ambassador from Nouvê, long-suffering resident of Erit, half-Jêpolissan, one-quarter Sogox, one-quarter Ghoupalle, beefy in a rugged, handsome way, stood on the stage and with his thick arms gesturing persuasively gave the speech of his life as Jinetta-d'Elous stood in the front row to cheer for him. To the greater good of all humanity, he insisted, though he did not use the word 'humanity'—*ghoumæ* was the Ghoupalle word referring to all the peoples of the planet. That tactfully smoothed over endless conflicts between the major races and ethnic groups: Ghoupalle, Rouê, Zetin, Danid, Sogoê, Tigu, Jêpolissi, Kobarêli, Lapughê, and the Dikondran and Bæro people on the separate continent of Bæronak. Instead of addressing the congregation as 'fellow-Ghoupalles' his word choice had the effect of calling to 'fellow humans' and won their attention. He outlined the plan in eloquent words Gina could only imagine being able to speak.

Sebastian could've done it, she mused, but he was nowhere in this time zone so far into the future from the days of glory and savagery and romantic love and children who grew into heroes and goddesses. No, he was left long ago and far behind. She was on her own and could not leave. Even if she had found the right tangent to escape Kobarêl safely with her children, now there was Vazak, her buffalo-man, her lover.

And a comet.

The vote went as she expected, yet she never considered that she would be elected to oversee the preparations, a kind of Queen of Aerospace Industry, as it were. She would macro-manage and coordinate the various spaceports to be sure maximum efficiency was maintained through conformity to the models approved by the science council. In short, one model for all construction efforts. Everyone agreed—or enough of them did to form a solid majority—that the construction of spacecraft was paramount and the resources of the planet would be put forth toward that goal: to have as many space vessels ready as possible in the 31 years remaining.

Of course, not all agreed. The main refutations came from the religious legions and the optimistic hordes. The religious believed they should welcome the comet as their punishment; to attempt to avoid it would be an affront to the seven gods and nine goddesses. The F'eng followers were the worst, choosing a masochistic lifestyle full of self-inflicted pain. The most extreme of them would cut their faces to the bone in sympathy with the prophet F'eng who had no face. Their horrible blood was found everywhere they congregated, spotting park benches, street corners, door handles, and trees. They were forbidden on public transportation. All Gina knew was that their leader, a mystic named F'eng, had supposedly gained enlightenment from surviving a severe disease which left him disfigured and in perpetual pain. She thought he might be glad to end the pain as soon as a comet strike could be arranged, but he eventually died. Now his disciples carried forth his message.

The optimistic denizens of the planet, furthermore, believed the comet would miss them, fly right past without so much as a wink. Or, barring that, a few well-aimed rockets with explosives could be launched at the comet to break it up and send the smaller chunks harmlessly away. Some at the conference had proposed the idea. The scientist who stood and answered their concerns had posed the question *What if we miss?* If that were the case, they would have no time left to build the fleet of spacecraft in order to evacuate. Go ahead and build them, he said, so we have them if we need them; and if we do not need them then we have them available for interplanetary exploration at leisure.

The degree of error in calculating the comet's trajectory had been accounted for, leaving the target on track, as feared. A shallow trajectory could sweep a continent off the globe, one scientist warned. A more straight-on arrival might set in motion destructive forces which would split the planet apart. The odds were not good for buying property thirty-two years in the future.

Gina gazed at the schematics of the proposed vessel, the R-10

Transport Frame and the V-7 Residential Capsule, on easels positioned to the side of the wide stage. She thought of Buck Rogers, decided the gold surface would be pretty, and the tune "Ticket to Ride" came into her head, causing her to smile. Better safe than sorry. Better a tangent than a rocket.

After the conference they said their goodbyes in Vazak's room, pledging to visit each other, first she in Erit, then he in Kobarêl. After all, she would be visiting each construction site around the globe, and there were already eight of them hard at work on different designs. He, however, would need to consult with her from time to time in order to be sure his team's timetable was on track.

"I'm one hundred-thirteen years old," he told her, breathing hard beside her. "I may not need a ticket."

"Of course you will." She stretch up and kissed his forehead. "I have pledged not to go, yet my children will go. You can be their mentor."

"We would be on separate vessels," he said. "I shall depart from Erit...if I go. Oh, it's no matter to me. I would care for them if I could, if you trusted me to do so. You are much younger than me—what are you? seventy? eighty?"

Gina grinned, never giving her age much thought, but she supposed that in Ghoupalle years she probably did resemble a seventy-year old woman. For that, she could call herself a middle-aged woman of forty or forty-five back on Earth.

"Yes, seventy-five," she lied. "Too young for you?"

He laughed, like a buffalo snorting. "You, *Kalmonê*, are perfect at any age."

"We shall see how I am in thirty years."

"I shall be dead in thirty years most likely."

"Do you have a son or daughter?"

"You are an easily-aroused lady!" he chortled. "No, I have no children. So I am thankful we have been able to share this week together. I shall see if I can find a suitable replacement for you when I can no longer please you. Perhaps you may enjoy one of my partners."

"Thank you, Vazak."

In the morning they went their separate ways. Gina boarded the airship flying south across the sea to Kobarêl. She was able to look down through the window as they pulled away from the tether and saw Vazak staring up, waving his big arms at her. Then he turned toward the gangway for the walk over to his own airship, heading northwest.

The clouds were green and obscured the view until just before they arrived. She could clearly see the construction zone on the peninsula extending north from the mainland, the construction teams looking busy as a nest of *ajii*—Aivanan red bees. As the airship arrived at Kobarêl, she knew her work was just beginning.

✻ ❋ ✻

"It's not our fault," cried the headmistress of the school. "I told you before that your son is a Miracle Child. It is expected that his head would tear open someday. The other Miracle Children are also sprouting wherever they are around the world."

"So it's true?" asked Gina. She crossed her arms over her chest, breathed in the fresh, filtered air of the school interior. "I thought it was only a legend."

"He is the only one in Kobarêl. Other Miracle Children have been found in Aupl, Majjer, Sanduu, Ilarat, Erê, Kipzon, Debrêk, and Rox."

"You said Kipzon? In Adanê? Fancy that."

"They are sprouted this week."

They both turned to gaze at Xix, the swarthy boy with no hair on his large head. His body seemed to remain the size of a toddler yet his head was adult size and growing. Along the top a ridge had formed, then the skin had torn, exposing the bone of his skull. Through it all, the boy had not cried out in pain, nor gave any indication of discomfort. Now the bone was thinning and with light shining at a proper angle the working of his brain could be seen there.

"He will die," said the headmistress. "Yet not before he reveals the message of the seven gods and nine goddesses."

"What an awful way to send a message." She thought of the letter she wrote to Sebastian long ago, when she was settled in a tropical resort in Liêta and had grown tired of so many lives lived. That letter was 29 pages, all handwritten. Then she did not kill herself as she said she would in the letter.

"Is he in pain? What can we do?" asked Gina.

"He seems not to notice. He still does not speak. Never has."

"He also refused my milk when he was born, as though he had enough stores of fat to live on."

"I told you he was a Miracle Child."

"I believe you now."

"We can only wait for his head to open and see the message."

"See?"

"It should be written in the ancient languages of the gods and only understood by a high priest."

"Are there any left?"

"Oh, yes, though they usually keep to themselves in caves or on the tops of mountains."

"Naturally," Gina said with a groan, then continued to herself in English: "Why make it easy? It's beginning to feel like some B-movie I'm in." *Next they will find pyramids here or a blue police box!*

When she had escaped from Kipzon with her daughter, she had wandered eastward across Gotanka and found a tangent in the foothills of the Zissekap mountains that led to somewhere in southern Megank, near the Trêsz Sea. To save herself from the wrath of the jungle people there, she allowed them to worship her blonde hair, even allowed them to cut off snatches of it for their own adornment. She became nearly bald. And she had slept with the shaman of the tribe. Soon a boy was born and she hesitantly accepted him, despite his odd appearance. The folk of the community thought she was cursed to give birth to such a child and sent them all away. The three of them crossed grassy plains and rocky deserts and eventually found another tangent on a sandbar beside a wide marsh. Believing it had to be better than continuing on by foot, she took it. That was how they had tripped into the volcanic plain of western Kobarêl.

It is a B-movie I'm in! She glared at the headmistress.

"Your daughter Zaura, on the other hand, is doing very well in our school," said the headmistress. "She has passed her exams with top scores and is on the priority list for advancement. She is likely to be selected to take a seat on the spacecraft. She has so much potential as a fertile maiden and a mother."

"I thought you were teaching them mathematics, engineering, and astrophysics," said Gina, sternly.

"Those subjects are for the boys. They need knowledge and skills to get tickets. As a girl, your daughter only needs to score high in fertility and motherhood skills. Which she has. Very high scores, indeed. She is rated the second-most fertile among her class cohort."

Gina laughed, thinking of the twenty-some children she had birthed in her various lifetimes on Ghoupallesz. Certainly fertility ran in her bloodline.

"When the boys die, who will run the spacecraft?"

"Other boys, I suppose. There will be enough of them aboard the vessel. They also will have physical needs, for their health—"

"And if they all die?"

"How would that happen?" The headmistress smiled politely. "All your daughter need do is mate with five males during the flight and upon landing at the destination. Five children is the mark the agency has set for maiden tickets. It doesn't matter if she knows engineering or—what was the other?"

"Astrophysics," said Gina. "Like what I do. I'm in charge of the entire space program, I'm sure you're aware. I can decide who gets a ticket or not. While I have chosen not to take a ticket for myself, my daughter Zaura must be on one of the vessels and she must know how to operate it, how to resolve problems that may arise, and how to lead the five hundred people aboard her vessel. If she wants to mate and have babies, that is her choice, not some government agency's command!"

"But—" The headmistress stopped herself. She did not want to say anything more which might get her kicked off the list, if she were even on the list. "I apologize, First Director. Certainly, it would be good even for the fertile maidens to know something of the vessel's operations. In case trouble occurred."

"I think so, too."

Chapter 25

Prophecy

Gina tried not to smile as she read the letter from her dear Buffalo Bob visible on the comm pad screen while leaning against her work station in the Aerospace Council's high-rise office building. His words were as eloquent as always. He included a sketch someone had done of him on the beach near Erit—obviously cold water in the Navadi Sea: his hair stood straight out like one of those things back on Earth, what, a sea urchin? She could not contain herself and laughed, drawing the annoyed attention of her colleagues.

She dared not say the letter had nothing whatsoever to do with spacecraft; that would be not only rude but highly inappropriate since all of their thoughts and actions were devoted exclusively to the goal of saving as many people as possible from planetary annihilation.

Vazak did mention news of the Aikavo spaceworks going rogue, deciding they would tether in orbit for a couple years while the worst effects dissipated, then return to the surface and rebuild. The Ilarat council also was leaning that way: sail above the fray for a while, then return to the surface. The residential capsules they were building—intended to be used by the four medium-sized vessels Kobarêl was building would go on; the evacuees from Bæronak, however, would not link up with deep space transport frames. Vazak told her the Erit spaceworks were slightly ahead of schedule with the heavy-lift rockets that would take the residential capsules into orbit. And he commented on Kobarêl's grand sub-orbital heavy-lift mechanism—basically, a "space elevator"—stating that Erit's space council had declined to build one, relying instead on shuttles to take parts into orbit for assembly there. He had been hoping he would be sent to Kobarêl to observe the space elevator in action, get a guided tour from Gina, but now the trip was off.

She flicked on her calendar pad and checked her schedule. Two trips next week, one the week after: Typeg, Lyas, and Sanduu. All were building deep space transport frames and launching them into orbit. Questions about the specs kept coming up. There was no time or resources to indulge in constructing different models. The International Council of Aerospace had approved three: the largest one the V-7 Residential Capsule with a capacity of 500 fully conscious passengers and a crew of 55; the V-20, a large dormitory vessel carrying 2000 passengers in hibernation and a crew of 35; and the smaller V-100 which was designed to carry 150 actively conscious passengers, mostly military, and a crew of 70, prepared for defense. The Council had approved the R-10 Transport Frame to which each residential capsule would be docked. The transport frames were under constant debate: should they be tethered or be of interplanetary or of interstellar capacity?

Vazak, with training in jet propulsion and having patents in airship propulsions systems that had not been approved because of their excessive pollution output were now being used; no need to worry about leaving pollution when evacuating the planet. For the quick launch, chemical-based rocket engines would be used and their fuel tanks jettisoned once the vessels were away. Then, once clear of orbit, the pulsed plasma propulsion systems would be initiated—a long, slow build up of speed, certainly, yet efficient for long distance travel such as between star systems. She knew there was a need to carry as little fuel as possible, and carrying a collection of nuclear bombs would be dangerous enough. If only they had the time to develop Warp Drive, she pondered, playing an episode of *Star Trek* she remembered through her head: "The Trouble with Tribbles"—was that the title? It did not matter now; she was so far from home, television, and science-fiction shows.

She had to make do with whatever was available on Ghoupallesz in the summer of 2148.

So she set down her calendar pad and picked up her dictation baton, pressed the button on the side and began speaking into the end of it. When she finished her reply letter to Vazak, she set the baton upright on the recessed catch on her work station panel and the message was immediately sent off, arriving at his work station in Erit in minutes—in exactly 2.5 *pon*.

Let's meet in Rox in seven weeks, she suggested.

Meanwhile, the nations of Lapughê and Majjer, in conflict with each other for centuries, decided to work together, combining their military technology and adapting it for space warfare— should it be needed. Who would want to hurt a peaceful fleet of evacuees on their way to a new home? And should that new home be inhabited already? The Lapugh-Majjeraxii Consortium would be prepared, both with onboard weaponry and security weapons for the surface.

Even the isolationist Zetin nations were becoming involved. Initially opposed to whatever the "unclean nations of the world" were planning, they began to come around to the reality of annihilation. However, their plan was to shoot down the comet. They proposed that a series of missiles be designed, built, and launched in succession. If it worked, they would demand tribute from all the other nations as compensation. They were welcome to try, many said; if they did truly succeed then a better future would be enjoyed by everyone. If it failed, of course, the Zetin would have no seats aboard any vessel. They would have spent their time and resources on missiles instead of spacecraft.

Her personal assistant reminded her of the meeting with the representatives of Biological Services. She was invited to look at the plans for the hydroponic gardens that were to be placed in each residential capsule. Each would provide a self-replicating food source. With banks of seeds on board and elements sucked from space, they could grow a variety of plant foods, enough to feed the active personnel of a capsule. She nodded, gathered her electronic notepad and stylus and headed to the upper floor.

Riding the clear fiberglass-enclosed external lift, she gazed out at the distant spires. Not buildings rising among the emerald clouds but a row of gleaming spacecraft. Six bullet-shaped towers pointed to their new home, wherever it might be. As she studied them, moving up the side of the building, she heard heroic music wafting between her ears and felt proud.

She was nobody, after all. Sure, she had married well and eventually became a queen. However, they were all lives of leisure. Sometimes there was drama, of course, but mostly she cared only for herself. Here she was doing something important, perhaps the last thing she would ever do. She watched the golden rocket cones and as she did, the large yellow sun peeked out from behind the green clouds and the small, blue sun cast its light at an angle to create a portrait of heaven she had once seen in stained-glass when her grandmother had taken her to the cathedral as a child.

Maybe there is a heaven out there, after all, she dared to think, regretting her decision to give up her seat aboard one of the vessels.

Maybe I'm giving up the chance to shake hands with God.

Two guards in brown and red uniforms opened the double doors to the conference room. Seated around the long table were thirteen administrators and scientists. Besides her own boss, she knew only one of them: her daughter, Zaura-d'Elous, Fourth Assistant Manager to the First Director of Biological Services, Aerospace Contingent. It was her first assignment following completion of her education requirements. She had also passed her fertility assessment and wore the cherished white scarf of A-grade womanhood. Maintaining their professionalism, mother only glanced and quickly nodded at her grown daughter. Then the meeting began.

In the Ghoupalle year of 2149, in the month of Gouö, on the twenty-fifth day, at the highpoint of the sunlight, the first Miracle Child made international news. Within two days, all the identified children had given up their lives to reveal their messages from the seven gods and nine goddesses. In each location, the child had shouted madly for several *pon*, then collapsed. Each head broke open like an egg shell and brains were exposed. In the curling, winding lines of the brain organ were supposedly the messages shown in the ancient divine script.

"As you said," Gina whispered to her unmoving son, Xix, "he will not live long, and he will give up the divine message for the people of this world. So he is a hero, isn't he? And I gave birth to him. His father was a shaman of the Xig people, yet they said nothing of this possibility." She regarded her daughter. "We never knew him." She sniffled back a tear. "He had no personality, never spoke, and I could detect none of his thoughts." She looked at the physician. "He was given life for one purpose—"

"What's the message?" asked the daughter.

"Patience," said Gina.

"There is a priest," said the physician, "who comes this night from Valek. He will read the script. Then we will know what to do."

She instinctively gazed at the map on the wall screen and calculated the distance such a priest would have to travel to reach Kobarêl. She wondered how they found him. Valek was a nation built on a vast field of volcanoes—she always linked the name of the country west of Kobarêl with its chief geologic feature. Many products made based on lava and volcanic stone. Exported energy from geothermic heat sources. Barren volcanic deserts. Wind-swept mountains free of vegetation. Other than the cities along the coast, the country was a wasteland. Perfect for ascetic priests to hide themselves away.

"I shall wait for him."

She instructed her daughter to return home and prepare for a funeral, knowing that no resources were available for a ceremony deemed pointless on a world that was doomed to die. How to honor the dead when everyone, almost everyone, would soon be dead?

Plenty had decided not to wait. News of mass suicides filled the reports. Not all were religious-based. A family here, a group of friends, a team of coworkers, a lone woman or a pair of children. They would take multiple kinds *bôb* and wait for the arteries to burst. Or jump from the tallest buildings they could find. A few had done violence to themselves with knives or other weapons. Most seemed to want to go to sleep peacefully and never awaken. Probably a new *bôb* was being produced for the final days, to ease the passage of those left behind.

And there was terror, too. The latest was the group that had bombed the Lyas spaceworks facility, apparently in protest to being left off the list.

"Lyas is gone," she had told her staff as she set down the communication baton, getting the information directly from the facility director. "Five years' work lost. All because of a rivalry with Typeg. Who can build vessels faster? Ridiculous! So Typeg workers have to blow up the Lyas facility? Fewer seats for everyone now!"

She ranted on and her staff feared to say anything, perhaps wondering if they would lose some seats because of the incident. Security was bolstered at all remaining facilities. The difficulty was to assure that those entering as workers were truly workers and not terrorists in disguise. There was slim enough chance of surviving but now the odds were every day in jeopardy by those small-minded ants who could not think beyond their own bodily survival!

"It's not about any of us!" Gina raged. "It's about *all* of us— something of us continuing on through the universe. I don't care if it is my genes or your genes or his genes or someone else's genes. Somebody must go on. Someone must continue us." She stared at her staff, challenging them around the table. "Or we give up now and drink away the remaining days in hedonistic pleasure."

One staffer snickered and she sent him out of the room.

"If you are finished, I'll buy you a bottle of *gor* and you can enjoy the end lounging in a gutter somewhere." Her calm tone sent heart-shaking vibrations through those who remained.

"We are with you," one woman had dared speak. Others gave their index finger salutes to signal agreement—

Gina noticed her hand was shaking, remembering that angry day a few weeks past. She questioned her presence in this time zone, her work with and for people she did not know. She wondered how she had turned into such a stupid humanitarian.

Need to spend more time looking for an escape tangent.

She lifted her son from her lap and the physician helped her stretch out the body on the examination table. A hood had been placed over the boy's head to shield the open brain cavity from the environment until the priest could arrive and study the divine message. Or it's simply the normal squiggles of a child's brain, she thought.

Outside the medical facility, a crowd of journalists was banging on the doors, demanding access. The world needed to know the message from the gods and goddesses. Gina could hear their shouts, feel the building shutter with their pounding fists. She feared they might break in and, in their fury for the truth, somehow desecrate the body of her son.

"I'm sorry, Xix," she whispered in English, holding his hand.

Word came just before dawn that seven of the nine Miracle Children had been examined and their messages decoded. The messages had all matched, apparently, which left those who believed in that sort of prophecy greatly unnerved. The final announcement would await the eighth and ninth messages.

Gina was jostled awake by the physician when the sky outside was beginning to lighten into a pastel lime. She saw the priest had arrived—or she presumed the man with the ankle-length gray beard, wearing the purple robe, head bald and eyes protected by goggles, was the holy man they were expecting. She stood and brushed her hair, straightened her kaftan.

The physician introduced her as the child's mother and, as explained earlier, she gave her permission for the priest to examine her son. The priest nodded, his beard touching the floor. She almost stepped on it as she tried to move out of the way.

Standing to the side of the table, she saw that the priest seemed to be praying. Meditating. Preparing for the exorcism. Waiting for a dramatic moment to unfold. Then he glanced at the physician and the hood was removed from the child's head. The priest knelt and was face-to-brain with the divine message. He stared without touching anything for at least three *peth*, Gina noted.

She turned to the physician.

"What is the message, O Holy One," the physician spoke.

The priest did not move, staring at the revealed brain and its curly lines.

A while later someone on the staff brought lunch for the physician. Gina declined food.

Still later, the physician slipped out for a toilet break.

Even later, Gina regretfully bowed out for a toilet break.

By nightfall, the priest had not spoken or moved from his kneeling position at the head of the examination table, his eyes focused intently on the boy's brain.

Gina yawned.

The light in the room kept her from sleeping deeply.

"Gourran ghêra Zaul sartuzen têla aof-se y naz-barlor," the priest mumbled, then repeated his words in a stronger, more confident voice.

Gina awoke and sat up, rubbing her eyes.

"Gaq-se zerren bul ghêra Memitha," the priest spoke solemnly, almost chanting in a steady rhythm.

Somehow the physician knew to return and the door suddenly opened as he rushed in. The priest did not move, continued in a soft monotone:

"Ourran isên zamen-jê zu T'hem-se ashê masten temaromma, afê itin-se loqêsen pætir! Ghêra Memitha fipen zex adul keañ en ost noren al an-se!"

"I should've known that Memitha would be involved," Gina muttered. The physician shot a glance at her.

"Avêtadaxii ge-hulgen ourran il framson-d'Ur-tha," the priest went on without pause, *"kejê ghêra Memitha-r dexas. Ashê baresen ymedæ kem Memitha-r pejaxii en ariën t'aril-d'isênaxii."*

He sat back on his heels and licked his lips. Bowing his head, his inhalation was a long rasp and the exhalation a few *pon* later was equally noisy.

"Doesn't seem to be good news," Gina spoke to the physician.

"I could not understand all of his words," the physician offered.

He sat on the bench beside her. After a moment he took her hand and held it tightly. They waited.

The lunch hour came and went. The priest remained in his seated position at the head of the table.

Again the clamor of the journalists rattled their peace. It seemed that a mob of the religious had joined them, demanding to know the message from this Miracle Child.

Gina could make out one particularly loud voice outside.

"He is not some Miracle Child," she said as though forming a prayer, "he was my son."

The physician squeezed her hand, released it as the priest stood slowly, grabbing the table for support. Once upright, the priest regarded the boy's brain, shook his head twice, and kissed the boy's forehead.

Without a word, the priest stepped to the door.

"That's it?" cried Gina, jumping up. "What's the message? That's my son there on the table, not some messenger boy. What is it that you think you can read there among the curls of his brain? Tell me!"

The priest stopped, squinting at her, then took a surgical laser from a side table and began writing on the wall, burning the symbols into the plaster.

The physician pulled Gina back from the doorway and together they mumbled the words as they became visible on the wall:

'Great God Zaul sacrifices this child being a messenger,' Gina translated in her head. 'This message spoken by Goddess Memitha. All living beings must call attention to Heaven before requesting grace, then the light causes blindness! Goddess Memitha cries for some time while flesh and stone merge as one. Faithfulness will hide all in a closet of Hell until Goddess Memitha's death. Then survivors should suckle from Memitha's nipples and sing a song of life.'

"We are doomed," the physician grunted, wiping tears from his eyes. He ran out.

The priest casually dropped the laser on the floor and without regarding Gina, stepped out of the room, moving slowly along the corridor as if weighed down by the tonnage of all the planet's hopes and fears.

Chapter 26

Progress

Although Ghoupalle society in the middle of the twenty-first century was, on its surface, scientifically-oriented and secular, much of the populace nevertheless gave credence to and carried various beliefs adopted from Danid and Rouê cultures regarding the divine pantheon which guarded the planet. The emergence of the F'eng movement in the late 1500s and early 1600s enhanced the spiritual outlook of many citizens. The seven gods and nine goddesses were thought to control all the heavenly bodies, the seasons and weather across the planet, and occasionally meddle in human activities if the mood struck any of them.

Memitha was a mid-ranking goddess yet she carried unusual power by being the goddess associated with death, destruction, cleansing, and sorrow. In the standard mythology, she had killed her lover at the end of their act of lovemaking, then ate him piece by piece over the course of the week, feeding some of him to their baby girl, Mara, when she was born on the last day of the week. Mother and daughter often went about seducing unworthy males, both gods and mortals, taking their essence and growing their own power from it while leaving the corpses to become dust in their wakes. People would pray to Memitha to request vengeance upon an enemy or to avoid bad luck themselves. Memitha hated mortals the most of any of the pantheon and so was widely appeased through regular rituals and on-going customs.

When the messages of the nine Miracle Children were shared and confirmed, and the messages found to be near duplicates, the highest priest in the highest ranking temple that still remained on the planet, set in the ancient mountains of Ilait in central Zissekap, stepped upon the holy dais and grabbed the communication baton from an assistant. With long, gray beard brushing the floor and the hot, arid breeze blowing perspiration off his bald pate, the highest priest carefully shook his purple robes straight before speaking the pronouncement that everyone seemed to already know.

"The high god Zaul says that Memitha has chosen to doom this planet, thus everyone should hide underground unless they want to be blinded by the light. Stay hidden until Memitha has died, then rise and resettle the land and sea."

That is what Gina said to her daughter, Zaura, as they sat before the communication beacon set into the wall panel, blinking blue with every vowel phoneme and gray with every consonant, yellow zigzags crackling across the bulb to measure the speaker's emotional investment. A red glowing diamond in the lower right corner of the device measured the truthfulness of each word, dimming when vocal tones suggested the speaker may have doubts about what was said. For this announcement, the red diamond glowed steady and bright throughout.

"It's mythology, my dear daughter," said Gina.

"Should we go underground?" asked Zaura.

Gina's aerospace engineering certification required her to work on spacecraft design. Already she was scheduled for a trip to inspect the bio-units being built in Sanduu for inclusion in the residential capsules under construction in Kobarêl and Erit. She wondered if these priests were serious about abandoning plans to evacuate the planet and instead have everyone hide in caves.

"I'm not," Gina responded. "I will continue my work with the evacuation plan. With luck, I will die of old age before the comet strikes."

"Yet I will not grow too old," said Zaura. "I will see it."

"You will have a seat aboard one of the vessels. You will go forth into the void and settle on a new world. You will be the future of us."

"I've already made a pact with Latol-Uessa to be my first mate."

"Already?"

"We decided to choose each other for making a first child." She regarded her mother's grim face. "If you approve, of course."

"Do I know him?"

"You met him at the consolidation ceremony. He wore a yellow cap. He was first in his rank and earned the yellow cap. You see? I only choose smart boys."

"Good for you," she responded, amused, thinking of that boy she met in high school named Sebastian and all the stupid things they had done together.

"We matched our gene profiles and found we have a high compatibility rate, nearly 98 percent—which is better than 99.6 percent of everyone eligible, that is, those among our age classification. And we cross-referenced our scores with our intelligence ratings and fertility scores."

"So you believe he is the best possible mate for you?"

"Oh, yes, Mother. In fact, our headmaster has approved our mating. He signed our certificate. We only need to wait until we are safely off this world and well on our way to deep space. We are first on the list for using the mating quarters on our vessel."

Gina could not help but grin.

"At least it will be clean for you two."

"With our high ratings, we should have conception on the first try. Headmistress Suda says we shouldn't wear out our vaginas with needless practice. I sure wouldn't want to have to keep trying it if I didn't have to."

"You may want to practice often, my dear," said Gina.

Of all the children Gina had given birth to over so many years and in so many locations on Ghoupallesz, this child, now grown to adulthood, made her the proudest. In a flash, she wished Sebastian could be there to share their family conversation. He would be proud of Zaura, too. However, he was likely busy doing his own thing, somewhere in the past where he liked to play. Probably doing something to change history again, she considered, something he'd had minimal success with, something he certainly had no business tinkering with, yet, like all Voyagers, could not resist.

"So you intended to follow through with all the plans for interplanetary travel?"

"Yes, Mother."

"And marry this Latol-Uessa boy?"

"Marry?" She had a puzzled look. "You mean 'mate,' don't you?"

Gina smiled whimsically. "I suppose I do."

"Then yes. After our child is born and develops for three years, I will select my second mate. And so on. That is the plan as outlined in the Reproductive Council's Third Official Concord, 2151 edition. All my sister-maidens have signed the agreement. We have all pledged to have at least five mates and, thus, five children—once we are away from this planet. We will consider exchanging boys within our cohort. I would like to see what children Latol and my friend Alouh would make."

Gina laid her hand on Zaura's head, softly stroked her golden hair. "Please name one child after me."

It did not surprise Gina that resources were suddenly being diverted from spacecraft production to the preparation of underground shelters following the announcement of the Miracle Children's message. Immediately three shafts were started in the mountains of Bezua-hü, Sekuate, and Aivana. Others were called for in Tebbicousimankalê and Feasfend but were rejected by government councils. Protests erupted. Desperate people died fighting for the right to hide from the comet. Others insisted the spacecraft program be sped up.

Gina called her staff together and demanded they stand up for the plan agreed upon by the International Aerospace Council and go forth to assure the necessary labor staff and resources to continue production. Otherwise, their legacy would be nothing more than millions of broken skeletons buried in the bowels of the planet, hidden for all eternity. She had used her most forceful voice and added a slam of her hand to the table as exclamation point.

The staff dispersed to pursue their assignments.

"Where is that bastard Sebastian when I need him?" she growled in English. "When I really, really do need him?"

She sat on the floor and crossed her legs, made difficult in that green kaftan she wore. She hiked it above her knees, then put her hands to her face. It had been a while, perhaps a hundred years in Ghoupalle time, since she had last felt so overwhelmed and lost. She never worried. That was her gift. Being born one of those happy-go-lucky girls, she seldom believed anything truly bad would ever happen to her. Sure, there had been several situations where she'd pondered her fate, wondered how she had let herself get involved in this or that problem, why she chose the way she did, and then, only then, did she dare to question whether Sebastian was close enough to hear her thoughts, or if she really, really needed him—needed him simply to cheer for her as she got herself out of trouble, showing off, just to be mean, to tease him as she always had. No matter whether he was a simple IRS clerk now or the warrior Set-d'Elous of legend, he always seemed to show up unannounced whenever a situation was most desperate. Perhaps he and she actually were soul mates. Perhaps they could hear each other's thoughts—well, if the thoughts were strong enough. Could he hear her now? Would he appear? She had to smile at that before wiping away a couple tears.

She did not need to stay; nothing here required her special attention. She could walk away, leave everyone to their fate, escape with her daughter back to Earth, or to an earlier time on Ghoupallesz, long before anyone ever looked up into the skies and saw a bright light approaching. If the assassins hadn't come looking for her in Kipzon after she escaped from the Zetin high priest's castle, she quite likely would never have arrived in this time zone, facing this problem.

"Isn't this about the time when the handsome, helpful alien arrives? Someone like...I dunno, Superman?"

She was breathing heavier, her insides tense. *Stress. Need to relax.* She chuckled.

"I'm the alien visitor, but I'm ordinary, no super powers. I can't fly or look through walls or leap over tall buildings or stop a locomotive in its tracks. And all I ever learned was in some classes at Washington University in St. Louis, Missouri, USA, Earth"—which were mostly useless, she added. Then she had dropped out to move to Ghoupallesz. In fact, most of her time at the university was spent in the library reading books and in the labs reviewing the experiments of the Ph.D. students. Nothing there had prepared her for a life on this world. *Much less for me to be able to solve their problems* "with a snap of my fingers."

Gazing at the tiles in the ceiling, ironically set in a pattern of interlocking 12-pointed stars, she tried imagining a route that would take her across the room to the farthest star while touching each of the other stars along the way.

She worked on the geometry puzzle for nearly two *peth*, then thought of her books, the science-fiction ones, the Asimov and Clarke she read in high school when she was training to be a nerd, the *Foundation* books and *2001*, that silly space odyssey story—after seeing the film. Sebastian had given her the books. There was a story, too, in a book by Clifford Simak, but she could not recall the title: something about a multi-generational spacecraft seeking a new home. She pursed her lips, thinking how wonderful it would be to have that in her hands now.

Besides books and movies, television came to mind. She thought of the *Star Trek* show Sebastian was always watching. They could fly faster than the speed of light using something called Warp Drive. That had to be fiction, of course. Matter and Anti-Matter were real, however. Their spaceship operated on Dilithium crystals. How convenient! Easy enough using some magical mineral to run a deep space propulsion system! What if there was something similar on Ghoupallesz? It could take decades to locate anything new and test its properties.

"Not enough time," she grumbled, then took as big a breath as her lungs could hold and let it slowly seep out. "I'm not in some damn sci-fi TV show."

Her stomach felt tight. She rubbed her belly, smoothed away some cramps, realizing how little she had been eating. Many people were starving. Eating seemed pointless now—unless it was an end of days feast hosted by one of the elite families here and there around the planet.

"Come on, Gina," she said with a slap to the floor. "You're not a quitter. You don't give up on a challenge. And there's no reason to wait for Sebastian to show up. He's probably back on Earth, safe and sound, dreaming of you, his so-called 'long lost love' or whatever he calls you. Doesn't matter now. You have work to do."

She pushed herself up from the floor, caught her balance, and went over to the windows of her fifty-second floor office to stare out at the green haze that filled the sky to the horizon. Far below was a sports field and teams of students were in training. Actually, they could not be students if they were training there, she understood after a moment. That field was for selected space personnel. She could not see well enough from that height but it was possible Zaura was down there running and being put through calisthenics to be ready for anything the rigors of space travel might have for her. The cadre of red-suited athletes were running drills and she thought of her own school days on the field hockey team.

"I just want to go home," she said barely aloud. "I don't belong here."

In Sanduu the toilets were coming along very well. That was something to be pleased about, at least.

Gina was walked through the plant for the inspection, even got to test one of them—without an actual deposit.

"So I just squat on top of this pipe?" she asked, removing her green and blue kaftan. One of her assistants held up the opened kaftan as a kind of curtain.

The space toilet consisted of a long tube rising like an elephant's trunk from the floor of a closet-sized capsule barely large enough for a normal-sized adult to stand within. The upper end was open and featured a slightly wider lip coated in ceramic. The person using the device lowered his or her back end directly down upon the ceramic ring. The oblong opening in the center of the ring, being less than the width of a human hand, made precise placement crucial. A tight seal needed to be maintained because of the suction involved. As the material was released from the body, the suction within the tube would remove it completely from the person's orifice and the tube. Jets of disinfectant would follow down the tube from the underside of the ceramic ring. For urination, the reverse position was to be used. However, that presented problems when the same device was switched on. Suction! Gentlemen needed to be cognizant of the g-forces applied to their family orbs. Ladies needed to be aware of the possible stretching effects of the suction upon their fleshy nether regions, as well.

"Can it be adjusted according to a person's tolerance?" Gina asked quite seriously once she had hooked up her kaftan again.

"There is only one setting," said First Director of Aerospace Toiletry Services Rogar-Tolourus. "We expect to give lessons on the proper way to sit on the device. As you can see, in the forward-facing position, a male would not have the capacity there for the orbs to slip into the tube. Not even width for accidental slippage. Females would be more at risk since—because of their...parts."

"Could a supplemental panel be added to the ceramic ring or held in place by the user so as to restrict the area that is submitted to suction?"

"Most definitely," said Tolourus. "Nobody wants bodily materials floating about the cabin area willy-nilly."

Gina had to smile. She instantly translated in her head his phrase as 'willy-nilly' and was amused at her choice of words. *Sauresk* meant 'haphazardly' in Ghoupallêan, which was the word he had spoken, yet somehow discussing bodily fluids was better served using 'willy-nilly.' Poor willy. All the poor willies subjected to that suction, she thought. And the poor nillies of each female crew member!

"So each crew member must place his or her fleshy parts directly against the ceramic ring to maintain the suction area?"

"Yes, that's it."

"Is there any provision for disinfecting the ceramic ring between users?"

"Oh, yes. We thought of that." Tolourus grinned like he did when she first removed her kaftan to test the toilet. "After the user has exited the cubicle and confirmed the closure of the hatch, there is a switch the user presses which starts a process of irradiation. That kills all life forms within the cubicle."

"I understand."

"The irradiation takes about a *pon* so no one may use the toilet until the irradiation process is finished."

Tolourus seemed quite proud of their product. It did the job, took minimal space, was self-cleaning, and could be fitted into any model of vessel.

"And where does it all go?" Gina asked, returning to a straight face.

"The suction prevents the material from escaping into the cabin environment, of course."

He waved his hand in front of his face as though trying to expel a bad smell. She was momentarily offended. Never mind that she had boldly squatted before them to test the device.

"The materials are pulled down the tube and remain in a holding tank. From there, they are treated with appropriate chemicals and can then be used as fertilizer in the on-board garden units."

It was beginning to make sense to her why the Sanduu facility was charged with constructing both spaceship toilets and food production units.

"If the holding tank should become full," Tolourus explained, a little giddy, "the excess can be jettisoned into space."

"Such a welcoming card," she muttered with a smirk. She regarded the others in the inspection team. None were amused. "However, it is necessary. Better the feces and urine burn up being bombarded by gamma rays than staying aboard to freshen the air."

They chuckled.

"Speaking of gamma rays," Tolourus spoke, "I read your report. It was news to me—indeed, to many of us in the toiletry science community—yet we know the seriousness of preventing, umm, that kind of radiation. So given our work with various kinds of fecal matter, I believe we may have a solution."

Gamma radiation, with its highly charged photons, could easily penetrate the walls of a spacecraft and over time do great harm to the humans inside. Building stronger vessel outer skin did not seem to be the answer. She had always considered a layer of lead in her vessel designs. Nor could she imagine a crew living inside lead-shielded flight suits for many years. The best that could be done was to reduce the effect of gamma radiation by half. Granite or concrete seemed to work well, but she could not believe a granite spacecraft would get off the ground. Right now, her job was less about how many people would survive to reach their destination than getting them off this planet in time.

"There is an empty interval between the outer and inner walls of the vessel, right?"

She nodded.

"We can pack it with ordinary soil. In fact, we have a unique clay here in Sanduu that would be perfect for that purpose. And when it shifts or a gap becomes detected, it can be filled with run-off from the toilet holding tanks."

"You want to fill the walls of our space vessels with shit?"

"According to your calculations—most impressive, by the way, for someone who is not an expert in the field of fecal properties— such organic materials would absorb the radiation, thereby reducing it. When the material should be deemed saturated, it could be flushed out into space and restocked with fresh..."

"Fresh shit."

"Exactly."

"So we will be out there cruising in our spaceshit?"

It wasn't complicated. She took the word for 'shit' (*ush*) and added it to the word invented for 'spacecraft' (*xænafi*) to form the word *xænush*.

"Yes, ma'am," said Tolourus and everyone laughed.

Then someone broke wind.

"There will, of course, be adequate ventilation onboard the vessels," said Tolourus.

Chapter 27

Miracle

From the airship, Gina had a sobering view of the ruins of the Lyas spaceworks, still being scavenged, before continuing north to Herêbout to check the progress of residential capsules. On schedule. The space lift was nearly complete, too, and a small rocket had taken a prototype transport frame into low-orbit. She was pleased.

From Herêbout, she went by KOHAX to the Rox construction zone in the eastern region of that nation, in the foothills buttressed against the Sogoê plateau. Propulsion systems were being tested at ground level in the rocky canyons there. The ion pulse system seemed the most promising for long-range travel and she stamped the documents approving continuation of the work.

"Still too much bureaucratic bullshit," she snarled to no one in particular.

Twice a year she made these trips to keep up with each spaceworks' progress. She was satisfied, although it was going to be close. They could only save a small number of people, anyway, and many were already abandoning hope of getting a seat, so many others were digging into the ground, either in construction projects or a family hole in the yard. Other people were content to enjoy parties that would last to the Final Day. Because of those developments, the destruction of the Lyas plant, and the Aikavo and Ilarat councils opting for tethering and resettlement after a couple years, she had less to worry about. The Zetin were cooperating, too, with their scheduled missiles to break up the comet ready for testing. It seemed every base had been covered.

She got on the airship and flew north to Terl, not because there was a plant to inspect and not because she wanted to sunbathe on an arctic beach, but because it was the only way around the towering Hikbok mountain range. She had refused to believe the statements of ordinary Ghoupalles that the highest peaks there literally stuck out of the atmosphere. She doubted that, though she did acknowledge they rose much higher than Mount Everest did on Earth, something like 40,000 feet, she once calculated. Therefore, airship travel between east and west needed to swing north or south where the mountains were lower. Being closer to her destination of Erit in Nouvê, she chose the northern route. If she had left directly from Sanduu in the far south, a mostly Tigu-populated city backed by red mountains and fronted by a brilliant tropical sea, she would have taken the southern route via Umavê, Pêpon, and Kobarêl. Stopping again in Kobarêl would defeat the second purpose she had of taking a vacation from that place.

And so it was that she arrived in Erit, dirty industrial complex shrouded in gray snow flurries, the gloomiest city she had ever seen. Yet there was smiling Vazak-Mixerran to greet her when she stepped off the descending platform. He had a big fur coat for her to put on.

"Welcome to Erit," he howled. "So many times we meet and now finally you come to my city!"

"It took some time for me to be brave!"

She hugged him and kissed his bearded cheeks, and he pushed her back.

"Not in public, *Kalmonê*," he cautioned. "Not the custom here, though I very much want to do that with you."

Vazak led her to an awaiting carriage, helped her aboard and took the reins himself, whistling to the two *Jêpe* to go. Each of the beasts wore a fur blanket made from *jalo* skins, he explained, then helped stretch a *jalo* skin over Gina's lap.

"With resources diverted to spacecraft production," he said as they entered the grand avenue of the city, lost in a stream of other carriages, "*Jêpe* are popular once more. The only problem is, the

Jêpe being tropical animals, they do not last long in Erit."

They pulled up to the entrance of a large gray townhouse and a footman in golden uniform rushed out to tend to the carriage. Vazak helped Gina down and into the building where two women, hairy and broad-shouldered, took care of her. One dropped down to remove her shoes and replace them with fur-lined slippers. The other took off the fur coat Vazak had lent Gina and replaced it with a fur-lined robe that extended to the floor. A man appeared then in a black skin-tight suit bearing a tray of items: a balm for lips, lotion for hands and face, a small thimble of a hot energy potion, and a mirror he held up for Gina to recompose her hair. The comb offered for guests to fix their hair looked to be made of gold.

"Shall we...?" said Vazak, extending his arm, palm open.

She lay her index finger in his palm and his thumb locked her in. They strode across the tiled floor of the large room filled with ornate wall decorations and furs covering furniture and some of the floor. The stairs rose magnificently, like something on which a bride would wish to descend. At the top, he led her down the corridor, passing two more female servants who raised their chins, exposing their throats.

Pausing at one door, Vazak knocked and the door was opened by a male servant, who bowed and quickly stood aside. Inside was Vazak's partner. One of them. The language was vague in the matter, Gina understood, but she was still surprised at what his words actually meant. After greetings and small talk with the man inside, they proceeded down the corridor and stopped briefly at three other doors, at each one greeting and chatting with other partners: two females and one more male. It was the Jêpolissan way.

"You are not upset?" asked Vazak once they were safely in his private quarters.

"I did not imagine how it would be in reality."

"It is not unusual compared to Ghoupalle society. There, you have a primary partner and each of you may spend time with others, what you call lovers. And you must keep them secret, do you not? You fight constantly about who feels jealous, who has envy, who is left out, who is getting too much affection and from who, yes?"

"I suppose," she responded softly, slipping out of the robe and slippers.

"We choose to keep our lovers close. More natural. More convenient. We like a 'star' pattern. Five partners. That is best, we believe: three males and two females, the most common, or two males and three females, almost as common. It is allowed to have one male or female and four of the other, though not so common. One of this and two of that is common, also, when starting a family. Sometimes, we hear of a family of six or seven partners. My parents were in a ten-partner family, but that was common in their day. You see, it is not only about matching a male and a female for mating. It is about life—companionship—love. My partners are my friends and my lovers. Or, they used to be. I'm the senior now so I take a different role. That is the reason they do not mind you being my guest. They expect me to find someone to complete this star for them when I die. Are you interested?"

"I can't do that, Vazak. I'll be somewhere in deep space by then."

He laughed, having been stripping down as he spoke. He set his final garment in a basket and faced her wearing only his natural fur, brown like a bear's, silver and thinning in spots. He reached for her gown, which she had unhooked, and let it drop to the floor.

"It has been such a long time," Gina said with a sigh.

"We have been so busy—both of us."

"Let's not talk about space."

"Certainly not—not until we have exhausted ourselves in this ancient ritual."

"I'm ready for some serious ravaging."

"Even from an old man?"

"I want you, Vazak." She pulled him to the *qala*. "I want you to make me forget everything. Just for a while. I want to dream and never awaken."

"Of course you want to awaken, *Kalmonê*. It is your duty to lead everyone to their destiny."

"That is what I want to forget. Please, Vazak. Make me forget for a while."

He reached from the *qala*, stretching over her for the side stand. Retrieving the canister sitting there, he flicked open the lid with his thick fingers and poured out a few tablets onto the cushion. He selected two of the red ones, offered one to Gina and popped the other into his mouth.

"Do you still like red-*bôb*?" he asked.

She grinned at him like a teenager, and wrapped her arms around him, squeezed him tightly like a big teddy bear.

"I haven't had any since the last time we were together."

Her teeth cracked the tablet and her tongue felt the burn, her tongue measuring sweet then bitter. She swallowed and felt the fire warm her belly, spreading down to her dream land, where the sun would soon rise and meet the horizon.

"Nuclear-electric or plasma engines, operating long-term at low thrust and powered by fission reactors, do have the potential to reach speeds much greater than chemically powered vessels or nuclear-thermal rockets," said Gina. She lay beside Vazak on the *qala*, both of them covered by a great white *jalo* skin. The red-*bôb* long ago had worn off and the green-*bôb* was starting to make her feel mellow. "We've been over this a hundred times. Such systems have the potential to power interstellar vessels with a reasonable travel duration. It's perfect for deep-space operation."

Vazak coughed and turned toward her. "Such a journey would take to the end of time, *Kalmonê*."

"We don't need to be fast, just last a long time." She sat up and let the *jalo* skin fall away. "It is like sex," she said, then thought better of her word choice in Ghoupallêan. "What I mean is, like this mating ritual we enjoy, what is important is not how quickly we do it but how long it can last."

Grinning through his beard, he sat up, pointing to her.

"You are the universe and I am the space vessel."

"That's it. I will always be here, always ready to receive a big space vessel full of little people. However, you must be able to make the full journey. Pace yourself, my dear. The end justifies the means, or something like that." It sounded better in English and she was willing to explain it but he had moved on in the conversation, dissecting the argument for each propulsion system

289

the council had already rejected.

"You have the right idea," he said, mild regret seeping out, "the only idea that will work, no matter what the others on the council say. I have kept count of the capacity of our vessels. We could carry only about ten-thousand people. That is all. Yet enough to start a new civilization, I believe. It's a good number as breeding stock."

"Just what humanity needs," she grunted, "to be treated as cattle." She sighed and sat up further, crossing her legs under the *jalo* skin. "That's what we've been doing, isn't it? All our silly councils are just ranchers herding the people around, deciding who gets to be slaughtered and who gets to live on and breed. And you and me are cowboys."

"Kau-boez?" he asked with a hairy smirk.

She explained what the English word meant, then went on with her rant: "We cannot save very many and who lives on has little to do with each individual person's worth or morality. It's still a lottery. And in the end, none of them will make it to the destination. The distances are too far. They will finish their lives aboard the vessels, reproduce and die. Like cattle. And someday in the far future, their children's children's children will arrive at a world that may not fit them, that may be uninhabitable after all, or that may be quite inhabitable, yes, but inhabited by a race who does not much fancy invaders, much less desperate, ragged, starving space refugees. There is no scenario in which the people who get a seat on a vessel are not committing suicide. Those who remain on this world will simply die quicker and perhaps in more horrific fashion. I don't mean the groups who line up in town squares and set themselves ablaze to escape the comet years in advance. I don't even refer to the circles of F'eng followers who drink to excess while popping *bôbs* and die in bliss with their bodies exploding soon after, splattering their flesh and blood everywhere—which is what they enjoy, I know: the blood being shared with everyone, as though blood was the only thing which unites each of us to every other one of us, as though blood was the only thing we could ever share—"

"*Kalmonê*, please make yourself calm."

"How can I be calm when there is so much horror in the world today and much more headed our way?"

"You said it: they are cattle and we are 'kau-boez' who have jobs to do. Concentrate on doing our jobs and we need not think of other things."

"My job, Vazak, is to think of everyone else's job!"

"Hah! An impossible task. How can you do it?"

"I accepted the appointment before I knew what it would involve."

"Yet you do it very well, and perhaps no one else could do it half as well as you."

"You are kind. Or bought and paid for."

"Bawt'n pey-dvur?" He scratched his cheek with two fingers. "You use strange words this morning, *Kalmonê*."

She rested her hand on his head, stroked his hair. "You are my only vacation, my only break from reality."

"Did I make you forget?"

She breathed deeply. "Yes, I forgot. Thank you. Now I am awake and everything is still there for me to deal with."

"If it will make you feel better, I also forgot my reality in your arms. It was a wonderful dream. You as the universe, me as the big space vessel blasting into the void...."

"If only it could continue." She rolled against him, gazed up into his eyes. "I'm ready to give up this reality and take hold of the dream. Let us dive into the dream forever."

He seemed startled, eyebrows pinching together, almost covering his eyes. "Are you serious now, *Kalmonê*? You want to go deep into the void?"

She looked away, then wiped a tear from her face. "I don't know. I'm at the end of my rope." She met his eyes again. "It's an old expression. From my homeland. It means I am overwhelmed and cannot go further."

"*Kalmonê*, I understand." He snorted, shook his head, let out a full breath and sucked in another. "I have been holding back from you."

"You mean about your polyamorous family?"

"No, this is about science."

"Science? Are we talking about that again?"

"How long have we been together? I mean, visiting each other. Ten years? Only twelve times we have been together."

"Yes, but one of them was the entire summer we spent in

Uadikuu, living on the beach, remember?"

"I have not forgotten."

"It's not the quantity of visits but the quality of our time together. Now I'm here in Erit, pleasing you."

"I enjoy how you please me. Of course, merely having you stand or sit within view of my eyes with your hairless body is pleasure enough for me, yet you do more—we do more, together. This time, like other times, we played the mating ritual. We always begin with me being a soft hearted fool and end with you talking about science."

"Because I need your soft heart at the beginning. When we are done, I naturally return to science."

"I'm older now. I need the red-*bôb* to please you. My partners don't bother with me now. So I spend my time with science. Once again I have been working in my laboratory, often late into the morning. I have—"

He stared at her, smiling. "Would you climb on top of me, as you did last night?"

She moved herself over his outstretched body and lay against him. His hands caressed her shoulders. One hand slid down her body, rested on her hip. "I like your hairless body. So smooth, so naked."

"You were talking about science."

"Yes. I want to show you something. It's a design from my academy days. I decided to work on it again."

"Your jet engine?"

"No. More advanced."

"What is it?"

"I looked again at the schematics for the conversion of hydrogen into helium and I realized with some adjustments and a new boilerplate assembly it might be safe even for an interstellar vessel. At increased scale, sure. As you said, like sex, interstellar travel need not be quick just long-lasting."

"I did say that."

"If you will allow me to watch you as you cover your naked body, I will take you to the laboratory and show you this device."

"A fuel cell?"

"You may call it that, *Kalmonê*. I call it the Mixerran fuel cell. If duplicated at five times the size of my model, it could power the medium-sized vessels. At ten-times the size it could power the large vessels. And the fuel is everywhere available in the universe. And, as you said, the universe is wide open, waiting for a big vessel to make that long journey."

"Yes, I did say that." She frowned. "Now stop repeating me and show me your toy!"

Chapter 28

Airborne

Once inside his laboratory, Vazak locked the hatch behind them. He turned to Gina with a scowl. "I have to trust you with this. There is no one else."

"Vazak, I've been trusting you for more than ten years," she responded, a bit on edge, "so why do you worry about me now?"

"Now everything is critical."

He pointed to a yellow coverall suit on the opposite wall, indicating she should change into it. Then he grabbed the other suit hanging on the nearby hook and began changing his clothes.

"Before, you and I were playing lovers' games," Vazak spoke as he suited up. "It was temporary. A fling at a conference. A mystery woman. A playful dalliance. A friend who was crazy enough to trust me in the *qala. Kalmonê*, I never thought we would continue meeting and playing all this time. Ten years, you say? It was easy to believe everything you did was for your pleasure. Or you felt pity for an old *jalo* well past his prime days. So then you did it all for my sake. I like to believe that so do not correct me. Now, everything has changed. Now, everything you do might be because you want this device."

"I don't even know what it does," she replied in a harsh tone, snapping up the suit and reaching for the helmet.

He took the other helmet off its hook.

"Now that the lovers' play is done, you want to talk science,

Kalmonê. So, I respect that. It is all for the greater good, as you say." And he lowered the helmet over his head and buckled the throat ring connector to the suit collar.

He checked her fit and tapped her helmet to let her know she was set. With a flick of a switch on the wrist panel, the communication link was connected.

"Hear me?" he called.

"I hear you."

He raised his index finger to signal a positive response.

"Let us begin."

He went to a giant chair suspended from the ceiling, and pushing a few buttons, brought it down to where he could sit in it. Taking the controls, he maneuvered the exo-body to retrieve the device.

As Gina watched, the robot hands opened a case and lifted out the device. In its horizontal position, it had no distinctive features, nothing that would give any hint what it was or what it was capable of doing. The robot hands turned the device upright and set it on the long workbench.

The silvery module stood about two meters high, she calculated, and had the diameter of a chubby man's waist. Each end was flat. Between the two ends the casing turned in and back out, forming a double hour-glass shape. Some panels seemed to be made of transparent material which allowed the workings beneath them to show blinking red and yellow lights. She knew it would be too heavy for a man to lift, or even two men. Hence, the need for the exo-body assist. It also protected him, she stopped to consider, if anything were to go wrong.

"Must be careful not to drop it," said Vazak through the comm link. "Fifty years of work lost in one flash."

"Don't talk," Gina responded. "Concentrate on your work. I will watch."

He proceeded to make a few checks on the device, then turned the exo-body to panels along the wall and worked a lever and pushed some buttons, checked several dials. She heard a whistle which rose and fell in intensity, a hiss of steam, perhaps, but she knew it could not be.

Using the robot arm, he attached a long, narrow hose to a port on the device, connected another hose to another port. The device had two lights which began to flicker, red and blue, beneath the semi-transparent side panels.

"It's really very simple, if you think about it," Vazak narrated. "Hydrogen goes in here. Helium comes out there. Just like—"

"Like a star!"

The moment of silence caught both of them by surprise.

"You should cover your ears and lower the blast visor," said Vazak. "It could explode."

"Are you sure about starting this thing?"

"That is why we are here, is it not?"

"I thought it was payback for getting you excited last night."

"That, too."

The exo-body turned slightly, as if Vazak were looking back over his shoulder. "Stand back."

The finger of the right robot hand extended twice and pressed a red hexagonal button at one end of the device. The robot arm withdrew and the exo-body swung backwards, away from the device.

She watched the device laying on the table like a kid's model car, plastic pieces painstakingly glued together, decals lovingly applied, now awaiting a parent's approval, the praise of modeling peers, then fearing the smashing of the car by some bully's boot. She held her breath.

It hummed, soft at first, but grew steadily in volume and pitch. Her helmet protected her ears. The device glowed in each of its transparent section covers: red, yellow, blue—like the tangent had just before she and Sebastian stepped through it that first night.

Then the humming became a roar, like a whirlwind, but even, smooth, steady, like...a jet engine.

"This is your jet engine, isn't it?" she called through the comm link. "You're tricking me, aren't you?"

"No, *Kalmonê*, this is the fuel cell. Give it time."

She continued to watch but nothing more happened. The device did not shake the table nor did its cylindrical shape cause it to roll around. The lights remained on and the roar remained at a tolerable level, lessening her fear that something bad would happen.

"That's it?" she called.

The robot arm reached toward the device and the finger again extended twice and pressed the red hexagonal button. The arm withdrew as the lights on the device went off and the roar slid down to a hum, then fell silent. In all, the full demonstration lasted barely one *peth*—18 minutes of Earth impatience, Gina calculated.

"That's all there is to it?" she called again.

"Yes."

"You stopped pleasuring me for this?"

"You were not impressed?"

"It did not do anything."

"Oh, but it did." He unbelted himself and stepped out from the exo-body, then sent it into storage above them. "If it worked properly, you will see the power readings on the monitor."

"Power readings?" She unlatched her helmet when he gave her the index finger salute. "There was no exhaust, no projection, no...nothing."

Vazak removed his helmet and went to her.

"It is supposed to be that way: quiet, stable, yet powerful. Let's check the read-outs."

He directed her to the panel of gauges, pointed to one and smiled. He showed her two more, again smiling.

"This is the longest I've ever let it run," he said, his yellow suited arm coming up behind her shoulders and giving them a squeeze. "You have witnessed history."

"What history? You are playing with me. You can pleasure me just fine but you will never fool me with your weekend science project."

"Look, *Kalmonê:* The read-out shows that within only the time it was fully operational, a duration of, say, 0.821629 *peth*, it would have propelled a space vessel of medium weight, like the V-100 military cruiser model under construction at Herêbout, approximately, mmm, 283,364.75 *radit*—"

Her mind froze on his last phoneme, put it in a closet and shifted to calculation mode: in 18 minutes the vessel would have, could have traveled 170,000 miles. Not bad for a toy. That would be 637,500 miles per hour. Not bad at all. Using an engine the size of God's cigar. Hydrogen fuel. Quiet. Stable. No radiation.

"Not bad at all."

"You see the potential?" He watched her thinking. "It's not a quick starter yet over the course of a year it will continue acceleration exponentially. I don't mean to boast, but you could theoretically reach one-tenth light speed after several years."

She closed her eyes, her lips moving silently.

"I know it won't get the fleet to the closest star and its planets within one generation, but it has other advantages. You would not need to carry extra fuel aboard the vessel. I could tinker more with it, try to get the production values higher."

She held her gloved hand up to his lips, shushing him.

"This changes everything."

"It does?"

She stretched up to kiss him. "It does."

"Then I'm so glad I was able to please you, enough to make you forget reality, as you wanted."

"This is everything I never dreamed of!"

"It's yours, if you want it." He picked her up in his bear hug. "I give it to you. For making my last days so joyful. I don't need it. I already signed the pledge not to take a seat. As you did."

"Then we will applaud you for conceiving of this device."

"The Mixerran fuel cell?"

"Everyone will know who built this, Vazak. I will tell them. I will tell the world."

"If you want to do that." He smiled, embarrassed. "Perhaps we should test it more."

Her eyes were twinkling when she met his. "Yes, but let's hook it up to a space vessel and see if it flies!"

In the days that followed, Gina took the airship to Kobarêl and fought with administrators over production quotas and resource allocation. She spoke with her daughter Zaura's supervisor, made sure her work was up to standard, inquired about her promotion. She visited the memorial to the Miracle Children built in a garden left green and floral in the center of the blighted rust-brown city. Two F'eng followers, easily recognized by their uniquely scarred faces, questioned her. They apparently knew who she was and chastised her for pushing for the evacuation rockets against the wishes of the seven gods and nine goddesses. The discussion became heated and two public order guardians stepped in and roused the F'eng ladies into state of fury. Gina hurried away.

When next she visited Erit a few months later, Vazak was delighted to announce a special romantic odyssey for their time together.

"Where are we going?" she asked, half worried, half curious. "Not to a wintry resort again, I hope."

He refused to answer and kept the ETUR-KV on the track, soon crossing the border from Nouvê into Jêpolissa. The track went through a medium-sized city, then entered some low mountains covered in a gray forest, the leaves long and narrow, the cones dull orange. Gina had been expecting to be shuttled away for a secret weekend but she had no idea that the isolated location was where Vazak had hidden his new toy.

Pulling up to the cottage, she could see the long fuselage and stubby wings of an aircraft parked down by the lake.

"You see? It's a surprise for you," he called as she went across the yard to the jet.

"Is it...?" She turned to him as he arrived next to her. "It has the Mixerran fuel cell in it?"

"Of course. We must test it, you said."

"Who will pilot it?"

He grinned and she noticed more gray hairs around his face. "I am too big to fit in the pilot box."

They talked more over dinner, planning the test flights. She was too excited for the mating ritual. "In fact," she said, "I've been feeling strange for a few months now. Perhaps I'm finally getting old."

"You don't look any different to me," said Vazak. "You are as beautiful now as when I first saw you—as though you have not gotten older at all."

When he had fallen asleep, she went to the personal hygiene room and looked into the mirror. She did not look bad, but she could tell there were changes. Most of the changes, she had to admit, were inside. Her abdomen cramped often and her skin felt hot with no reason. Headaches and heartburn, too. She brushed her hair back, staring at herself.

"Could it be...?" She counted in her head. "After three-hundred and eighty years lived around this planet, *now* I'm finally hitting menopause?"

The next morning he showed her the aircraft and went over the controls with her. Two recessed balls were set in the front of each armrest which the palm of the hand moved in any direction. Clips fastened to the thumbs, also leading to controls. The helmet was fitted with information and communication screens, as well as earpieces for audio. The panel ahead of her showed all the readings a pilot would need.

"I will strap you in so you will be safe," said Vazak. "If you want to see the sky up close."

"Yes, I do." She could not remember flying even in an ordinary airplane back on Earth other than the flights home to Kansas City from her college in St. Louis, only an hour. On Ghoupallesz, her airborne experiences were always on airships.

By then, four technicians had arrived to help Vazak with the test. The vehicle they drove pulled a large trailer containing flight control equipment. They set up a miniature airport on the strip of flat shoreline along the lake below the cottage. The shoreline was packed clay and served well as a 'runway'—a word Vazak did not know when Gina used it.

"We will control the craft from here," said Vazak. "We have a no-cable connection to the craft. Everything is by invisible radio strings. We will be out of range at some time today. Yet I made sure to program the flight. You need not do anything." He kissed her forehead. "Enjoy the ride, *Kalmonê.*"

They sealed her up inside the pilot box and waved goodbye. Her stomach began to tighten as she watched them manipulate the buttons on the control panels of the portable station. Her throat was dry. She blinked several times and thought of her daughter back in Kobarêl; sure, Zaura was an adult leading her own life now but she still felt responsible for her. What if this experiment went wrong? What would the International Aerospace Council do to complete the project without her to guide them? Or bully them into doing something, anything?

The engine fired behind her and she felt its power kick her forward, then throw her back.

"Wait a moment," she spoke into the comm line. "Can you wait a while, please?"

They could not hear her, she decided, feeling the craft slide forward along the shoreline.

"Are you calm?" asked Vazak unexpectedly over the comm line. He chuckled.

"I'm not sure about this—"

Then she was grabbing tightly to the handles on either side of her seat as the craft thrust forward like the worst rollercoaster ride of her life, grazing the shoreline and streaking out over the lake, dragging its surface up into the air as it went. The craft barely missed the treeline and then was heading toward the next mountain.

She fell back, pressed into the seat cushion, as the craft shot high into the sky at an impossible angle: the emerald clouds breaking away, the fading of familiar sights below, the darkening of the sky above, and suddenly there was the arc of the planet, curling away from her in all directions. There before her was the entire inverted bowl of the northern hemisphere: Jêpolissa and its T-shaped peninsula, the ice of the northern sea. Then just as quickly she was sinking, falling—no, it was the planet turning, as usual, as it was meant to do; everything was normal. There was the arctic coast of the Zetin nations in northern Megank, ahead the mountainous bowl of the Alaun plateau. And as she streaked southward, the subcontinent of Tebbicousimankalê! She could pick out the industrial cities of Debrêk, Cousi, and Sendask, then the blue of the Tebbi Sea. Then Kipzon, and Gotanka, and down the middle plain of Filopê, Saunicêa, then Typeg, where a new transport frame was currently under assembly in orbit. And across the strait to the jungle-choked west end of the continent of Lapughê.

She was crossing the continent when she was struck by a bright light: the yellow sun, Abæda, was rising and the blue sun, Siila, was there, too. She lowered the shade screen on her helmet and announced the moment through her comm set to those on the ground.

"That's wonderful, *Kalmonê!*"

"And I can see the orbital assembly zone now!"

As she approached Kobarêl, there was the space elevator, the heavy lift machinery, and four transport frames, all of them in nearly complete condition. They floated like empty squares of metal skeletons along the curvature of the planet's atmosphere, two with the propulsion assembly already in place and two still awaiting their nuclear pulse engine modules. She told her ground crew how magnificent it all looked.

Suddenly, she was startled by a loud thump and held her breath, listening for more.

"I've been hit by something," she said, rather frantically. "I think it was a rock of some kind."

"All part of the wonders of space," came Vazak's calming voice at the other end. "You're almost home now anyway. Hold on. We'll bring you down."

She breathed deeply, blinked, then watched the curve of the planet draw closer as they pulled her down. And as she arched over Kobarêl and the Jassera Sea, another light caught her attention. She had turned away from the twin suns by then so she knew what it was: the bright light, bluish-white with a trail like glowing embers. It was the comet Xôsz that was causing so much hardship and fear. Ghoupallesz would circle the suns several more times, the comet chasing it, until at last they would meet. She studied it until the craft curved out of view and she soon saw the rough forest cover of Jêpolissa once more.

Setting the craft on the shoreline, Vazak hurried to release her from the pilot box. He slid the canopy back and unhooked the straps. Gina tried to stand, instead, bent over the side of the craft and let go two days' worth of food rations down the side of the fuselage.

"That's normal, *Kalmonê*," he said, then patted her shoulder.

As she recovered, he examined the dent in the nose cone, a fist-sized mark that disappointed him. His beautiful rocket was damaged. His beautiful pilot could have been hurt.

He helped her out of the pilot box and half-carried her up the path to the cottage while his assistants tended to the aircraft.

"You liked the ride?" he asked.

She nodded weakly. Her headache was growing.

"You won't believe how little fuel was used. You won't believe what speed you attained. You were a vessel piercing the opening of the universe. And you returned to me."

She tugged at his beard.

"I want to lie down now. I must sleep. Let the world stop spinning. Please stop spinning."

"You may rest now. I will give you a green-*bôb*."

"Would it be all right if you just held me tonight?"

He seemed puzzled at first, then nodded. "Whatever you wish, I shall grant for you."

"Thank you, Vazak."

She felt weak, knowing it was only partly from the flight around the planet—*the planet!* In only 1.75 *peth*! Thirty-five minutes in Earth time. Less than full speed, according to Vazak. She realized the rest of her troubles came from the fact she was getting older, older than she had ever been in all her many voyages in and out of interdimensional doorways. Tangents could be kind, she knew; they could also be cruel.

Chapter 29

Truth

Gina was nervous just setting foot in Tebbicousimankalê again but she had to be at the conference. She was the chair, after all. This year the International Aerospace Council's worldwide conference was meeting in Debrêk, the industrial metropolis west of the Tebbi capital. It was the home of the Debrêk spaceworks. In fact, after the general assembly, the gathering would witness the first launching of the V-8 Residential Capsule that would dock with the R-12 Transport Frame already in orbit, launched from the Kobarêl spaceport. At long last some tangible progress would be visible. And yet, at this conference, Gina would try to convince the council members to try the Mixerran fuel cell as a new, better propulsion system for upcoming transports.

As she walked the avenues of Debrêk after setting her bag in the inn, she was amazed at how well the city had been rebuilt following the wars. She stopped—*wars?* Ignoring her doubts, she gazed upward, admiring the tall, silvery buildings with their conical crowns topped by statues of the 48 dragons of Zetin mythology. Well, she called them dragons: reptilian, winged beasts. They also had made up the décor of the Grand Palace in Siti, she recalled. Somehow the invading Zissekap settlers long ago chose to retain the dragon symbols for each of their states as the Zetin people were pushed north. Over the centuries, however, the dragons had been reduced to little more than cartoon characters, curiosities, and children's toys—which, of course, angered the Zetin to no end. Debrêk was Disneyland, she decided, and laughed, much to the consternation of the dirty beggars holding out their boxes. Not smiling, she dropped a few food tickets into their boxes and continued on her way.

Walking along, she vaguely recalled seeing pictures of this very avenue, set with the five statues of Tebbi generals and statesmen, one at each of the grand intersections, then destroyed by steady bombardment from the Sekuatean army in 1532. She felt she had been here before, perhaps talking to a soldier. It wasn't clear. Her dreams and memories were becoming colluded. Another time, she had visited the city as the wife of the Prime Minister of Tebbicousimankalê. She remembered waving at the crowds along this avenue. That was long ago. Perhaps it never happened. Just like the war that some people remembered and others swore never happened.

"That Sebastian, always changing history," she said with a warm smile. There never was a great war, not after her high school sweetheart changed everything. If only he could change history now, save her from the end of the world—at least save her from this conference. She had no hope of that. She glanced about, hoping to see a hand mysteriously reaching for her from out of thin air. He might be able to change history, she pondered, but he could not change a comet.

She wore her new emerald green kaftan with red lapels, getting tired of the fashion trend now extending into its tenth year. It fit her mood, however, wanting to look regal, to command authority and respect, and hide her extra weight. Well-fed people were not welcomed in most places because many were starving with the diminished food production and distribution. Already the planet was dividing into the haves and have-nots, fighting and defending instead of sharing and cooperating. Yet how could anyone help in a project they would never benefit from? She didn't know the answer, but she knew many proposed the *bôb* system of drugs to keep laborers working steadily and blissfully unaware of the future. A day's work was rewarded with food rations. There used to be sports or dull-witted dramas and comedies performed in community centers. Those innocent pastimes were considered frivolous now; no one was in the mood for comedy with the comet bearing down on them. An evening dose of the right *bôb* and a good night's sleep would prepare them for another day's conscientious effort. That more than anything made her glad she was not taking a seat on any vessel. That decision was not completely altruistic; she expected to find that elusive tangent before the Final Day.

"Today there are more than three million applications for a seat on Homeland Project vessels," Gina calmly announced before the assembled crowd of perhaps five thousand scientists, engineers, administrators, and heads of religious communities. "Our staff is overwhelmed sorting through them. Naturally, they skip over those having physical or mental defects. Also skipped over are those of excessive age, height, weight, and low intelligence ratings. Certain proclivities are grounds for exclusion. We estimate that Kobarêl's vessels will be able to carry about four thousand crew and passengers. Total. This includes both active members and those in suspension. There are plans for an embryo craft carrying ten-thousand units. What other spaceports may yield we have yet to determine; Kobarêl's program is the most advanced, so we have been using it as a baseline."

"What of the tether programs?" asked a woman.

"We are not including their statistics in our assessment. They have chosen to separate from the International Aerospace Council's protocol. I understand that both Aikavo and Ilarat have or soon will be able to launch four vessels of short-term capacity, with the expectation of a two-year hibernation in orbit followed by resettlement. The government of Dikondra has also expressed a desire to construct their own tethering vessels."

"Any estimate of the numbers destined for underground accommodation as recommended by the testimony of the Miracle Children?"

"We know of seventeen underground projects in operation. That is, sufficiently deep and furnished as to be useable even now. There are at least twelve others in progress. Most are in mountainous regions because of the belief that mountain shields will provide better resistance. That all depends on the strike zone, of course."

"Strike zone! What a ghastly term," a man in the front row shouted.

"Yes, what is the latest trajectory data?" asked another.

"The Astronomical Observation Agency sent us a report this morning, as requested. The comet remains on track for a strike in 2175, the same data we have operated from for twenty-two years. However, as it moves closer, they are able to better measure its course. The latest data indicates strike likely in the months of Denio or Azit of that year, late summer. If that changes, and we are told it probably will, the timing will likely shift to Azit and Shæ, or even as late as the month of Batou. The position of the planet in that season will put the western hemisphere at more of a risk than the eastern hemisphere."

The crowd noise rose. Those from Zissekap, on the west side of the supercontinent, seemed most vocal.

"So how long do we have until Final Day?" someone shouted.

"We have less than eleven years," Gina called over them.

The assistant flashed the lights and the crowd calmed.

"How soon will the interstellar vessels be loaded?" one person asked.

"How far in advance of the strike will people be put aboard?" asked another.

"The question is whether they will be ready for loading in time." She scanned the crowd. "Some vessels will be ready soon but we do not want to load them too early and be using resources needed for the, mmm, voyage."

Voyage.... She thought of the day she and Sebastian stepped through the doorway, when they first became voyagers, and how that special talent had made them like gods, roaming back and forth across the timelines, past, present, future, of Ghoupallesz, never considering when the end might come. *All things must end.*

"Our spaceports have the following quotas...."

Charts were projected on the walls, outlining in great detail the number of transport frames completed and how many were still under construction, along with completion schedules of each spaceworks facility. The same data was displayed for the various residential capsules. Large hibernation capsules. Medium split-crew capsules. Small active-crew vessels for security. Supply vessels. Kobarêl had five transport frames in production, three completed and in orbit. Two residential capsules were under construction. The first was being used as a test model so the work was proceeding slowly, carefully. One of the security vessels was considered complete and was about to begin testing in orbit.

In orbit.... She had been there, had seen the transport frames in their spacedock at the top of the space elevator. She knew what she was talking about. Soon she would ride on one of those vessels—and not on Vazak's little toy rocket with the new fuel cell providing almost endless energy. He would be introducing it in the afternoon to a gathering of engineers. If they approved of his design, he would reveal it to the entire world.

"Then I can sit back and enjoy my last years," he had told her the night before.

"If we were not leaving soon, you would be paid handsomely and be a wealthy inventor the rest of your life," she said.

"I care not about being a wealthy man," he said with a laugh. "I care only about sensual pleasures: a hot bath, a rough massage, a warm sleepmate, fine food and drink, and music. Lots of music! Let the stars sing our song! Let the galaxy dance for us, *Kalmonê!*"

She held her smile until she realized others were again asking questions.

"Yes," she responded, "there is a rumor of a new propulsion system. We shall have to wait until that is revealed—or not. You know how rumors can be. The Miracle Children, for example. And the F'eng movement. All started with rumors. All we know for certain is that our comet has not slowed or turned and still intends to meet us near the original, appointed date, whether we like it or not. Some have chosen to hide underground. Others have decided to wait in orbit. Still others expect total annihilation and are making plans to find a new home among the stars. And, sadly, there are some who dare not wait to see how the end will come and take it upon themselves to choose the time and method of their end, which is their right. I do not judge anyone's choice. I— and many of us here today—have pledged to give up our seat on a vessel. We pledge to stay behind and accept that fate so that others may carry forth our genes, our culture, our civilization—"

"*Kalmonê* d'Elous!" someone shouted from the middle of the

room. "You must choose a vessel and take yourself aboard it to prove it is safe and space-worthy."

Others shouted similar declarations. The crowd noise rose. Gina glanced at the co-chairperson. He shrugged.

"How can we be sure these rocket pods are not a conspiracy to exile us? Or even to kill us out there? So you and your cohorts can inherit the planet?"

"Colleagues," she called, holding up her arms, index fingers extended to signal for calm. "Please hear me clearly. I made a pledge for the good of all. There is no deception. No agency plots to exile anyone. There are many conspiracies perpetrated by so-called wisemen. Look at the F'eng self-immolation in Foixe last week. Several hundred people looked to the skies and set themselves ablaze. They believed the seven gods and nine goddesses were calling them and they did not want to wait for the comet. No, I am here to save you, yet I do not ask for you to set yourselves on fire, or crawl into caves or do anything else but save yourselves. I cannot ask laborers to build me an evacuation vessel and then not allow them, any of them, not even their families, to be saved with me. So I have pledged not to take a seat. I promise you that, and you elected me to oversee the Homeland Project, which I have done for fourteen years."

Half the crowd jeered while others whistled in support of her.

She scanned the crowd, met some eyes while other eyes turned away.

"Perhaps it is time for me to step down."

More people, especially from the western delegations, sent jeers to the stage. Those in support of her fell silent.

"I shall resign this position at the end of this year," she spoke out, "so you have some time to find a replacement overseer. I will be happy to act as mentor and consultant for whoever is chosen to follow me."

"Are you resigning so you can break your pledge and grab a seat?"

More angry words from the crowd.

"No, I continue my pledge," she shouted back. "I will not leave this planet on any vessel."

She stepped back as the crowd shouted their questions, suggestions where she could go, and what she should do with her remaining time—such vulgar language coming from respected scientists and politicians! She was shocked. How could so many feel so angry at her? She never pushed them into anything that did not make sense from a biological or anthropological perspective. Nor did she hide anything from them. She had always been quite transparent in everything she did.

I truly am a goddess to them. She exited the stage, the roar of colleagues still hurting her. *Yet they know not what they do.*

She would take a welcome vacation, just relax, and in her spare time she would try again to find a good tangent.

"Ah, have no regret, *Kalmonê*," said Vazak, holding her in his big arms. "It is to their regret, they will soon see. They will be like children abandoned by their mother. They will cry and whine like naughty babies. They will realize they are hungry and they have already refused the breast!"

There was always a warm hug waiting for her, she knew, whenever Vazak-Mixerran was close. And yet that too would end soon. He was not in good health, she knew, though he hid it well. His project had taken his last energy even as it gave him a reason to press on with the remaining days.

"You rest here," he told her, gesturing to the *qala* in the inn's room, "and I will give my presentation of the Mixerran fuel cell."

"I should go there to support you," said Gina.

"I thank you for your constant support. Today I am ready to fly on my own. You know everything about the fuel cell already. You know what I will say. There is no reason to be among such a group of engineers and wait for my talk to end. Rest here and I will return after perhaps five *peth*."

And he did return, the door opening serving to startle her from her nap.

"Is everything all right?" she asked, rubbing her eyes.

He pouted. "They are idiots!"

First, he was accused of a hoax, making something to trick them. That turned into an argument about him seeking to profit from his invention at a time when money had no more value. The engineers were the worst, Vazak explained, challenging him at every turn. He described the flight tests, without mentioning Gina, and proposed that models five-times the size of the test unit be constructed and used in the interstellar transports. Objections rained down about having to redesign couplings and docking assemblies on the transport frames. There was not enough time for a complete propulsion system makeover many insisted.

"I can give you a hug," she offered.

"Better than that, I want to take their words and crush them in my hands!" He crunched his fists together and howled. "I'm sorry, *Kalmonê*. I cannot bear idiots."

"No one liked your new propulsion system?"

"First the hug you promised," he said, reaching for her, "then the explanation."

Chapter 30

Childhood

When Gina returned to Kobarêl, she made her way wearily from the airship terminal through the dirty streets to her high-rise apartment in the Third Ward compound where many of the administrators and scientists lived, guarded and safe from the mindless masses sucking *bôb* and laboring for a steady fix.

She was surprised to find her daughter, Zaura, lounging at home. Gina was also surprised to find her sitting naked on the learning chair, wearing only the white scarf that marked her status as an approved fertility club member, virgin rank, with a seat on a vessel guaranteed.

"You really must wear some clothing, my dear," said Gina, dropping her bags on the floor.

"Nobody is here," Zaura replied, not looking up from her tablet, quickly dabbing the stylus on colorful buttons on the screen.

The learning chair was more like a chaise-longue with embedded computer interfaces. Their use was approved for space cadets whenever the environment was on alert for high pollution levels or there was a riot of the mindless hordes; school lessons could be maintained that way.

"Besides, it's the trendy thing for youth to do." She glanced over her shoulder at Gina. "Headmistress Dero says there's no harm in looking. We need to get used to it for such a long journey. Besides, it's only Latol. You already said he was allowed to sit in our family unit some day."

"I did?" She regarded the screen set into the wall and saw there a naked boy, sitting on his own learning chair, playing with his stylus and apparently unaware that Zaura's mother had returned home. "Hello, Latol."

He startled. "Greetings to you, Mother of Zaura," said Latol, not at all embarrassed.

"So formal?"

"Yes. You will be a grandmother for us some day, true?"

Gina grinned. "Not too soon, I hope."

"Mama, we're discussing the coupling specifications for the residential pods' docking assembly and we discovered that if they started Design Protocol 431 precisely when Design Protocol 394 was 55.5 percent completed, the teams could save 14.33 *peth* in time, which translates into 1,815 *merin* in cost savings—and that would allow the purchase of 45 more food processor units, for example, which is enough to outfit 86.2 percent of one V-100 military cruiser's standard allotment—"

"I'm relieved you are actually studying." She laughed for the first time since she had left for the conference in Debrêk. "I worried about pre-marital sex, like my mother always did. I know there's no marriage now, only state-authorized coupling that maximizes fertility and produces the best of the species. Eugenics returns. I approve of it if only ten-thousand or so can be saved from certain doom."

"Mama, you are so zero-grade. Did the conference go well?"

"No, it certainly did not."

"I have sorry feelings spinning around you."

"You didn't learn the latest news?"

Zaura looked up. "We have been manning the Calculus orb, Mama, not slinking the Events channel."

Gina pursed her lips, amused at her daughter's youthful slang, then took a seat by the dining loft.

"My dear, there was an accident." She tried to laugh, choked instead. "After my keynote address. The launch of the first residential capsule from the Debrêk spaceworks went bad. There was an imbalance in the chemical rockets which sent the capsule off trajectory and it crashed nearby. There were five crew aboard. Fortunately. They were only sending it up to dock with the transport frame already in orbit."

"That's horrible!" Zaura turned to Latol poised on the screen. "Did you copy my mother's words?"

"Yes," he said. "Let me eye the Events channel for video food. Communicate after an interval." He blinked out and the screen returned to a static picture of a lush green valley that could be somewhere in Switzerland—or Sogoê.

"We stood on the observation platform," Gina continued, "and everyone was happy, excited, waiting to see this momentous event. I cheered for them when the engines ignited. It was only a little way into the air when it spun sideways and went nose-first into a hillside. The fire was horrible and everyone ran. Someone threw a fire-cover over me and held me down. When it was clear, two medical staff helped me but I was not injured in anyway."

"I feel a sympathetic pain in my chest on your behalf. What an experience!" Zaura went to her mother, embraced her. "Take a black-*bôb*."

"Then everyone began accusing me of setting them up! I did not make the vessel crash. I had nothing to do with it, nor did the Debrêk spaceworks. They have an outstanding work record. They said I wanted everyone to go onto the vessels so they would be killed and I and 'all my friends' could take over the planet. How ridiculous! Evacuation is the only way to survive the coming catastrophe. I even offered to take a seat on a vessel, if they so wished, so they would know I had not booby-trapped it."

"Buubii-turapt?" asked Zaura with a smirk. "Who would want to design something to catch breasts?"

"An English word," said Gina in English and continued in that archaic language: "Like if a bomb were set to go off. Ah, daughter, you must not forget the language of your ancestral homeland."

"I was born in Kipzon," Zaura replied in English. "You said it like a truth in stone."

"But your mother and father were born on a planet far, far away and long, long ago. The planet is called Earth. Well, some call it Terra. Others no doubt call it Shithole. It doesn't matter unless we go back to it."

"It exists still?" asked Zaura.

Gina wiped a tear from her cheek. "I think it does. We need to find it. Staying here is not a good idea. Going aboard a spacecraft for the rest of your life isn't much better."

"You feel exploding seashells, Mama?" asked Zaura, returning to Ghoupallêan. "Pop a black-*bôb* and sleep deep."

"I don't need any drugs!" she snapped in English.

She threw her hands to her face as the tears came fast. Many years ago she was happy to take drugs—purely for recreational purposes, of course. Anything to get through the days and nights of college life, hanging out with other druggies when it was all so counter-everything. Now the drug culture had gone mainstream and she was the old-fashioned witch-mom denying the youth their pleasures.

"You need a vacation, Mama."

Gina lowered her hands, her eyes red. "I certainly do. So I quit the council. I promised to stay on to the end of the year but I did resign at the conference. Right before we watched the residential capsule crash. If it had launched full, there would have been five hundred people dead instead of only five." She teared up again.

"Mama, cut an interval."

"You should come with me. I don't want to go alone."

"I have cadet training. I cannot quit or cut an interval from the schedule."

Gina nodded, realizing that she had little control over anything now. Only herself. And that was becoming so maddening as the planet was trying so hard to turn its years over into months. They would soon be under a decade until the end.

"I'll go then," she said. "Be good. Resist the *bôb*. Stay as happy as you can. And dream. Everything is perfect in your dreams, daughter."

The scene was like something from a dream: white sand beach, turquoise water, pastel green sky and the two suns adding their light from different angles. It was just as she remembered it from several lifetimes before.

Gina stood up from the lounge chair and gazed out at the bright sea, feeling the warm breeze on her face. She untied the belt of her white robe and let it slip off her shoulders and drop to the deck of the beach house she had rented. The air touched her skin and let her know that the clocks had been destroyed, the calendars burned, and all that remained was one perfect moment when everything turned inward, sank into deep, luxurious cushions, and yawned without apology. She felt alive again, as though the world of cutthroat aerospace councils never existed, as though she had always been on this beach, had always stood nude on the sand, wanting to slip quietly into that warm sea and swim until the days turned to nights and back to days again.

And she did: stepping down the beach until the crystal clear water caressed her ankles, then her knees, then hips and belly and breasts, and tickled her chin. She swept back her hair in the water, shook it free. She launched herself across the waters, arms paddling and legs slowly kicking; she was not in any race. She sighted a point of land about a half-*radit* away, and swam toward it, letting her head vent all its frustration as she went.

Liêta, on the west coast of Bæronak, on the tropical Soguirê Sea, straight across the ocean from Kobarêl. No other guests were around. The resort was run down now, quite understandable given that no one had money for vacationing. The clip of money, such as it was, would buy a lot of food rations for the proprietor's family so they were happy to welcome her. They quickly made a room available, what used to be their honeymoon suite, and once more staffed the office in case she needed anything. She slept for a day, read a book of poetry she found in the room for part of the second day, then walked the beach on the third day. Each night she had sat on the deck gazing skyward, eyes focused on the light, the blue trail of doom, almost twinkling like a star people made wishes to, or pledged eternal love before it could stop shining. How many more close passes would the planet make before they united in profane matrimony?

Today she had welcomed the sunshine. And the silence. She pretended that nothing before dawn had happened, that none of those years stuck in her memories ever happened. The tropical forest presented bird song and monkey chatter but everything else was mute. The waves rhythmically licking the shoreline reminded her of Vazak-Mixerran and his winter cottage, the *jalo* skin coverings—

So long ago, another world, possibly a dream....

It seemed like yesterday she was in charge of the planet. She was responsible for everything in the International Aerospace Council's protocols. *Yes, responsible.* Whatever went wrong, she was responsible. She would never get a seat on a vessel now. She laughed, her hands cutting the waves as she swam. A seat on a vessel did not matter to her. That her daughter was going was all that concerned her; yet how could she watch her daughter blast away into the void, never to see her again? And how could she sit back and watch the comet coming in, see it approach, growing larger, predict the trajectory and feel the crash and the ripples of quaking cross the globe, the ground beneath her shattering, she and her chair falling into a crevasse, being swallowed and then to have that chunk of ground ripped from the mantle beneath and flung up into the atmosphere like a giant plume of lava?

Where is a damn tangent when I need one?

She came to the opposite shore and rose slowly from the water, streams running down her slick body. She shook the water from her hair and lay on the sand, feeling young again, feeling sexy. The sunshine warmed her, matching the heat from the sand under her. Arms tucked back under her head, she closed her eyes and dreamed of tomorrow.

Dreams...intimations of reality, predictions of agency, warnings of consequences, role playing scenarios, virtual reality, the quest for immortality on a finite world in an infinite universe. And here she was, a mortal being renting time and space on a world not of her birth, worrying about strangers and their silly fate. And here she was, with a daughter grown to adulthood, a daughter who would sail away. And here she was, still secretly mourning a son she never knew. And the other children she had borne through so many lifetimes lived in so many places, lived and died, and their children who had lived and died, and theirs, too. And she never knew them or their lives. And once upon a time she had lived right here in Liêta, beside a lake in a different district of this isolated paradise that seemed like a dream, as though she were in some sensory-deprivation chamber, in some kind of experiment she had never signed up for. She would open her eyes and see that the sky was a ceiling and the suns merely fluorescent lamps glowing in a laboratory, and she would be home, safe and sound, and her mother would wipe the sweat from her forehead and ask how she felt, and she would say "Much better, thanks" and then wonder where she had been for the past three hundred years or so and yet still be a child in that room in that little town of Blue Springs, Missouri, back on Earth, somewhere back on Earth, where tangents did not exist, where a boy she stood in front of in Choir suggested they go make-out one summer day at some abandoned quarry hidden in the woods, and that would be all there was to it, only the making-out, only kissing and touching, only that and nothing more.

When she opened her eyes, many *peth* had passed and the skies were dark overhead. Across the sea, only half of the yellow sun's orb was above the horizon, the blue sun already gone. The breeze turned cooler against her skin. She sat up, yawning. Was this still the dream?

She stood and gazed across the little bay to where her swim had begun, wondering if she dared swim back in the dark. On this new beach she had nothing, no towel, no robe, so walking back along the shore was no easier a choice.

Stretching her arms into the sky, she felt relaxed, rested, and ready for a new adventure. She toyed with the idea of a strange, handsome hunk of man coming upon her and seducing her, then dismissed the idea as the ravings of a madwoman who was already over the hill and hopelessly perverse.

She brushed the sand off herself and headed back to the resort, following the line of surf in a wide curve that left half of her steps in the water and half on the sand. As she walked, slowly so as to be careful where she stepped, she listened to the chattering of nocturnal life in the forest beside her. When the chattering stopped and the breeze became the loudest sound, she paused, concerned whether something bad was about to happen. She imagined the natives of the jungle were watching her. Seeing her nude, they might abduct her for their fertility rituals—unless they found her to be too old. Or it could be some wild animal looking for dinner. She stepped quicker, fearful of being followed. She wished she had brought her laser stick with her but, obviously, not a good idea when swimming.

Alone—all alone on a beach in the dying light, as nude as a newborn, an uncomfortably noisy jungle beside her—

She saw the lights of the resort and breathed easier. It was difficult being alone, completely alone in the world, out there on a secluded beach with only the suns and sand. And her inevitable cacophony of thoughts. She glanced back a few times as she approached the resort, feeling more confident.

It took her three times as long to walk back as her swim had taken, and when she finally arrived and set foot on the deck where she had left her robe, the proprietor was waiting for her, worried his only customer had fled.

He held out a small parchment scroll, announcing that she had received a communication from Kobarêl.

She pulled on the robe and took the parchment, unscrolled it, and read about the death of Vazak-Mixerran in Erit.

Gina wore a white sari-like gown with gold patterns running in orbits around her curves, one of the latest fashions among the élite class of Kobarêl. There was still time to enjoy life, it seemed. No point in spending the final years in utter gloom. That was the attitude now: be colorful, have parties, live it up, enjoy reckless abandon!

Despite the new glamour, she stood stiffly before First Director Hanar-Santorak, who had replaced Atox-Dassel several months before. Dassel had gone insane, the report read, and one night took a fistful of mixed *bôb*, causing him to experience, so they surmised, a lavish bliss of several *peth* followed by a sudden and extreme explosion: head, belly, knees. Quite a mess in his office. The night custodian had found him all over everything. It was unexpected for Dassel, but becoming more common among the masses. It was time to check out if one did not have a ticket to ride. Not everyone was living it up.

"I did the best I could," Gina stated solemnly. "The accident could hardly be my fault." She meant the residential pod launch in Tebbicousimankalê. "Debrêk was exemplary. Their work protocol and production rates were in line with our standards, neither behind schedule nor in a rush to complete the vessel. I suspect sabotage. That would fall in line with the times and the mood of many who see our efforts as elitist."

"Our efforts our elitist," said Santorak, rearranging personal items on the desktop. "It is good to be among the élite, isn't it? We fund construction of vessels which will save us. We pay the laborers, who will not catch a ride, with whatever they desire in entertainment, fashions, sports, food, and drugs, and for mostly they are satisfied: work all shift then lounge all interval. Media Services gives them all kinds of sports and comedy and sexual instruction shows to placate them. That's seems a fair exchange, eh?"

"You're concerned about a fair exchange?"

"Concerned? No."

He looked up and his grin was evil. The spiked red hair did not amuse her; another style trend. The black skin-tight suit with red collar did not impress her. In fact, he made her think of a vampire, and the similarities were not superficial.

"That is the way of the world," he said. "We cannot all be the same. Everywhere people will sort themselves into appropriate levels and within each level each shall make their way doing what they can. You, First Director d'Elous, have special talents none of us cannot ignore, and so I am obliged to welcome you back to your former position—since you resigned from the International Aerospace Council."

"My resignation is not until the end of the year," she spoke up, narrowing her eyes. "Until then, I do believe I outrank you."

He seemed to choke, catch his breath and fake a smile.

"Perhaps."

"And since I outrank you, I need some assistance from you. I will attend the memorial ceremony for my friend Vazak-Mixerran in Erit. That part is easy—"

"I should tell you we cannot afford another trip for you with this year's budget. All trips must be business-related."

"It is." She stared down the vampire. "After the memorial ceremony I will see if I can obtain the fuel cell he built. He said I could have it."

"I heard he presented a lecture on that device and was roundly ridiculed. It was a clever hoax—"

"It was not a hoax!" She stepped forward and he fell back. "I saw it in operation. He put it in...." She decided better to say less about it. "It has potential so I think we should make a play for it.

Because he was my special friend, I may be able to obtain it fairly easily. I would like to see the fuel cell used in all Kobarêl vessels."

"You know we have a proven design that serves our needs. No point of starting over from scratch."

She translated his words and was amused at the idea of 'scratching' his eyes out. "It won't require any redesign. I'll show you when I get it back."

He seemed defeated, sulking as he went to the windows and gazed out at the green haze.

"As you wish. Go to your lover and beg for his toy."

"I will go."

She turned to leave. She could take the airship there, then if it was available, fly the aircraft back to Kobarêl. If she still remembered how the controls worked.

"I will need a landing license before I go."

He turned and glared at her. "Landing license?"

"Yes. I may be flying myself home."

He laughed, tried to make it more forceful just to show her how silly her idea was, but she held her ground. "Using your wings?"

"Yes. And I really detest that hair style of yours," she sneered. "What are you, thirty years old?"

Chapter 31

Resignation

The stately, broad-shouldered woman casually brushed back her drooping moustache and smiled at Gina, then placed her thick hands on Gina's shoulders and looked into her eyes.

"We are pleased you granted him the favor of the mating ritual in his final days," she said. "We never knew he had any fondness for women with yellow hair or bare faces. Perhaps it was an old age realignment of his senses. You never can tell with men. His head was full of clouds."

Gina smiled softly, remembering the warm, protective rumble of Vazak's bass voice.

The four women who gathered around her after the memorial ceremony of Vazak-Mixerran welcomed her as one of their own. She was surprised he had four wives—polyamorous partners. Each had been a part of his star at one time, then each moved on after several years, as custom dictated.

Gina was also surprised he had no children. She assumed they were grown and living their own lives and so he never interacted with them. It was not something either of them had talked about. She was not certain if he had known of her daughter in Kobarêl. Whenever they were together, they discussed science or were too busy with sex to discuss science. Nothing else.

Vazak had also been Erit's *boiar*—its mayor—for twelve years before he retired to his science projects, eventually appointed to be ambassador to the International Aerospace Council.

The four women invited Gina to join them in the ceremonial cleansing ritual. Off to the bathhouse they went, stripping down and lowering themselves into the hot water. Gina was relieved all that was involved was washing each other. She had feared more would be required but she left the pool feeling refreshed. The woman who had greeted her at the ceremony got out with her and showed her how to dry herself with the special towels they used: small squares of cloth which reminded her of the cleaning rituals she had endured by the *utê* while in Zetin captivity.

They struck up a conversation about Vazak's inventions as Gina combed out the woman's back hair. He had many of them locked away in a warehouse, she said. His papers and designs were in a vault, too. So many things nobody knew what to do with.

"We never concern ourselves with his fantasy toys," said the ex-wife. "As long as he pleased us on schedule, we left him alone at other times. I never saw anything. He never showed them to me. I don't have any concern for them now. I don't even know what they do."

"I know," said Gina, turning the woman around to work on her shorter front hair, careful to maneuver the comb around her nipples. "I know what he was working on and I know how to operate his toys."

"I suppose you and Vazak were scientists first and lovers second."

"That's true."

"So I'm sure my sisters will let you see what he has. You can take what you like. Less for us to be concerned with."

"Oh, thank you! That will be so helpful."

With the combing finished, the woman embraced Gina, released her.

"I cannot comb you, sorry." She stroked Gina's blond hair. You are such a naked woman, I don't know how Vazak was attracted to you. No offense intended."

"None taken."

*   *   *

Vazak's partner #3, who was a member of the city council herself, lent her personal assistant to take Gina to the warehouse where Vazak's 'toys' were housed. The young man in light brown coveralls with yellow collar and shoulder identification tags, seemed irritated to have to show this woman around. He kept scratching his meager beard every time she asked a question. Two clerks at the warehouse quickly produced an inventory list on the tablet and Gina scrolled back and forth through the list. Finally she found it: FUEL CELL, ATN-14, DESIGN 18, BUILD 4F, GP2159. Apparently, it already had been designated "for Jinetta-d'Elous"—without tax or penalty.

Gina took seven *peth* going through the aisles of items he had collected, built, or had some part in. Boxes, crates, tables and shelving, endless piles of parchment scrolls—a lifetime in itself for someone to go through. However, Vazak was nothing if not organized, and the catalog made it easy for his staff to find what they were looking for.

"Here it is," said the snooty assistant, pointing to the long bulge of canvas set on a support harness. He yanked back the cover. "Hmm! Looks like a sex toy, only bigger."

Gina smiled. "Not a sex toy, dear boy. It's a jet engine. More accurately, a prototype for an interstellar vessel's engine. It will power the vessels that—"

"Oh, I don't believe in that hoax," said the assistant, making a show of scratching his baby beard. "That comet will pass right by us without even so much as a friendly wink."

"Friendly wink? I doubt that."

"Anyway, no reason to worry. The Zetin are scheduled to shoot it out of the sky next year. That's what I heard."

She glared at the young man. He was not too hairy yet.

"Let us hope it works."

"I heard if they succeed, every nation will have to pay them one-tenth of their wealth."

"That's a high tax."

They packed up the fuel cell, 2.2 *mest* in length and 0.72 *mest* in diameter, set the device into a crate that was 1 by 1.2 by 2.8 *mest*, added protective padding, sealed and labeled it, then wheeled it out of the warehouse on a robo-cart. Gina called with her comm baton for an ETUR-KV to transport it to the airship terminal.

"That kind of cargo is forbidden on airships," the sleepy inspector there told her. "Too heavy. Send it on a boat."

"How about if it's only me and the box? I'll buy the whole airship."

"You can pay for that?"

She supposed not. So she had it transported to the docks. A voyage from Erit around the north cape of Qekolin and down the east coast of Aupl-zonê, then south across the Jassera Sea to Kobarêl would take too long, put the device at risk of damage or theft, and simply cost too much—more than the airship.

She returned to the airship terminal with the crate and initiated a comm link.

"I need a *merin* authorization from you," she demanded of First Director Hanar-Santorak over the special comm link allowed for authorized personnel.

He chuckled for a *pon*. "You know the budget." His voice rang of smugness. "We can barely afford to pay your way back here. You were advised not to go."

"It was a matter of professional etiquette. And business. A business trip, all for the Kobarêl spaceworks."

"We cannot be obligated to use so many resources in these desperate days simply for a show of politeness."

"I told you this device I'm trying to obtain is a crucial element in the construction of the vessels. We need it."

"I will see what can be done," Hanar said with a grunt. "I do not have much confidence in your request being fulfilled, I want you to know."

"Just get it done." She thought of her tone, decided to sweeten it. "First Director, this device will pay for its recovery very quickly. Authorize the funding and you will be a hero when it lifts our vessels into orbit, and powers them on their way."

"A hero, eh? I like the sound of that."

"I thought you would." She breathed easier. "But I need extra funding to bring it home."

"Perhaps we can get that extra funding by shifting your residence to the laborer quarters."

"You wouldn't!"

"It is the only way."

"Stop joking."

"Are you not scheduled to resign your head position with the International Aerospace Council at year's end? At that time, you will no longer be eligible for top level housing. You will need to move, and all that is available is in the Fifth Ward. Probably something can be found on the ground floor. I'm sure you'll enjoy the howling of the *bôb* hordes all night, perhaps get to share your bed with any vagabonds who break into your quaint little residence. No way to predict what could happen."

Gina lost her breath. She wanted to slam down the comm baton but held her anger in check.

"You cannot do that until I actually resign—at the end of the year!"

"Authorization has already gone through. It should return to me with the Overlord's stamp within another *peth*." It sounded as though he was trying to muffle his laughter. "When you return home, First Director, you will be homeless. Such irony. Poor planning. And poor performance. And do not worry about your daughter. She has already been moved."

"Moved? Where?"

"To the education facility."

"What! For what reason? She's a model cadet."

"And yet, there apparently are rules to follow and some of them were unfortunately broken."

"What's she accused of?"

"Wearing the white scarf, you know she is not allowed to mate, yes? And yet, she did. I can show you the video when you return. It's quite thrilling. We all agree. I'm sure you will agree, too. Take your time, Jinetta-d'Elous—if that is your real name."

The comm line went dead.

❋ ❋ ❋

The mechanical device which would save ten-thousand people or get her daughter out of jail? Gina did not hesitate. She had the fuel cell in its crate moved to a storage facility near the airship terminal, then went to a store and bought new labels, tore off the old labels, and wrote that the crate contained "Parsoud Eturag Maxapathi"—'refurbished automobile parts'; nobody would touch such a crate, she thought. She purchased several other boxes and stacked them empty around and on top of the crate, then locked up the unit. She would have to get back to it later.

On the airship, she thought of her options, decided on two. She would first confront Hanar-Santorak to assess his threat level. Then, if he seemed serious, she would go to the Overlord's office and charge Hanar with kidnapping, unlawful imprisonment, and a personal attack without provocation on a sitting Council member. Perhaps Hanar would lose his seat on a vessel.

The Overlord was Samot-Artexus, essentially the prince of the city. The city being such a huge metropolis and the center of everything in the nation of Kobarêl, he was like the president of the country. Technically, he was only the mayor but he carried the power of a minor god. What Gina knew of him was that he lived lavishly despite the poor lifestyle of most of the citizens. She thought he had been married then became a widower, but she was not sure. There was a rumor of his grown son being an engineer at the spaceworks and assured a seat aboard one of the vessels. With so many First Director (*senex-pirenor*) of this and that everywhere, *Æx-Kalmonê*—Overlord—was the only title that outranked them.

As soon as the airship was tethered, she saw a scramble of police below.

"What's this? An escort?" she mumbled.

Arriving on the ground, she greeted them: "Gentlemen, so good of you to welcome me home!"

"First Director Jinetta-d'Elous?" asked the captain.

"Yes, I am. Want an autograph?"

The captain was not amused. "Come with us."

Gina stood with her arms folded across her chest in the chilly, windowless room. The vertical light panels in the corners glowed pale blue, the horizontal panels in hexagons overhead projected yellow light down upon her, yet none added any warmth to the room. Before her were five men, three in the dark blue uniforms with red collars of the Public Protocol Commission. To the far right, as Gina stood, was First Director Hanar-Santorak, sitting at the end of the table, clearly enjoying the proceedings.

The chunky, bald man in the center asked all the questions. She did not know him and he did not introduce himself. They had been quietly questioning her for what felt like an hour—three *peth*—to the guardians of public behavior.

Gina's legs were growing tired.

"I assume you've been entertained enough?" she spoke after a long silence. "I would appreciate having my clothes back and I'd like to see my daughter now, too."

"Not yet," said the one she thought of as Mr. Chunky. "We have more questions."

"There's nothing strange about me," Gina said with a sarcastic twang. "You've been through my service record thoroughly and you've checked all my body cavities. I don't know what you were looking for, but you didn't find anything unusual in those cavities, did you?" She waited as Mr. Chunky looked at his tablet. "It's not like I'm some alien monster from another world come to eat your children." She chuckled weakly.

"And yet you did produce one of the Miracle Children," said Mr. Chunky without looking up.

"I certainly had no control over that. Being raped by a Xig shaman caused that conception. It was not my idea. They wanted my daughter but she was too young so I offered myself. The rest is well-documented in my personnel file."

"First Director Santorak believes you are not who you say you are."

"First Director Santorak doesn't know what he's talking about. The truth is he's had a romantic interest in me ever since we worked together as Second Directors in Biosciences. He was quite the flirter." She extended her arms to each side. "He's always wanted to catch a look at my naked body—my highly fit body." She turned sideways, then showed her other side. "Hope you're pleased, Hanar!" She returned her attention to Mr. Chunky. "All he had to do was invite me to dinner and flirt nicely." She placed her hands on her hips, defiantly. "Yes, I know it's the epitome of decadence to dine out while the workers cannot afford to do so. There's not many restaurants left in the city, anyway. No business for them. No problem. Hanar could have prepared dinner himself in his residence. Ah, but his wife likely would not have wanted him to demonstrate his perversions, play out his fantasies about me right in front of her. Poor man."

"Not true!" said Hanar with a grunt.

"It is true," said Gina. "Why else would he take all of these complicated steps just to see my body? And a woman my age, at that! He has quite a few perversions and one, obviously, is older women. I don't mean the usual five-year age difference common in Ghoupalle marriages but the age difference that would make the two of us more akin to mother and adult son. He probably wants to suck some milk. I'm sure you will agree that smacks of impropriety, wouldn't you?"

"You are mistaken about all that," said Hanar. "I have no wife. Yet that does not mean I am a perverse man."

Gina acted surprised. "Oh, now I understand. You are one of those weak men who need the state to assist him with his perversions. Now I get it."

"I apply all my time and effort for the good of the state!"

"Just as you are now? Wasting everyone's time today just to get a look at me?"

"We are not here to question Hanar-Santorak—"

"He has a fetish for yellow hair. Now he knows the carpet matches the drapes. So let us be done with this silliness."

Mr. Chunky asked what she meant by carpet and drapes, both uncommon in Ghoupalle residences. She explained the terms but no one was amused.

"So then...Jinetta-d'Elous...." Mr. Chunky stared straight at her. "Is that your true name?"

They had been over her identity several times. She had no proof available of who she seemed to be and they had no proof she was not. There simply were no records either way.

"I was named for two legends," said Gina. "The warrior known as Set-d'Elous and the Queen of Fenula, Jinetta. To my knowledge, I am not actually related to them by either bloodline or marriage contracts. The names appealed to my parents, I suppose."

She knew the only person better at telling convincing lies was

Sebastian Talbot, but he would never rat her out.

Mr. Chunky turned to Hanar-Santorak. "You said she was a demon, or spoke with them?"

"Ah, yes. She said she was from Ur-tha." He glared at Gina. "Didn't you?"

"Ur-tha?" She had always found it amusing that the people of Ghoupallesz referred to their version of the underworld or hell as *Ur-tha*. They took the Zetin name for a post-death paradise, flipped it on its backside and used it for a place of punishment. That *Ur-tha* sounded close to 'Earth' always made her laugh. She tried to laugh now.

"Isn't that a mythological place?" she asked Hanar. "I had thought you'd get the joke. But you did not—despite your advanced training." She regarded Mr. Chunky. "I would like my clothes now. And I want to see my daughter."

"But she met with that Jêpolissan several times," Hanar blurted out, standing. "She met him at the Siti conference and so many times since then, even meeting him in Erit! And she she she had s-s-sex with him! With a Jêpolissan—a big, hairy Jêpolissan man!"

Gina shook her head. "Hanar, you are an idiot."

She used the word *sorêjix*, which did not mean someone of low intelligence but someone who ignores the consequences of his actions, the closest word Ghoupallêan offered.

"How do you think I was able to get access to the fuel cell I've been trying to bring home?" She shook her head again, made sure Mr. Chunky was watching. "Hanar, you are such a poor judge of everything." She turned to the others at the table. "Because I was able to gain his trust over several years, Vazak-Mixerran showed me his invention, the fuel cell I told Hanar about. It was offered to me when Vazak died. I went to pay my respects at his memorial and his wives, not knowing what it was exactly, gave it to me. I had it in my hands, ready to load onto an airship. The steward said it was too heavy so I wanted to hire the entire airship solely for the crate and me. I was trying to bring the device home to Kobarêl, for use in our own vessels—but that idiot would not authorize funding for the airship. Then he had the audacity to threaten my daughter!"

The panel turned as one to regard Hanar-Santorak.

"I—I thought she was fleeing with some state secrets," Hanar explained.

Mr. Chunky pressed a button on the table controls.

"Bring in the suspect's clothing."

"Now, I want to see my daughter."

The men shared glances, then Mr. Chunky raised a tablet which showed a report within the video display.

"We are convinced of your honest intentions, First Director d'Elous," said Mr. Chunky, "but it appears that accusations against your daughter are true."

"I want to speak with her."

A woman in green staff uniform entered with clothing hanging over her arms. She went up to Gina and stood as Gina took each article of clothing and dressed herself.

"We will arrange that for tomorrow."

"Tomorrow? I need to talk with her now."

"We will arrange a place for you to stay the night."

"Can't I go to my residence?" She glared at Hanar. "Or did he really give away my apartment?"

"It is under contract for a new resident. The items there which were deemed common were placed in a public vend box. Obvious personal items were collected and put in storage. You will be able to access it tomorrow."

"May I speak to my daughter over a comm line?"

"She is in seclusion. She is safe." Mr. Chunky stood, put his fists on the table top. "On behalf of the Public Protocol Commission, we apologize for the false accusation by First Director Hanar-Santorak. You are free to go. Someone will escort you to comfortable accommodations for tonight. That is all."

Dressed again, Gina waved her hand.

"I have a request, if I may, *Kalmonê*."

"What is it?"

"Since I stood in this room for about eight *peth* without any clothes—and went through the body cavity search when I was first stripped—could I request that my esteemed colleague, First Director Santorak, be treated in similar fashion?"

Mr. Chunky grinned, then tried to wipe it away. "Granted. Proceed, First Director Santorak. Disrobe."

Chapter 32

Discipline

The door panel slid open to the right and Gina immediately saw her daughter, naked and frightened, standing in the center of the small cubicle, her feet planted inside a red circle on the floor.

"Oh, Mama!" cried Zaura, wanting to run and embrace Gina. She held back so as to stay in the circle. Gina went to her and they hugged.

"Can she have a gown?" Gina called back to the staff woman. "What's the purpose of keeping her naked?"

"All sorts of things can be hidden in clothing," said the stern-faced woman.

"Like what? Everything in this cubicle is bolted down."

The staff woman closed the panel. The lock buzzed a moment, then beeped.

"I'm sorry, Mama. I didn't mean to do anything wrong—"

"Speak English," said Gina, "so they won't understand us."

Gina took off her shawl and wrapped it around Zaura as she stepped out of the red circle. The circle was only for when the door panel was open. Zaura sat on the bunk projecting from the side wall and Gina sat beside her.

"It's all a big mistake," said Gina, putting her arm around her daughter's shoulders. "I'm working on getting you out. Then we will leave this place."

"Mama, they said I'm off the manifest. No seat. I can't go away from here. And Latol is no longer my mate. But I want him. We started to feel love together. I feel so squiggly when I'm with him. You know what I mean?"

"Yes, I know, dear." She stroked her daughter's short golden hair. They had cut it short, she guessed, as part of the intake protocol. Easier to manage. It looked feminine and neat, at least.

"I saw the video," said Gina softly. "They asked me a lot of questions, too. Of course, I was shocked—not at seeing two beautiful young people exploring each other that way, but that they were able to watch you at all and capture a video. That cannot be legal."

"We could not wait—"

"You know the screen can be two-way, didn't you? There is a green light in the lower right corner that comes on when the Public Protocol Commission observers are checking into each residence. The law does allow them to check up to five times per day and observe up to a full *peth* each time. It's for our benefit—for our security. So they say."

"But, Mama, there was no light."

"There wasn't?"

"No." She thought a moment. "While you were gone, a man came to our residence and fixed the screen. He said the signal was corrupt and he was called to fix it. I did not call. He simply arrived one day to fix it."

Gina sighed. She knew what was going on.

"That so-called repairman was likely from the Public Protocol Commission. He was sent to disable the warning light so you wouldn't know when they were watching you."

She muttered a vulgarity.

Zaura burst into tears, hands to her face.

"It's not your fault, dear," said Gina, rubbing her daughter's back. "I don't believe you did anything wrong. I remember what it's like to be in love, to feel like you have to be with that person. It's Nature pulling you together, and it's a beautiful thing. There is no shame in that. But there are rules and customs we try to follow to make living in a crowded society easier. It's not what you did, it's that you had a contract with the Aerospace Agency promising not to do it. I remember when I was your age...."

Zaura looked up at Gina. "Is there anything that can be done? I want to be with Latol so much. He always makes me feel so squiggly."

"That may not be possible. Not now. I can only imagine what punishment he is undergoing."

Of course, Gina had her own memories of punishment, mostly at the hands of Zetin priests. She recalled being in the Zetin ambassador's castle. She recalled being rescued by Set-d'Elous and his team of mercenaries. She also recalled that memory being false. It was one of those dreams that seemed real and got stuck in her head as a memory. The longer she lived on Ghoupallesz, the more she doubted the things that had happened, events that seemed to have happened long ago.

"What we need to do is get you out of here," said Gina, thinking it through. "Then we need to leave, just go away. I no longer care about saving people from this planet. I already pledged not to take a seat on any vessel. But that wasn't good enough for the International Aerospace Council, so I resigned, effective the end of this year. Before then, we need to find a way out of here. I need to find one of those tangents that used to be almost everywhere. Now I don't think I could find one in a whole barnful of tangents."

"What's a tangent? What are you talking about?"

Gina grinned. "I suppose you don't know much about that. When you were a little girl we passed through one and here we are in Kobarêl. A lot has happened since then." She stared into Zaura's eyes for a while, saw her daughter's sorrow there, and the heartbreak, the shame, the fear. "A tangent is a spot in a three-dimensional space where a weakness in the fabric of the universe allows one who is sensitive enough to exploit it, to...to pry it open, open enough for a person to slip through. We slip through to another world, sometimes also to another time period."

"Like a fun house trick?"

"Yes, I suppose so." There were no fun houses in Kobarêl yet back in Kipzon they had gone to a summer carnival—what passed for one on Ghoupallesz—and the mirrors made it seem as though they could walk through walls. Zaura was a toddler and her father had carried her through the fun house. "Except there are no walls, just air. We poke a finger into the air and feel a sensation that lets us know where the weakness is."

Her mind flashed back to Liêta and her walk along the beach, returning in the dark to the resort. She had felt a weakness—as a sensation of resistance—but, at the time, she was too overcome with worry that someone was about to pounce upon her from the jungle to stop and check it.

Was that a tangent? Could it be?

"Would Latol be able to come with us?" asked Zaura.

"Would he want to? As a full-blooded Ghoupalle, it may not be wise. I don't know what would happen to him or his body being on Earth."

"How about me, Mama? I've never been on Earth. Will I die if I go there?"

Gina paused, felt her heart stop then restart.

"Better there than out in the depths of space." She tried to smile, just to reassure her. "You're a full-blooded Earth girl who just happened to be born on Ghoupallesz. You seem to be aging at a Ghoupallean rate, though. I think you were eleven Ghoupalle years when we came to Kobarêl, and it's been twenty-two years since. And yet you look like a teenager in Earth years. So you're probably older than Latol by five years, biologically. You're fine, it seems. Except for the damn rules and customs of this place!" Gina instinctively glanced at the camera in the corner, returned to Zaura. "First, we need to get you out of here. I'm going to meet with the Overlord tomorrow. I will offer to trade the Mixerran fuel cell for my daughter. Only I know where it is, and they need it to power a vessel as far as it takes to find a habitable planet—two or three generations."

A long buzz sounded and grew louder. Zaura jumped up and went to the red circle, tossing off the shawl before the beep came. The door panel opened and two staff women were waiting. One carried a laser marker, the other a tablet.

"End of visit."

"I guessed that," said Gina in Ghoupallêan. She turned to Zaura and spoke in English: "So it was worth it? The sex?"

Zaura was not allowed to speak but she smiled.

"Good," said Gina, exiting.

❋ ❋ ❋

"*Êivallas-se Æx-Kalmonê*," said Gina with a sharp bow, using the most formal Ghoupallêan she could muster. "Gracious Overlord, grant me an audience with you, so I may beg for your counsel."

"She has yellow hair," said Samot-Artexus with a whiny laugh, lounging on his posh divan, to his stiff-collared secretary standing nearby. "Have you ever seen anything so extraordinary? I'd heard there were a few in the city but obviously it is not a trait of most Kobarêli."

"It is extraordinary, Overlord."

Gina kept her head bowed. "I come to you to tell you of one thing and request another thing. You alone, Overlord, can solve two problems at once."

Samot-Artexus grinned. "Like those vessels up there: two things working together as one."

"You are observant, analytical, and wise, Overlord."

"Tell me your problem, First Director d'Elous."

So Gina told him everything. Almost everything. She had gone to Erit to retrieve an important propulsion device that would make interstellar travel a lot easier for their vessels. While she was away performing her official duties, thus demonstrating her loyalty to Kobarêl, the dastardly Hanar-Santorak stepped in with his plot to humiliate her. First, he was premature in acting prior to her actual resignation date at the end of the year. She still carried VIP credentials, yet he refused to grant extra funding to enable her to transport the device to Kobarêl. At the same time, Hanar took it upon himself to capture video of her daughter making love with her boyfriend—granted, that was against the manifest contract, but his obtaining of the video was done illegally. Her daughter was in a re-education facility undergoing training, never again to be a white-scarf wearing virgin destined to populate an interstellar vessel. That was fine, said Gina; she just wanted her daughter to be returned to her. In his evil plan, Hanar also had most of her belongings distributed to the public and her residence reassigned to a lesser ranking staff member. She had no place to stay even now—last night or tonight. So she was desperate. But she had something to offer: she had put the

Mixerran fuel cell in a safe place and she promised to deliver it to the Kobarêl Science Commission in exchange for her daughter's freedom, white-scarf or not, ticket or not. Samot-Artexus asked what the fuel cell did, what made it so special, and she explained in some detail until she recognized he was bored.

"We already have rocket engines," said the Overlord, "don't we?" He turned to the secretary. "They are already being installed in orbit, true?"

"Yes, Overlord."

"That propulsion system is the best we had a few years ago when this all started," Gina rebutted, "but the Mixerran fuel cell will give limitless power on minimal fuel. The current system will require a many-generation journey. The Mixerran system will cut that travel time significantly."

"If the cruise is leisurely, I should like to enjoy it longer."

"It's not a luxury cruise, Overlord, it's an escape from death. There will not be any returning."

"Someone on my staff has already arranged my seat. And for my loyal staff, of course. Up and around the planet a few times, then a gentle return. We pick up a few pieces and carry on. And I shall still be the Overlord of this city."

Gina gave him the latest data: trajectory, timing, destruction forecasts, and the difference between the current propulsion system and what the Mixerran system could do. He seemed impatient, so she rushed to the bottom line: "It makes possible a chance of reaching distant habitable planets if applied to our vessels."

"This claim has been proven?"

"I've seen it in action. I've run the numbers. I have the design plans and a working model."

He seemed tired, distracted.

"We are lucky to have you on our side," he intoned.

"I shall be grateful to help Kobarêl's endeavors in any way possible. I am at your service, Overlord—always."

Samot-Artexus rubbed his chin, thoughtfully.

"That yellow hair is wonderful," he muttered to his secretary. Standing slowly, the mayor went to Gina and paused.

"May I touch it?"

Gina nodded, bowed her head. The government's hand touched

her locks, pulled gently, slid up to the top of her head and with fingers spread raked down through her hair.

"So soft...."

"Overlord, did you understand my situation? Can you help me help you?"

He turned back to his secretary, asked for a cutter.

"May I have a sample of this?" he asked her.

"Your wish is my golden hair," she said, not sure whether to feel flattered or disgusted. He was a handsome enough man who looked slightly younger than her, but she had no interest in his interests. This was a business meeting. "You can take it all if you grant me my two requests: let me bring you the Mixerran fuel cell and return my daughter to me."

"Are you serious?" he asked her, seemingly amazed. He turned to his secretary, "Can she be serious?"

"I believe she is serious, Overlord."

The Overlord grinned as wide as the Jassera Sea.

"Then I approve your mission."

"Overlord...?"

"I want that yellow hair," he said, rubbing his finger across his lower lip, "as much as you can spare. Perhaps I'll have something made of it. A scarf, perhaps. Or a codpiece. Yes, that's it! It shall make a very comfortable codpiece."

"Speaking of scarves," said Gina, as gently as she could, "I would like clarification on my daughter's status." She paused, watching him studying her, lost in thought about her golden hair. "As I explained before, my daughter wore the white scarf of the fertility club, something she proudly earned. Even so, now that she has allegedly experienced the mating act, I know she is no longer eligible for a seat on any vessel—although why an unproven virgin would be a better choice to populate a new world than a couple with a proven record of fertility by producing a healthy child prior to the voyage, I do not know. That's who should get to go, in my opinion. Anyway, the rules stand. So, as regards my daughter, is there any way she might regain her seat aboard a vessel? For myself, I pledged years ago to give up my seat to her, specifically to her, so...that seat is, in effect, my seat. I should be able to give it to anyone I choose, isn't that right? So, even if my daughter is no longer a white-scarf girl, I can give my seat to her. And I shall stay on the surface to face the Final Day."

The cutting had begun, she noticed, as long strands of her yellow hair dropped into a basket held by another staff member.

"Please leave it neat," she said, "not like some street whore."

"Ah! The street whores...." Samot-Artexus had a smirk, as though he was embarrassed by the topic. "The Public Protocol Commission has clear guidelines about your daughter's case. Once removed from white-scarf status and re-educated, she may be eligible for yellow scarf status. She could be selected as an alternate—say, if a white-scarf girl is unable to go aboard, dies or has an accident, or partakes of mating activities prior to launch— that sort of situation. Then it is possible your daughter may take her place. She will be on a list. Failing the re-education program, however, would demote her further to orange-scarf status."

"And that is...?"

"Street whore status." He gazed at her and their eyes met. He seemed pleased to tell her that bit of information. She looked away as he continued. "Someone whom anyone may take for the night, though with proper compensation. People of such a status are only allowed to earn credits through their sexual labor. They are unclean for any other kind of work. The red-scarf women do not require any compensation. They are slaves of the state, quite popular with the gangs. They do not last very long on these streets. Most are eventually eaten." He turned to his secretary. "Isn't that true?"

The secretary nodded awkwardly, and Gina struggled to hold back her emotions. She did not know whether the Overlord was plain insensitive or he was actively calculating how to maximize her discomfort.

Just give me my daughter back! You can have everything else— everything else.

"What if she doesn't wear any scarf?" asked Gina.

"She must. That is the law for females between the age of education and partnership. She may wear blue or green scarves if she does not like yellow or orange. However, she should then carry her status tag clearly visible somewhere on her garments."

"Yet I've never worn a scarf."

"You are clearly a mother. And, I presume, also a widow. The father of your daughter was...?"

Her throat tightened. "My daughter never knew him. And I guess I didn't either."

"She can join with some male in a temple union—if a suitable partner can be found. Nobody is doing that these days. Who can blame them? Why start a life together when it all will end in seven years? What is the point of marriage in that case? If they were going away together on the vessel, that would be different."

"It's actually six years now—"

"These days I only have time for one-night concubines wearing black scarves, or specially trained courtesans from Uadikuu; not some rude, chit-chatting, lazy partner who only wants—"

"We can solve the problem easily, Overlord—if you will release my daughter in exchange for the Mixerran fuel cell. Then my daughter and I will leave this place. We will be out of your way. We will return to our ancestral home and wait for the light to shine bright. We will pray to the seven gods and nine goddesses until the last *pii*."

Samot-Artexus turned to his secretary: "Have you ever heard an offer like that?"

"No, I have not, Overlord."

"And she gives me her glorious yellow hair, too!"

"It is a blessèd day, Overlord."

Gina stepped forward, resisting the urge to check her haircut with her fingers. She kept her hand against her hip, pinching herself tightly.

"Thank you for your generosity, Overlord."

"I am happy to help my people. Come see me sometime when duty does not call. We may have a service position for you in my office. I would like to see your yellow hair every day, and watch it grow back."

"You are very gracious, Overlord."

We are ready, came the announcement from the Zetin Rocketry Agency in all communication formats. Prepare your tributes! A long and winding explanation followed, describing the missile in glowing terms, allusions to the great phallus of the Zetin High God

HʀN were included, and its powerful explosives were described in equally lucid terminology. Two more missiles were available if the first should have any problem. When the comet was close in its next pass, the missile would be sent skyward. According to Zetin propaganda, the missile would strike the comet and shatter it into a million snowflakes. It was passable poetry the way it was written in Ghoupallêan and Gina was momentarily amused.

She set down the tablet, flicked it off and lay her head back against the seat. Her short, stubbly hair was covered by a brown, leather skullcap that was popular with married women in Kobarêl. It made her feel like a monk. Outside the airship window were only the lime-colored clouds. In the cabin with her were only two businessmen. In the lower deck, there were a dozen or so second-class passengers. These days, even second-class was a rarity; few could afford the airship as transportation. Fortunately, as a VIP, Gina carried her credentials in plain sight. She smiled to herself; anyone who could take an airship was a VIP.

After the others had disembarked and were descending to terminal level in Erit, she remained in the airship. She breathed deeply, running through her plan. Counting to a hundred, she got up and exited.

Inside the terminal, she took her time, stopping for dinner, browsing the gift shop of Erit handicrafts: a lot of things involving fur and bone. She wanted everyone to go ahead of her before she went out.

Undressing and sitting on the edge of the *qala* in the inn, she thought of Zaura, feeling some relief that officials had promised to move her to a dormitory and allow her to wear a uniform. She would continue her re-education training—a crash course in following rules and protocols and caring for one's body properly. Gina expected to return before that training got very far. Then Zaura would be let out and the two of them would get the hell out of Kobarêl.

The door suddenly slid open and a girl in a white gown was there with a tray of ointments.

"Shall I warm the *qala* for you?" she asked.

"No thanks."

"Shall I add healing balm to your body?"

"I think I'm all right, thanks."

The girl exited as smoothly as she had appeared.

Shortly after Gina had stretched out on the *qala*, the door slid open again. This time a young man greeted her. He wore only a white loincloth, his shoulders broad and his chest well-muscled and hairless. He smelled good as he stepped into her room.

"I came to warm the *qala* for you, " he said with a slight grin, "but it seems you've already warmed it."

Gina looked him over. "It's still not warm enough."

"Shall I warm you tonight?"

"If that is the custom in Erit."

"No, it isn't, *Kanê*. This inn sits within the international quarter and many travelers request these services."

She waved him over and he climbed onto the *qala* and settled next to her, his chest to her back, his arms wrapped around her, holding her tightly. One of his legs pressed between hers.

"I shall stay until you are asleep," he said softly. "I will lock the door when I exit. You should not go outside during the night. F'eng followers occupy the park."

Chapter 33

Launch

Gina awoke in the middle of the night from a dream: back in Liêta, surrounded by the turquoise water, oddly swimming with Vazak-Mixerran, who was quite shy about letting his hairy body be seen unclothed outdoors. She laughed at him. Then that high school boy showed up. Sebastian was his name. Now he was hairy, too, had a beard and muscles. 'I'm ready for you,' he said to her. She looked back at Vazak and he was gone. She turned to Sebastian but he was gone, too. In the sky was a wide jet trail. An aircraft was streaking away toward the horizon. After that, she could not return to a deep sleep and tossed until dawn.

She dressed in a beige kaftan with brass buckles and a black leather waist sash. The black leather collar gave it the appearance of a uniform but it was not. Black calf-high boots completed her ensemble.

The morning was cool in Erit. Flying in an airship was usually on the cool side, as well.

Breakfast in Erit was some kind of yellow fish mush with green herbs; thin, crispy black wafers with embedded seeds; a bowl of small green berries with red spots. She drank water with a long *hemmux* twisting around in the tall, wide-throated bottle. She'd heard the healthful properties of *hemmux*, yet she'd never been confronted previously with the white, almost transparent worm. Some people swore by them: the flat worm would wiggle through the digestive tract, eating the toxins it found and exit harmlessly when finished.

Not today, she decided, pressing the pay button on her tablet and hearing the *ding* from the café's control panel on the wall behind the serving counter.

Waiting on the front steps, she could see the robed F'eng people gathering in circles in the park. They were beginning their morning ritual: washing each other. Off came the robes and out came the buckets of water. A few apparently saw her: one waved for her to join them; another gave her a vile gesture. Anyone staying at an inn had to be a member of the hated establishment. She turned her back to them and went inside. Through the clerk she hired an ETUR-TM to take her to the storage facility near the airship terminal.

Inside, she made her way to the unit where she had left the crate, each step causing nervousness to course through her, fearing it would be stolen.

Opening the storage unit's door, she saw the stack of boxes just as she had left them.

"Thank goodness," she mumbled in English, then turned to wave off the facility staff person.

When she was alone, Gina removed the empty boxes and set them to the side and stood staring at the crate. It was the same as it was almost a month before: too big for anything but a robo-cart to lift. She pulled out the comm baton and tapped several buttons along the side. She called a transport company and waited.

To the airship terminal was her plan. Then negotiating a fair price for the use of the airship, just her and the box. It's official business. Documents? She had VIP clearance, still a member of the International Aerospace Commission—who, for the sake of the planet, were not to be impeded in their activities. Sure, some had long ago begun abusing their privileges, but not her. She saw the corruption in the Commission: members trying to fatten their own vaults as though they thought they could take the wealth with them when the Final Day dawned. Others were consumed with age-old petty jealousies, territorial squabbles, cultural differences, any affront they believed could be corrected through participation in the Commission. She was right to resign.

And yet, even less seemed to be getting done since she had

announced her departure. Did she really owe these people any consideration? Next year they would hold another conference, planned for Typeg. That would include another launching. She hoped it would go smoothly for everyone's sake. The world did not need more negativity as the end approached. If she were quick enough, she might be able to attend the conference. And from there, she could go to Aivana...and from there to the tangent she knew well...out in the desert. That was the one leading straight back to the quarry on Earth where the whole adventure began.

Four men with a robo-cart arrived and packed up the crate, hauled it to their waiting ETUR-KV and, at Gina's direction, drove slowly to the airship terminal a short distance away.

"You again?" said the terminal clerk.

She explained that she wanted to hire the entire airship and showed her VIP tag and the documents authorizing funding for the project. Managers were consulted. They discussed at length all the possible ramifications. Gina offered them bonuses of food ration tickets for expediting the registration process.

"Contents?"

The crate still had the labels she had put on it before.

"Used machine parts," she said, pointing to the label.

One manager gave a smirk. "They are so valuable you must hire the entire airship?"

Gina grinned. "My boss thinks they are antiques, so he is willing to pay the shipping bill. Strange fellow, I admit."

"Very strange."

The second manager was tapping through a checklist on his tablet. He looked up at Gina. "Your weight?"

"You think that crate weighs the same as forty-nine other passengers and their bags?"

"I need to enter it."

"I don't know."

"Step on the scale over there."

"You're kidding."

"We cannot guess. It must be entered accurately."

She stepped on the square outlined on the floor and a steady beeping began, rising in pitch until a soft chime rang.

"One *nelsa* two *leva*," the clerk announced.

"Not too heavy," said Gina. "Right?"

"We must calculate everything. If there is an error, the airship could lose buoyancy. Not good."

They finished the manifest and loaded the crate into the second-class deck, centering it from bow to stern. They had to remove the inside rows of seats to widen the aisle enough so the crate could be accommodated—incurring additional charges which she was prepared to pay. Gina took a seat on the upper level, directly over where the crate was anchored, regretting not loading the latest Science Foundation report onto her tablet to read on the flight. She would probably sleep most of the way, anyway.

Because of the cargo, they'd had to lower the airship, a slow slide down the tethering pole. Now they were rising along the pole. It was a leisurely process which Gina did not mind. Below, she could see the F'eng in the park, about a hundred of them, sitting in small groups and having their meal. Some of them had wandered from the park down the street to the gates of the terminal. Probably begging for food.

She sat back, no longer interested in what the rebels below were doing. They were anti-technology and hated all science projects. They were saboteurs, responsible for serious set-backs at spaceports around the planet. She had no idea where all their hate originated and did not especially care. All she knew was something about their founder being injured and disfigured by some technology mishap. He had vowed to destroy anything man-made. He preached that Ghoupalles were doomed and their day of judgment would eventually come. Born in a time of war, as he apparently was, it would be easy for anyone to think that. But that was some five hundred years earlier. If they wanted to stay on the surface when the comet arrived, they were welcome to it. The only thing that surprised her was Erit being of interest to them. The nation of Nouvê was not their usual territory. Perhaps the success of Erit's spaceport construction zone had brought them out to protest.

To pass the time while the airship was being raised, Gina took out her comm baton, amused that she was making a wireless telephone call from an airship. If only they'd had these portable telephones back when she was in high school!

First came the *maxa-d'anno*, a device that could send coded data across a network of communication lines strung between major cities. Then, in 1889, Roumak-Venark invented the system for converting the phonemes of Ghoupallêan into the symbols of a new data protocol, thus enabling voice to be sent from point A to point B. Of course, it was so expensive that only élites of society could afford it. The device worked by converting the spoken voice pattern into raw data, which was then sent across the network. At the other end, the device converted the data file back into a voice pattern. In essence, the communication baton, looking like a giant lipstick tube with a microphone at the top, spoke back to the listener in an artificial voice whatever the original speaker had said. One did not actually hear the voice of the original speaker. Fortunately, the system had been refined so that comprehension was good—although there was a slight delay between speakers, much like using a walkie-talkie.

And yet they still used airships to go from city to city, all while design plans for airplanes were locked away in dusty archives, relegated to fantasy conventions. Aircraft were possible, she knew, but besides concerns for air pollution from burning fossil fuels, there simply was not much fossil fuel available on the planet, anyway.

Shaking her head, she input the code for her nemesis, Hanar-Santorak.

"I have the Mixerran fuel cell onboard now, so get my daughter ready to leave that facility," she spoke calmly but firmly.

"Who is this?" said Hanar-Santorak.

"You know damn-well who this is, puppy!"

"First Director Jinetta-d'Elous, I presume? I heard you left town, that you went on vacation."

"It's a business trip and you know it. We are about to depart and the fuel cell is with me. Get my daughter ready to leave. I want to see her when I land."

"That won't be possible," said Hanar, his voice full of delight. "As you know, she is in the re-education program. She must finish the curriculum before she can be released. You know the rules. She's doing very well th—"

"Switch this comm line to that facility. I want to talk with her. Now!"

"Such an itchy witchy! All right...switching...."

The two beeps sounded and a woman's voice responded. Gina stated her demand and the woman politely put her off with the usual excuses. Gina pulled rank and got the woman to put the link on pause while she retrieved Zaura from the classroom.

After a longer than expected interval, Zaura spoke the usual greeting into the comm line: "*Stê.*" Her voice sounded tired.

"Zaura! This is your mother," she spoke in English, expecting the line would be monitored. "I'm in Erit now with the fuel cell. We're on the airship."

"With the what?"

"Never mind. I'll catch you up when I return."

"Where are you?"

"Erit. In Nouvê. Anyway, I told Hanar-Santorak to get you out of there by the time I arrive. He says you have to complete the program. Is that true?"

"They said if I am in the program I must complete the program to earn a yellow scarf. Then I might be selected. It's the only chance I have to get a seat on a vessel."

"It's not the only way...." She thought a moment. "Are you all right, Zaura? Treating you well? Hanging on?"

"I follow all the rules."

"Do what you have to do, but don't give in to them. They are brainwashing you."

"Brain...? Washing...?"

"Getting you to follow their rules, not your rules."

"Mama, I want to see you."

"I know, dear. I'll see you soon. We are about to depart here."

"I must disconnect now."

"Are you all right? You sound sleepy."

"I'm in perfect health, Mama."

"Then I'll see you soon."

The comm link went silent. Gina replayed her daughter's words in her head, not convinced she was as well as she should have been. Her tablet buzzed and the cost of her international communication link, which the Kobarêl Science Commission would pay, blinked in red numbers on the indigo screen. She tapped the yellow approval button and lay her head back, breathing deeply.

She dozed off a moment, then was awakened by the departure instructions. With a sense of relief, she listened to the calm voice of the pilot telling her, and the other passengers who should have been aboard, exactly what to do in the event of a water landing or, as could happen on an airship, a rapid deflation event. She had heard the speech many times already. Feeling drowsy, she closed her eyes again. Before she drifted into sleep, she sensed the forward movement of the airship, uncoupled from the tethering pole, turning gently southeast over the city, then the Nouvan countryside.

"Attention all passengers of Airship E-15: The Skylark!" It was the captain's voice, startling Gina out of her dozing. "I do not wish to upset anyone, however, we are being ordered to change our course. We will be turning to the north and move over the Navadi Sea. After a short time we will then return to the terminal in Erit. We apologize for causing you hardship and confusion."

Gina yawned. *What's happening?* She shook her head a few times to awaken herself, then pulled herself up straight.

The co-pilot in his white uniform hurried down the aisle.

"First Director d'Elous," he spoke excitedly, "do you know anything about a bomb possibly being put aboard this airship?"

"A bomb? You mean the crate on the second deck? That's mine and it definitely is not a bomb. It's a jet engine, actually—a model, of one, anyway."

"Are you sure?"

"Yes, I've seen it. Before it was crated up I inspected it."

"I have to inform you that we have been ordered to fly out over the sea and jettison the crate."

"What? No! You can't! It's not a bomb. It's the Mixerran fuel cell. It's the answer to our hopes and dreams, the only thing that will save us from the comet. I'm bringing it home to Kobarêl so more can be made for our transport frames."

"I'm sorry, First Director—"

"What is this madness?"

"It's either the crate or us. If it explodes, we will all go down."

"The crate is just a fuel cell. It's my only reason for being on this flight. It must arrive in Kobarêl! It must!"

"We must follow orders."

"Show me how to fly this thing and the crew can jump out with escape packs. Then you won't need to worry about any explosion. I hired this airship so I'm responsible for it. You and your crew can escape and I will take full responsibility."

"You don't understand. There have been several airships with bomb reports. One has already exploded. It happened over Ghoupalleme just after uncoupling. Several people killed on the ground and all aboard the airship died. Another landed safely in Zefer and the bomb was deactivated. There are threats to nine airships departing today. It appears to be the F'eng terrorists."

"But not my crate! This is a charter flight. Only me and that crate. That's the only cargo and I vouch for it myself." She was losing her breath. "I—I'll show you."

She took his arm, jerked him toward the stairs, pulled him down to the second deck. The crate sat in the center of the deck, straps from each side of the fuselage keeping it in place, preventing it from rocking or shifting which might throw off the balance of the airship.

"I need a tool to open this box," she said, glancing around for anything that looked like a crowbar.

"First Director, we should not open it," said the co-pilot. "Usually the triggers for these things are set to go when they are touched or if someone tries to deactivate them."

She dug her fingers into the gap, trying to force it open, but could not move the lid at all. Her nails tore and bled.

"Please! Please don't!" she cried out.

"I'm sorry. We must."

Chapter 34

Terminal

The airship slowly descended as it skirted the coastline and Gina saw out the window two rivulets wriggling through the grassy dunes to join and form a small lagoon in the beach. Nearby, several *akua* surrounded a beached *jurrent*, something like a blue beluga whale with a white spiny crest running from head to tail, its body twice the length of the airship. The big *akua* birds, the height of a man, were padding around the sand, squawking about the order of dining as the *jurrent*'s body heaved with its last breaths. Finally, the feasting began.

She could understand how it felt: the world taking bites from your living flesh and there's nothing you can do about it.

"After we drop the crate, we are required to return to the terminal for inspection," said the co-pilot to the three men who were always aboard an airship: the flight engineer, the fireman, and the 'hanger'—the man who, if needed, would climb around on the outside of the airship to make repairs while in flight. "The report says all flights are grounded until further notice."

"If you're going back to the terminal anyway," said Gina, licking blood from her fingertips, "can't we just go to the terminal and you inspect it there? I'm on the International Aerospace Council. I saw the crate packed. I know it is not a bomb. I am no suicide bomber!"

"You know," the flight engineer spoke up, "she's probably right.

I wouldn't hire an empty airship to haul one big box then blow up the airship. What's the point of that without a full manifest?"

"Yeah, where's the terror in destroying an empty airship?" asked the hanger, hands on hips in the aisle at the far end of the crate.

"We are aboard, aren't we?" said the fireman. "We still could die. But who would care?"

"Who cares about anything nowadays with that comet coming down on us in a few years?"

And the debate went on, louder and louder as the airship angled further away from the beach and out over the sea.

The co-pilot waved his hands for silence.

"So you believe her?" he asked softly.

"Please believe me," said Gina, her voice raspy. "You will see I am telling you the truth. This is bound for the Kobarêl Science Commission. I promised I would deliver it."

Again, she showed them the documents that authorized the cargo transport.

"It looks authentic," said the co-pilot.

Gina watched him studying the documents, flipping back between them, nodding. He glanced at the flight engineer.

"I'll tell the pilot."

"Thank you!" said Gina. "Oh, thank you! So much I thank you!" and on she went thanking them as the other three crew members returned to their seats at the rear of the lower deck and resumed their dice game.

The airship soon left the land completely, circling over the choppy waves, and after a few more *pon* she felt it turning again. The yellow sun was dim behind the pastel clouds but it gave her hope. The sunlight shifted to the other side of the airship as it completed its turn to continue on to Erit.

Gina was too exhausted to nap, fidgeting in her seat next to the crate, guarding her baby. She knew she would not be arriving in Kobarêl tonight. One bomb threat and all airship traffic was grounded across possibly six nations! Ridiculous!

She grabbed the comm baton from her travel bag and punched in the code she had been given for the Overlord. The receptionist had to be convinced who Gina was and that the Overlord would wish to speak with her. She went through the same routine with the personal secretary, then was made to wait. The battery light began to blink yellow; she had one *peth* remaining—18 minutes. She would need half of that to explain the situation and the other half to beg for an alternate plan.

"Jinetta, so good to hear your voice after all this time!" came the joyful greeting of Samot-Artexus. "I must tell you your golden hair is delightfully soft. As I told you previously, I had it skillfully woven into a lovely codpiece. I'm wearing it now, as we speak. Such comfort! I have you to thank for that. We must make a production line and share these with the world!"

Gina was not sure what to make of his remarks. Clearly he was a jerk, but there was nothing to be done about that facet of his personality today. She had a problem; it did not matter what he had done with her hair.

Biting her lip, she reminded him of her mission, the one he had approved, to fetch the Mixerran fuel cell in Erit so the Kobarêl spaceworks could engineer duplicates and use them to power the interstellar vessels. The existing propulsion systems would not get them all the way to distant habitable planets, she feared, leaving the vessels as man-made rogue moons floating aimlessly for all eternity. She sighed, waited.

It all sounded much better when he said it back to her to check his comprehension. Yes, he did know about her mission; he wished first to thank her for her hair, for her personal sacrifice. He was being polite. Now, what's the problem?

"Terror threats have grounded all airships," said Gina, trying to keep calm. "We are heading back to Erit. There are reports of bombs aboard a few airships. They wanted to throw my fuel cell out because they thought it was a bomb. I convinced them it wasn't but we still must return to the home terminal. How shall I get the fuel cell to Kobarêl now?"

There was a moment of silence except for faint talking in the background at the Overlord's end of the line.

"Did you hear me, Overlord?"

"I heard your words, golden-haired lady."

"I am actually First Director—"

"You do not have the thing we agreed upon? That machine?"

"I have it but I cannot bring it to you for possibly a few more days. Whenever they allow airship flights again."

"So what will you do?"

"I am asking you what I should do."

"If you are not returning with the thing you promised, what else do you have?"

"What do you mean? I will bring the fuel cell to you. It will just take a little while longer."

"You are running from your promise?"

"No!" she exclaimed, thinking *Listen, you jackass, I'm doing the best I can!*

She caught herself and apologized for being rude.

"I heard you have a daughter. She has golden hair like yours? Your colleague told me."

Gina hesitated. The battery light had changed to red. "I am almost out of battery on this comm baton, Overlord. I'll recharge when we are at the terminal and I'll call you back."

"She has your golden hair, yes?"

"Yes—but please do not shave her head—"

The comm line went dead and she threw the baton hard across the cabin, disgusted and frustrated. It hit the opposite wall and broke apart. She shook her head for another *peth*, then got up and retrieved the parts of the comm baton and reassembled it.

"Prepare for terminal docking," came the announcement from the pilot.

The airship crossed over the dirty, smoky-brown city of Erit, passing over the working class districts of abandoned factories. With a few short years until death, nobody needed the products once made in them. Instead, people huddled among the bricks and mortar, killing each other for food, selling their children for food, eating their neighbors in the night. That's what was reported. Similar stories in all the major cities. Anarchy. Hopelessness. Or bliss through drugs for those who knew they would not get a seat aboard an escape vessel. Yet, *bôb* production was becoming sporadic now, too. So they wandered the streets looking for food, seeing each other as greasy-spoon dives, cutting off strips of meat, scooping out brains, licking up spilled blood, roasting/grilling/frying what they could—whole families gorging on some unfortunate stranger who had become lost in the bad part of the city.

As they approached the terminal, Gina again saw the crowd of F'eng followers pushing against the fence, shouting at the airship, making scissor-cutting gestures with their fingers. What could they have against a marvel of old-age technology such as an airship? Instead of throwing away their lives following some masochistic guru preaching submission to death, they could apply themselves to solving the problems of the world. As she was doing.

She was chastising herself for almost surrendering to fate when suddenly she heard a loud crack followed by a frightful whirring noise—

"Brace for rapid descent!" the pilot called. "We've been hit! Bladder deflating! Hold on!"

Gina strapped herself into her seat just as she felt the gondola crash against something, perhaps a building. The cabin tilted severely, bow up—then righted itself a moment before dropping further. They hit the ground roughly and the crate tore loose from its straps and slid heavily to the stern, breaking open the exit door. Gina felt the weight of the collapsing bladder pressing down upon the passenger decks. The ceiling of her deck broke open and she jumped to the aisle, crawling on her hands and knees to the rear exit, blocked by the crate.

Outside, she heard the angry F'eng crowd calling for their destruction. They hated technology. They hated anyone who was associated with technology. They especially loathed the people building the space vessels, those they called hopeless fools bent on flying to heaven, daring to be gods themselves, challenging the seven gods and nine goddesses with their acts of insubordination! They deserved to die!

Suddenly the bladder was being sliced open above her and several arms in the brown robes of the F'eng were reaching inside to pull her out. As she was lifted, she saw the head of the 'hanger' smashed by the corner of the crate. Others outside the airship found the crate and were maneuvering it out the doorway. They brought out hammers and began beating them against the box, breaking it open.

"No! Don't touch it! Leave that alone!" Gina cried out as two women holding her by the arms dragged her off the hissing bladder skin and dropped her roughly on the pavement. She shook her head, trying to clear the daze she felt. She got to her feet, a little dizzy, then shouted for them to stop what they were doing. "It's not a bomb! It's an engine!" she cried out to them. "It will save us!"

"It will save you, not us!" one man holding a hammer growled at her. He rushed to her, the hammer shoved in her face. "You're a scientist? Is this your device? Did you create this?"

"No, I didn't create it," Gina frantically explained. "My friend did. He's from Erit."

"None from Erit would do this blasphemy!"

"It's not blasphemy to use the minds the seven gods and nine goddesses programmed in us!"

"They have a plan for us! It's not to fly to heaven and dance with them, mate with them, entertain them like little children!"

"You don't have to destroy everything you hate!"

The man raised the hammer over his head. His face was scarred, patches of skin cut from his cheeks in ritualistic fashion, emulating the original F'eng prophet. He waved the hammer, his grin pure evil.

Gina cringed as he swung the hammer down. She threw up her arms to block the strike but the hammer caught her under the arm, striking her ribs. She fell back, stopped by the side of the crushed airship gondola. The man raised the hammer again. This time as he swung it down, Gina caught his wrist and wrestled the hammer out of his hand. She thrust it back at him, handle first, striking his mouth. Teeth fell out and blood spurted, ran down his chin.

"Yes!" he cried, eyes wide in apparent joy. "That's it! Do it again! You know what to do!"

So she flipped the hammer around in her hand, grasped the handle, and swung it with all her might at the man's head. The vibration of her hit rippled up her arm and exploded into her shoulders. He fell to the ground, a bloody dent in the curve of his skull.

"Thank you," he muttered.

She was not sure she heard him clearly.

Gina turned her attention to the crowd. They were working hard to destroy the Mixerran fuel cell. Bashing it with hammers and axes, ripping out wires and tubes, tossing parts out on the ground. Someone had started a fire and others were collecting anything they thought might be useful from the growing pile of debris. Anything left over was tossed into the fire.

Several F'eng followers danced around the fire, singing. Others were taking delight in what they could salvage from the downed airship. A few were crouched by the fire, eating something.

She looked for the crew but saw only the F'eng in their brown robes. Her beige kaftan was torn, but perhaps she had not been identified as a crewmember. She shrank from the chaos, crawling through the wreckage to the other side.

"You made it," said the co-pilot, laying bloodied but alive.

Nearby was the pilot, unconscious. His forehead was a mess, his arm bent backwards awkwardly.

"He didn't make it," said the co-pilot.

Gina tried to help up the co-pilot but her ribs hurt too much to be of service.

"That's all right," he said, "I think I can manage."

"I'm sorry," she wept. "I'm sorry for everything."

"Let's get inside the terminal—quick! Before they tear us apart for dinner like they did our fireman and engineer!"

Chapter 35

Touch

She could not recall the last time she had embraced for so long but when she finally did release the airship co-pilot from her arms, it felt like years.

"First Director d'Elous," the naked co-pilot gasped, "thank you. I needed that. I really needed that."

"Me, too," she replied with a long exhale.

Then she cried.

Violence. Death. Ugliness. Madness. And the Mixerran fuel cell destroyed. She had almost forgotten that fact as the physician treated her ribs. A balm was applied to deaden the pain. She had let them remove the kaftan she wore, ignoring the stare of the co-pilot as she lay nearly nude in the clear bubble of the treatment pod. After that, straps were applied to hold the two cracked ribs in place, but it still hurt to take normal breaths.

The co-pilot helped her slip into the kaftan afterwards.

"What's the world coming to?" she asked.

"This is what the world is coming to." He touched his forehead, pressing the medical patch there, confirming the adhesive was strong enough. "More days of chaos. Waiting for the end.... What's a person to do? There's no point of making anything—no reason to go to a job, nobody growing food, nobody cleaning up, nobody caring for anyone else. It's every person for himself. Why go to the trouble of fighting for survival. The comet makes everything we have done during the past centuries all without purpose. Or meaning. We worked hard to build something and called it civilization, then a non-thinking entity destroys us."

"You're more depressing than the F'eng, dear co-pilot."

He turned to her, extended his index finger. She touched her fingertip to his. Jêpolissan custom. This man, however, did not appear to be of that ethnicity. He was not hairy like Vazak-Mixerran. In fact, this fellow was thin and balding; he gave her the impression of being a stork.

"I'm Kag-Jugarrus," he said with hesitation. "You can call me 'Jugs' like all my friends do."

Gina smiled. He had no idea how ridiculous he sounded.

"Call me Jinetta."

Once inside the terminal, the locked doors had held off the F'eng while the military squads arrived to deal with the crowd. Of course the 'accident' was newsworthy. A journalist got into the terminal and questioned Gina about what she had seen. Learning she had been aboard the airship, the inevitable questions about her destination and business followed. Gina was a VIP, a member of the International Aerospace Council, someone newsworthy. She tried to dodge the questions, throwing attention back to the crime scene: people had died in the crash, others had been killed by the crowd, some of the killers had eaten the bodies. Two soldiers were killed. More F'eng were killed. A fleet of ETUR-KV arrived to haul away the bodies. A quick ritual in a fiery pit, then covering it with dirt and planting trees.

One military vehicle took them to a medical office where their injuries were treated.

Jugs said he was married. More accurately, they had a three year contract. They also had a child, so it was likely they would renew the contract another three years. Or longer if they could find a third adult whom they both liked. They were eager to expand their duo into a polyamorous star—perhaps a little too quickly, he laughed. And her?

She lay back on the cushions of the *qala* in her room at the inn, staring at the ceiling. The black *bôb* the physician gave her was making her mind dull. She felt no pain.

"I have a complicated life. I've been so many places and loved so many. I've had many children, too. It seems as though I must live forever, that I cannot ever die. I'm not saying I want to die, though. Hah! The choice is no longer mine, is it? One day soon I will watch the comet coming down and all the moments of my life will flicker before my eyes, every day I've lived and every night I've dreamed. I will gaze skyward and welcome the end, knowing I have lived as full a life as I could and did everything I could to please myself and everyone around me."

Jugs nodded, steepling his fingers in his lap as he sat on the cushion beside the *qala*. "I think I understand."

"Then tell me what I meant because I sure do not know. The black-*bôb* is working. The words spilled out without any thought. I'm so tired."

"Like all of us," he said, "you started your life with purpose and determination, wanting something to be good, or something you wanted to represent you, to last after you are old then gone. Children, or art, or deeds, or sharing ideas. I tried that: went to the academy but I had no talent in those serious subjects. I met my partner there, however."

"Then it was a good choice."

"Perhaps. She is a teacher now. And I fly airships between Erit and five other cities. My life is in the air among the clouds. I'm a dreamer, I suppose."

"I knew a dreamer," said Gina, turning on her good side. "Long ago. He took me by my hand and led me here. I mean, here to Ghoupallesz. Our first stop was Biznuik. You know it? On the far tip of Zissekap."

"Yes, I know its location yet I never visited. Is it a happy place?"

"It was back then. I think it was 1927. We had no idea what we were doing. A kindly old couple helped us. We had some *gealan* that paid for our life there. Then we moved on to Feasfend, then Selauê—"

"You said 1927." He blinked twice. "You were in Biznuik in 1927?"

"Of course I skipped some years between then and now. Don't be so alarmed."

"I apologize, Jinetta. I intend no insult, yet how can you be more than two-hundred years old?"

She was certain she heard him accurately and realized then she had misspoken.

"I'm teasing you, Jugs. It's a joke. Certainly I cannot be two-hundred thirty-three years of age. That's impossible. There is no way for me to have lived three-hundred-eighty years on this planet and still look like a forty-eight year old matron of Ur-tha. True?"

Jugs moved off the cushion, rose on his knees, elbows on the edge of the *qala*, his intense eyes regarding her there: feet bare and legs bearing faint blonde hairs. With the cap she had worn on the airship now removed, he saw her stubbly blond scalp and knew she had been beautiful not too long before her trip. Golden hair had covered her head.

"Ur-tha?" he asked, his eyes narrowing. "How are the years counted in Ur-tha?"

"Very carefully," she said and laughed.

He laughed with her, weakly. Then he extended his hand, took hold of her heel, massaged the arch of her foot with his thumb, pressed down into the arch. He seemed to be searching for something, not merely massaging her foot. Apparently satisfied, he released her foot.

"That felt good. You have the touch, it seems."

He leveled his gaze at her. "Are you a goddess?"

The room was deathly still, as though all sound waves had been sucked out of it.

Gina sat up, crossing her legs, her ten toes attracting his eyes. She reached for him and he held out his hands, refusing her. After a moment he looked up and their eyes met. She tried to smile.

"There are some people who think I am."

His throat seemed to tighten, his breath shallow.

"I—I was suspicious—from the start—on the airship."

She grabbed his hands, squeezed them between her fingers.

"Come up here and lay beside me."

He pulled his hands away.

"Come join me. I want to tell you a story. A true story."

He relaxed, possibly believing he was in no danger. She gave the cushions a pat, added a dope-smudged smirk. Only then did he give in. He stretched out beside her on the *qala* and storytime began.

❋ ❋ ❋

Gina winced at the pain in her ribs as she turned herself on the *qala*, then fell back with a satisfied exhalation.

"So now I need to get to the other fuel cell at that country house. They can back-engineer it. I still have the designs. Yet, if I can bring them the working model, it would certainly advance our production tremendously. I wonder if I could fly the aircraft myself."

Jugs laughed, blushed, pulled the corner of the fur cover over them.

"I never imagined someone would ever want to do such a thing as we did. And with me, especially." He still breathed hard. "Is it considered normal to do that in your country?"

She reached out, pinched his face between her fingers.

"I'm sure the gods and goddesses have many customs which mortals are forbidden to try."

"Should I pay a tribute at the temple?"

"Not required, Jugs. I felt like being wild. It's a way to forget what happened for a little while. Almost dying brings out that urge in me. I want to live so brightly, burn so hot, while I still can. You know?"

He did not know. So she went on with her commentary, her voice sanguine yet halting. So many years, she repeated as though the words were her personal mantra. With everything coming to an end soon, she tried to think back to that summer when everything began but could not fix it firmly, clearly in her mind. Now this man was asking her if she was a goddess and she was so enjoying teasing him, wanting to believe she really was divine. No, she was simply a survivor. She had the luck of the gods but none of their fluffy clouds or lightning bolts—

She noticed he was complimenting her in a voice as hopeful as a little boy wanting more candy.

"You are so beautiful, Jinetta. Especially beautiful for being three-hundred years of age."

"I didn't say I was three-hundred years of age." She gave his hairless chest a tap. "I said I have been visiting here for three-hundred-eighty years. I visit for a few years at a time, then I move on. I find a good place to live. I meet new people. I find kindness and love. I make children, watch them grow. Then I depart for a new life. This one, now, has been the longest I've ever visited a place. I want to leave, but I've pledged to help everyone in any way I can—even if nobody wants my help."

"I think what you're doing is wonderful—"

"Why did you feel my foot like you did?" she asked. Her foot rubbed against his ankle under the fur cover. "Is it an obsession? Do you want to worship my feet?"

"No, not an obsession," he said, adding a chuckle to try to play along with what he thought was another joke. "It was a test."

"Really? A test?"

"Before this trip," he spoke, pausing to reflect, "I spoke a story written on a scroll. For my little boy. It was mythology, the stories about the gods. His mother chose it. So I spoke one story to him— a story that revealed how the gods did not need strong feet because they lived in heaven, in the clouds. The story said gods have no need for the knob on the bone at the high end of the inside arch—where the tendons of the heel attach. I studied anatomy for a while, then failed the exams; I became an airship pilot instead. Because the gods actually float mere breaths above the ground, the story said, they have weak feet. And you...."

"And my foot was right there, so you thought 'I should confirm my suspicions'—true?"

His lips pursed, holding back a response.

"You checked my feet to see if I am a goddess. That's a bit flattering."

A beep interrupted the silence.

"The comm baton battery is finished loading," she said. "I need to call Kobarêl."

"Should I leave you now?"

"Oh, no, Jugs. I need you to help me with the aircraft."

She climbed off the *qala*, holding her ribs with one hand. Standing, she gazed back at her new friend, a thinner, balder version of Sebastian. *Poor boy, what trouble you must be in.*

"First, I need to fix everything in Kobarêl. Then we will go to Jêpolissa and try to fly that aircraft to Kobarêl—or, if matters there are settled, then...." She paused to think, her fist holding up her chin, index finger poking her cheek. "Next year, in Typeg. I should be there. If I can unresign, I'll regain my power and can make everything happen the way it should. But I don't know if I can go to Kobarêl then go to Typeg. First, I need to be sure my daughter is unharmed, preferably free, whether or not she regains a seat on a vessel. Then I could go to—as long as I'm on the same continent—go check the tangent south of Aivana and maybe the one near Lyas. If I have to, I'll go back to Biznuik. Either way, I absolutely must—"

"You have a busy schedule, don't you?"

"I do."

"And you want my help?"

"I do.

Jugs knelt on the floor, play-acting, and gazed up at her.

"I shall be at your service, goddess!"

She placed her hand on the top of his head.

"Are you sure? The last six years of a planet are not easy ones. You should understand that before you come with me."

Goddess, she thought, delighting in the sound of the word—*ghêra* in Ghoupallêan: a single sex-neutral word for both gods and goddesses. Dressed in a new outfit from her bag, a dark red pleated gown with tan epaulets and collar, a few golden sprigs of flora on the sleeves, she felt in charge again as she punched in the code for the Overlord, then glanced at Jugs, still naked on the *qala*.

"Don't waste my time," she growled at the receptionist. "Switch me to Samot-Artexus immediately!" She did not even use the title *Æx-Kalmonê*. She could hear the shocked gasp of the receptionist.

"*Stê*," the Overlord spoke—'What's up?'

"This is First Director d'Elous! I'm not dead, though you may have heard of the attacks in Erit. The fuel cell was destroyed in the airship crash and by the crowd of F'eng followers there. But, I have—"

"Lady, so good to hear your voice, rough as it may be. Certainly you have reasons for being full of alarm. The days grow shorter, the people more desperate, the cities crumble and the stars call for offerings. However, you, Jinetta-d'Elous of the golden hair, float above all the chaos."

"What's that supposed to mean?"

He seemed to want to chuckle, then cleared his throat. "I have read the report on you."

"What report?"

"The report by your colleague, Hanar-Santorak."

"What? That buffoon is always making reports that are nothing but his paranoid fantasies and schoolboy imagination!"

"Nevertheless—"

"What's it say about me?"

He exhaled loudly. "Yes...."

Gina glanced at the light on the side of the comm baton, expecting it to be flashing again. The light was off; she had plenty of time to talk. Each battery was good for a month.

"You were examined previously," the Overlord continued in a voice that sounded as though he was trying to hide his apparent amusement. "Very interesting data. I am puzzled by it, however. The laboratory readings, especially. Blood. Essence. Other fluids. Chemicals. The whole mélange. Yes.... Either you were able to trick us for such a long time, or the data is in error. Or it is true."

Gina let go the breath she had been holding.

The Overlord cleared his throat again. "How can I put this? I mean, delicately? Don't want to offend you. Hmm...."

She waited, wondering how many were listening on the comm line.

"Yes, uh...let me ask you, Jinetta-d'Elous: Are you a Ghoupalle woman? Or not?"

"I am." She held her breath again. Did she give the right answer? Was there a right answer? What were they looking for? The comm line was quiet a little too long.

"We think not. The data we have does not support your statement."

She uttered a spontaneous vulgarity. "Does it matter? I've been helping you—all the people of Kobarêl—all the people of this planet for so long I can't believe I'm even being questioned about something so ridiculous as that at a time like this! There is so much work to be done. We must make ready to depart! Whoever are selected for the journey need to be trained—and I've already said I won't take a seat. I give my seat to my daughter. No matter what silly rules you say she's broken, I give her my seat—and that will be her ticket to the stars. So how is she? Where is she? I need to speak to her, too. Get her on the comm line. Is she all right? Tell me about my daughter!"

"Calm yourself," the Overlord suggested. "I understand your daughter is doing very well with her re-education. I've been told she will graduate on schedule and therefore be eligible for an alternate position for a seat aboard a vessel."

"She shouldn't even be in that re-education facility! It was false evidence! Hanar-Santorak is responsible for that!"

"What's her name? Zaura? Ah, yes. The one with the golden hair, like you. She has been assigned additional work. Extra tasks the instructors look favorably upon. She works as the personal assistant to First Director Hanar-Santorak, and he reports that she is—"

"You get her away from that pervert!"

"It's nothing like that."

"What is it then?"

She heard the Overlord's exhalation. What was it, frustration? Fatigue? Putting up with a crazy woman from another planet? There could be worse things for him to have to deal with today, at least more than being bothered by one of his staff members, indeed a First Director at the Kobarêl Science Commission—

"Are you a goddess?" he asked in a suddenly different voice, a stream of phonemes coated in sugar, running fluidly from his tongue as though he had rehearsed the question for a week. "And if so, which goddess are you?"

Chapter 36

Goddess

The clanging she knew to be the wheels that turned to raise or lower the metal gates of the great castle in heaven where mortals were invited to stay for all eternity if they sufficiently displeased the gods and goddesses. Torture was routine, agony the order of the day, hopelessness the new blood flowing out of their veins. Not many managed to return from such fate. Certainly not Interdimensional Voyagers, no matter what their class might be. Gina was a First-Class Voyager, but it had been so many years since she had traversed a tangent that she was not very confident of being able to do so. She feared that instead of stepping through to an Earth she barely knew, she would find herself there outside the gates of heaven and see the chains pulling up the bars and the huge Guardian Jur-Fux swinging his thick, muscular arm toward the castle, a bull voice roaring "*Sata!*"—'Welcome!'

Gina remembered the lessons of her children, lifetime after lifetime, teaching them what all good Ghoupalle children should know.

Nourii stands tallest among the goddesses, presumed the eldest of Great God Zaul, red hair and pink skin, scars of war across her chest, breastless (one lost in battle, the other the result of self-mutilation after being outraged by her cheating lover, the god Katoux); long, sharpened teeth and fingernails; rides a three-wheeled chariot pulled by three *bintur*—giant red badgers.

People pray to her for strength during difficult times, though she seldom listens.

Pemaa, the quiet sister, loves to cook and enjoys a clean home; plays with small animals; eats only three plants: *eguo*, *blith*, and *resh*, usually together in the same meal. Believed to care about young lovers, popular with girls who are popular with boys. She sleeps with snakes and plays with fish, often acting as a mermaid and tricking sailors.

Roloura is the smart one, the scientist of the family, the holder of stars and worlds, the measurer of everything, the decider of days and nights and lifetimes. People call to her for longer lives, shorter work hours, extra tries in sporting events, and a full growing season for crops. She seldom grants favors other than a single extra day for the truly righteous people who are on their death beds.

Garou has hair blacker than night, eyes of red, hands that sweat blood, six fingers on each hand, feet with six toes; long feet and long legs that stride the world, from kingdom to kingdom; who hovers over croplands to water the soil from her loins; who calls women to bow to the earth before giving birth. Mothers-to-be sometimes sacrifice to her, leaving one of their fingers buried in the soil of a garden.

Emmau is the child of innocence, the irrational waif who prefers to play games than take the fate of mortals seriously. She is often chastised for her lack of concern. She responds that eternity is long enough for both work and play; she will do her work later. The lazy people of Ghoupallesz pray to her, begging for excuses to skip work or school or come home to spouses after cheating them. She laughs a lot, too much, and almost always at inappropriate moments.

Furanna, the matron saint of the Furank people, is a warrior goddess with a silver shield who lives deep in the forests and rides a *jalo*. Always surrounded by fairies, often sung to by birds, given fish and fowl for food by mountain gnomes whom she prefers as bedmates. She carries a silver spear that can penetrate anything and is forever sharp. She takes it to bed with her.

Aburra is the happy one, arms full of juicy fruit and cuddly animals; the one who dances across the clouds. She wears flowers and nothing else, and carries a small, divine *pugua* named Tix in her arms at all times. She never sits, not wanting to compress her buttocks, believing her bottom has the most perfect curves in the universe. She is often painted as a nude figure admired by a circle of lusty old men.

Sethi is thoughtful, and kind when it suits her, helpful with household matters, yet believed responsible for the deaths of babies whenever the mothers are deemed unsuitable. Men pray to her for a woman who will please them in the *qala*; they pray to Pemaa for a good, faithful wife, however. Most young couples have a Sethi icon hanging on the wall over the *qala*. Her icon is a popular symbol used as a tattoo by sexually promiscuous young women.

Memitha is the ornery one, always looking for ways to hinder progress. She loves throwing down obstacles before mortals and delights in their consternation. Traditionally, she has brown hair with streaks of golden locks throughout. Yet she is never vain; she cares about others' fear of her, not their admiration of her. Still, her body is the one men dream of as they mate with their wives, yet were they to be welcomed by her they would die before they could satisfy her. She never takes shit from anyone—god, goddess, or mortal. Most of all, she loves playing handball with human heads and she never loses.

"So which goddess are you?" the Overlord repeated.

Gina took a breath, let it out slowly, patiently.

"I am Memitha. And you are toast."

The Overlord did not understand her reference to burnt bread but he got the gist of her demeanor: the Overlord was a mortal and had not been acting very decently in recent weeks. He was therefore subject to discipline and Goddess Memitha had been assigned to dispense it.

First, however, she needed to get to Vazak-Mixerran's country house and fly the aircraft to Kobarêl. Only then could the spanking begin.

* * *

She closed off the comm line with the instruction, the demand, that the Overlord release her daughter from the re-education center at once and assure that her health was good before handing her over to Gina, a.k.a. the Goddess Memitha, when she arrived.

"Hurry, Jugs! We need to get moving!" she called out, slipping the comm baton into her travel bag. "I want to be in Kobarêl by tomorrow night!"

Turning, she was surprised to find him fully dressed, posing as if to defend himself. In his hand was a knife—no, it was a sharp length of metal, she saw, perhaps a scrap from the airship he had grabbed to fight against the F'eng.

"Aren't you going to help me?"

"I'm sorry, Jinetta—or whatever your name is, whoever you really are, goddess or mortal doesn't matter—but I can't let you do what you're planning to do. It's evil and it's a lie."

"It's the only way to survive," said Gina in Ghoupallêan, then slipped into English as she muttered to herself: "The end justifies the means. And I have to free my daughter from the clutches of the evil re-education ministry—or whatever the hell they call it. Damn, this is just like some stupid sci-fi novel of Big Brother! I thought I left all that behind on Earth. Overlord...warlord.... Am I dreaming this?"

She faced him, taking him seriously but keeping up the act.

"I thought you determined I was a goddess," she spoke in an overtly Jêpolissan-accented Ghoupallêan, sounding like she had marbles in her mouth. "Or at least I had the feet of a goddess—which is a wonderful pick-up line, by the way."

Pick-up line? he questioned. She had to stop thinking in English and translating into Ghoupallêan. Idioms did not transfer well.

"You say something clever to make me want to mate with you. That's all it means."

"I said nothing for that purpose."

"Of course you didn't. And that innocence worked very well on me. After a trauma, I like to be comforted: rough sex then lots of cuddling. Now I've recovered from yesterday's trauma. Let the F'eng all burn under the comet's fire—well, I suppose it's really ice. Never mind—"

"I must stop you," he said, his voice shaking.

"So you want to stop me from going to Kobarêl and destroying the Overlord and his minions. Is that it?"

He relaxed slightly, continued holding up the shank of metal.

"I've heard all the temple speeches since I was a child," he said, "and I've read most of the religious scrolls, too. All the important ones. I have to believe you are who you say you are, Jinetta, so I must ask you not to harm anyone. Most mortals are innocent fools who mean the gods no harm. I don't believe any of you have sent the comet to destroy us. I believe it is an astronomical phenomena. Perhaps not even divine entities could stop it. I know there were Miracle Children who had a message and many people believed it. They dig tunnels and underground homes to escape the comet—"

"I knew one of the Miracle Children."

"Then you know what we all have been through these past thirty years. Half my life! I wish it would all end. Let the comet come tonight!"

"If you want to help me, I welcome you." She watched him weaken. "I need to go to Jêpolissa. Just across the border. Then I can do what's needed to at least save some of the people of this planet."

"Why?" He shook his head, eyes focused on the floor. "Why do you want to save any of us?"

"Because I believe in life."

She stopped to think. Was that the right answer? She could have left years ago. She gave up her seat on an escape vessel. Even if she could escape through a tangent in the nick of time, why stay and help these desperate people? Perhaps in three-hundred-eighty years she had learned something about people—Ghoupalles, Earthers, humans in general, and the hybrids she had borne. Perhaps she had also learned something about herself: how strong she could be when needed and how weak she also could be.

She took a breath, expelled it with force.

"I believe in people—Ghoupalles—and the best they can be. Who will survive? What will remain? Everything is a test, gods or no gods. This comet is a test. How much disaster can you endure and still keep your humanity?"

"This is all a test?" He tried to laugh. "The gods do have the disease of humor."

"It's seriously twisted humor, but...yes, humor."

He laughed cynically and resumed his defensive stance.

"I don't believe you. If you are Goddess Memitha, you always favor death and destruction."

"Listen, Jugs...." She let a smirk burst upon her face. "I am no goddess. I said that because it was fun to tease you. It was also useful to let the Overlord of Kobarêl think so. I want him to be afraid of me. I am quite mortal—like you and your family and the crew on the airship and everyone in Kobarêl, Nouvê, Sekuate, Typeg, Gotanka, and any other place people live on this planet. But I do have a few things about me that are special. I have secret knowledge that lets me live a different life, a different kind of life than everyone else. I told you before I've lived about three-hundred-eighty years over the past ten centuries of history. Now I happen to be here."

"I shall call you a goddess for that."

"I am a lucky woman, not a goddess." She smiled sincerely at the co-pilot. "Jugs.... You know, dear, in my culture, that means a woman's breasts, big ones. I recommend you use your real name."

"Kag?" He made a face. "I never liked it. I will continue with Jugs."

"As you like."

She turned to grab her travel bag, ready to leave.

"Are you going ahead with your plan?" he asked weakly, perhaps afraid of being left alone in the room.

"Jugs, or whatever your real name is, I am going to save my daughter. If you do not want to help me, then you should go to your home and love your partner and play with your child. Yesterday you earned my admiration, saving me from the F'eng. Tomorrow you will fly another airship, but tonight you may be at peace. You can tell people you met a goddess and lived to tell about it."

"We seemed to agree on what to do with the F'eng, but when it comes to regular Ghoupalles, I humbly request you reconsider your plan."

"It's the only plan I have. I have killed people in my previous lives, but only when necessary. I don't like doing it. I am not a vengeful goddess—or woman."

"We were just fighting for our lives," Jugs explained. "We were right to fight them. I think I stabbed two and they may die from what I did. We can be forgiven for that. We did not plan to do it. Now you want to go kill someone deliberately?"

"Not kill, perhaps only hurt. Persuade that person to see things clearly. To act responsibly."

"I disagree with your plan. Maybe I cannot stop you, but I beg you to reconsider doing harm."

"Is it bad to harm a bad person? Should I allow evil to continue disrupting my life? And the lives of everyone in Kobarêl?"

"You cannot fight against evil by being evil!"

She sighed, shaking her head. "I once knew a man who changed history." She took a deep breath. "Do you recall the Sekuatean wars in the early 1500s? When the Sekuatean Empire invaded Tebbicousimankalê?"

Jugs looked puzzled; perhaps he had not been a good student. "You refer to that scroll everyone dismisses? I remember learning about the Sekuatean Empire but I don't remember there being any war with the Tebbis. I think that would have been explained in history scrolls."

"Yes, it should. But there's nothing about the siege of Siaa in 1533. Nor the retreat from Tebbicousimankalê, is there? That's because he changed it. That man was able to prevent a war by killing one person."

"One person? Who? A general?"

"No, a girl. A young girl who wrote poetry."

"How could she stop a war."

"She didn't. Her death prevented the war from happening."

"How can that be so?"

"That girl was supposed to grow up and lead a group of rebels against the government of Sekuate. There would be a revolution. The armies would conquer surrounding nations and eventually invade Tebbicousimankalê. All because she lived to become the Empress of Sekuate."

"Ah! Basura-Kanoun, you mean?"

"Yes, her."

"She was only a girl. And he killed her? Is that how the scrolls tell the story?"

"He regretted it, of course, yet he knew the greater good would be served. Unfortunately, he didn't know what would happen. He prevented the war and thus the deaths of millions of people, but his own family suffered great harm. He regretted that, too, and tried to change history again. And now, I'm here. I can't change history and I certainly cannot stop a comet. But I intend to get my daughter back, no matter what I have to do. If a death occurs, I'll call it necessary and I'll sleep well and smile in the morning! I have sacrificed too much for her already."

Jugs nodded, finally understanding. He tossed the metal shank in the waste slot in the wall.

"Then I wish you and your daughter peace at all costs."

They parted outside the airship terminal, taking an ETUR-TM there and sharing breakfast at the café inside. Despite it being against the custom in Erit, she hugged him, then planted a kiss on his lips. Caught in a flash of memory of their days together, he kissed her in return, deeply. She wished him love and peace. He wished her success in her mission—and a pardon, in advance, for whatever she might do as long as it resulted in her saving her daughter.

* ❋ *

"So this is what it's like to play in a Jêpolissan star, huh?" asked Gina. Her arms were growing tired, numb, tied up over her head as they were. She was almost at her limit.

"No. This is not a star. We are only two, not five. This is you and me having another talk." The warden was gruff, could never appreciate her sense of humor, especially in desperate times. "This is interrogation. You have experience with it, don't you?"

The chill she felt initially had eased. Her skin no longer was covered with goosebumps, or whatever they were called in Erit. As much as they seemed to enjoy stringing her up naked and asking her stupid questions, they should have a name for it. Perhaps a literal translation: *terust*, the bird that most closely resembled a goose, plus *mak*, meaning bump, nob, pimple. Yes, that's it: *terust-mak*, or in the plural, as a general condition of the skin, *terust-makaxii*. There! She had finally solved that linguistic conundrum.

The question was repeated.

"No, of course not. I have no experience with interrogation, at least not Erit-style."

Every day the same thing. Questions. About everything. All because she was seen kissing in public with a man wearing a co-pilot's uniform. A public servant, as it were. A man of respect. And she, a common whore by the look of her, dressed in dirty clothes, was yet another disruption to a well-oiled society. The first to respond was a low ranking street patrol cadet, a zealous fanatic who seemed delighted to mark her first prey. And Gina did not help the situation by being her usual sarcastic self, berating the young officer and trying to hold that First Director rank over her.

Jugs was given a reprimand on the spot when the officer's superior arrived. Fined and sent on his way, he had gazed back at her with what seemed a pleasant grin yet which somehow unnerved her, almost as though he was glad for her capture—as the quartet of officers bundled her into a sanitation cart and wheeled her away with the collected trash, despite her cries of innocence and the injustice of it all.

Taken to some kind of warehouse, she saw it was actually a prison facility. Perhaps once a warehouse, it was now divided into individual wire cages containing hundreds of females and several males, all stripped and kept like cattle awaiting slaughter, four levels high, she could see from the uptake station.

First, she was force-fed a black-*bôb*, which made her body limp and her mind dull. Easy to manipulate, easy to lead around. There was no phone call, no lawyer, no chance to speak to a judge and straighten things out. She had been caught red-handed ('red-lipped' in Ghoupallêan) engaging in unlicensed mouth-to-mouth "sexual inducement" in public—a violation of Public Order Code 88, section 29(b) and (c). Then she resisted arrest and continued her string of expletives, resulting in additional charges: Code 116, section (a), (b), and (g).

"You mean prostitution?" she had laughed when hearing the charge. "It was all consensual and no money was exchanged."

"Was your partner a member of your family?"

She grinned, suddenly feeling she should be careful what she said. "No, we met on the airship. He saved me from the F'eng."

"Are you registered in a family?" the supervising officer had inquired. "If so, give me its official name and most recent license number. Plus any membership changes made during the past five years."

"No, I'm not in any of those polyamorous groups, if that's what you mean. I'm not even a citizen of Nouvê."

"In Erit, morality decrees people only participate in amorous activities with members of their own family. If you want to play a game or such with some other family, you must register for that. A temporary or permanent license."

"Why so strict? Doesn't anyone just fall in love? Just get horny?"

"We must record and track all genetic materials. It is the only way to ensure compliance with health regulations."

"I'm completely clean," said Gina.

To be certain of her claim, she was run through the usual protocol: stripped, examined, bodily fluids collected and tested, applicable treatments applied. She protested at each step.

Disposition: 50 days of detention with weekly counseling sessions and, once released, one year of public order counseling with a certified psyche examiner. There was obviously some flaw in the structure of her brainwaves that needed to be monitored for public safety. Couldn't have someone like her let loose in society unsupervised! Hand stamped with a registration number, she was clamped and braced, and presented to the detention facility, full of black-*bôb*.

Most days were a haze of sitting naked in her cage among all the other wire cages, bare floor and without a bench or blanket. The toilet was a tube set in the floor of the cage, much like the one designed for the interstellar spacecraft she had inspected in Sanduu. That seemed so ironic to her and she began to question what language she was thinking in, and what the meaning of 'ironic' was. It seemed way too harsh a sentence for possessing a small bag of weed. Cheap stuff at that. It was all a daze now.

Other days had her following a strict regimen of examination, testing, inspection, submission to authority and cleaning duties. It was nothing too different from a juvenile delinquent's schedule at some work farm in Missouri. Just for cursing the guards. Just for playing around with a cell mate. Was it all a memory or was it happening now? Unable to distinguish which world she was on, she resisted everything as best she could, waiting for her time to be up so she could go home.

However, her continued resistance and her lack of submission to required bodily inspections during the initial sentence caused her detention to be doubled. Then extended 20 more days—twice—for defiant language. Then 10 more days for displeasing one of the wardens, Second Director #3, who had weird tastes in interpersonal engagement, and another 10 days for resisting Second Director #4, a female, one night after the prisoners' communal bathing session.

"Failure to comply with a second-degree warden's level-B command earns you a ten day extension," he reminded her.

"Even so, that is not something I am willing to do," she had responded.

"So you state."

Her sentence was extended another ten days and she was still forced to perform for the warden, then dragged back to her cage by her feet.

I'm just a political prisoner, she decided. Her stay really had little to do with a thankful kiss on the cheek. They knew who she was and perhaps they were in cahoots with her colleagues in Kobarêl. Anything to keep her away, keep her from causing trouble, from thwarting their plans. Hanar-Santorak had to be behind her continuing detention. He and the Overlord. With the comet arriving soon, they needed to let her out so she could save them, all of them, even the ones who hated her.

She had asked her neighbor among the wire cages what her crime had been and when the woman turned to respond, she saw the deliberately disfigured face of a F'eng follower. The young woman was quite sullen, as though her rebelliousness had been beaten out of her. Her bare skin showed bruises and scars, but she could not guess how much of it was because of the prison staff or her previous life with the cult of the F'eng. Despite whispering, Gina was called out and once more brought to the interrogation room. The questions were the same, her answers a little more creative this time.

"Are you enjoying your stay in this special luxury inn?" asked the warden.

"Yes, I love it here," she spoke in plain Ghoupallêan.

"Yet you cannot wait longer to return to your star, yes?"

"Yes, I cannot wait longer."

"Yet you will need to wait longer, yes?"

"Yes, I will wait longer."

The warden sat back with a satisfied sigh, turned and entered information into the tablet on the desk.

"I am delighted you have finally learned to obey protocols," he said, standing. "I can reduce your sentence by one day. Therefore, you will be released tomorrow."

"Thank you."

"Do not thank me. I am not kind. I am doing my job." He stood close to her, examining her from chin to hips. "If you mistake my following of protocols for personal kindness, I could be accused and charged with favoritism. I won't permit that."

"Yes, I will not thank you."

"Correct."

He ran his index finger down her body from her throat to her navel, then called in two uniformed matrons to take her down from the wall. They released the cables and her arms dropped heavily to her sides, blood flowing into her hands. She rubbed her arms as she stood weakly before the warden.

"Tonight you will stay in the transition center. Food, bath, clothes will be yours. Tomorrow you will receive the certificate of completion for your re-education session. If you are found again to be in violation of public order protocols, your sentence will be double to this one—that is, all of your time here, not only the original detention period."

She nodded rather than risk saying something that might be against the protocols, and was shown out by the two matrons.

In the morning, belly full and body refreshed, she dressed in her old outfit—it had been sanitized after her arrival—and was escorted to the exit. There, she was finally given back her travel bag containing her personal possessions. Even the credits and food ration tickets she had when she arrived were there. Inside also was the comm baton, which she powered up as soon as she was dismissed from the facility.

However, its battery had gone down so much that only local communication was possible, and not much time available even for that.

She wanted desperately to check on Zaura, worried that her daughter may have taken a turn for the worse, worse than before, without the constant pushing Gina was known for. She had let up on those Kobarêl people during her incarceration. And if they had finally released her, would Zaura even know where to find her? Would she have a home to go to? She had not been able to let them know what had happened for several months. First, she needed to find a place to recharge the battery.

She was still a VIP, she wanted to believe. Not sure of the date, she guessed there were yet a few weeks before her resignation became official. With a few credits in her bag, she walked to the nearest inn and bought a room and a sleepmate. Without concern for the prison stamp on her hand, the man held her in his arms through the night and drew her bath in the morning. He invited her to have a nice day and departed.

Well, if nice day means no more sexual assaults or confinement or worrying about your daughter's freedom....

Bathed and dressed, she stepped outside the inn and finally felt free. With a few deep breaths and a quick walk out of sight of the inn, she took the comm baton from her bag and called for an ETUR-TM. When it arrived, she directed it through the city and onto the road west, riding as far as the driver would take her.

No, not across the border. Against company policy. She would pay extra—whatever she had left. No deal.

"Fine," she said with a huff, paying the fare.

She stood on the side of the road with her bag, watching the vehicle head back to Erit.

Around her was dense forest; above the treetops, a gray-green sky of haze, smudged in the corner where a sun was descending. She tightened the buckles on her boots and took off along the road, trying not to be fearful of whoever might pass by and stop for her. Or the chance that some *jalo*, the horned bear-like beast, or *jax*, the long-necked wolf-like carnivore would think she might make a tasty dinner. She kept the laser marker in her hand.

Staying the night in the deep woods, she found a fork in some tree branches, up off the ground to sleep in, and ate berries and herbs for her dinner. She thought of Zaura, hoping she was strong, hoping she would stay strong and do what was right, that is, right for her. Zaura was the daughter of the legendary warrior Set-d'Elous and the Queen of Fenula, after all.

The next morning, she continued walking along the road.

Five days later, she turned up the driveway leading to the country house of her former lover, Vazak-Mixerran. It was near nightfall when she arrived and she was tired and hungry. That was not part of her plan. She had made no provision for anything but getting the aircraft aloft. She expected the house would have been cleared out by Vazak's many relatives and partners, and those partners' relatives. However, when she turned up the drive to the house, she saw it was occupied. Lights beckoned.

Looking to her left as she marched up the slope to the front entrance, she spied through the trees the fuselage of the aircraft she had once upon a time ridden to the edge of space and back. Her heart pounded quicker at the sight of the aircraft. It had been a longshot coming here, but she had nowhere else to go. The aircraft might have been taken by one of Vazak's relations. Or, possibly, nobody knew what to do with it, how to fly it, and simply left it.

Holding her travel bag, she wondered if she should greet whoever was in the house first or simply climb into the aircraft and fly away.

"If I even remember how to do that," she mumbled.

Chapter 37

Countdown

Gina padded around the aircraft, inspecting it as best she could in the fading light, unsure what she might be looking for. Everything seemed the same as before. What else did she need? Would the fuel cell still work? Did it need fuel to get started? And how about the control equipment they had used for her previous flight? Could she fly it herself? She sighed, then sighed again, louder, punching her hands to her hips, feeling a twinge of pain in her side.

"*Fan-dar?*" called a female voice among the trees.

Gina turned as the woman, wrapped in a big parka, came through the trees.

"Who are you?" asked the woman in rough Ghoupallêan. Gina guessed that it was the same Jêpolissan accent that Vazak had sometimes slipped into.

"I am Jinetta-d'Elous," Gina responded, not trying to hide or be deceptive. The woman looked familiar, too. She had probably met her at Vazak's memorial ceremony, perhaps one of his partners. "Are you the occupant of the house?"

"I am. It's my house now. My partner said it was mine. Who are you, Jinetta-d'Elous? Why are you here? Not a good time to be sneaking around someone's house in the dark. In these days we might shoot you before we ask who you are. You are fortunate I'm a polite person."

Gina knew whatever shooting might be done would use a variation of the military AT pulse gun that launched not a bullet but a blob of molten metal. It left a nasty burn at best; it burned through a body at its worst.

"I'm not here to bother you," said Gina, holding out her open palms as Vazak had done: the Jêpolissan greeting. "I also knew Vazak-Mixerran. We worked together the past ten years. Up to his death."

The woman squinted, hand spread above her unibrow, staring hard at Gina.

"Oh, yes! I see you now. Why would you come all the way here? Did he leave something for you? I thought we had already divided everything."

Gina assured the woman she had no designs on anything in the house, nor the house itself. So the woman invited her back to the house and served some kind of beverage: a thick green drink that was bitter. The woman dropped a few sprigs of a yellow herb into the mug and Gina tried it again. Not her cup of tea.

Sipping the drinks, they talked late into the night, mostly about their memories of Vazak. The woman, whose name Gina learned was Zif-Exorran, had indeed been one of his partners, his second. That is, the first partner added to the original couple he had formed with the woman who had looked after Gina at the baths following the memorial gathering. This woman, Zif, became the third member of that family. Now she was elderly, alone in this house with her memories of a life lived long ago. Gina could certainly empathize.

"So then you probably don't even know what that thing is that's sitting by the lake," said Gina when the subject came up.

No, she had no idea what it was. One of his experiments. It looked pretty, like the beak of a *batalu*, only longer and without the cheek feathers. The thing had wings; was it meant to fly? How do they flap?

Gina explained his invention. They agreed he was quite the clever man. He designed several flying machines and the engines to power them. This one, however, was special. First, because he had built a complete, working model himself. Second, because it was a model intended to be used to power the interstellar space vessels.

Zif laughed, a birdy chirping that did not match her stout body and wide, hairy face.

"He had so many dreams! Yet to go up to the stars is not our destiny. We were put on this world to care for this world. We are not meant to leave it."

Gina wondered what her religious beliefs might be, and if they would hinder her obtaining the aircraft.

"He intended it to serve the people of this world," said Gina. "He offered it freely to the International Aerospace Commission, but they did not want it. They believe what they currently have to power the space vessels is sufficient to enable them to reach their destinations in adequate time. Of course, adequate time to them means a trip of several generations. Hundreds of years. The longer such a journey takes, the more chance for trouble to occur. Vazak's fuel cell would be more efficient and also faster. It could cut the journey time by half, or better. The one he put in that flying machine by the lake was only a test. For the interstellar vessels, it would have to be made larger by a factor of six."

Zif seemed interested although Gina decided the woman could not really understand it all. Rocket science. Separating the women from the girls for generations, she thought.

She knelt at the feet of Zif, her host, following Jêpolissan custom. It was the way to ask a favor. She gently stroked the hair on the top of Zif's furry feet.

"Vazak wanted me to be sure it was used properly by the Commission. He trusted no one else. I tried to help him by taking a model of the fuel cell to them but it was destroyed. Did you hear about the airship crash in Erit caused by the F'eng followers? I was part of that. I was aboard that airship they shot down. I managed to escape the wreckage. The fuel cell was destroyed, though—by people who hate technology, people who don't want to leave this world before the comet strikes! And they don't want anyone else to survive, either!"

Zif grinned like she held a big secret. "Everyone worries about this comet thing. Not me. I am a mature woman. I have done everything I have wanted to do. I have had a happy life. For me, it's only a special way to see my life end. I'm content to sit by the lake and watch it come down."

"I feel that way, too—sometimes." She slowed the foot stroking ritual. "Long ago I made a pledge to the people of this world. I promised I would find a way to save as many of them as possible. Vazak believed in that goal, too. That's the reason we worked together."

Around and around they went discussing the comet and all that had ensued from its existence. They grew closer and Zif began stroking Gina's feet, joking how if she stroked forcefully, she might get hair to grow on them. Gina thought Zif was merely being polite.

Zif suggested some balm to make her feet heal quickly from the hike. She went and retrieved a large tin and began applying the balm, rubbing it thoroughly upon Gina's feet.

Eventually Gina realized she could not think straight. After five days of walking and meager food rations, her strength was failing. Zif acknowledged Gina needed to sleep. There was an awkward moment before Zif offered her a place to sleep.

"You may share my furs, if you don't mind a hairy woman beside you. There isn't much else in the house. The relations took everything. There is no *qala* as you Ghoupalles prefer. So you'll need to sleep Jêpolissan style: on the floor with a pile of *jalo* furs. You may snuggle against me if you get cold."

"I can do that," said Gina, followed by a long yawn. "In the morning, we can see about getting that flying machine out of your way."

Her host, Zif, lay beside her, stroking her bare arm, long ago remarking how odd she appeared having little hair on her body. The blond stubble on her head had grown a bit. Gina no longer felt awkward about it and paid no attention to it. Besides, she had helped Zif comb out her body hair each night and each morning after bathing. She felt like an honorary Jêpolissan.

After dinner, they had talked about the troubles in Erit and Kobarêl. The world was ending and there was much to do. Yet so many people had given up. According to the latest news bulletin, both the Kobarêl and Erit spaceworks had scaled back their production. They did not have enough workers to meet the goals they had originally set. Instead of building a fleet of nine vessels, the Kobarêl officials were acknowledging only six could be completed in time. Thankfully, four were already finished and parked in orbit. Erit was behind schedule and only expected to have five completed before the comet arrived.

"There are things I must do soon," said Gina, allowing some impatience to leak out. She explained again how her itinerary had been so disrupted that her only option was to come to this country house of Vazak's and plead to use the aircraft he had built, simply to return to Kobarêl. Once there, she would free her daughter from the re-education facility.

Zif was sympathetic, sharing a heart-wrenching story of how her two daughters were taken from her and forced to serve government ministers in the Jêpolissa capital. That was before she met Vazak; they never had children together. Anything she could do to help Gina....

"Take that flying thing, if you wish it. I don't know how it works. I don't know what to do with it. I have no need to fly away and see how my house looks from the sky. The birds are not impressed with it so why would I be?"

Gina thanked her profusely. She massaged Zif's hairy, meaty shoulders.

"I know now the reasons Vazak adored you so much," said Zif, purring beneath the work of Gina's fingers.

"You said, back when we met, that you would shoot someone who was sneaking around the house. Does that mean you have such a weapon?"

"Yes, dear. I never make a claim I cannot support."

"May I borrow it? I need to be safe in this crazy world of terrorists and F'eng minions."

"No one but you have called on me here. Take it. I'll give it to you after we finish this exercise."

"Exercise? It's called 'massage' in the language of my ancestors. It's *smotaxii* in Ghoupallêan."

"In Jêpolissan custom we do not touch another's body as you are touching mine unless we are partners in the same star-family. Do you want to be my partner? It's perfectly legal. We can be the only two members."

"You and Vazak have been so kind to me, I feel I'm a Jêpolissan, too. A naked, hairless Jêpolissan—if you don't mind that aspect of me. I apologize for showing my hairless skin to you. It must be rather disconcerting for you."

"It's taken a few days but now I see you as beautiful, even with no hair. In fact, now I can see the benefit of going without hair on your body. With the right skin texture and color, it can be a different kind of beauty. It's right for warm climates."

"And I have grown accustomed to you having lots of hair all over your body, even your face. You are like a teddy bear." There she went again, thinking in English, translating to Ghoupallêan. "It's a toy for children, covered in fur, soft and always ready to be hugged."

"Wonderful! I enjoy hugs." Zif let out a long exhale. Her eyes seemed to twinkle. "I think now we can join our mouths. If you are ready."

"You mean a kiss?"

"Is that what you call it?"

"Yes."

"I think you may be imagining something different. In our custom, I cough up food and pass it to you. The act shows my willingness to feed you my spirit. And you feed me yours. Are you ready?"

Gina grimaced, realized she could not be rude.

She leaned down as Zif placed her hand behind Gina's neck, pulled her close. Their lips touched lightly. Gina felt Zif's tongue push into her mouth and find her tongue. She fell into a trance and pressed the kiss harder against Zif's lips. Then came the cough and a bit of partly digested fish. Coated in saliva, it had no real flavor. Perhaps a bit smoky. Gina swallowed and returned to kissing her, this time in Earth style.

Gina wondered if she needed to wear some kind of leather bikini with some metal arm bands and thigh-high boots. Would that say 'badass warrior chick'? Carry a huge sword or a battle axe? A tiara? Lacey corset? More important was how she acted. Lots of attitude. And weaponry. The sword would fit in the cockpit. So would her laser marker.

She would waltz right into the Overlord's office on the top floor of his high-rise palace and demand her daughter. She would quickly snatch him in a headlock, press the laser marker to his throat, and make her demands. Silly man that he was, he would let her in quite willingly because he loved her golden hair. She would sweet-talk her way inside, offering him more as soon as it grew out.

Standing before the tall mirror, she nodded, satisfied with her appearance. Maybe she was approaching fifty in Earth years, she guessed, but she was fit. Very fit. Muscular shoulders and arms. Strong thighs. She could fit into a warrior bikini if she had to. She stared at her body, belly firm and tight, wondering. Perhaps it was the bare midriff that served to disarm opponents. The sight of the belly weakened opposing warriors. Was that the magic of the bikini warrior chick outfit?

"I can pull it off, I'm sure."

She closed the mirror cabinet and ran her fingers through the short hair on her head.

Yawning and ready for bed, she went to the sleeping room and settled down upon the furs, stretched her arms and legs, then curled up. Soon Zif joined her, and held her through the night, her furry arms and body keeping Gina warm.

"Jinetta! Jinetta!" cried Zif first thing in the morning. She ran unclothed back into the room on her thick, bare feet, her long nails, more like claws, clattering on the wooden floor. Her body hair, though thinning with age, still covered her well. "Come! See the news report! It's horrible!"

Gina jumped up in her sleeping gown and followed Zif back to the public room where they stared at the communication screen, reading the words displayed there.

The Zetin Rocketry Agency had launched their missile at the comet as it came to its next approach to Ghoupallesz. This was the event everyone had been waiting for: break up the comet and worry no more. In their excitement, however, the Zetin had launched the missile a little early and it had missed.

"The fools! Never trust Zetin to do anything right," Gina growled.

"They launched three missiles," said Zif, pointing to the smaller text at the bottom of the screen.

Realizing their mistake, the Zetin then launched their second missile as the first one should have been scheduled. It came closer to striking the comet yet it, too, missed, and continued on. In a panic, they adjusted their launch parameters and sent their third and final missile skyward. Telescopes confirmed the third missile did indeed strike the comet. The blast tore off a chunk of it. Cheers went up in the Zetin launch control office and news reports were sent around the world announcing their success and reminding the world of the tribute they owed the Zetin.

"Oh no...." Gina's hands went to her face.

The chunk broken free of the comet spun downward into the atmosphere. It did not burn up—not much anyway.

As the planet turned on its axis, the Bær Sea moved into the target zone. The main chunk of the comet, about 6 x 2 *radit*, descended rapidly, striking the water near the coast of the southern district of Sekuate-north, near the capital city of Seas. Smaller pieces broke off during entry and showered the Seas metropolis with debris. The main portion hit off-shore, causing a huge wave that swept over the coastal city of Koern and plunged upriver to swamp part of Seas.

"One million dead," Zif muttered, breathless.

Gina took her hand. "Of five million citizens...."

Zif turned and roared her shock, filling the house with her anguish.

"Four miles long," Gina calculated, studying the map of the devastated area on the comm screen. Just that sliver was four miles in length, she gasped. What remained of its angry parent was reduced by only two percent. In less than six years, 98 percent of the original comet would still strike the planet like this mere pebble had yesterday.

That was the bump we felt during the night. Seas was on the opposite side of the planet. *And we felt it here in Jêpolissa!*

Zif ripped fingerfuls of hair from her chest, tore at the hair on her shoulders and whatever she could reach of her back, and tossed it into the air, forming a cloud of dark brown confetti. She dropped to the wooden floor and pounded her fists and banged her knees. She raised her face and roared like a wounded beast.

Gina was frightened yet dug into her soul and made herself drop to the floor and hold Zif tightly. They rocked back and forth together. Gina tried screaming as loudly as she could. She beat the floor with her hands, kicked it with her feet as she held Zif. After a while they had become exhausted and lay together on the floor, Zif whimpering and Gina weeping softly. The end was drawing closer, had come to their doorstep and was rapping hard on the door.

With a slow draw of breath, Gina looked out at the bright green curve of the planet turning against the darkness of space, thinking of the last embrace she had with Zif-Exorran before climbing into the cockpit of the sleek aircraft that Vazak-Mixerran had named STARLIGHT—*Espæxii* in Ghoupallêan. This time, she was not fazed by the experience. She kept calm and remained serious. She was confident as she studied the control panel, read through the instruction manual, and made sure her skin-tight coverall flight suit, white with pink trim, was in good condition. She fitted her helmet on securely, tested her gloves and boots—all taken from the closet Zif had shown her once they stopped crying at the destruction of the city of Seas. After that horrific event, Gina knew what she had to do.

The POWER ON button was yellow, ENGINE SEQUENCE buttons were blue and numbered in the order she should push them. Everything was planned for her, it seemed. The data screen before her displayed text of each step she had to follow. She complied and the aircraft hummed as it came to life. Then she pressed the red diamond button and the fuel cell ignited—that was the closest word she could think of. She saw on the data screen rows of figures fluctuating, lights flashing, a colored graph appearing: as the propulsion came nearer to take-off, the red line moved up the graph. The next instruction appeared:

PRESS GREEN DIAMOND #1

She did.

Instantly the trees outside the canopy shook and she felt herself rolling forward, faster and faster. She was heading toward the opposite row of trees across the lake. Suddenly she was tilted backward and the aircraft rose at a sharp angle into the sky.

ENGAGE STEERING CONTROLS

She took hold of the round pads in each armrest, placed her palms on each disk. She remembered that to steer the aircraft she only need roll the disk left or right, forward or back with the palm of her hand. So she did, directing the aircraft northeast to the coast then due north over the arctic sea. The aircraft rose higher and higher until she was threatening to leave the stratosphere.

An alarm beeped, and as she arched higher it became an irritating siren.

The data screen displayed the all-important question:

LEAVING ATMOSPHERE - APPROVE?

No, she did not want to leave the atmosphere and be launched into space; this was not actually a spacecraft. She knew it was dangerous to be unprotected from radiation while in the upper atmosphere.

She looked at the rows of buttons, glancing at the data screen. Press the left yellow diamond button? Or press the right yellow diamond button? The air seemed stale and she took as deep a breath as she could but felt dizzy. What to do? The data screen flashed for attention.

"What do I do?" she mumbled, then repeated it louder.

"Need help?" a voice spoke into her comm set. "Press yellow circle button above data screen."

What? Her eyes found the button: ADAIN.

She pressed it hard. Of course the button that said 'help' in Ghoupallêan was the one to press, but what good would that do? She was quickly heading out of the atmosphere and into space! She was not even going into orbit around Ghoupallesz but straight on to the next planet, Gouö!

The data screen vanished and was immediately replaced by a cartoonish image of Vazak-Mixerran's face. He was speaking to her! He was programmed into the data screen.

"You called for help," said the data screen Vazak. "How may I help you? Speak the problem."

"I am heading straight out into space! How do I stop?"

"Press the red diamond button under the data screen."

She did and the cartoon image disappeared. Now rows of numbers again flickered before her.

"That doesn't do anything!"

"Speak the numbers in the left column," said the voice.

She read them off, top to bottom."

"Press the blue triangle on the left control panel."

"Done." She waited. "Nothing's happening!"

"Press the second blue triangle on the left control panel."

She shook her head. "Don't joke with me!"

"I am not programmed to joke."

"I pressed the button. Now what?"

"Check all straps and protective gear."

She tugged at her straps, adjusted her helmet. "Done."

"Prepare for Rapid Reverse."

"Rapid Reverse? What's that?"

"Rapid Reverse is Emergency Procedure to halt exit from atmosphere. You asked for help with this problem."

"Yes, I did, but—"

"When you are secure, press large yellow triangle above data screen. Hold on tightly."

She took a big breath as though she were about to dive into a deep pool. *Nothing deeper than space*, she thought, *except death.*

Her arm stretched out and her finger reached the button. She pushed it and immediately was thrown back against the seat cushions as the propulsion system shut off its forward thrust and the nose of the aircraft split open along the sides and two nozzles appeared; a third nozzle under the nose cone was out of view. All three had columns of data on the screen. At the same instant, some kind of thrust shot out of the three nozzles and her forward speed slowed dramatically. She was thrown forward but the straps held her, still unable to reach for any buttons.

"What do I do?" she cried out.

"Wait."

"Did I do it right? Is this what's supposed to happen?"

"Wait."

The alarm siren stopped. There was only a ringing silence inside the cockpit. A faint roar continued as the nozzles pumped out power to halt her forward progress.

"Is it working?"

"All systems are operating properly."

"Will I return to Earth?"

"Unable to answer. Restate."

"Will I be able to return to the planet's surface?"

"Yes. State new destination."

"I'm trying to get back to Kobarêl to rescue my daughter. Oh, I wish you were with me, Vazak."

"I am with you."

"I mean in person, with your big, hairy body next to me."

"Operation not possible in present venue."

"Silly man!"

The aircraft had slowed to a point where it seemed to float in the weightlessness of space. Loose objects were hovering in the cockpit. She waved them out of the way.

"We're in orbit! That's not what I want."

"State new destination."

"I want to go to Kobarêl."

"Insufficient fuel for destination."

"What? You built this new fuel cell. I thought it lasts forever. That's why you said it should be used for the interstellar vessels. Isn't that right?"

"Present fuel cell is not capable of use in interstellar vessels."

"Where am I? What's the closest landing zone?"

"Closest suitable landing site is Typeg spaceworks."

"You're kidding!"

"I am not programmed to joke."

She let out a frustrated sigh. The air was thin in the cockpit and she was dizzy. "Vazak?"

"Recommend: Apply additional breathing module."

A panel popped open on the side of the cockpit and she saw the apparatus there. Just like what the stewardesses on Ozark Airlines had demonstrated when she'd flown between Kansas City and St. Louis as a college student. She pulled the apparatus out of the storage cabinet and fitted it over her nose and mouth.

"Was problem solved?"

"Which one? I've got lots of problems!"

"Problem one: Exiting atmosphere not recommended. Rapid

Reverse Protocol. Problem Solved. Problem two: Pilot box environment dangerous—"

"Okay, solved. Thanks." She breathed comfortably. "Thank you, Vazak. Even as a cartoon, you are wonderful."

The dancing columns of numbers on the data screen switched to his cartoon face again, smiling, eyes twinkling.

"Destination Typeg. Prepare for Autopilot Engagement. Flight Plan Entered. Final Approval?"

"You think of everything, don't you, Vazak?"

"I am programmed to solve problems most likely to occur when Jinetta-d'Elous occupies the pilot box."

"Well, geez, thanks!"

"Final Approval?"

"Yes. Approved. Typeg, it is." She felt the aircraft power up and shift direction. "With time in jail for a stupid kiss, maybe I'm in time for the conference. I want to hear what they all have to say after the Zetin messed up their missile plan. They have no idea what they're doing—"

"Speak the problem."

"Where do I begin?"

"Begin with Most Urgent Problem."

"That would be landing this thing."

"Autopilot Engaged. Problem Solved."

Chapter 38

Flight Plan

Gina swept into the front hall, glancing at the sign and grabbing a program card. She drew the attention of everyone, dressed in her crisp white flight suit, carrying her helmet, strutting confidently like a biker chick out of a comic book.

INTERNATIONAL AEROSPACE COMMISSION
ANNUAL CONFERENCE - TYPEG
BATOU-10: 2169

KEYNOTE SPEAKER: OLARK-SENJARUS,
FIRST DIRECTOR OF TYPEG AEROSPACE EXECUTIVE COMMITTEE

"AFTER MISSILES FAIL: OPTIONS FOR RENEWED PRODUCTION
AND EVACUATION"

She was amused to see the cute logo at the bottom of the card depicting a smiling countdown dial.
It's not like Christmas is coming!
Taking a seat in the back of the hall, she thought of putting on the helmet to escape the stares of her fellow scientists. Did they even recognize her with her short hair? Did it matter? She was nobody here now.
The keynote speaker was introduced following a few moments

of silence for those killed in the 'missile mishap'; it was not polite to accuse the Zetin of aiming deliberately in such a way as to get a piece of the comet to wipe out one of their enemies' cities. No, thought Gina, the Zetin could not possibly calculate something like that with any accuracy. Pure bad luck. That's all it was.

She listened to what Olark-Senjarus had to say, noting he was not much at pep talks. The mood was desperate in the hall, most sitting on their hands hoping for good news, fearing someone would dare tell them the truth. Of course, she knew the truth: she had seen it from space. The comet would make one more orbit, one which would end with the whole thing coming down like that tiny piece did on Seas.

She also knew what she had to do. For herself, her daughter, and perhaps some of the people around her. They all had tickets to ride. She waited patiently through the question and answer session, wishing those in the hall took greater interest in the scientific rather than the social aspects. Too many Q&A on the F'eng and whether their thinking had merit. And the underground shelters? Whole cities had been built, able to house tens of thousands of people each, stocked with supplies to last ten years. Then they would peek out, like Punxsutawney Phil seeing his shadow on February 2nd, and decide it was time to resettle the surface.

She chuckled and those beside her were annoyed.

The audience's roar knocked her out of her thoughts. The Zetin ambassador—some representative of the Zetin Rocketry Agency, anyway—was declaring they would not apologize.

"Although we did not plan it, and we could not have predicted the result, we nevertheless rejoice that our age-old enemy has been struck by the hand of the Zetin High God Tʜ'T!"

More recriminations, accusations, bitter insults and the worst of offensive words flying everywhere. She wanted to run out but she stayed. When the hall was about to erupt into complete chaos, she made her move, rushing up to the stage.

As she stepped upon the stage, carrying her helmet, the hall became less noisy as people became curious who this person was. Looking so sexy in the skin-tight white flight suit with pink lines down the arms and legs. They were not quite sure if this was a man or a woman, but she stood boldly beside the lectern. She sat the helmet down and picked up the amplifier baton.

"Citizens of the world," she spoke resolutely, her calm voice sounding over the din, "please allow me to speak for one *pon*. I have solutions to the problems spoken here." More people fell silent, willing to give her a chance. "I am Jinetta-d'Elous. Some of you may remember me. I resigned from this Commission almost a year ago. Yet, in the interval since, I have found new technology which—"

"Your time is almost done," shouted someone on the side.

"This new technology will make it possible to journey to interstellar destinations in less than half the time as using current propulsion system technology—"

"She is only pushing the escape plan!" cried out another.

"Many people want to stay here!"

"Underground is the place to be if you want to survive!"

"We won't go into space!"

She held up her right hand, wiggling her fingers in Typegan fashion to call for quiet.

"Commission members! You witnessed the results of the Zetin missile fiasco. Yes, fiasco! It is clear that another set of missiles will not be enough to protect this planet. Stay or go: the only choices. If a chunk of comet hits the site of any underground city, they will perish. If a chunk of comet hits any of the evacuation pods tethered in orbit, they will perish. What will be left when the full weight of the comet strikes this planet? Remember: only two percent of the comet's mass hit Seas! The remaining ninety-eight percent will split this planet apart. The largest quakes ever seen. Rips through the center of the planet, down to its core. Continents tossed about. Debris thrown into the atmosphere, surrounding the entire planet, choking and killing all life everywhere. It is the end of Ghoupallesz!"

"We've had a good run of it," yelled someone in front.

"I agree! We are tired!"

"It's time to accept our fate!"

She clapped her hands, a rude gesture in Typeg.

"Commission members! If you will allow me—"

"Your one *pon* is long done!"

A man in dark green uniform with red lapels leaped onto the stage and she was momentarily startled, snapping into the too-familiar defensive stance learned in the Erit prison.

"You, Jinetta-d'Elous, are not who you say you are!"

The crowd hushed. A murmur rose and spread.

"We all know about your background. It's the scandal of the year. That is your reason for resigning. You did not want to face the tribunal! You're a fake. First, you haven't any academic credentials. No academy claims you. And you have no history of residence in the nation you call home. You gave birth to one of the Miracle Children, yet heed their message not at all—"

"He was my son! How dare you—"

"Some say you are not even Ghoupalle. You are an alien. You have different blood. You cannot trick us, or gain our sympathy, with your fancy spacesuit and your personal flying machine. Oh, yes, we saw you arrive in grand style—a sleek metal bird that can carry only two passengers. Is that what you invented to save us? Seems you only care to save yourself and your daughter!"

She did not know who the man was but he was dressed in the uniform of a First Director of something. His hostility took her by surprise. What was the crowd thinking?

"Commission members! I came here to ask all of you to allow me to lead the Commission again. There are solutions! There is time! We can survive!"

"You have more pockets to line with the wealth of dying nations? That's it, isn't it?"

"I have not taken any funds from the Commission, unlike some members. Instead, I have risked so much to help the people of Ghoupallesz. I've risked my life countless times to bring the best technology to the space program. I've been attacked by F'eng followers. I've been in an airship crash! I've been at war with my own government to secure what we need—what we all need—to succeed and achieve our goal: survival! And I still do not accept a seat on any vessel. You cannot lose with me as your leader again! I un-resign!"

"You cannot un-resign! You gave up your position and you cannot return. How can we trust you now?"

She gazed at the audience, scanning the faces of a dozen ethnicities from wall to wall and back to the center of the hall. Mouth agape, she could not focus, could not think. She felt helpless and embarrassed. Her gut tightened.

"Who the hell are you?" she growled, turning to her accuser on stage.

"I am the current First Director of the Commission," he spoke, adding a bow like it was a formal introduction. "I am Guxod-Uek, from the Free Danid state of Sorêg. It's in—"

"Yes, yes, I know where Sorêg is."

"Ever been there?"

"No, but my friend...he was there. It was long ago. Sadly."

"It must have been before we gained our freedom from Sekuate, if it was a sad occasion. Once more demonstrating your ambivalence for groups different than your own. Tell us, Jinetta-d'Elous, if that is your real name...where are you from? Name your birthplace."

She froze, not sure what to say. In most of her lives she had used either Siti or Selauê as her hometown, but she knew they could easily check records now.

"It doesn't matter where I was born. What matters is I am here, ready to help in every way I can. That's all you need to know."

"Ah, I see!"

"What do you see?"

The audience seemed to be enjoying the debate on stage. They laughed and whistled at the barbs being flung at her and her reactions to them.

"I heard that you were trying to pass yourself off as a goddess, saying you had special powers."

"Who would say such a stupid thing?"

"Your boss. The Overlord of Kobarêl, Samot-Artexus."

"What did he say?"

"You threatened him when he was exposing your false identity. You said you were Goddess Memitha!"

She tried to chuckle, throat dry. The audience thought it was hilarious.

"That was a silly game we play. He is the kind of pervert who enjoys being dominated by a strong woman. He likes to play goddess and priest. A sex game. That's all it is."

Only then did she notice the audience's collective gasp.

"Sex games?" asked Uek.

She eyed the audience. Some were tilting their heads, a negative response. Others were pressing their index fingers to their foreheads. A few were standing and holding their left hands over their right shoulders. One couple who seemed to be from Aikavo or Dikondra opened their split skirts in protest and shook their urine bags in her direction.

"Slip of the tongue," she muttered in English.

"And what language is that you speak?"

"It's my language. My mother taught it to me."

First Director Uek had a moribund grin, as though he knew she was disgraced enough now and his attack could turn to pitying her.

She took a deep breath, holding her head high.

"I offered my help, my knowledge of space, and my mind and soul and body for the people of all races on Ghoupallesz. I have been on this planet a long time and I've come to love it despite the hardships I've often faced. I have lived here a lot longer than even my home world. So now, if I cannot be of further service to you, then I shall be on my way."

"Wait! You said your 'home world'?" He seemed truly shocked, perhaps not expecting her to actually confess something like that. "You're not from Ghoupallesz? How can that be?"

Gina pursed her lips, thinking of her twenty-nine lives, the places she had been, the sunrises and mountains and deserts and children and forests and cities and new constellations overhead and that one damn comet. She thought of Zaura.

"All I ask is that my daughter be released and be allowed to join me. Can you—will you?—speak on my behalf to Artexus—to Overlord Artexus? Will you? Please?"

Uek smiled, raising his arms to quiet the crowd.

"I am Danid. From Sorêg. Thus, I have no connections to your country or its governor. There is nothing I can do. However, I do wish you well and hope to see you aboard some vessel in the near future—if you change your mind by Final Day."

He turned to the audience.

"First Director Jinetta-d'Elous served us excellently for a full fourteen years. She has been a leader and an engineer and a scientist. We can credit her with the basic design of the transport frames and the residential pods. We can also thank her for the astrobiology work she has done, locating four habitable planets. Her leadership has impressed us and enriched us, taken us to new heights and given us hope. Let us show our appreciation to her!"

The audience roared and whistled, many jumping to their feet and waving their hands over their heads. They seemed sincere, yet in the back of her mind she knew they were humoring her.

"Thank you again, Jinetta-d'Elous, for all of your service."

Uek stepped to the side of the lectern as two guards moved to gently escort her off the stage.

"Easy with her," he said. "She needs kindness now, most of all. Did you notice that detention facility stamp on her hand?"

As she was led out she heard his final remark:

"It's sad when a once brilliant Ghoupalle advances in age and enters the senile period. And she looks so young...."

Outside the conference hall, standing on the upper plaza, Gina bit her lip as she snatched the comm baton from her pocket and punched in the code for the Overlord. She could hardly breathe as she fought her emotions. People on the street stared at her: sleek white and pink flight suit, carrying the white and pink helmet.

It was noisy there on the street so she turned to face the building.

"Unauthorized use," came a message on the comm baton.

What? Had they shut off her access already? She thought she still had a month left. *A month?* How long had she been in prison? Her resignation was long past now, she realized. And the comet was closer.

She dialed a different code: the receptionist for the Overlord.

"International service prohibited. Local service available."

Fine! She called for an ETUR-TM to take her out to the Typeg spaceworks where her aircraft waited.

She needed to speak to the Overlord before anyone at this conference could. Before Guxod-Uek especially. She wanted to speak with her daughter, too, and assure she was at least in reasonable condition. Zaura had not sounded well the last time they spoke—how many months before? She'd sounded drugged or sleepy or both, repeating what she was expected to say. Gina could only hope for the best. Zaura was an adult now, as far as

Kobarêl laws were concerned, so there was little she could do if Zaura did not want her help.

She tried again to call Kobarêl from the spaceworks Tarmac, punching in six different numbers, all denied. Her service had been downgraded, or she was out of range to make a call to the far side of the planet. This was not Earth, after all—where AT&T could connect you, for a price, to any other phone on the planet.

The flight service personnel were gathered around the aircraft, admiring it, studying it, examining it as Gina approached. She held the laser marker in her hand in case there was any trouble. When they saw her, they began asking questions about the aircraft, more interested in learning about the futuristic vehicle than flirting with her as she expected. She did not know any of the details, of course, so she put them off politely.

"I'm just the test pilot," she said, smiling. "Kind of in a hurry now, gentlemen. Please step back."

They moved away, remaining in a semicircle between the tip of the port wing and the nose of the jet, watching her climb up the side of the fuselage and punch in a code that made the cockpit canopy slide open.

QOBÂ-ZIMON was the password Vazak had programmed—'hairy man'—perfect.

She settled into the seat and quickly closed and locked the canopy. Pressing the red square button above the data screen, she secured her helmet as she waited for the power to activate. When the engine was humming, she saw data appear on the screen, updating the aircraft's systems. Everything was fine except the fuel cell.

"What's wrong?" she asked after pushing the round yellow ADAIN button.

"Fuel Cell Low Power," came Vazak's bass voice.

"What's possible now? Can I return to Kobarêl?"

"Calculating."

"Range: 32 percent via northern route, 77 percent via southern route. Select."

She thought for a moment. To go around the mighty Hikbok mountains, she would have to swing north around them or south. Typeg was south already, so less of a detour to stay south. Either way, she did not have enough power for the route.

"How about going across Bæronak and the ocean to Kobarêl?" After all, what was displayed on the screen failed to show the western route.

"Range: 93 percent."

"You mean I can only go 93 percent of the way before the fuel cell runs out?"

"Correct."

She ran her fingers over her face, expelled a hard breath.

"What should I do?"

"State the problem."

"Yes, of course. State the damn problem!" She glanced out the canopy at the men in coveralls watching her. No doubt they were waiting to see how the aircraft worked when it launched. "How do I make the fuel cell fully powered again?"

"Fuel Cell may be recharged following Protocol Seven."

"What is Protocol Seven?"

"All Protocols are available in the manual associated with this machine."

The tablet with the full manual installed was in her bag, which was in the second seat, behind hers. It was impossible to get to it while sitting in the front seat.

"Can you give me an overview of Protocol Seven?"

"Yes."

She waited.

"*Will* you give me an overview of Protocol Seven?"

"Yes. Protocol Seven has instructions for the recharging of the Mixerran-d'Elous Fuel Cell. First, remove the fuel cell core unit. Second, place fuel cell core unit into prepared mixture (Follow Protocol Eight). Third, allow fuel cell core unit to become completely dry. Fourth, install fuel cell core unit in its designated location. Fifth, calibrate fuel cell capacity. Proceed as usual."

"Can you repeat that?"

"Yes."

"Come on! Gimme a break! Repeat the damn Protocol Seven overview."

The voice of Vazak remained relaxed and steady as the words were repeated. She followed along with the printed text on the data screen.

"What are the ingredients of that mixture you referred to for

Protocol Eight?"

The voice listed 23 ingredients before Gina stopped it.

"Is there any substitute? Can I find the mixture already made?"

"Yes."

"Where? Name the closest fuel cell shop in Typeg."

"Not available in Typeg."

"Where else can I get it?"

"Calculating. Nearest location is Trêsz Sea."

"The Trêsz Sea? What the hell's there that would have the mixture?"

"The sea."

"What do you mean?"

"Closest substitute to mixture described in Protocol Eight is seawater."

Gina cursed and the voice of Vazak reacted with a mechanical laugh: "Hah-hah, hah-hah." That caused her to curse more and the mechanical voice to laugh more.

"You really thought this out, didn't you? You knew what dumb questions I would ask. I hate you! I love you!"

"I am programmed to solve problems most likely to occur when Jinetta-d'Elous occupies the pilot box."

"By the way, on my world we call it a cockpit."

"Filing. Pilot Box is Cockpit."

"Thank you."

"State new destination."

"If all we need is seawater, let's go to Aivana. I'll use the Bær Sea instead of the Trêsz Sea. Do we have enough power for that trip?"

"Range: 233 percent. Approve destination?"

"Take me one hundred *radit* south by southwest of the capital city. Then ask me again what to do. I'm looking for a small object in the desert there."

"Calculating. Destination confirmed."

She sighed, feeling relief at last. "Fire when ready."

"Launch sequence initiated."

The humming around her transformed into a lurch of power.

"Engage Steering Controls."

She could not simply lay her head back and nap on this trip. Not until she was airborne, at least. So she used the two disks on the armrests to maneuver the aircraft onto the long strip of flat stone. She saw the spaceworks personnel behind her and hoped they were far enough away for the backblast. Then she pressed the red button again and the aircraft slid down the stone-topped plaza—not intended as an aircraft runway—and was launched into the sky, soon turning west to Aivana, and became lost among the pale green clouds.

The monument stood as it had the first time she and Sebastian encountered it. He'd always insisted he found it before her, when he was dabbling in interdimensional travel without her. Probably one of those trips he took with girlfriend of the week, the naughty boy. Nevertheless, there it was—however many millennia it had been lost in the desert. Four stone pillars, stone floor, seemingly all carved of one large rock. In the center of the floor a stone pillar rose half the height of the corners, like a lectern. On top of the pillar was a large gemstone of dark blue.

She stood several steps away from it, barefoot in the loose reddish-brown sand, her flight suit stripped off, drying on the wing of the aircraft. In leggings she had torn off at mid-thigh and a camisole she'd worn under the suit, she marched down the sandy slope from the relatively level plateau the sensors of the aircraft had detected as a suitable landing spot. And up the next slope, imagining she was on a beach, prancing around in her short shorts and tanktop like a flirty teenager.

Now she gazed at the device—a machine of some kind built by who knows who sometime long, long ago.

"I have no idea how old I really am," she spoke to the wind, expecting it to be sympathetic, "but I know I've spent a total of three-hundred-eighty-some years on this world. Ghoupalle years. At the same time my body has aged at its normal Earth pace. So I'm guessing it's been thirty Earth years since I was last here at this stargate thing."

Suddenly she looked around, feeling someone watching her. The desert could be that way. Or perhaps someone was about to step out from the monument, arriving from some distant world to save her. Or kill her. The odds were about equal. No one was in sight; she could see the aircraft sitting on the plateau.

She returned her gaze to the monument, knowing a five mile hike in that direction would get her to the coast of the Bær Sea. First, she would have to disconnect and remove the fuel cell core unit from the aircraft.

"First things first," she mumbled.

She walked around the monument, concluding it had not succumbed to any damage from natural elements or deliberate sabotage over the centuries. Her path wound inward until she was ready to step upon the stone platform. That would not in itself do anything, she knew—expected. So she stepped up, and strolled around the central post with its gemstone.

What else can I do? She studied the gemstone, fearing to touch it, worried what would happen if she did. According to Sebastian, when he placed his hands upon the gemstone the world began spinning until he could see the abandoned quarry on the east side of Independence, Missouri outside of the monument's perimeter. Sebastian had simply leaped off the platform and found himself rolling in the wet clay at the center of the quarry, surprised that something as silly as a mysterious cosmic 'transporter' would actually work. Whoever had built it was smarter than they were. They might have ended up in an even stranger, more dangerous place if not for concentrating on that quarry's appearance in their minds. So he never used it again.

Her right hand, fingers spread, dropped over the gemstone, hovering a thumbnail's width above it. Then she dared to cover it with her palm. Expecting a sizzle of energy, she closed her eyes and gritted her teeth.

Nothing happened.

She added her left hand, covering all of the gemstone. There was some sensation, she thought. Electricity? Perhaps it was only her imagination, wanting to feel something, anything—wishing desperately for something, anything to happen.

All she wanted was to go home—and take her daughter with her—

She pulled her hands back quickly. If anything was about to happen, she might be pulled into that transporter, wrestled into a vortex, and arrive at the quarry on Earth—or some other place.

Years on Ghoupallesz could pass while she blinked in that quarry. The comet might arrive before she could return. Then how would she save her daughter?

"Zaura...." A pang of regret floated up from her gut. "You are all I have now."

Determined once again, she jumped off the stone platform and marched down the slope, up the next slope, back to the aircraft. She retrieved the flight suit, pulled it on, stepped into the boots and slipped on the gloves. She unlocked the canopy and climbed into the cockpit, secured the canopy, then her helmet. She pushed the red round button, felt the machine hum around her.

Where to go now?

She regarded the data screen.

STATE NEW DESTINATION

She found it easier to interact with a voice than a screen of text and numbers. "Vazak, are you there?"

"Yes," came the voice after two beeps.

"How much range do I have now?"

"State new destination."

"Liêta. West coast of Bæronak. I like the seawater there." She pursed her lips. "It's where I was when I heard you died."

"Calculating. Range: 100.5 percent."

"So I can arrive there before the fuel cell runs out?"

"Yes."

"Great. I'll dunk it in the seawater there. The sea is prettier there, anyway. Then I'll go back to Kobarêl and free my daughter. If it's the last thing I do! You hear me? If it's the last thing I do!"

"Speak the problem."

"My daughter's being held captive by a jerk!"

"Unable to solve problem in this venue."

"Take me to Liêta."

"Destination Liêta. Prepare for Autopilot Engagement. Flight Plan Entered. Final Approval?"

"Approved."

Chapter 39

Penultimatum

She swam across the little bay outside the same resort where she stayed months earlier, and the warm, turquoise water soothed her tired body and tortured mind as she left the fuel cell core unit to soak.

Stretching on the sand, she rested, slipping in and out of naps. Between swims she ran through her exercises on the beach, recalling the moves she had learned across a hundred years on Ghoupallesz. She had studied with the best masters in Feasfend, Typeg, and Têfos in Fenula back when she was the queen. She even had some instruction while held captive in Zetinê. Over thirteen days she tried to make herself ready for combat. She took the sword from the cockpit and began swinging it up and down and around herself, feeling her muscles obeying, nerves igniting. It felt good to wield the blade. She felt young again. Until her back became strained and her arms were too sore to lift. On the patio, she caught sight of herself in the resort's windows and liked what she saw: a badass warrior chick! She needed some epic music for her workout. She needed a masseuse, too.

Daily workouts and swims, followed by massages, and she soon achieved fighting condition. The woman from the resort would stretch her out, pull back on her arms and legs, pop joints, dig with her thumbs into the arches of her feet, her thighs, hips, then bend shoulders back and forth. She would pummel her back, up and down her spine, knuckles loosening tension, pinching her neck and poking fingertips around her shoulder blades. At first it was worse than the workout she put herself through, then better. In time, neither the workout nor the massage hurt. She was ready for war!

She waited another four days for the fuel cell to completely dry. The installation was not complicated following the steps in the manual. Vazak had made them simple—so simple she felt insulted, but let it go.

Recharged and refreshed, she settled the bill with the resort owners, then powered up the aircraft and launched out across the turquoise bay.

She flew across the southern portion of the Great Ocean separating the west coast of Bæronak from the east coast of Lapughê, then angled northwest across a vast delta plain and over the narrow Uadikuu Sea. She approached the city of Kobarêl from the south, passing over the brown, choking cesspool and on out to the spaceworks on the northern peninsula, landing the aircraft flawlessly—on autopilot. The workers there knew her well from her many inspections. When she landed, she was met by a crowd of cheering workers who were impressed not only with the sleek, new flying machine but with her skill as pilot. Some suggested she should be a pilot of one of the interstellar vessels, to which she simply smiled.

"Guard this with your lives," she said with a sexy grin. "No one but me touches it. Got it?"

"Yes, Kanê," they responded.

She noticed the top buckle of her flight suit had been torn off somewhere along her journey. The next one was loose, so she jerked it free to be rid of it. Vazak did not know much about aerospace fashion, it seemed, but she forgave him. The open V that was formed at the front of her flight suit and the bounce of breasts gave her the look she wanted. When they were in awe, mouths agape, then she'd smite their heads off.

Boarding the KOHAX for the ride into the city, Gina was swarmed by the mindless stares of workers calmed by drugs. Zombies. Their glassy eyes and gelatinous bodies probably did not speculate about her motives, consider her plans, or wonder how she might escape. She knew the plan and her eyes showed confidence and strength. Besides, she carried the Sword of Namag with her in a cloth bag, its hilt made of the vertebrae of a slain Zetin warrior; yes, the one named N'HMG whom Set-d'Elous had bested in one-on-one combat.

(She recalled the tale from her daughter's textbook. It was during the Sekuatean invasion of Tebbicousimankalê in 1533, when Zetin warriors had fought alongside their arch enemy, the Tebbi. The two warriors had met on a snowfield outside Siaa and fought to a draw after ten *peth*. Agreeing to fight another day, both had turned to go when N'HMG suddenly threw his sword at Set-d'Elous, striking him across the back of the knees. He fell and the Zetin grabbed the sword and hacked at his knees, removing the lower legs, tossing each to the side, allowing blood to splatter the snow. Both sets of onlookers were aghast at the deception and savagery—more so when they saw Set-d'Elous rise on his bloody stumps and hurl his own sword through the back of the Zetin, a thrust as mighty as a lightning bolt, the blade running through the Zetin's backplate and out the chestplate, pushing a piece of heart out, red strips dangling from the tip of the blade. And there the Zetin fell. Or so the story read. She wondered how true it could possibly be; she'd never seen Set-d'Elous, her high school sweetheart Sebastian, without his feet.)

She entered the sliding doors of the First City Council building, also called the Overlord's palace. His suite was at the top, the fiftieth through fifty-fifth levels. At this time of day he would most likely be in the conference room, getting the daily reports. She knew how to get there and so walked deliberately to the entrance gate. Her white and pink flight suit continued to attract attention.

The guard called after her as she went through the gate. She ignored him and he called for backup on his comm baton. Two more guards arrived as she went for the elevator. It was one of those inventions introduced in 1574 by Jason Aronstein, consort of the Queen of Aivana, she recalled again from her daughter's textbook. It made a trip up to the sky possible and city buildings suddenly began to grow taller. Then the space elevator was constructed.

"Here, hold this!" she called out as she unsheathed the sword and tossed it to the guards. One of them tried to catch it, juggled and grabbed it by the blade, shredding his hands in the process.

As they dealt with that emergency, she boarded the lift box and started skyward. So much for an old Zetin's sword, she grumbled; antique or not, it was useful as a decoy.

Now she was unarmed, they would think and not worry about her. They would be wrong. She carried the laser marker inside her sleeve.

The lift stopped, the doors remaining closed.

"Level Fifty," said the artificial voice in the lift box. "Welcome to the Overlord's Suite. If you have not been invited and have not been given a First Class Access Pass, you will be subject to Level 3 Discipline, up to and including the penalty of death."

With the word 'death,' the voice included a jarring echo, like some haunted house gimmick.

Gina cursed at the speaker.

"Password incorrect. You have one more attempt. If incorrect, a security team will escort you to a Discipline Facility."

She ground her teeth a moment, breathing deeply.

"Stupid security system," she growled. "I'm First Director of Bioservices. I'm Jinetta-d'Elous. I'm important, dammit. I'm not just the Overlord's whore."

"Voice recognition confirmed on *Jinetta-d'Elous* and *Overlord's whore*. You may Proceed."

She cursed again.

"Password used. There is no need for additional passwords."

The doors opened and into the Audience room she stepped.

A dozen or so people were present, most of them off to the side of the room, to her left as she entered. It appeared that a meeting had just ended and two small groups were huddled in opposite corners discussing matters. Straight ahead and slightly to her right was the Overlord, dressed in an all white uniform with blue epaulets and gold trim, the Kobarêl-style hem swaying against his calves. His back was turned to her, speaking with a staff member. One of the others noticed her and gasped—no doubt struck by her sexy flight suit, opened in front to reveal her chest, moist and shiny from her exertion. The short blond hair made her extra stunning. The staff member opened his mouth to speak—

She charged the Overlord and threw an arm around his neck, catching him in a headlock, in the same motion jabbing the laser marker against his throat, flicking it to the strongest setting—

warm, bake, broil. Pressing the 'launch' button would send the laser beam through his flesh; at close range, a narrow hole would burn all the way through his neck, severing his spinal cord.

"What are you doing?" cried the Overlord in a muffled, strained voice.

"Stand back!" Gina shouted, glancing about the room.

The staff members stood in shock, frozen. One reached for a panel on the wall.

"Don't touch that or your Overlord loses his head!"

"Please, *Kanê*, do no harm," cried the Overlord's secretary, down on one knee in front of her.

"I won't do harm if you follow my instructions."

The Overlord finally realized who had attacked him, twisting slightly to spy her face.

"Good afternoon, First Director Jinetta-d'Elous," he said, trying to seem relaxed. His voice was strained by her grip around his neck. "Or should I call you Memitha?"

"Whichever you like. The result will be the same."

"So what business brings you to my office today?"

"I want my daughter and I want her now!"

"Your daughter?"

"Yes." He could not play dumb. "You know what I mean. We had a deal: the Mixerran fuel cell in exchange for my daughter's freedom."

"So where is this fuel cell thing you promised? Did you bring it in your pocket? I can't quite see for myself in this position."

"It's at the spaceworks, well-guarded. You can have it when I get my daughter."

Some of the staff fidgeted and she glared at them.

"But I distinctly heard you say it was destroyed in your airship crash. And some F'eng were involved? Is that true? Then how is it you have this fuel cell to barter?"

"There was a second one. A small one. However, our clever engineers can figure it out and construct larger sizes, big enough to power interstellar vessels. This small one powers the aircraft I arrived in. You hear me? That's how I got here, Samot-Artexus!" She knew how it irked them all to hear her call the Overlord by his name. "In fact, Samot, I flew it from Jêpolissa to Typeg, then to Liêta and on to Kobarêl. All that on one charge. You can have the whole aircraft—with the Mixerran fuel cell in it. Fly it around the planet for your pleasure, I don't care. Just give me my daughter. Do that and I will also let you live!"

"Overlord, shall I order the woman released?" asked the timid secretary from his kneeling position.

"What is she in?" asked the Overlord.

"The re-education facility," said Gina.

"Is she?"

The secretary scanned information on a tablet.

"You'd better be reading information, not sending any," Gina growled.

"She has finished the re-education facility protocol. All levels," the secretary reported.

"Good. Find her!"

"Go on, look," the Overlord instructed the secretary. "We can track her location by the comm bead those who went through the re-education facilities always have implanted in their hand."

Gina gasped. "You put a bug in her?"

Another staff member stepped forward, trying to grin. "No, not an insect. A communication device. It is standard procedure—in the event of escape."

"If she completed the regimen then there's no need to keep tabs on her."

"It's done for life," said the staff member. "Once assigned to re-education, she is always a re-education participant."

"Who are you?" asked Gina with a scowl.

"I am First Director of Re-Education, Latol-Mendarrus."

"Another Latol," Gina sighed. She wondered what had become of her daughter's one-time boyfriend when the two of them were captured in the act of breaking rules. That boy did not, could not, concern her; only her daughter was important now. "You've got some racket going on here, don't you?" she said. "Catch kids in the act, exactly what they naturally want to experiment with, then turn them into slave labor!"

"We will have the comm device removed," said the Overlord, trying on his righteous voice. "She will be as good as new. Like she never broke the rules."

"She never did break the rules!"

"Actually, it has been verified," said Mendarrus. He reached for a tablet on a desk. "May I check the record?"

"Go ahead. But don't you dare send any message."

Mendarrus scrolled down the screen, pushed a couple buttons on the side, paused to read the information.

"First Director d'Elous...your daughter would not have been assigned to the re-education protocol were it not for her flaunting the rules she was properly taught in school. Upon capture, her breaking of the rules was legally confirmed. Two physicians on the capture team examined and confirmed her condition, as is the protocol. Let's see.... That's rule 14, subsections (a) and (b); rule 16, subsection (c), and 18 (a), (b), (c) and (g). Also, while under the care of the re-education facility, she was also charged with breaking rule 22, subsections (b) and (d). On Denio-12:2168 she had the mark of re-education confirmation, Class F, affixed to her left hand and right shoulder, as specified in the Re-Education Procedures manual, Revised Edition of 2159. She has completed her re-education and been released into society. Everything has been done according to those rules."

"You would not even know she broke any rules if that Hanar-Santorak hadn't sent someone to illegally change the observation indicator signal on the comm screen in our residence. That was deception and fraud. She has a right to privacy."

"As someone under legal age, she does not have a right to privacy. To gain such rights, the individual must be an adult."

"So perverts can spy on young girls but not older women? Ridiculous!"

"Dear Overlord," Mendarrus spoke, "this Zaura-d'Elous has completed her re-education and has been assigned to a work group. That is the normal, proper procedure. She was assigned to work with the First Director of Aerospace Designs. As a personal assistant."

"Personal assistant? What's that?" asked Gina.

"Like a secretary," said Mendarrus. "Answering the comm line, writing reports, cleaning the office, things like that. It's standard procedure to initiate the re-educated person back into society."

"At Aerospace Designs? She's better than that place."

"A position was available there."

"So it's an assigned position? Then she's free to leave if she wishes, right?"

The Overlord, still in a headlock with the laser marker against his throat, struggled to cough and clear his throat.

"If we are going to chat for a while, my dear, might we all sit down and be comfortable?"

"No, Samot. I need to keep this marker against your throat. Otherwise, I may come to harm. I'd rather it be you than me. Now get my daughter! Whatever she is doing, bring her to me here. Now. Then I shall leave you to all your perversions and political skullduggery, comet or no comet. I don't care any longer."

"It's a job like any other," said Mendarrus. "If she leaves it, however, she may not be able to get another job and, thus, she would lose her chance at a seat on a vessel."

Gina tightened her arm around his neck. "Samot and I have argued about that before. Haven't we? I gave her my seat a long time ago."

"Jinetta, dear Jinetta," said the Overlord, struggling to raise his eyes to her, bent as he was, "you have no seat to give. When you pledged not to take a seat, it was given to someone else. That person was selected according to the protocol you established during your time in Bioservices. There's nothing I can do about that."

She glanced at the secretary. "Is she on the way here?"

He glanced at the Overlord.

"Yes, bring her here." The Overlord rolled his eyes to the side as far as he could to see Gina's face. "I could use a fresh look at some golden hair."

She wanted to slap him but dared not release her grip.

"Are you wearing my hair today?"

"Not today," he said, sounding delighted she had asked, "but if I had known you were visiting me, I certainly would have had it washed and be wearing it now in your honor."

She glanced around the room, eyeing each staff member. They stood impatiently, waiting for it all to be over. Probably some of them would not mind if the Overlord were to be harmed when one of them tried to escape. Yet most of them had settled into a passive ponderance of the proceedings. If a single woman could barge in and take the Overlord hostage, Gina thought they must be wondering, then how strong can he really be? How much in control of the city is he? What a lack of security, too! And her complaint? The mistreatment of her daughter by Re-Education officials. Even if it were somehow true, how could that one woman's complaint gets to this high level?

"If we are to wait for your daughter to be brought here, may we sit down?" asked the Overlord.

"Of course," she replied, not moving. "You gentlemen may sit on the floor." She regarded the Overlord. "Samot, darling, would you mind if I sat on your lap?"

Before he could say anything, she had pushed him backward into a chair, forcing him down, and plopped her whole body into his lap. She maintained her arm around his neck and her other hand held the marker against his throat. He lost his breath.

"So now we wait...." he finally said, weakly.

"As long as it takes for my daughter to arrive," said Gina. "And if she's not in good condition, you still lose your head."

"You are a bold woman. I wish only we could have met in different circumstances. I'd like to see how you play on the *qala*."

"Not me."

"No? I'm certain you could excite me."

"You have a vivid imagination, Samot."

"Lady, how can you be so cruel?"

"Three-hundred-eighty years of living on this planet."

"A joke, certainly!"

"I have the diary to prove it. Somewhere."

"You're a clever woman."

"You noticed."

As they waited, Gina imagined the staff members might try to charge her, attempting to rescue the Overlord. She was ready for them. The laser marker, though intended as personal defense, could easily cut skin. She had tried it on vegetables. If one of them rushed at her, she would slash with the marker: shoulder, chest, elbow. Then slash at the next man: hip, groin, thigh. And the next: forearm, throat, ear. Rather like one of those light sabers in that movie. The space movie...what was it called? *The Star Wars*? The laser marker wouldn't kill them but they would be cut/burned seriously enough that they would tend to their wounds rather than carry on the attack.

"You're getting heavy," said the Overlord.

The door to the Audience room suddenly slid open and out

stepped two figures from the lift box. From her position holding the Overlord captive, she could not clearly see who they were, only that one was in a white gown and the other was taller and dressed in black. She caught flashes of orange in the corner of her eye.

"Come in," said the secretary. "Stand here."

"Welcome to my office," said the Overlord.

"Zaura...? Is that you? Is it really you?" cried Gina.

She wanted to jump up and embrace her daughter but she needed to keep the Overlord in check. She examined her daughter: the filmy gown hid little of her womanly shape and she noticed the men in the room were immediately interested. The hair on her head had been cut short, but neatly styled, bobbing at her collar, grown out from the much shorter cut at her induction into the re-education facility. Her face was pink, cheeks rosy, a smile hiding under her nose, afraid to shine. She was beautiful, thought Gina, so proud that Zaura had survived the re-education protocol. She seemed fine, undrugged, alert.

"I've come to take you home, Zaura. I don't know where that will be yet, but we will make a home somewhere. Then we will watch the comet come down and get drunk together. Or whatever you want to do." She switched to English: "I found a tangent that will save us. I checked it out but I didn't want to risk me getting through and not being able to come back for you. So I returned for you, to get you out of here. A year is long enough to be in captivity. Now we will go to Earth."

"Ur-tha? Did you say Ur-tha?" asked the Overlord.

"It's a different word," said Gina in Ghoupallêan.

She glared at the man standing behind Zaura, acting like her master: First Director Hanar-Santorak.

"What are you doing here? You think you're in charge of her? Is that it? You can take your hands off her, puppy!"

He neither smiled nor frowned. The orange hair remained though there was less of it, only in the middle, a stripe. He was the same terrible man who had tried to humiliate her, then when he could not, took it upon himself to spy on her daughter and order her arrest when he saw her making love with her boyfriend in her residence. Sentenced to the re-education facility: relearn the rules of polite society. Hah! A society on the verge of annihilation! What did the rules mean now? How could they matter? It was every person for himself, for herself. Any deal made to get a seat on the evacuation vessels. Lots of sexual favors, she guessed. Anyone with the power to have a ticket to board had access to whatever the desperate buffet could offer. But that did not concern her. She had won. She had reclaimed her daughter. Now to get out of the First City Council building free and clear—

"First Director d'Elous," Hanar spoke up, as solemn as death, "I am your puppy no more."

"What do you mean by that?"

"I'm sorry, Mama," the young woman spoke in English. "I'm sorry to disappoint you."

"What do you mean?" Gina responded, also in English. "You haven't disappointed me. I'm proud of you, how tough you are."

"I'm not going to go with you, Mama," said Zaura. She glanced up at Hanar. "I can't go. I must go aboard the vessel. I must go with the others to a new home far, far away, and start a new life. A new life with my new partner."

Gina's eyes grew large. "What's this?"

Hanar reached around from behind Zaura and took hold of her gown, slowly opening the folds of translucent fabric to reveal her belly. The slightest of newly formed curve would be noticeable only to a woman who'd had babies previously. Gina recognized it and knew what it meant. New life. She cursed herself. If only she had not been kept away for so long. If only she had not had to overcome so many obstacles or deal with so much interference to try to save her daughter, flying back and forth, being attacked and injured, having to recover, stuck in a stupid jail, then trying to get her job back, everything a First Director is supposed to do before the world can end.

Her hand went to her face, wrinkles tightening, tears bursting forth.

In that emotional lapse, the Overlord felt his chance had come. He snapped back his elbow, catching Gina in the face and knocked her off his lap. She fell to the floor and he grabbed the laser marker. Blood ran from her nose as she sat up, then slowly pulled herself to a knee. Her attention was still on Zaura.

Hanar closed the gown. He showed no emotion as he placed his hands on her shoulders.

"You were right about one thing, Mama."

Gina regarded her, sniffling, hands pressed against the floor. "And what's that?"

"Your proposal was good. Remember? You said only couples who were proven to be fertile should be selected for the vessels. I guess they approved your recommendation. Once this baby is born and it is proven to be healthy, then I will be upgraded to First-Class status. I will have a seat on the vessel guaranteed."

Gina knelt on the floor. "Is that the only reason? To get a seat?"

"No, Mama. We—" She gazed up at Hanar. "We are together now. I will stay with him. He's the father of this baby. That proves his fertility."

"But you can't take a baby into space, Zaura."

"We know. You can have it if you want it. We only need to prove we could conceive successfully. And we got it on the third timed attempt—which is within the specifications."

The Overlord had stood when Gina was knocked to the floor and was still rubbing his throat. He stretched his back, added a groan.

"Now then, Lady, you see how foolish you are? I heard about the wild display at Typeg. It was only a matter of time before you would try to fight your way in here. A lot quicker than I expected, however. No, I certainly was not prepared. Where is my Security Chief, anyway? Bring him up here at once."

He stood over her, waving his thumb from side to side to scold her like a little girl.

"I understand how you thought you could build yourself up, make yourself into some kind of hero, even dare to mock the goddesses. You could almost pass for a goddess, I'll grant. You tried to instill fear in all of us. Then you burst in here like you are some avenging demon—and with a laser marker as your only weapon! Well planned. At least that. Performance? Hmmm. So you are mortal after all. It's nothing to be ashamed of. We are all mortal, although some are more mortal than others."

The doors to the Audience room opened and a security team entered, weapons drawn.

"You're late," snapped the Overlord.

"I apologize," said the Chief, beefy and bald.

"You see this woman on the floor? She held me hostage for

more than three *peth*. I didn't like that. Do you know how she got in here? She walked in. What kind of security is that?"

"Bad, Overlord." The man swallowed hard. "Bad security."

"Then we agree."

"Yes, Overlord."

The Overlord returned his attention to Gina. "So how shall we end this fiasco of yours?"

"I—I think—"

She tried to stand but her knee suddenly burned with pain and gave way.

"Just stay on the floor. It suits you." He glanced at his secretary. "How about getting that stinking uniform or whatever it is off her? She smells like she's been wearing it for a month or more. I could hardly stand having her so close to me. And this room will need to be cleaned, too."

The secretary and two of the security team pulled at the flight suit. One security team member used a knife to cut away the lower part of the flight suit, then the top half, until Gina lay on the floor in only what remained of her torn leggings, and the boots.

"Much better, I think." The Overlord walked around her slowly. "You must have been through an awful lot to get so smelly, and if there were a wash room close at hand I'd scrub you down myself. Could be fun. There remains a lot you could offer a man, even a man like me, who has discriminating tastes. I know your golden hair will grow out and then you will be attractive to me again. As it is, you have nothing now. Not even your precious daughter. Hah! I could have an orange scarf put on you and drop you outside in less than a *pon*. In the streets, it would not be long before someone found you attractive. And another. And another. You would be popular. And not long after that someone would find you delicious. That's the way our fine city is heading, you know. To barbarism."

"I have the Mixerran fuel cell," she blurted breathlessly. "You brought my daughter here, true. You did your part. So you may have the Mixerran fuel cell, as we agreed. Our deal is done."

The Overlord laughed. "The Mixerran fuel cell...."

"It's in the aircraft," she grumbled. "It's yours. Take it—take the whole aircraft. Let me leave here and you'll never be bothered by me again."

"How is the Mixerran fuel cell supposed to power any of our interstellar vessels? Tell me, Jinetta-d'Elous. Especially if it can be recharged so easily with seawater. How much seawater is there in space?"

He let out a chuckle.

Then the room was silent. Gina held her breath.

"Long before these political games, I studied Aerospace. Can you believe that? It seemed a good place to do some dreaming; we had no rockets, after all, and no plans for any in those days. Even so, I thought that would be my career. I read about this Mixerran fellow's ideas. Yes, he had influence on airship designs. Then he went mad, thinking he could fly through the sky like birds—like bolts of lightning! He gave a presentation many years ago—in Siti, I think; perhaps you attended?—on this fuel cell idea of his. All the scientists of the world laughed at him. Laughed at his designs. No, Jinetta-d'Elous, what we have now on our interstellar transports will have to do. We have nothing else. No magical solution. There is no miraculous stone or mineral yet to be discovered deep in our mountains that will suddenly power our engines. We must deal with the reality we are given. No matter how much we want to, we cannot live our lives in dreams. Because every day we awaken and there it is again: the harshness of reality. Then what do we do? We must press on. We cannot return to the dream."

The Overlord paused, glanced at the secretary who was busy scribbling something on the tablet with a thin stylus. Probably recording his words, thought Gina.

"Even the shortest space journey, as you have so eloquently explained at previous conferences, is longer than the longest Ghoupalle life. Those who depart Ghoupallesz will die on those vessels. Those born on those vessels will die on those vessels. And someday the people born on those vessels will see a bright disk ahead and they will orbit it, then descend to the surface, and never return to the stars. That is our destiny, no matter how long it takes. Yes, you were one of us—a pioneer, a scientist, perhaps also a goddess who sought to lead us. I had high hopes for you...."

"The Mixerran fuel cell is a fake?"

"No, not a fake. I'm sure it works perfectly in the atmosphere of Ghoupallesz. Haven't you judged its performance in your travels?

It simply does not work in space. He was probably teasing you with it, like any man would, I suppose, when confronted with an intelligent, beautiful goddess. It was inevitable he'd fall in love with you. But the scroll has been rolled up now."

The Overlord nodded at his secretary, who had brought a new tablet over to him. Buttons were tapped, information read. He returned the tablet to the secretary.

"What shall we do with you, First Director Jinetta-d'Elous? After all, how can you be First Director of anything now—after this ridiculous display? Kobarêl is no longer your home. I'm going to have to banish you."

Gina looked up from her crumpled position on the floor, first at the Overlord, in whose grinning face was pure evil, then at her daughter, whose face registered sympathy, perhaps seeing there in the Audience room what she herself had been through in the re-education facility.

"All right, I'll leave," she said. "Plenty of places to go. I still have some power. I have connections. People will support me. After all, I've been helping everyone survive the coming comet—"

"You flatter yourself! You want to know who has power?" he roared. His eyes were angry, red like a wild *jalo*, his shoulders suddenly hulking like a *galguin*, the sasquatch-like beast of the Uadikuu jungle.

"You do," Gina grumbled, "...*Æx-Kalmonê*."

"Pick her up," the Overlord commanded of the security team. He nodded toward the desk. "Put her there."

Two guards bent her over the desk far enough that only the tips of her toes touched the floor.

"This is power." He stepped behind her. "I can do this and no one will stop me—or even file a criminal accusation. I am immune from all that." He slapped her hip. "Hah! Meanwhile, I can indulge my lust for you, and at the same time make you feel humiliation for being treated this way—and in front of your daughter."

He took the waistband of her tattered leggings and pulled it hard, ripping it and tearing it off her. With an admiring smile, he dropped the rags to the floor.

"Please do not hurt my mother," Zaura spoke out. She took a step forward but Hanar's hand on her shoulder halted her.

"If she doesn't fight me, it will not hurt," said the Overlord. "I

427

only wish to show her who has power. In our civilization, as I am sure you know, this is how a man shows a woman which of them has power. This is our basic, primal way of enforcing submission. Every culture has its customs for putting members in their proper place. The Danid burn marks into the flesh of their property. In Uadikuu, the primitives like to chop off the toes to keep lower ranking people in line. The Tigu, I've read, force their errant females to mate with various animals. And I hear the Xig like to designate a disobedient wife as the village whore for a year. Even those wild Javonnê, where females have the power, like to keep their men in check by mutilating their genitalia, keeping them on leashes, forcing them to growl like beasts. We are much kinder in Kobarêl, are we not? This is our way: forcing the mating ritual upon an unwilling partner. Natural, yet also perverse. It has a welcoming kind of balance to it. Much more civilized, don't you think?"

He shifted his codpiece aside. Admiring her body, his fingers tested her flesh, sliding over her hips.

"Does this make you feel strong?" said Gina fiercely.

"You'll feel my strength soon enough."

She grunted as he pressed forward. "How about a fair fight? With swords?"

"Hah!" said the Overlord, rubbing against her, exploring. "You would cut me apart, I'm certain, perhaps remove my manhood altogether with a quick snip of your blade. This exercise is much better for showing everyone who really has power."

Gina took a breath. "I should have killed you right away."

He stroked the curve of bare back as he pushed against her. "Calm, now." His hand slid around her belly and down between her thighs. "How does it feel to be my toy?"

As the Overlord waited for an answer, he lay his chest upon her back, digging his chin in as he nibbled at the meat of her shoulder, teeth cutting into her flesh until she cried out—

"Æx-Kalmonê," Hanar-Santorak spoke with a step forward, "please do not do that. It is not suitable behavior for the leader of our city. It is not suitable for the leader of our interstellar fleet."

The Overlord glanced back. "The puppy barks!"

"Overlord, I humbly ask you to release her. Think of your dear mother...."

The Overlord straightened himself. "My mother?"

"Everyone has a mother, *Æx-Kalmonê*."

He laughed. "That ruins it for me." He gave Gina's hip a playful slap. "You're old, Jinetta! Like my mother. I should send you to a work camp—like my mother. I hear you're fond of Valek, all the volcanos there. Or we shall put you in a cage for all to see."

"Please let her go," Zaura cried out. "She cannot survive being locked up. She needs freedom or she goes crazy. I will stay. I will stay here for her sake."

The Overlord threw his hand up, halting her.

"For the sake of your golden hair, I will let your mother go free. I'm not that kind of despot. I want a woman who wants to be submissive to me, not one who must be forced into it."

"Thank you, *Æx-Kalmonê*," said Zaura, bowing.

He regarded Gina, bent over the desk. "You're a fine looking female, Jinetta, yet now you know who has the power. Right?" He spanked her. "Stand up, lady. Or I'll appoint someone to finish the task. How about this husky security guard? Perhaps we should call upon First Director Santorak for that duty. He seems to fancy you well enough—though I'm certain in different ways than me."

The secretary came over with a towel for her shoulder, wiping away the spots of blood the Overlord's teeth had drawn.

"I like you, Jinetta, so I shall be kind—kinder than before. I apologize for my misbehavior, too." He put his codpiece in place, smoothed his suit, grinning like a thief caught in the act, claiming that he was merely looking at the merchandise. "I've ordered new clothes for you. They are coming. Please wait. And you can keep that fuel cell; I have no need of it. Museums will be obsolete in a few years."

He waved at Zaura and Hanar, dismissing them.

As they turned to exit, Gina asked the Overlord: "May I hug her one last time?"

He grunted. "No, I don't think so. That's your punishment, Jinetta. No last hug."

Pointing toward the doorway, he said: "Go on, Santorak. Take your bride out. Return to your tasks."

When they had departed, the Overlord turned to his secretary. "For letting this woman get to me, possibly to end my precious life, I must blame someone." He glared at the Chief of the Security

Force. "You have not fulfilled your mission."

Two security team members snapped to attention, then took their leader by the arms. As the staff members who remained watched, other security team members shackled the Chief's hands and ankles.

"I'm sorry, Overlord," said the Chief.

"I don't like apologies." Then, to the next-in-command: "Take him to Execution Field #3—where the largest crowd will see him. Let them count him as an example. Make a spectacle of it. Say he defied the Overlord, and this is the punishment. Something like that. You know what to do. Make it horrible."

The secretary was on the comm line as soon as they exited.

Two women in dark blue uniforms with yellow stripes down the arms and legs arrived. They brought a big, yellow package tied with green string and opened it on the desk as Gina stood naked and roughed up in the center of the room.

The last members of the staff filed out. Only the Overlord and his secretary remained to observe the washing of the woman by the two assistants, followed by dressing her in suitable attire. The emerald green kaftan clashed with her white and pink boots, but the red sash made her feel like Christmas was just around the corner. The brown leather brimless cap made her feel like a little girl again, just like a Girl Scout Brownie. The slap of the laser marker into her open palm surprised her but gave her hope that she would live another day.

The door slid open again.

"Farewell, Jinetta-d'Elous," said the Overlord. "I will not meet you again. However, I shall continue to wear your golden hair from time to time, and I shall think of you when I do. May the comet not catch you sleeping."

Chapter 40

Retirement

Long...warm...wavelets rolled over her toes...ran up to her knees, as Gina reclined on the white sand beach in Liêta. The golden sun was dropping toward the turquoise horizon and the azure sun hid behind the crest of the jungle. The breeze was a caress from a lover's hand, an invitation to enjoy the profound nothingness of the final years. No questions asked.

Another day drawing to a close. How many had passed since she returned to this paradise? How many more days would she count? In this tropical cove, every day seemed the same, week by week, season by season. One day she would come out to the beach, take her morning swim, lounge under the sun, admire her deepening tan and her golden locks cascading down her back. One day the sky would be different. The pale green would be darker, more blue perhaps. She would watch that chunk of rock and ice wink at her. She and ten million more would wave hands in welcome, for there would be nothing else to do. A last meal, a final embrace, trivial words spoken, desperate prayers sent, and knees crashing to the ground, tears streaming, hearts breaking. It would be all for nothing. The word 'nothing' seemed to come into her head more often, in different contexts: a line of symbols, a bunch of sounds, together representing all that had ever been and all that never would be.

She gazed at the sky, pondered the clouds, waiting for a sign that she could finally go home—

Years before, she had gazed up at the sky, a brown, chalky one whistling of decay, as she left the First City Council building. She had stood thinking of the horror of everything. She observed the people coming and going across the plaza, following their daily protocols. Watching them, she could not feel anything. Moments before she was raped by the lord of the city—the man put there wash away all her emotions and memory of that abuse and leave her clean again. Then she boiled with rage, wanting to return to the Overlord's suite and run him straight through with a Zetin *holka*. She would not be concerned with what might happen next, what punishment she would get, but delight in the fountain of blood rising from the Overlord's chest.

She took a step, hesitated, thinking—then collapsed onto the plaza, her knees hitting the pavement hard. Why was this world ending? Why was she there to witness it? Wasn't she supposed to be back on Earth, finishing college, starting a family, a career, enjoying her menopause among friends, growing old with them?

I don't belong here, she had sighed before tumbling over.

Her hands went to her face, tears running between her fingers, dripping onto her chest.

Sensing the approach of someone likely in need of food, she pulled herself up and stood tall and strong. Three men and a woman in ragged clothing halted before her. No, this woman freshly escaped from the First City Council Building is not ready to give up, her stance told them. No, she is not a meal waiting to be claimed. She stared them down—until they turned and went hunting for another desperate person.

She had walked toward the closest KOHAX station, avoiding as best she could all the hungry predators, the homeless denizens, and hapless vagrants hibernating in *bôb*-induced stupors on the streets. Food no longer was a commodity—only the endless drugs which calmed people's frantic minds.

"Hey, got any *bôb*? Any black *bôb*? I'll take green or blue *bôb* if that's all you have. Give you food tickets for *bôb*."

She hurried past them, feeling lucky to be walking the streets at all but fearful of what she might find there. And yet, being full of regrets slowed her pace.

A man called her by name, adding *Kalmonê*. It was the Chief of

Security, she recognized when he opened his dark cowl to show himself. Dressed in a black robe that was torn and dirty, he sidled up to her and gripped her arm, narrowing his eyes.

"You got past us," he snarled.

"I had a job to do." She tried to jerk her arm away. "I thought you were supposed to be executed."

He laughed, a strange grating noise that set her on edge.

"Like you would care! No, we don't really do that."

"Won't they know you skipped out of your execution?"

"The Overlord is arrogant and stupid. We just shoot a dozen or so miserable vagrants and the homeless gangs scramble to divide up the meat. Nobody wants a public execution. It's a waste of food."

Gina stared at him, deciding if he was serious. He was out of uniform so perhaps he was in hiding. He had lost his job, for sure; staying alive was a bonus. Like herself.

"What will you do now?" she asked.

"I need to get out of this fecal city!"

In Ghoupallêan, the word was *todo-Ghêraxiin*, which meant the waste products of the gods and goddesses. Kobarêl was literally what they had ejected from their bowels and were glad to be rid of. Gina had to smile.

The man dipped his head, a polite bow, held his gaze down.

"Me, too," she had said.

When he raised his eyes, she met them sternly. "You sad, sad man. Think you're so tough. Top of the city tower one moment, in homeless rags the next. And you thought you were so strong and in charge. Chief of Security! Hah! You cannot even take care of yourself without your minions to order about. You come running after me now—a woman you were happy to watch being raped— asking, no, begging, for a favor. What makes you think I can help you? Or want to help you?"

"I don't know that, *Kalmonê*. It is my sincere hope you will be compassionate in ways I was not able to be."

She nodded, regarding him. He was hunched over, acting like a beggar, cowering within his robe and hood. A good actor.

"Do you have somewhere to go?"

"I was sincerely hoping I could go with you, *Kalmonê*. It's a strange request, I know. You hate me. Yet you can get me out of

Kobarêl. You have the flying machine. Then I'll make my way somewhere."

"You don't know where I'm going." She scratched her nose. "I don't know, either. I'll probably go to Siti first."

"Anywhere but here. Siti will be satisfactory." He seemed to study her a moment, seeing a strong woman, perhaps recalling how she came to get her daughter, risking everything. And for what? "It does not matter, true? Only a few years more to wait, no matter what we do. Then everything ends. Five years—is that all? What's the point of being enemies now? Let us be at peace."

She nodded, still feeling the strain of the past hours' conflict rummaging through her like a bad meal.

"I can't hate you. I don't even know you. But I'm glad you were not executed."

She reached for him, took hold of his arm, pulled him close and jostled him into a hug.

"We are friends now," she said when she released him. "I spent time in jail for doing this, but Kobarêl is a different city."

He seemed surprised. "It's been a while since I did that."

"A hug?"

"Is that what it's called?"

"Come with me and you will learn more."

They hurried along the streets, staying ahead of the cleaning squads who each evening ran the vagrants out of the central business district. Hiding a few times in alleys, they eventually arrived at the station and took the automated KOHAX out to the northern peninsula, to the spaceworks where her aircraft sat, guarded faithfully by the work crew.

"Thank you so much," she said, greeting them.

She gave them food ration tickets and they smiled. They had a few more questions about the aircraft and she tried patiently to answer them. She had no place to go, anyway. She had no home left in Kobarêl. The Overlord had decreed it.

Unless she dared to stay with Zaura and her partner. No, she could never sleep under the same ceiling as that hideous man. He's not that way, her daughter had explained via comm line after Gina had flown away and landed first in Siti where she dropped off her husky escort—then, after a few weeks, continued on to other places, seeking a new life but finding none; after a year of wandering, she arrived in Liêta. Sure, Hanar never has kind words for you, Zaura explained, yet he treats me well. At first we worked together and he told jokes about you. I endured the teasing. One day, he stopped doing that and asked me what I thought of him. I told him the truth, no matter what punishment might come upon me. He asked me if I would forgive him. He said he admired me. He said I'm smart and efficient. We became friends and then we agreed to apply for a ticket on a vessel as a couple. We thought we would be a suitable couple for the flight. High marks in all categories. First, we had to prove we were compatible and you saw we are, Mama. Now your granddaughter is already three years old, and as golden-haired as you and me. I remembered your request so we named her Gina. Your Earth name. I know you will go home someday, as you always said in your sleep, so I thought it best to give her that Earth name instead of a Ghoupalle name like Jinetta. Was that all right? Did I do well? Are you proud of me? Do you love me, Mama?

"Yes to all those," Gina had whispered.

Usually Gina would walk down the beach in the lamplight after dinner—Ghoupallesz had no moon to light her path—down to where the aircraft sat. She liked to sit in the cockpit and listen to Vazak's artificial voice. The fake conversations were comforting. He would always say "Speak the problem" and she would respond "Too many to count" or "I'm all alone now" or "How do I return to Earth?" He never had an answer yet hearing his voice made her feel less alone.

The Taxar family, who strangely spelled their name 'Tucker' and had owned the resort for generations, had left, so it was all hers now. The husband, Qiyukar, and his wife Fojê had been very kind to her during her many visits. Before they left, they showed her pictures of their family, all the way back to when their great-ancestor walked out of the jungle onto this beach and declared he would never leave. They chose to move, after all: away to one of the underground cities, in their case one of three built outside of Aikavo, the metropolis to the south of Liêta. The cities were designed to accommodate 125,000 people for up to ten years.

Money had no worth by then so they let Gina have the place; she could rent it out to any other tourists who happened along. It would be a great spot to watch the comet come down: the bright star sailing over the blue-green waters....

* ❈ *

Mama, I have great news! Gina read on her tablet after the message beep awoke her. The Overlord had granted her and Hanar a special license to board the vessel with a child. The rules had been bent, it seemed; now children of at least five years were allowed for couples having First-Class rank, which they did. Hanar had been promoted to Chief-of-Staff for the Overlord. They would both serve aboard the vessel. *So your granddaughter will be one of the first to go into space! There is no need for you to care for her as we expected. I will teach her about you.*

She clicked off the tablet, unable to think of a reply.

The stars continued to blink overhead. The jungle was dark and noisy. The birds seemed to believe all was well. If they could be blissfully ignorant, so could she. There was no reason to fear. It was only a dream. She was certain of that. Only the scar on her shoulder convinced her it wasn't.

* ❈ *

One year and seventy-nine days later, she awoke with a start, a strange feeling that she was not alone in the resort lodge. She grabbed the laser marker, threw on a gown, and went outside. The sky was dark and red. Clouds boiled. Trees bent. A storm was coming.

Grabbing her few possessions from the house, she went to the aircraft and powered it up.

"Select destination."

"Kipzon."

"Calculating. Range: 102 percent."

"Wonderful. I don't want to be here during a mere hurricane.

I'm saving myself for the comet."

"Destination Kipzon. Prepare for Autopilot Engagement. Flight Plan Entered. Final Approval?"

"Approved."

The airship terminal in Kipzon was closed, abandoned, as she expected, but it did not possess enough area to safely land her aircraft anyway. The cartoon Vazak found a place close by: a long, flat valley where the autopilot could set down the aircraft. The fuel cell would be near empty by then. From there, however, she had to borrow a *Jêpe* to ride to the next town and catch the KOHAX to Kipzon.

She thought of all the times she had flown in the machine Vazak had made, feeling as though he made it just for her. This was the final trip, she contemplated. Once she got to Kipzon, she would be reluctant to move again. She had too little power left in the fuel cell to go anywhere else and the sea was too far away to recharge the fuel cell. She locked up the aircraft and bid it farewell, kissed the nose cone of the *Starlight*.

Kipzon, she sighed, stepping off the KOHAX in the central business district. The streets were mostly deserted. Shops had been closed long ago, it seemed. Buildings had not been maintained. She thought the small city would stay sane a little longer than a crazy metropolis like Kobarêl would.

After a while, she found a sign directing residents to the new city underground: the entrance was in the side of a nearby mountain where ore had once been mined. Residential passes could be obtained from a certain office in town—now closed.

"Help yourself to whatever you fancy," said an old man sitting on a bench. "Nobody needs anything from now on."

She smiled and thanked him.

Except for constant reminders that life had vanished from the surface months before the comet would end it, her stroll through the town was pleasant. An autumnal warmth spread around her, so different from life in the tropics. She had not lived in Kipzon very long the previous time. But there were memories here and they were what she sought by returning. She would bathe in soft nostalgia to the end.

The house where she had lived before had been replaced by a newer house, looking as rustic as the one she used to know. The door to the upper apartment was unlocked. Inside was some of the furniture the family had left, most of it broken and dirty. It all seemed similar to what she remembered having in the older house. Kipzon style, of course. She contemplated the time, sitting on the edge of the cot, holding another colorful quilt reminiscent of the one she had used there centuries before. She wondered about the family who had lived there, about why they had left the quilt behind. Shaking it out, she wrapped it around herself and thought back.

After many adventures on Ghoupallesz, she had somehow become a captive of the Zetin ambassador, Ut'r-BkanN. Was that in 1533 or 1534? The details were dim. What she did recall was that her friend, Set-d'Elous, whom she knew as Sebastian Talbot from high school, met her when she landed in northern Fenula, safe and sound. She had flown from the castle on a hang-glider. So full of joy he had been at her safe arrival that they had practically lived in bed for a full year in that old house in Kipzon. And they made a baby there. He had insisted she be named Zaura, after his deceased Ghoupalle wife.

In her escape from the Zetin castle, however, she had to kill the Ut'r-BkanN. Since then, a team of assassins had been on her trail, bent on revenge. One night the assassins came. Sebastian was gone, away on business, perhaps; she could not remember. She managed to sneak out with the baby, yet in their haste she was unable to let him know where they were going.

They went through hell—then arrived in Kobarêl, a new kind of hell.

By coming to Kipzon, she desired only to complete the cosmic circle, even though she had neither that daughter or that lover to accompany her. She felt very old.

Sitting cross-legged on the floor, she retrieved from her travel bag the square government-issue pill box with the Bioservices logo on it. She held the small container in the palm of her hand and thought of the day she first was introduced to *bôb*, and how her co-workers lived for a few capsules at the end of their shifts, how the vagabonds in the streets would choose the drug over food. Even her old friend Vazak-Mixerran had shared some with her. She had to admit that it probably did help a lot of people handle the day to day fears of the coming comet.

The container held four black-*bôb* capsules. That was all she had left. They would be enough, she knew, to relax her to the point of falling into a deep sleep—if she took them all at once. It would be best if she had five capsules; that would push her over the edge, into an unrecoverable coma. With only four, however, she would sleep for five or six days—long enough to allow the comet to do its damnedest. Then she would not need to awaken.

Outside, the pastel lime sky was burnt through by the blinding blue fire of Comet Xôsz, growing wider and brighter as it came closer, rivaling the smaller sun, Siila. 'Xôsz' meant 'Finality' in the Danid language. The final comet. She dared not peek at it. She did not wish to see its grimace, its sarcastic smirk, or feel its cold humor and icy embrace.

Come to me, Ghoupallesz, and kiss my ass! she imagined the comet laughing. She was not its friend. Not its worshipper.

She held up the first capsule, staring at it: a small black pearl that signaled she was giving up, that she would no longer await the end, would not stay to see the light, feel the crash, be swept away in the fiery flush of energy, and become a soul free-floating in the ether of space....

Damn comet! Why'd you have to ruin everything?

She froze, unable to count any other times she had given up, then broke from her trance and swallowed the first black-*bôb* capsule, guzzling water from a glass bottle after it. She counted to a hundred, then swallowed the second one. Stretching out on the floor, she studied the wooden beams of the ceiling for a while. When her toes and fingers became numb, she swallowed the third capsule and tried to count the stars she was seeing swirling around the room. They twinkled for her: red, yellow, blue—just like the lights that had sparkled at the first opening of that first interdimensional tangent in that abandoned quarry so long, long ago.

Alone at last.

Alone at the end. That seemed appropriate.

Alone at the end of time. She knew her daughter would be fine—far away and safe, heading into the greatest adventure ever. She hoped that Sebastian was safe, too, wherever he might be in another, earlier time zone, or possibly all the way back on Earth, living the dull life of an IRS clerk, or perhaps he had finally found someone to love him. Poor guy. If mythology was based on any set of facts, they might still meet again on some distant world, some place with fluffy clouds and melodic harps, though she did not need the wings.

She slid the last capsule into her mouth and bit it in half, just to make it work quicker, then drank more water to wash down the bitter taste. Laying her head back, she breathed deeply, deeply, closed her eyes and slowly, slowly exhaled.

✳ ✴ ✳

"Gina," a voice called to her, almost covered by the din of *arixou* in the bushes outside, oblivious to tired people trying to sleep.

She felt a hand on her shoulder, a jiggle.

"Gina...wake up," the voice whispered frantically. "It's me: Sebastian. You need to get up. Now!"

"What...?"

"The assassins are here."

Her eyes popped open, looked around, saw the face near hers. She recognized him, then gasped at the sight of blood on his shirt.

"We must go—quickly," he said. "I've got a bag ready."

She climbed off the *qala* as though she were fully awake, dressing automatically in a loose gown and short boots, a leather jacket and knitted shawl that was laid across the foot of the *qala*.

"And Zaura?" she asked, glancing around the dark room, a room that seemed both familiar and foreign.

He took her by the hand, leading her down the outside stairs.

"Who?"

"Zaura—our baby. Where is she?"

He stopped midway down the stairs, and grinned. "So you've decided to name her for my wife, after all? I'm glad. But we must be going now."

He patted her belly and helped her down to the bottom of the stairs. A carriage was waiting, two *Jêpe* hitched up. He got her and her protruding belly up onto the seat, then followed. Grabbing the reins, he started the carriage rolling. He turned it around in the street and hurried away.

"Someday," he said a few blocks later, "ETUR will be popular enough everyone can afford to have one."

The carriage raced down the midnight streets, left the town, and took a country road through the forest.

"I hate living in 1546—but I love living with you, Gina. You're the Love of my Life. You always have been."

She felt a strange pull and decided to lean against him as the carriage slowed, winding along the road in the middle of the night. She felt a cut on his hand. His sleeve was wet, perhaps bloody. She asked about the blood.

"The assassins," he said, concentrating on the road. "I killed two of them. A third got away. We'll be safe where we're going. Don't worry—"

"You said the year is 1546?"

"Yes—has been for months," he said with a chuckle.

The carriage rolled to a halt, the twin *Jêpe* snorting in the cool night air.

"It's time to move to a new time and place. I found a tangent in a meadow between those hills. It leads to somewhere in Canada circa 1999. I only stayed a few days, but it checks out. I could see the Falls from where I was."

"Sebastian.... Did you change history again?"

He stopped, met her eyes.

"Possibly. I really can't tell any more. Sometimes it seems every breath I take changes something. I can hardly control it. The last thing I recall is waking from a deep sleep. There was a note in my hand telling me to go to Kipzon."

She took his clean hand, grasped it tightly as he led her up the trail to the meadow. It was a perfect place to be alone with a lover.

"I think I wrote the note," he said, pausing among the trees.

The autumn air was chilling but her skin was flushed from the hike. As he moved carefully through the grass, measuring steps, she slid her fingers inside her gown, reaching for her shoulder. She felt for the scar, the bite of a man she used to know.

"What are you doing?" he asked, waving her over.

"Checking for something." She studied him a few moments. "Do you have any scars? Anything you got on Ghoupallesz?"

He was surprised. "Well, I do have the one from when that Zetin priest, ambassador, whatever he was, stabbed me. Why?"

Her eyebrows twisted, her brow furrowed. "Was it Ut'r-BkanN who stabbed you?"

"I think that was his name. It's been a while since—"

"Sebastian, will you show me your scar?"

"It's right where my thigh meets my groin. Very bad spot to take a dagger, you know. I could've bled out from—"

"Show me, will you?"

He laughed. "We don't have time to get naked here, Gina."

"Drop your pants, big boy. I want to see it."

There was never any use arguing with her, he knew. He loosened his trousers and slid them down. She touched the cleft where his thigh slid into his groin. The triangular scar was there. As he pulled up his trousers, she opened her gown, turned and showed him her shoulder.

"Can you see a scar here?"

He touched her shoulder, young and smooth—except for the teeth marks.

"You have a scar, also." He grinned. "Now we're even."

She closed her gown and embraced him.

"Happy now?" he asked.

"I suppose so." She kissed his cheek, her fingers caressing his head. She felt something behind his ear: a round disk. "What's that?"

"My brain plug." He chuckled.

"Brain plug?"

"Yep. Got to keep the hole to my brain closed, you know. Especially when it rains. Long story. I'll tell you later. After we're home."

"Are we really going home?"

"Yes, this time for sure."

"To Canada? I've never been there."

"We never visited the Dream Land, either—until we arrived."

She hugged him, as much as her belly would allow.

"On to Canada!"

"That's the spirit."

A light in the sky caught his attention. For a planet with no moon, it was a rare event.

"Look at that!" he called. "A comet!"

She gazed at the light streaking across the sky, trailing a blue fountain behind the white bulb. She held her breath until he became worried. Then she pressed her face into his chest.

"You're not afraid of a comet, are you?" he asked.

She snuggled against him, clapped her hand against his cheek, kissed his mouth, and held him tight.

"Not now," she said, one hand resting on her belly. "And never again."

ADDENDUM

[Audio recordings found on communication baton belonging to Jinetta-d'Elous (a.k.a. Gina Parton), discovered in travel bag, at Niagara Falls, Ontario, Canada, on 5 October 1999]

[1.2] I'm at the window of the general meeting room. I can see the whole planet. It's beautiful! Blue seas and green and brown land, some snow on the mountains. I can see the comet, too. It's blue around the edges but bright white in the center. I can see the stream behind it. Everything is beautiful, Mama. I hope you can hear me. Are you safe? Did you go underground or are you on a beach somewhere watching it? Don't worry about me. I'm safe with your granddaughter and my partner. We are aboard the MEMITHA. That's the name of this interstellar vessel, launched from Kobarêl.

[1.3] In total there are nine vessels in orbit, each named for one of the goddesses. It was amazing to be lifted into the sky and I walked from the shuttle into the vessel with all our trunks. The Overlord was very kind to us; we have a large suite. Besides the interstellar vessels, there are three pods in tether, floating above Aikavo. They hope the comet will not be too bad and they can return to the surface after only a year or two. Others went underground, as you know. I counted 36 cities built underground. Most are in Zissekap. They hope to be protected for up to ten years, then return to the surface to clean up and continue living.

[2.1] Now I see the comet is closer. Like a diamond in the sky. There was an announcement to strap ourselves. They are firing the engines soon. We should all be secure in our quarters. I have my daughter in my arms as I speak to you. Little Gina looks just like you! Such golden hair! She says hello!

[2.2.1] I can see the other transports. The lights are going on and off. The engines are firing up. Orange and blue streams of energy project out the back.

[2.2.2] Below me I can see Bæronak—the whole continent! The mountains in the east, the wide jungle across the northern half, the savannas across the southern half. On the west coast is Aikavo and the three tethered pods floating like balloons high in the sky. They are lit up, too.

[2.3] Bæronak is turning away from us. I see Kobarêl now. And the Hikbok mountains! So magnificent! Now the Sogoê plateau, and the Zissekap mountains, and Gotanka and Sekuate, and the Bær Sea, and here comes Dikondra again!

[3.0] The comet is closer. It's difficult to look now, it's so bright.

[4.0] I just heard an announcement that one vessel has some kind of engine trouble. The NOURII, the first vessel to be built long ago. There is a leak in some system. They will not be able to make the journey to another star system like us. They are being told to head for Gouö, try to make a go of it there in that frozen place, maybe return to Ghoupallesz if they can. If the planet still exists.

[5.1] The comet is blinding now!

[5.2] Looking down, I can see the continent of Bæronak again as the planet turns.

[5.4] There are two shuttles coming up to dock with vessels now. There are more people on the surface waiting to be brought up. They should hurry! The comet is close now. It fills the window, Mama!

[5.5] Our vessel is fine. The engines rumble and I can feel the vibration through the girders and flooring. We will make it. Our destination is Tumark-C. That is 17 *Utark* from here. Probably four generations. That is our best hope, Mama. I wish you were with me. I don't know where you are on the planet but I hope you are safe.

[6.1] The comet is dropping—arching, I mean—to Bæronak! It looks like it will hit Bæronak. It's shooting straight for that inlet— what's it called? Boila Inlet? West of the Dikondra mountains. It's filling the entire sky! I can't look. Too bright!

[6.2] (random noise)

[6.6] The comet crashed! There's a chunk of mountains that's been hurled into the sky. The Dikondra mountains are in orbit! They hit a vessel, the SETHI, I think, and it's falling from orbit. The vessel was struck by a mountain and it's done! It's going down! More chunks of the planet were kicked into space! One giant rock hit the GAROU! Then it exploded! I see lots of people shot out into space!

[6.7] Sirens are blasting now! We are ordered to be secure for emergency launch. They want to move us away before we can be hit. The engines are firing, Mama! I fell down, but I'm all right. So is little Gina. She is all right but crying. We are breaking from orbit! Moving away! We are starting the journey to Tumark-C!

[6.9] I see the shock wave spreading around the planet. A line of fire and debris rolling across the surface. I see the continents tearing apart. I don't see the tethered pods any longer. Maybe they were pulled down, I don't know. Wait! Is it...? Yes, I see one of the tethered pods. It's no longer tethered. It's going out into space! It's turning end over end! They have no engines—how can they return?

[7.0] The oceans are shifting, washing over continents now! I see half of Zissekap is covered in water, as far as the mountains of Bezua-hü. I see Tebbicousimankalê pulling apart! The continents are pulling apart! They all look like they are on fire—any place there's not water. It's horrible! The people in underground cities are doomed! They never had a chance! And anyone on the surface is either burned or drowned! Not all the passengers were brought up by the shuttles. Not enough time. They must be dead now! It's horrible, Mama! Horrible!

[8.0] (garbled audio)

[9.1] We are away from the planet now. Out into space, away from orbit. Can you get this message? Am I still in range? They don't know what to do. We are waiting to see the end, I think. The vessel is silent. Everyone is praying. Then they will fire the H-10 departure engines at maximum power and we will start our journey. When they are spent, the H-10s will be dropped and the K-77 propulsion pods will fire.

[9.2] Everyone is watching Ghoupallesz break apart. Continents are drifting into space; they're becoming asteroids. I recognize the peninsula of Zitoir, drifting into space, dripping its shattered cities, trailing debris, perhaps people. Kipzon is an asteroid! The planet is torn apart! There are rips in it, deep crevasses down to the core. I can see molten rock at the center. It's done now, Mama. You were right. There will be no more Ghoupallesz. The only safe option was to leave the planet. Thank you for everything you did for me, for the people of Kobarêl, for all Ghoupallesz! I will make certain no one forgets you!

[9.3] We are a safe distance now. Six of the vessels are safely away. One will go to Gouö, and the other five to our planned destinations: four star systems with five habitable planets, all in different directions. We won't see each other again. Cousins in the galaxy, that's all. We are on our own now, Mama. Like you told me.

[9.4] I remember what you said in your last message. I still have it on my tablet: "You do not need to please anyone but who you choose. Do not allow anyone to push you down an alley and into a backdoor to some horror house unless that is what you, and only you, really want, and you have considered all the options—the possibilities and consequences, and have a backup plan for escaping if it turns bad. This is what I've been teaching you from the day you first could speak. And every day after. Comet or no comet, I won't be with you forever, so I have to trust that you will be all right, that you will make good choices, that you will stand up for yourself and what you believe. Only then can I comfortably rest in my grave, daughter."

[9.5] Probably you are dead now, Mama. Either you died in one of the underground cities or you were washed away, or swallowed by the mountains, or you were sitting on the beach, getting drunk, maybe singing a hymn to the seven gods and nine goddesses. I don't know if you heard any of my messages. Maybe they will be lost in space for all time, these messages of Final Day.

[9.6] Today is Denio-5 in the Ghoupalle year 2175. The Final Day. I am Third Director of Reproductive Services Zaura-d'Elous, the daughter of Jinetta and Set, partner to Hanar-Santorak, birth-mother of Gina-d'Elous (6 years). I am a proud member of the administration staff of the interstellar vessel MEMITHA, bound for Tumark-C.

[9.8] Someone will hear this. Maybe someday. Until then, let me say I love you. I love you all. Be good to each other. It's a long journey we have to take.

[end of transmission]

NOTE: Because of the unit's depleted battery, the transmission was unable to be replayed.

Acknowledgements

Any work of imagination necessarily draws from a variety of sources. For inspiration, insight, and where applicable the gift of insouciance, I am greatly indebted to Roger Zelazny, Michael Moorcock, Robert Silverberg, and Gene Roddenberry. Special thanks go to my daughter who not only endured hearing all the tales of the Dream Land but produced the cover art.

About the Author

Stephen Swartz grew up in Kansas City, Missouri where he dreamed of traveling the world. His writing usually includes exotic locations, foreign characters, and splatterings of other languages—strangers in strange lands. After studying music, even composing a symphony, Stephen had planned on being a music teacher before deciding to turn to fiction writing.

The Dream Land was born from various childhood games, then forgotten until serendipitously reignited in adulthood by the musical album *The Celts* by Irish singer Enya. No correlation between the novel and that album is intended; the music simply evoked the necessary soundscape to allow interdimensional voyaging to occur.

After countless voyages, Stephen now teaches English at a university in Oklahoma and continues to write fiction late at night.

www.ingramcontent.com/pod-product-compliance
Lightning Source LLC
Chambersburg PA
CBHW051509250626
47156CB00001B/24